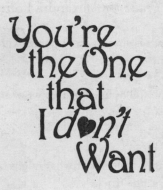

You're
the One
that
I don't
Want

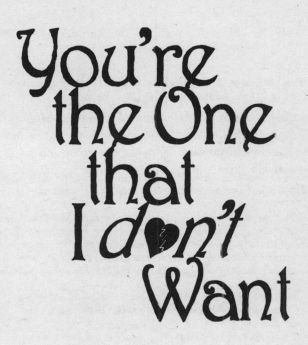

You're the One that I don't Want

ALEXANDRA POTTER

HODDER

First published in Great Britain in 2010 by Hodder & Stoughton
An Hachette Livre UK company

1

Copyright © Alexandra Potter 2010

A CIP catalogue record for this title is available from the British Library

Trade paperback ISBN 978 0 340 95413 3

Typeset in Plantin Light by Hewer Text UK Ltd, Edinburgh
Printed and bound by Clays Ltd, St Ives plc

Hodder & Stoughton policy is to use papers that are natural, renewable and recyclable products and made from wood grown in sustainable forests. The logging and manufacturing processes are expected to conform to the environmental regulations of the country of origin.

Hodder & Stoughton Ltd
338 Euston Road
London NW1 3BH

www.hodder.co.uk

For my beloved Barney

ACKNOWLEDGEMENTS

Thanks to my wonderful agent, Stephanie Cabot. A big thank-you to Sara Kinsella and Isobel Akenhead, and everyone at Hodder for all their support and enthusiasm. Thanks as always to my mum and dad and sister, Kelly, who have been amazing as ever. I really couldn't do this novel-writing business without you!

Thanks also to my great bunch of friends on both sides of the Atlantic: Beatrice, Sara, Dana, Pete, Melissa, Rachel, Matt, Tricia, Georgie, Kate and Bev, for cheering me on from the sidelines, making me smile, giving me inspiration and never telling me to shut up when I start talking about plots, characters and deadlines . . .

And finally a special mention for Barney, who sits beside me as I write. Never has there been a finer muse. Here's to the next one, kiddo.

Prologue

Venice, Italy, 1999

The summer heat creates a shimmering haze, through which Venice appears like a Canaletto brought to life. The dome of St Mark's Cathedral rises above the pastel-coloured buildings, with their peeling paint and time-weary elegance. Vaporetti buzz. Tourists throng. Among the crowds, children run in the square, scattering pigeons; men in sharp suits and designer shades sit smoking cigarettes; a guide with his umbrella talks history to a group of German tourists.

And two teenagers. They're weaving a lazy path across the cobbles, her arm wrapped round his denim hips, his arm slung loosely over her bare freckled shoulder. She's eating an ice cream and laughing at some joke he's making as he puffs on his cigarette, waving his arms around and making silly faces.

That's me and Nathaniel. We just rolled out of bed an hour ago and are spending Sunday in Venice like we always spend our Sundays in Venice: drinking espresso, eating ice cream and getting lost in the cat's cradle of alleyways that crisscross the maze of canals. I've been here the whole summer and I still get lost. Leaving the square, we turn a corner, and another, and another, until now we stumble across a market selling brightly coloured Murano glass and Venetian masks.

'Hey, what about this one?'

I turn to see Nathaniel holding a mask up to his face. It's got huge pink feathers and is covered in gold sequins. He does an absurd exaggerated bow.

'It suits you,' I giggle.

'You making fun of me?' He pulls it from his face and frowns.

'You? Never!' I laugh in mock indignation, as he tickles my nose with the feather.

'I thought I'd get it for my mom.' He puts it back and picks up another. This time it's a grotesque one with a long, hooked nose and beady eyes. 'Or what about this?'

'No, the first one. Definitely.' I shudder.

'Sure?'

'Sure.' I try to mimic his American accent, but my Manchester burr makes me sound ridiculous and he laughs at my rubbish attempt.

'What would I do without you?' He grins. 'Though I think we're gonna need to work on that American accent of yours.'

'It's better than your English one!' I protest.

'Awright, luv, let's 'ave a butcher's,' he replies in a jumble of Cockney and Lancashire, and I crack up laughing as he grabs hold of me and silences me with a kiss. 'Bad?' He pretends to look hurt.

'Terrible,' I say with mock-seriousness as he turns to pay for the mask.

Left standing in a patch of sunlight, I smile happily to myself. For a moment I watch him, puffing on his cigarette, trying to barter with the stallholder. Then, glancing away, I let my gaze drift absently over the market. I don't want to buy anything – I've already got all my souvenirs – but there's no harm in looking . . .

My eyes fall upon a stall. Tucked away in a shady corner, it's not really a stall, more a fold-up table, but it's the old man sitting behind it who attracts my attention. Wearing a battered fedora and with thick black-framed spectacles balanced on the end of his nose, he's peering at something under a small spotlight. Curious, I slip away from Nathaniel and wander over to see what he's doing.

'*Buon pomeriggio bello come sei oggi.*' He looks up at me.

I smile shyly. I'm useless at languages. Even after nearly three months in Venice studying Renaissance art, my Italian still only stretches to 'please', 'thank you' and 'Leonardo da Vinci'.

'*Inglese?*'

'Yes.' I nod, meeting his eyes.

They flash mischievously. 'What is a beautiful girl like you doing here alone?' He smiles, revealing teeth stained by a forty-year cigar habit. He reaches for one, burning in a nearby ashtray, and takes a satisfied puff.

'Oh, I'm not.' I shake my head and gesture to Nate, who's having his mask wrapped. Putting it under his arm, he strolls over and slides his arm casually round my shoulders.

'Ah, to be young and in love.' The old man nods approvingly as Nate and I look at each other, our faces splitting into embarrassed grins. 'I have just the thing for you.'

We turn back to see him holding out what appears to be an old coin.

I look at him in slight confusion. 'Um . . . thanks.' I smile, wondering what he's doing, and then suddenly it registers. Oh God, he's trying to give us money. Do we look that broke? OK, so we're students, and Nate looks a bit scruffy in his ripped jeans, and my dress had seen better days, but even so. 'Actually, we're fine,' I begin explaining hastily, and am about to tug on Nate's arm and drag him away when the old man places the coin on a small piece of machinery and breaks it in half.

I watch as he proceeds to punch a hole in either half, through which he threads a piece of leather. Then triumphantly he holds them up, letting them dangle like pendants. 'For you.' He smiles. 'Because you are like the coin,' he explains. 'You are two halves of one whole.'

I gaze at the jagged edges of the half-coins, like two pieces of a jigsaw puzzle. On their own they're just half a broken coin, but together they make a seamless whole.

'Wow, how romantic,' I murmur, turning to Nathaniel, who's watching me and grinning in amusement. I feel a flash of embarrassment. 'What? You don't think it is?' I yelp, poking him in the ribs.

'Of course it is,' he laughs. 'Don't I always call you "my other half", anyway?'

'Only three thousand lire,' says the old man.

I turn to see his palm outstretched expectantly.

'Even romance has a price,' quips Nathaniel, digging out his wallet.

And there was me thinking the old man was being all romantic, when the whole time he was just trying to sell us something, I realise, feeling foolish. Honestly, I'm such a sucker. Before I can protest, though, Nathaniel has handed him a note and is looping one of the pendants over his own head.

'See, we can never be apart now,' he jokes, putting the other half round my neck. 'Wherever you go, I go.'

Despite his attempt at humour, I can feel my mood immediately darkening. In just a few weeks we'll be leaving Italy and going back to our respective colleges and I'm dreading it. Ever since we met I've been counting down the days until we have to part.

'Hey.' Seeing my expression, Nate gives me a hug. 'We can do the whole long-distance thing,' he reassures, guessing immediately what's going through my mind. 'We'll write. I can call . . .'

I think back to my student digs in Manchester. I don't even have a landline, never mind a mobile, and letters might sound romantic in books, but in real life they aren't going to be a substitute for nuzzling my face into his neck, sharing a huge bowl of pistachio *gelato* with him on a Sunday afternoon or laughing at that terrible English accent of his.

'I guess so.' I nod, trying to put a brave face on it. I don't want to spoil the present by brooding about the future, but it's like a big, black cloud is just sitting there, waiting to descend.

'If you want to be together, you can always be together.'

I turn to see the old Italian watching us thoughtfully.

'I'm afraid it's not that simple—' I begin, but he interrupts.

'No, it is very simple,' he says firmly. 'Do you want to be together?'

Nathaniel cocks his head to one side as if thinking about it. 'Um . . . what do you reckon?' he asks teasingly, and I punch him playfully. 'Uh-huh, I think that's a yes, we do.' He grins, turning back to the stallholder.

'Well, then . . .' The old man gives a shrug of his shoulders and takes a puff of his cigar.

'We have to go back home,' I explain.

'Where's home?'

Nathaniel hugs me tighter. 'Lucy lives in England—'

'And Nate's from America,' I finish.

'But you are in Venice,' he replies, seemingly unfazed. 'Here, there is no need to say goodbye. You can be together for ever.'

He is a sweet old guy after all, I decide. And a bit of an old-fashioned romantic.

'I wish.' I force a laugh and squeeze Nate's hand. 'But it's impossible.'

Unexpectedly the Italian lets out a loud roar of laughter. 'No! No! It is not *impossible*,' he cries, slapping the table with the flat of his hand. 'Don't you know the legend of the Bridge of Sighs?'

Nathaniel frowns. 'You mean the bridge right here in Venice?'

'Yes. That is it! The very one!' he exclaims excitedly.

'Why, what's the legend?' I ask, suddenly intrigued.

Like a magician waiting for a drum roll before producing a rabbit, the old man pauses for dramatic effect. Only when we are both quiet does he start to speak.

'The legend is very famous,' he says gravely. His voice has the kind of hushed, awestruck respect reserved for churches and museums, and I almost have to stifle a giggle. 'It says that if you kiss underneath the bridge at sunset, on a gondola, when the bells of the church are ringing . . .'

'Wow, they don't make it easy for us,' whispers Nathaniel jokingly into my ear, but I swat him away

'Yes?' I urge, turning back to the old man. 'What happens?'

Dragging on his cigar, he exhales a cloud of smoke. It drifts upwards in front of his face, like a smokescreen. As it clears, his dark eyes meet mine, and despite the oppressive heat, a shiver suddenly runs down my spine and I feel goose bumps spring up on my arms. He leans closer, his voice almost a whisper. 'You will have everlasting and eternal love. You will be together for ever and nothing –' his eyes flick to Nathaniel, then back to me – '*nothing* will ever break you apart.'

'Nothing?' I repeat, my voice barely audible.

'*Niente.*' He nods, his face filled with conviction. 'You are bound together for ever, for eternity.'

I laugh nervously and press the pendant to the heat of my chest.

'So you like?' He gestures to the necklace.

'Oh . . .um . . .yes.' I nod, snapping back.

He smiles and holds out our change, and as I take it from him, his sandpapery fingers brush against mine.

'*Grazie,*' I whisper, managing one of the few words I know in Italian.

'*Prego.*' He smiles genially, tipping his hat.

Then Nathaniel puts his arm round me and we turn and start walking away through the market, but we've gone just a few steps when I hear the old Italian call after us, 'Remember, *niente,*' and I glance back. Only the funny thing is, he's not there any more. He's gone, swallowed up by the crowd. Almost like he simply vanished into thin air.

Chapter One

Everyone is looking for their soulmate.
Take our Love Test and find out:

Is He the One?

God, these things are so stupid.

I scan the quiz in the magazine. There's a photo of a couple looking into each other's eyes, all lovey-dovey, and it's decorated with cartoon drawings of Cupids and love-hearts. I mean, *please*. As if you can find out if he's 'the One' by answering a few silly multiple-choice questions.

Like, for example:

My guy and I go together like . . .
a) Batman and Robin
b) Posh and Becks
c) Lindsay Lohan and fake tan

Honestly, how ridiculous!

I'm jostled by someone squeezing themselves into the tiny space next to me. Looking up, I realise we've pulled into a station. I cast my eyes around the crowded carriage. It's Friday-afternoon rush-hour and I'm sitting squashed up on the subway, flicking through the pages of a magazine I found on my seat. The doors close, and as the train moves off with a judder, I turn back to the magazine. And that dumb quiz.

Dismissively I turn over the page. It's an article on cellulite. I frown.

Then again, maybe a dumb quiz isn't *so* bad. After all, it has got to be more fun than reading about how to get rid of dimpled

orange-peel thighs, I muse, glancing at the section on detox-
ing. Though, frankly, I don't think you *can* get rid of dimpled
orange-peel thighs. Everyone has cellulite. Even supermodels!

Well, that's what I like to tell myself, anyway.

I peer closely at the grainy paparazzi photo of Kate Moss's
bikini-clad bottom, which has been magnified a million times.
To tell the truth, I can't actually see any dimples. Or much
bottom. In fact, looking at this photo, I'm not sure Kate Moss
even *has* a bottom.

Suddenly I'm struck by what I'm doing: I'm sitting. In public. On
the New York subway. With my nose pressed up against a photograph of a left bum cheek. Or is it a right? I grab hold of myself.
For God's sake, Lucy. And you thought the quiz was ridiculous?

Quickly I turn back to it. I notice it hasn't been filled in. Oh,
what the hell. I've got five more stops.

Reaching into my bag, I pull out a biro.

OK, here we go . . .

1. Whenever you think about him, do you get
    butterflies?
    a) Yes, always
    b) Sometimes
    c) Never

Well, I wouldn't call them butterflies exactly. In fact, it's
been so long the butterflies have probably grown up and flown
away. Now it's more of an ache. Not like the terrible toothache
I got when I pulled out my filling at the cinema on a pic'n'mix
toffee . . . I wince at the memory. No, this is more of a twinge.
The occasional pang.

I plump for b) Sometimes.

2. How long have you liked him?
    a) Less than six months
    b) A year
    c) More than a year

My mind flicks back. We met in the summer of 1999. I was nineteen. Which makes it . . . As my mind does the calculation, I feel a thump of realisation. Quickly followed by a left jab of defensiveness.

OK, so it's ten years. So what? Ten years is nothing. My mum's known my dad for forty years.

Yes, but your mum's married to him, pipes up a little voice inside me.

Ignoring it, I quickly circle option c. Right. Next question.

3.   Can you see yourself getting married to this
      guy?
      a) 100%
      b) 50%
      c) Zero

Well, that's easy. It's zero.

In fact, I'd say the chances of marrying him are less than zero. But that's OK. I'm perfectly fine with it. That's just the way things are, and that's cool.

All right, so in the past I *might* have thought about it. And maybe for a moment I imagined myself in a white dress (actually, more of a calico, in antique lace, with full-length sleeves and a sweetheart neckline) and him in top hat and tails with his messy blond hair and tatty old Converses peeping out from underneath. Dancing our first dance under the stars to 'No Woman, No Cry', our favourite Bob Marley song. Leaving on our honeymoon in his old VW camper van . . .

Zoning back, I notice I've been absentmindedly doodling a love-heart around a) 100%. Shit. What did I do that for? Flustered, I grab my pen and start scribbling over it furiously. It's not as if that means anything. It's not like it's in my subconscious.

I suddenly realise I'm pressing so hard I've torn the page.

4. Do your friends think you're obsessed with this
    guy?

My body stiffens defensively.

I think about him from time to time, but I wouldn't say I'm
obsessed. Not at all. I mean, I'm not stalking him or anything.
Or hounding him with Facebook messages. Or Googling him
relentlessly.

OK, I confess. I Googled him once.

Maybe twice.

Oh, all right, so I've lost count over the years. But so what?
Who hasn't gone home and Googled a man they're in love with?

Hang on – did I just say the *L word*?

Out of the blue my stomach flips over like a pancake. I flip it
straight back again. I didn't mean that at all! It's this silly quiz –
it's making me think all kinds of things.

I circle b) No.

As the number six train makes its way uptown, I continue
through the questions. They get progressively more ludicrous,
but it passes the time. In fact, I'm just on the last question . . .

10. What film best describes your relationship?
     a) *Love Story*
     b) *Brief Encounter*
     c) *Nightmare on Elm Street*

. . .when I'm suddenly aware of the overhead announcement
– 'This is Forty-Second Street, Grand Central' – and I realise
I'm at my stop.

Stuffing the magazine into my bag, I start politely trying to
excuse my way through the packed carriage. Of course, no one
pays any attention. Since moving to New York from London
a few weeks ago, I've begun noticing that all my 'Oh, sorry's,
'Excuse me's and 'I beg your pardon's fall on deaf ears.

It's not that New Yorkers are rude. On the contrary, I'm finding them to be some of the friendliest, warmest people I've ever

met. It's just that our terribly British way of apologising for everything has zero effect. They don't understand what we're apologising for. To be honest, half the time *I* don't understand what I'm apologising for. It's just something I do. A habit. Like logging on to Facebook every five minutes.

For example, yesterday I was crossing the street when this man bashed right into me and spilled coffee all over me. And get this – *I* was the one who said sorry! Yes, me! About a million times! Even though it was totally his fault. He was on his mobile and not looking where he was going.

Sorry, I mean *cell phone* – well, I am in New York now.

At the thought I get a tingle all the way up my spine. I can't help it. Every time I catch myself glancing up at the skyscrapers towering above my head, or walking down Broadway on my way to work, or hailing one of those distinctive yellow cabs (which I've only done once, as I'm broke, but still), I feel as if I'm in a movie. I've been here six weeks and still can't believe it's real. I almost expect to see Carrie, Miranda, Charlotte and Samantha waltzing arm in arm towards me.

Exiting the subway station, I pause at the pedestrian crossing to study the little pop-up map of Manhattan I keep in my bag. Some people have this sort of inbuilt GPS, a bit like cats. You can drop them anywhere and they can find their way home. Not me. I get lost in Tesco. Once, I spent over half an hour wandering around the salad bar trying to find the checkout. Trust me. I've not been able to face coleslaw since.

I turn the map upside down, then back again. I'm stumped. I've arranged to go for a drink after work, but I haven't a clue where the bar is. I squint at the grid of streets. It all looks quite simple *in theory*, but in reality I'm forever getting lost. As if it wasn't hard enough, here in New York you can have East Whatever Street, or West Whatever Street. Which is just completely confusing. I mean, how on earth are you supposed to know which is which?

Looking up and down the street in frustration, I give up and do my little rhyme. I'm continually stopping dead in the middle of the street and doing it. You know the one: 'Never Eat Shredded Wheat.'

''Scuse me?'

I turn to see a fellow pedestrian standing next to me, waiting to cross. He's looking at me quizzically, his brow furrowed beneath his baseball cap.

Oh my God, did I just say that out loud?

'Er . . .' I fluster with embarrassment. 'Never . . . um . . . cross the dreaded street,' I manage hastily, gesturing to the little red man, 'until the little man says it's safe.'

He stares at me blankly. 'Sure,' he replies doubtfully.

He's got one of those really drawly *Noo* York accents and I notice he's carrying what looks like a large video camera and a furry microphone. Gosh, I wonder what he's doing. He's probably making a movie or something really cool.

Unlike me, who's reciting ridiculous rhymes and prattling on about the Green Cross Code, I realise, my cheeks flushing. Feeling totally *un*cool, I look away and pray for the lights to change. 'Oh, look, *now* we can cross,' I announce with a beat of relief, and shooting him an awkward smile, I stride off purposely into the crowd.

You see, that's the thing with New York. The city has this amazing energy that attracts all these interesting people. Turn a corner and you'll stumble across a film set, or a stallholder selling some wacky kind of jewellery, or a group of street artists doing amazing hip-hop routines. You never know what's going to happen.

Sometimes, late at night, when I see the Empire State Building lit up in different colours, I get this buzz of excitement. Anticipation. *Magic*. I almost have to pinch myself. For a girl who hails from deepest Manchester, it's the stuff of fairytales.

Only this particular fairytale is missing one thing.

Walking past a row of restaurants, I glance at the couples cosying up together over a romantic meal. Being a warm summer's evening, restaurants have flung open their doors, spilling their tables out on to the street. I feel a pang.

I brush it quickly away.

Once upon a time there was a prince of sorts, but we didn't end up living happily ever after. Like I said before, though, I'm fine with it. It was a long time ago. I've moved on. In fact, since then I've dated loads of different guys.

Well, perhaps not *loads*, but a few. And some of them have been really nice. Like, for example, my last boyfriend, Sean. We met at a party and dated for a couple of months, but it was never that serious. I mean, he was good fun, and the sex wasn't bad. It's just . . .

OK, I have this theory. Everyone dreams of finding their soulmate. It's a universal quest. All over the world millions of people are looking for their true love, their *amore* their *âme soeur*, that one special person with whom they will spend the rest of their life.

And I'm no different.

Except it doesn't happen for everyone. Some people spend their whole life looking and never find that person. It's the luck of the draw.

If, by some miracle, you're lucky enough to meet the One, whatever you do, don't let them go. Because you don't get another shot at it. Soulmates aren't like buses; there's not going to be another one along in a minute. That's why they're called 'the One'.

I mean, if there were loads of them, they'd be called 'the Five', or 'the Hundred', or 'the Never-Ending Supply'.

So I think maybe that's it for me. Because you see, I *was* lucky. I did find the One, but then I lost him. I blew it, or he blew it. At the end of the day it doesn't really matter. The details aren't important.

Besides, it's not like I'm *un*happy. What's that saying? Better to have loved and lost than never to have loved at all. To tell the truth, I rarely think about it any more.

And yet . . .

Sometimes, when I least expect it, something will remind me. Of him. Of us. Of long ago. It can be as random as a quiz in a magazine, or as inconsequential as a restaurant table on the street. And sometimes I can't help wondering what my life would be like if things had worked out. What if we were still together? What if we had lived happily ever after? What if, what if, *what if* . . .?

Sometimes I even try to imagine what it would be like to see him again. Which is crazy. It's been so long I doubt I'd even recognise him now. I could probably walk past him in the street and not even know it was him.

Oh, who am I kidding? I'd recognise him in an instant. Even in a crowd.

And do you want to know something else? Deep down inside, I know if I saw him again, I would still feel exactly the same.

Anyway, that's hardly likely, is it? I think, catching myself. It's been ten years since I last saw him. A whole decade. A brand-new millennium. Who knows where he is or what he's doing . . .?

Up ahead, a neon sign interrupts my thoughts. *Scott's.* That's it! That's the bar! Feeling a beat of relief, I start hurrying towards it.

Like I said, you get one shot and I had mine.

And dismissing the thought from my mind, I push open the door.

Chapter Two

Inside, it's dimly lit and busy with the after-work crowd. I pause at the doorway. It's one of those really cool New York bars you see in films and on TV. Several tables are squeezed inside, and running the whole length is a bar made of polished dark wood, with shiny brass fittings and hundreds of different bottles of spirits, all stacked in rows.

Sitting ramrod straight at the bar is a girl in a pinstripe suit. She's jabbing away at her BlackBerry. With her hair cut into a sharp blonde bob and an imposing black leather briefcase sitting beside her on a barstool, she cuts a rather formidable figure amid the relaxed early evening crowd. Think Michael Douglas as Gordon Gekko in *Wall Street* and then imagine a more imposing, female version.

That's my big sister, Kate. She's older, by five years, but it might as well be twenty the way she bosses me about like I'm a child. She's used to bossing people about, though. She has not one but *two* assistants working for her.

She's an associate at a major law firm here in Manhattan that specialises in mergers and acquisitions. Personally, I haven't got a clue what mergers and acquisitions *are*, let alone the ability to compile hundred-page reports on them and win cases worth millions of dollars.

But then my sister has always been the super-brainy one in the family. She spent seven years training to be a doctor, then as soon as she qualified, changed her mind and retrained as a lawyer. Like it was no biggie.

I swear I've agonised more over what sandwich to have for lunch at Prêt-à-Manger.

Kate got all the brains and I got all the creativity. At least, that's what my mum likes to tell me, though sometimes I wonder if it was just to make me feel better after flunking yet another maths test. While logarithms baffled me (and still do – could someone please tell me exactly *what* a logarithm is?), drawing and painting were like second nature and I ended up at art college.

Three glorious paint-splattered years later I graduated and moved to London. I had all these big dreams. I was going to have this amazing career as an artist. I was going to have exhibitions in galleries across the country. I was going to have my own studio in this super-cool loft in Shoreditch . . .

Er, actually, no, I wasn't.

For starters, have you any clue how expensive lofts in Shoreditch are?

No, neither did I. Well, let me tell you. They're an absolute *fortune*.

That wouldn't have been so bad if I'd been selling my artwork. I mean, at least then I could have saved up. For about eighty years, but still, it's *possible*.

But the truth is, I never actually sold one of my paintings. Well, OK, I sold one, but that was to my dad for fifty quid, and only then because he insisted on giving me my first commission.

As it turned out, it was also my last. After six months of sliding further and further into debt, I had to give up painting and look for a job. Consequently, my dreams of being an artist ended up just that. Dreams.

Still, it's probably for the best. I was young and naïve and unrealistic. I probably would never have made it anyway.

Excusing my way through the crowd, I make my way towards the bar.

After that I temped for a while, but I was pretty terrible. I can't type, and my filing is useless, but finally I got lucky and landed a job in an art gallery in the East End. At first I was only the receptionist, but over the years I clawed my way up from answering the phone to working with new artists, organising exhibitions and helping buyers with their collections. Then a few months ago I was offered the chance to work in a gallery in New York.

Of course I jumped at it. Who wouldn't? New York is where the art world is right now, and career-wise it's an amazing opportunity.

Except, if I'm entirely truthful, that's not the only reason I decided to pack up my stuff, move out of my flat-share and fly three thousand miles across the Atlantic. It was partly to get over my latest break-up, partly to escape the prospect of another terrible British summer, but mostly to get my life out of a bit of a rut.

Don't get me wrong – I love my job, my friends, my life in London. It's just . . .Well, recently I've had this feeling. As if there's something missing. As if I'm waiting for my life to begin. Waiting for something to happen.

Only problem is, I'm not exactly sure what.

My sister's still focused on her BlackBerry and hasn't seen me walking over to her yet. Since I arrived, I've been staying with her and Jeff, her husband. They have a two-bedroom apartment on the Upper East Side and it's been great. It's also been, shall we say, *challenging*. Put it this way, I've never stayed in army barracks, but I have a feeling they might be similar. Only without the polished wenge floors and flat-screen TV.

As soon as I told her I was moving here, she sent me a list of house rules. My sister's very organised like that. She draws up regimented lists and ticks things off, one by one, with special highlighter pens. Not that I'd call her anal . . .

Well, not to her face, anyway.

We're total opposites in everything really. She's blonde; I'm brunette. She likes to save; I like to spend. She's super tidy; I'm horribly messy. It's not that I don't try to keep things neat and tidy – in fact, I'm *forever* tidying, but for some strange reason that just seems to make things more untidy.

Kate's also a stickler for timekeeping, whereas I'm never on time. I don't know why. I really try to be punctual. I've tried all the tricks – setting off fifteen minutes early, putting my clocks forward, wearing two watches – but I still seem to end up running late.

Like now, for example.

Right on cue I hear my phone beep to signal I've got a text. Hastily I dig it out of my pocket. I'll let you in on a secret. I'm a teeny bit scared of my big sister.

I click the little envelope on the screen.

Five more minutes then you're dead.

Make that a lot scared.

'You're late.'

As I plop myself down next to her on the barstool, she doesn't even look up from her BlackBerry. Instead she continues replying to an email, a sharp crease etched down the middle of her forehead, like the ones down the front of her trouser legs.

Kate always wears trousers. In fact, I think the only time I've ever *not* seen her wearing them was on her wedding day, five years ago. And that was only because Mum got all upset when she found out she was going to be wearing a trouser suit ('But it's from Donna Karan,' my sister protested) and said the neighbours would think her daughter was a lesbian. Which seems a bit ridiculous, considering she was marrying Jeff.

'I know, I'm sorry,' I apologise briskly, giving her a kiss on the cheek. 'You know me – I'm useless with directions.'

'And timekeeping,' she reminds, hitting send with her thumb, then turning to me.

She looks pale, despite the fact it's sunny and seventy-five degrees outside. Kate rarely gets outside. During the week she's always at her desk in her air-conditioned office, and at weekends—

Well, she's usually at her desk then too.

'Guilty as charged.' I nod, pulling a remorseful expression. 'What do I get? Two years? Five?'

She smiles, despite herself. 'Well, this isn't my legal field of expertise, but let's see ... No prior convictions? Mitigating circumstances?' She drums her fingers on the bar. 'You'd probably get away with a warning and a good-behaviour bond.'

'That's it?' I'm laughing now.

'Plus a fine,' she adds, raising an eyebrow.

'A fine?' I frown. 'How much?'

'Hmm . . .' She taps the tip of her nose with her forefinger, like she always does when she's thinking. 'Three drinks. At ten dollars a drink. I reckon thirty bucks should do it.' My sister smiles at me slyly. 'Plus tip, of course.'

She's nothing if not a tough negotiator. Now I know how she wins those multi-million-dollar cases.

'Hang on – three drinks?'

'You, me and Robyn,' she explains.

'Oh, she's here?' I say in surprise, looking around for her.

'She went to the bathroom.' Kate gestures to the back of the bar, where at that moment I see a tall girl with wild, curly hair and wearing a tie-dye kaftan appear from the ladies'. Her face splits into a huge, excitable grin as she spots me.

'*Honnnneeeeyyyyy!*' she shrieks, waving manically as she rushes over, seemingly unaware of the people she's knocking into as she makes a beeline for me. She's like the human form of a heat-seeking missile.

I watch in amusement. A slightly different welcome from my sister, then.

Throwing her arms out, she envelops me in a haze of patchouli oil and a jingle-jangle of silver bracelets, which are stacked up her freckled forearms like Slinkys.

Anyone watching Robyn greet me would think we were life-long friends, but we only met a week ago, when I answered her ad for a roommate to share her apartment. I move in this weekend. After a few weeks of my sister's house rules – '1) Usage of electric toothbrush not permitted after 10 p.m.' Apparently it wakes her up, as she likes to be in bed by nine thirty so she can get up at 5 a.m. to go to the gym. Yup, that's right. *Five in the morning* – I knew it was time to move out and get my own space.

Well, maybe 'space' is something of a misnomer. 'Broom cupboard' would be a more accurate description. New York might be exciting, but it comes with a hefty price tag and on my salary I can only afford nine-foot square in a fourth-storey walk-up on the Lower East Side.

Still, the most important thing is it's all mine. Well, Robyn's really. Plus guess what? I can see the Empire State Building from my window!

Well. *Sort of.* It's not actually from *my* bedroom window. The view from my bedroom window is a brick wall, a fire escape and some pretty interesting graffiti. You can see it from Robyn's bedroom, though. If you sort of hang out of the window and squint a bit. It's definitely there. Promise.

'I didn't think you could make it,' I gasp, finally breaking free.

'My last client cancelled,' she explains, still grinning.

Americans, I've noticed, spend a lot of time grinning, but I haven't yet worked out if they're really happy or if it's an excuse to show off their teeth. Robyn has perfect straight white teeth. Like piano keys.

'Said he was afraid of needles. Which made things a little problematic, what with me being an acupuncturist.'

'What is it with men and little pricks?' quips Kate.

I stifle a giggle, but Robyn is oblivious to my sister's sense of humour. 'I don't know,' she says earnestly, her face falling serious. 'I think perhaps men have a much lower threshold when it comes to pain. Women endure the agony of childbirth . . . menstrual cramps—'

'Brazilian bikini waxes,' interjects my sister.

'Not to mention the emotional pain women suffer,' continues Robyn, ignoring her and chattering on regardless. 'We just feel things so much more deeply – like, for example, the other day I was watching *Oprah* and there was this whole section about comfort eating . . .'

I glance across at my sister. Eyebrows raised, she's staring at Robyn with a mixture of horror and disbelief. I feel a pang of concern. My sister's not the kind of person you talk to about emotions. She doesn't really get emotional. The only time I've seen her look slightly perturbed was when she scored 99 per cent in a chemistry exam.

' . . . Her husband had run off with her best friend and she gained two hundred pounds by eating cupcakes. Can you believe it? She was so devastated she used cupcakes to try to block out the pain. There were red velvet cupcakes for break-fast, double-chocolate fudge cupcakes for lunch, lemon butter cupcakes for—'

'OK, so what are we drinking?' I ask, butting in and changing the subject before we all die of thirst.

'Whisky sour,' says my sister without a moment's hesitation.

'Robyn?' Having got the attention of the barman, I turn to her expectantly.

'Er, wow, I have no idea,' she gasps, drawing breath for the first time in five minutes. 'Now let me think. What do I feel like . . .?' Tilting her head, she winds a brown curl round her finger thoughtfully. 'Something sweet . . '

'A lemon drop?' suggests the barman, smiling broadly.

She wrinkles her nose. ' . . . but not too sweet.'

'Well, in that case, what about a mojito?'

'Ooh!' She gives a little squeal of excitement. 'I *love* mojitos!'

'Great.' The barman reaches for a handful of mint and grabs the pestle and mortar.

'But not tonight,' she adds after a moment, shaking her head decisively.

The barman puts down the pestle, his jaw clenching.

'Tonight I feel like something a bit different,' she continues cheerily. Behind us a queue is forming, but she's chattering on, completely obliviously.

'Maybe a martini?' The barman passes her a menu. 'We have lots of different kinds. Like the ginger martini.'

'Mmm, that sounds yummy . . .' she coos.

The barman flashes a look of relief.

' . . . but so does the pomegranate one,' she says, reading from the menu. 'Wow, there are so many and they all sound delicious.

Oh, look, what about the one with lychees? What does that taste like?'

'Lychees,' deadpans my sister.

Robyn looks up, startled. 'Actually, you know what, I think I'll just have a glass of wine,' she says hastily, passing the barman the menu. 'Anything white. I'm not fussy,' she adds, avoiding my sister's glare.

'And I'll have a beer.' I smile. I've never been one for cocktails. I get *way* too drunk on them.

'Coming right up.' The barman reaches for a cocktail shaker.

'Oh, just one more thing . . .' On tiptoe, Robyn suddenly leans across the bar and studies the barman under the lights. 'What's your name?'

I'm taken aback. Crikey. I've heard American women are confident when it comes to asking men out, but this is so, well, *brazen*.

'Brad.' He grins, showing off by doing a little impersonation of Tom Cruise in *Cocktail* with the shaker. 'Why, do you want my number too?'

Robyn's face falls in disappointment. 'No, thanks.' Leaning back from the bar, she gives a little sigh. 'Not unless your name's Harold.'

'Who's Harold?' I ask in confusion.

'I dunno.' She shrugs. 'That's the problem.'

'If you're looking for a missing person, I've got some great contacts at the NYPD,' suggests Kate helpfully.

'My sister's married to a cop,' I explain.

'Really?' Robyn's eyes go wide. 'How exciting!'

'Not really,' laughs my sister. 'You haven't met Jeff.'

'Or Harold,' reminds the barman, who's been ear-wigging. He looks vaguely put out that he's been passed over for a total stranger with a name like someone's aged uncle.

'Not yet, but I know he's out there,' says Robyn with complete conviction. 'A psychic told me.'

'You went to see a *psychic*?' Kate looks at her in disbelief.

'About a year ago,' nods Robyn, her face serious. 'She said I was going to meet my soulmate and I have to be on the lookout for a Harold.' She reaches for the large pink crystal pendant hanging from her neck and clasps it tightly. 'When it comes to love, I just have to put my faith and trust in the power of the universe.'

I glance at my sister. She's struggling to contain her cynicism. 'Did she say what this Harold looked like?'

Robyn pauses and glances furtively around the bar to check no one is listening, as if she's afraid someone might overhear and steal off with this highly classified information and find Harold first. Satisfied the coast is clear, she whispers conspiratorially, 'Tall, dark and handsome.'

Out of the corner of my eye I see the barman puff out his chest.

'Well, there's a surprise,' remarks Kate drolly, rolling her eyes.

'There you go, ladies,' interrupts the barman, placing three drinks on the bar in front of us. 'That'll be twenty-eight bucks.'

'I'll get this,' I say, reaching for my bag 'It's my round.' I start rummaging around inside for my wallet, but it's so crammed full of stuff I can't find it. Big bags might *look* fashionable, but in reality you just end up carrying around a load of junk.

I pull out an old chocolate-brownie wrapper, a lip gloss that's covered in fluff, my subway pass . . . Damn it. It's got to be in here somewhere. Balancing my handbag on my lap, I'm just tipping it to one side to get a better look when it suddenly topples over on to the floor, spewing out its contents.

'Oh shoot, let me help,' cries Robyn. Bending down, she scrabbles around, helping me pick up my stuff. 'Ooh, what's this?'

I glance over to see her holding up the magazine I was reading on the train. 'Oh, nothing,' I say, reaching for it, but it's too late – she's already turned to the quiz.

She starts reading it out loudly. '"Everyone is looking for their soulmate. Take our Love Test and find out: Is He the One?"' She looks up at me, her eyes wide with excitement. 'Oh wow, I love these things!'

'Why does that not surprise me,' says Kate, paying the barman for me.

I throw her a grateful look. 'It's just a bit of silly nonsense,' I say, feeling my cheeks flush with embarrassment.

'But you filled it in!' refutes Robyn, waggling it in evidence.

Oh God. Now I feel like a complete idiot.

'I was bored on the subway, you know what it's like.' I'm trying to keep my voice casual while not looking at my sister. Once, when I was a teenager, she caught me secretly reading my horoscope and that of Ricky Johnston, whom I'd had a crush on for ever. She teased me about it for months afterwards.

Years later nothing's changed.

'Give it to me. I'll throw it away.' I laugh lightly and hold out my hand, but Robyn is poring over it, head bent, eyes narrowed in concentration.

'So what was your score? Was he the One?' She looks up, her face eager with expectation.

'Look, I hate to break this to you, but there's no such thing as the One,' dismisses my sister. 'It's bullshit.'

Robyn's face drops like a six-year-old who's just been told the Tooth Fairy doesn't exist. 'But you're married,' she protests urgently. 'What about your husband?'

'What about him?' replies Kate evenly. 'I love Jeff, don't get me wrong, but I wouldn't call him my soulmate.'

'You wouldn't?' asks Robyn in a hushed voice.

'No.' My sister shrugs nonchalantly and takes a sip of her drink. 'I call him plenty of other things, though,' she adds, and laughs throatily.

Robyn looks stricken. 'What about you, Lucy?' She turns to me desperately. 'What do you think? You believe in the One, don't you?'

I hesitate. 'Well, um . . .'

'Oh, I'm so sorry!' Robyn suddenly claps her hand to her forehead. 'I'm being so insensitive.' She looks at me, her face full of remorse. 'Your sister mentioned you'd broken up with someone recently. I didn't think.'

'You mean Sean? Oh, he wasn't anything serious,' I reassure her quickly.

'He wasn't the One?' she says knowingly, refusing to look at my sister.

My mind flashes up a picture of Sean in his purple Crocs. Even if things had been perfect, those Crocs would have always come between us. 'No, he wasn't the One,' I laugh, but deep down I feel that familiar twinge.

'Well, don't worry,' she encourages, patting my hand. 'I'm sure you'll find him.'

I smile ruefully. 'That's the thing. I already did.'

There's a loud groan from Kate. 'Oh God, not the Bridge Guy.'

'His name was Nathaniel,' I retort, shooting my sister a look.

She rolls her eyes impatiently. 'Lucy, when are you going to forget about him and move on?'

'I have moved on,' I snap back defensively. 'I've had loads of boyfriends.'

'You're still hung up on that guy.'

'No, I'm not!'

'So why are you doing some stupid quiz?'

'So what? It doesn't mean anything!'

'Not much!'

Robyn's head is flicking back and forth between me and Kate as if she's watching tennis. 'Whoa, you guys!' she cries, holding out her silver-ringed hands to break up what is in danger of turning into one of our sisterly quarrels.

Trust me, that's something we're *both* good at.

'Would someone mind filling me in?'

We exchange glances. Sheepishly Kate turns her attention back to her drink.

Which leaves me.

I hesitate.

'Well?' Robyn looks at me expectantly.

'Oh, it's nothing,' I mutter dismissively.

'It sure as hell doesn't sound like nothing,' remarks Robyn, raising her eyebrows. 'C'mon, I want all the juicy details.'

I think about resisting, but the beer is weaving a warm path inside me and I can feel my defences weakening.

'Do I have to remind you that I stick needles into people for a living?' She fires me her most threatening look, which couldn't be *less* threatening, but still.

I swallow hard, my mind flicking back. 'It was the summer of 1999. I was nineteen and studying art in Venice, Italy.' I start talking quickly, the words tumbling out. I'm keen to get it over and done with. 'His name was Nathaniel and he was twenty and an American on the Harvard summer programme, studying the Renaissance painters. Afterwards I went back to England and he went back to America—'

'You've missed out the bit about the bridge,' interrupts my sister.

My momentum broken, I throw her a furious glance, but she's pretending to focus on her drink as if she never said anything.

I turn back to Robyn. 'Sorry, I'm getting ahead of myself. First I should tell you how it all started.' As the memory comes flooding back, my stomach starts whooshing giddily and I take a deep breath to steady my voice. 'Let me tell you about the legend of the Bridge of Sighs . . .'

Chapter Three

'Wow, how romantic.' Robyn lets out a loud sigh.

As I finish telling the story, I zone back to the bar. Elbows leaning on the counter, chin cupped in her hands, Robyn's got a strange, dreamy expression on her face. Like she's in some kind of trance.

She's not the only one, I realise, noticing several people along the bar who have stopped their conversations and are leaning in to listen. Seeing my captivated audience, I feel a prickle of self-consciousness and glance around awkwardly, only to see a group of girls sitting at a table behind me, waiting expectantly.

'So did you kiss underneath the bridge?' asks one of them, mascaraed eyes wide.

I can feel my cheeks burning with embarrassment. I've never been much of a public speaker and now suddenly here I am, orating to an entire New York bar.

'Well?' coaxes her redheaded friend, clutching her martini glass to her cleavage with anticipation.

My mind wanders back to that evening, all those years ago. 'We didn't have enough money. We were totally broke in those days . . .'

There's an audible groan of disappointment.

' . . . but Nathaniel bribed a local gondolier with some pot,' I finish, laughing at the memory of the young Italian in his stripy shirt, stoned and giggly.

'So did he take you?'

I hear a male voice and turn to see a burly banker type, shirt unbuttoned, tie loosened. The hope on his face is tangible.

'Stop interrupting. Let her tell the story,' shushes someone else loudly.

'So we met at sunset . . .' I continue, an image of the tangerine sky popping into my mind. It had been such an amazing sunset. Multicoloured streaks had lit up the sky in a blaze of colour, bathing the ancient buildings of Venice in a fiery glow. I've seen many sunsets before and since, but none has ever seemed as special. ' . . . and he rowed us out on to the canal.'

I can see Nate's hand helping me into the gondola, feel his arm round my shoulder as we snuggle together on the worn velvet cushions, hear the water lapping against the banks of the canal.

'Just as the bells started ringing, we reached the bridge . . .'

For a brief moment I'm right back there. The distant echoes of Venetian life are filling the warm evening air and I'm looking at Nate and he's brushing the hair out of my face and we're laughing like a couple of lovestruck teenagers. Because that's what we are: a couple of lovestruck teenagers.

'So do you think this is really going to work?' he's asking, the corners of his eyes crinkling as he smiles.

Catching the laughter in my throat, I gaze up into his pale blue eyes, at the dark grey flecks around his irises, the pale blond eyelashes. I want to absorb every detail. I don't want to forget a single thing.

'I hope so.' I smile back, nuzzling my nose against his neck and inhaling the soft, warm scent of old T-shirt and second-hand suede jacket. Despite the heat of the evening, he insisted on wearing it, like always.

'You don't think it's some scam by the old man and we're going to get mugged under the bridge.'

'Mugged?' I laugh, jerking my head up. 'By who?'

He gestures to the gondolier and does a mock-scary face.

'You're crazy,' I giggle.

'You say that now, but . . .' He puts his mouth up close to my ear and whispers, 'Have you never seen *The Godfather*?' He draws a finger across his throat and makes a choking sound.

I crack up and punch him in the ribs

'Ow,' he yelps, flopping back against the cushion. 'That's a mean left hook you've got there. I need to be careful.' He grabs hold of my fist.

'Uh-huh.' I nod, meeting his eyes.

'Very, very careful.' He starts slowly uncurling my fingers, stretching out my palm and tracing the lines upon it with his fingertips.

I lie back, enjoying the sensation of his fingers brushing against mine, feeling the mood change, like a summer breeze. His touch is light, feathery, gentle, yet its effect upon me is like a thousand volts coursing through my veins. Now I know what people mean when they talk about electricity between two people. It's as if someone has just plugged me straight into the mains. I feel alive. As if I spent the first nineteen years of my life asleep and it was only when I met Nate that I finally woke up.

'Hey, can you hear that?'

Nate's voice brings me back. His head is tilted, his eyes searching the air around him, a smile spreading slowly across his face.

'What—' I begin, but he puts a finger to my lips.

'Ssh, listen.'

The warm evening air surrounds us with its pillow-softness, its scents of red wine and fresh pizza, cigarettes and aftershave, mingled with the sounds of music, voices, a woman in the apartment above us washing dishes . . .

And something else.

In the distance I can hear something. I listen closer. Is that . . .? Could that be . . .?

'*Bell*s,' I whisper, feeling a sudden thrill. I glance back at Nate. His eyes are twinkling with excitement.

'This is it.' He grins and my stomach releases a cage of butterflies. '*It's happening.*'

With the soft peal of bells being carried on the breeze, we glance up ahead to see the bridge. Arching majestically over the canal, it glows in the golden light, the white marble a blank canvas for the setting sun. Streaks of vermilion mixed with tinges of burnt umber and yellow ochre create a shimmering rainbow reflected in the water. We drift slowly towards it, both filled with anticipation, excitement, laughter, love . . .

Closer and closer . . .

And now the gondolier is falling into the shade and we are gliding slowly under the bridge. Inch by inch, by inch. We have only a few seconds. Our eyes lock. Our laughter falls silent. The joking stops. *Everything stops.*

In that split second everything slows right down. Like a movie gone into slow motion, the frame freezes. It's just me and Nate. The two of us. The only people to exist in the whole wide world.

Two halves of one whole . . . Out of nowhere the old Italian's voice pops into my head and I feel a shiver tingle all the way up my spine. *You will have everlasting and eternal love. You will be together for ever and nothing will ever break you apart.* As his words echo inside, the air suddenly turns cooler and goose bumps prickle my arms.

Something's different. There's an energy. A certainty. A powerful sensation all around me that I can't describe. It feels like . . . like . . .

I look at Nate. He's leaning towards me . . . The bells are chiming . . . The sky is blazing . . . and my breath is held so tight in my chest I feel as if I'm going to burst with the sheer exhilaration of the moment, of him pulling me close, of him telling me he loves me.

Magic. That's what it feels like.

It feels like magic.

'And?'

I snap back to see the barman standing stock still behind the bar, gripping the beer pumps as he waits anxiously.

A warm glow envelops me. 'And we kissed,' I reply simply.

It's as if the whole bar has been holding its breath. All at once there's a loud exhalation of giddy relief. There's even a slight ripple of applause, and someone, somewhere whoops.

'So what happened then?' gasps Robyn excitedly. She looks joyous. As does the rest of the audience, I realise, glancing around. Everyone, it seems, loves a love story.

I pause, collecting my thoughts. I feel the moment quickly ebbing away, vanishing back into the past, swallowed up by the present. Like Venice itself, it's fast disappearing into the water.

'Well, it was the end of the summer, so he went back to Harvard and I went back to Manchester,' I say matter-of-factly. 'There were lots of letters, the odd phone call when we could afford it – it was so expensive to call transatlantic in those days and I didn't even have the Internet.' I smile ruefully. 'We dated long-distance for almost a year . . .' I pause. I can see everyone waiting eagerly for the punchline. For the big happy ever after.

My stomach knots.

'And then?' The redhead with the martini glass is almost beside herself.

I suddenly feel a huge weight of responsibility for everyone's hopes. I don't want to disappoint them. I don't want to let them down. And yet . . .

I feel a lump in my throat. Even now, after all this time, I can't think about it without that crushing feeling in my chest. That feeling of not being able to draw breath. As if I'm swimming underwater and my lungs are going to burst.

I can remember it as if it was yesterday. I had just graduated and was sleeping on a friend's sofa in London while I looked for a studio to rent. It was summer. I remember seeing forget-me-nots in the park as I walked home, remember wondering if they had forget-me-nots in America, thinking how as I bent down to pick one that I'd press its pretty blue petals and send them to Nathaniel.

My friend yelled to me as I opened the front door. Standing in the hallway, she held out the phone to me, a bright, excited smile on her face. It was him, Nathaniel, my American boyfriend calling. I rushed towards her and snatched up the phone, trying to untangle the wires that twisted round my hand, breathless with excitement about speaking to him, telling him all my news, hearing his voice.

But the moment I heard it, I knew. In that split second I just knew.

Zoning back to the bar, I take a deep breath to steady my trembling voice and say as nonchalantly as I can, 'We broke up. He married someone else.'

The audience gasps. Robyn throws her hand over her mouth. Another girl looks gutted.

'No fucking way!' curses the barman in disbelief.

My sister, who until now has been silent, nods, partly in sympathy, partly because she's heard this story a million times. 'Way,' she says matter-of-factly, answering for me. 'I saw it in the *New York Times*. They got the full page.'

There's a sharp intake of breath around the bar. Feeling all eyes upon me, I focus on my beer, swallowing the amber bubbles, trying to block out my emotions, which are swirling around inside me . . . Him saying he was sorry, that this long-distance thing wasn't working and he'd met someone else, that he never wanted to hurt me but it had all happened so fast . . . Me dropping the phone, feeling my legs give way beneath me as I crumpled into a heap in the hallway, feeling as if my heart had split clean in half, just like that stupid coin pendant he bought me . . .

OK, stop right there. I pull myself up sharply. I'm getting carried away thinking about this stuff again. It's in the past, and that's where it's going to stay.

'See, that's what happens when you believe in silly fairy stories about everlasting love,' I say, quickly pulling myself together. And putting down my glass, I force a bright smile. 'Right, who's for more drinks?'

Chapter Four

The weekend comes and goes in a flurry of moving and unpacking. It takes several trips to move everything from my sister's apartment to Robyn's – trust me, it would have taken a lot more if it hadn't been for my sister and her obligatory lists. Clipboard in hand, she organised everything with military precision, which is not easy, considering my two suitcases had somehow transformed themselves into about eight bin liners full of stuff. I swear it was like magic porridge. The more I packed, the more I found to pack. Correction: the more my sister found to pack.

She was like something from *CSI*, going through the apartment with a fine-tooth comb, discovering random socks under radiators, my toothbrush in the kitchen (don't ask, I have no idea how it got there either), a do-it-yourself Pilates DVD in the recorder. I bought it in a burst of enthusiasm. According to the blurb on the back, in no time at all the unsightly roll over the top of my jeans would apparently be transformed into what the cheery, super-toned instructor called a 'steel corset'.

I say 'apparently' because trust me, two weeks later there is nothing underneath my T-shirt even *vaguely* resembling a corset, steel or otherwise. Admittedly I've only done it once. Twice, if you count fast-forwarding through the boring bits.

To be honest, I was secretly hoping I could 'accidentally' forget it and leave it at my sister's. That way, I'd have an excuse not to have to do it. I wasn't reckoning on Kate's sniffer-dog talents, though, and before I knew it, it was ejected from its hiding place and added to my mountain of luggage.

Thankfully Robyn was on hand to help me unpack it all at the other end. Her approach was slightly different to that of my sister. Hers was more along the lines of:

1. Rip open a bin liner.
2. Chuck everything all over the floor.
3. Then spend hours randomly picking things out with cries of 'Ooh, what's this?' (my new Butter Frosting bubble bath from Sephora – God, I *love* Sephora. It's my new spiritual home), 'Wow, can I try this on?' (a silver sequinned scarf I bought from Top Shop yonks ago and which I've never worn but still insist on taking with me every time I go away, just in case *this* time I get an uncontrollable urge for a silver sequinned scarf) and 'Oh my God, is this really you?' (my old photo albums, in particular a teenage picture of me when I was going through my goth stage and was all liquid eyeliner and dyed black hair).

Robyn, I quickly discover, is what they delicately describe in novels as 'loquacious'. In real life it means she never stops talking. Not for one moment over the weekend does she appear to draw breath. If it's not to me, her mum in Chicago or her numerous friends, it's to her two beloved dogs, Jenny and Simon, who follow her wherever she goes, heads cocked on one side, eyes beseeching, waiting for treats to drop from her pockets.

Both are strays that she rescued from an animal shelter. Simon is short and fat, snores like a pig. Jenny is thinner, hairier and has a terrible underbite. Robyn loves them like they're her children. In fact, the way she mothers them you'd almost think she gave birth to them herself. When Simon isn't having acupuncture for his arthritic hip, or Jenny isn't being given Chinese herbs for her allergies, they're sitting on the sofa having their bellies tickled and watching *Oprah*.

Oprah is to Robyn what the Pope is to a Catholic. Armed with a bowl of popcorn and the remote, she listens solemnly as Oprah discusses infidelity, dabs away tears during Oprah's interview with a couple who lost their cat to cancer and high-fives the sofa when Oprah appears in a pair of skinny jeans and announces she's lost twenty pounds. In forty-eight hours we cover sex, love and weight loss. By the time Monday morning rolls around, I'm relieved to leave Oprah behind and go to work.

Although Robyn promises me tonight's episode about a man who married a grizzly bear is going to be 'a good one'.

Work is at an art gallery in SoHo called Number Thirty-Eight, and with my new address I can now walk there, which means an extra twenty minutes in bed.

Well, that was the idea.

Only in practice my terrible timekeeping is made worse by sleeping through my alarm and those extra twenty minutes turn into an extra forty.

Which means I have to rush like a mad thing in my flip-flops (which is a bit of a non-sequitur. I mean, seriously, have you ever *tried* running in flip-flops?).

'Morning.' Smoothing down my shower-damp hair, I push open the glass door of the gallery. My heart is hammering in my chest, a sure sign that I need to do that DVD, if not for my muffin top, then so I don't have a heart attack before the age of thirty-five.

'Loozy!' booms a loud voice from the back office, heralding the appearance of Mrs Zuckerman, my boss, otherwise known as Magda. By the strength of her vocal chords you'd be forgiven for expecting someone over six feet tall and two hundred pounds. Instead she's a diminutive blonde woman who can't measure more than five feet, despite her skyscraper heels and carefully constructed beehive, which rises five inches from her scalp in a golden haystack.

'It is so good to see you!' Dressed head to toe in Chanel, she bustles into the gallery, her miniature Maltese dog scampering at her heels. Reaching up, she grabs my face firmly with her diamond-clad fingers and plants two brisk lipstick kisses on either cheek.

This is the way she greets me every morning. It's a bit of a departure from the clipped 'Hello' that I grew used to from Rupert, my old boss in London, but then Rupert was Gordonstoun-educated and mates with Prince Charles. He used to walk around the gallery as if he still had the coat hanger in his suit jacket and wore one of those rings on his little finger with his ancestral coat of arms or something on it.

Whenever anyone came into the gallery who wore one, he would fiddle with it, like it was some secret code and they could communicate telepathically through their pinkie rings.

Magda is the antithesis of that old-school pinkie-ring mentality of the British class system. A rambunctious Jewish lady with a thick Israeli accent, despite having moved to New York thirty years ago, she's not about subtleties, calling a serviette a napkin or saying, 'What?' instead of 'Pardon' (all lessons I learned from Rupert, who seemed to take it upon himself to play Henry Higgins to my Eliza Doolittle).

Instead everything is about extremes and exaggeration. Why call a spade a spade when you can call it something completely different? And preferably outrageous. She talks in exclamation marks and is forever regaling me with one of her outlandish stories, be it about an amazing dessert ('The apple pie was unbelievable!), her three ex-husbands (He was terrible I tell you, *terrible*!) or the time she was arrested ('I say to the police officer, "Why cannot I break his windows? He broke my heart. It is justice!"').

Like strong cheese, or Russell Brand, you're either going to love Magda or hate her.

Luckily for me, it's the former.

'Are you hungry? Did you have breakfast?' Without waiting for an answer, she dives into her large Louis Vuitton tote. Out of it she pulls an enormous paper bag filled with what appears to be the entire contents of a bakery. 'I bought bagels. Sesame, poppy seed, onion . . .'

'Thanks, but I'm fine with coffee.' I smile, reaching for the coffee-machine. 'I've never actually been much of a breakfast person.'

Magda looks at me like I've just told her I'm an alien from outer space. 'You don't eat breakfast?' Her eyes are wide with astonishment.

Saying that, Magda always has a certain astonished look about her. At first I just thought she was permanently surprised by things, but now I've figured out it's due to her eyebrows, which sit much higher on her forehead than normal, a result, I suspect, of having had 'work done'.

Which in the States is not in reference to a new loft conversion but to a series of nips and tucks performed by a man in a white coat at some fancy address on Fifth Avenue.

'Well, no, not usually.'

Magda is shaking her head violently. 'But this is terrible!' she cries, pounding the countertop with her fist for emphasis. '*Terrible!*'

I swear you'd think she'd just found out her entire family had died at sea, not that her employee skipped breakfast.

'No, honestly, it's fine. I'm not that hungry,' I try explaining, but Magda is having none of it.

'You must eat. You must eat to survive,' she insists dramatically.

I open my mouth to protest. Trust me, I eat. And I have the thighs to prove it. Remember that movie *Alive*, in which the survivors of a plane crash had to eat each other to survive? Well, those passengers could have lived for months on my thighs. Years, probably.

There's no point trying to point this out to Magda, I realise, looking at my boss's determined expression. I surrender and take a poppy-seed bagel.

Immediately her expression changes from tragic to comic, like one of those theatre masks. 'It's good, no?' she chuckles, beaming with pleasure.

'Mmm, yes, delicious.' I nod in agreement.

'I have cream cheese and lox.'

Lox, I've learned, means smoked salmon in New York.

'No, thanks,' I mutter through a mouthful of bagel.

'You want it toasted?'

'Mmph.' I shake my head.

'I have honey. You like it with honey?'

I'm still chewing.

'Peanut butter? Pickles?'

I had no idea there were so many different ways you could eat a bagel, and I'm sure she would have kept suggesting them if I hadn't swallowed hard and managed, 'Um . . . it's yummy just as it is,' nearly choking myself in the process.

'Hmm, well, OK.' She clucks her tongue reluctantly. 'It is important to keep up your strength as we have a very, *very* busy day today. We have some new paintings arriving by an amazing artist from Columbia. Oy, the colours!' She smacks her lips with her scarlet fingernails.

At the mention of the paintings, I feel the familiar tingle of excitement that I always get when I see work by a new artist. A sort of fluttering in my stomach, like when I was little and I would run downstairs on Christmas Day and see all my presents under the tree. The feeling of anticipation, followed by the discovery of something new and wonderful.

I'm sure the paintings will be amazing. Magda's judgement when it comes to husbands and broken windows might be questionable, but when it comes to art, she has great instincts.

I glance around the gallery. She's been running this place for over twenty years, ever since she won it in a divorce settlement from her second husband, a millionaire property mogul. By her own admission, she had no formal art background and just sort of fell into it, buying whatever took her fancy, whatever made her smile, and because of her unorthodox approach, it's totally unique.

When you think of art galleries, you often think of those huge, imposing white lofts with several floors, but Number Thirty-Eight is housed in the converted basement of a townhouse. Most people walk past it on their way to the big-name designer stores and never think to glance down at the sidewalk, through the railings and into our windows. They never notice an amazing abstract painting by a new artist, or a series of striking lithographs that form part of our latest exhibition.

But if you do happen across us, and take a few moments out of your busy schedule to look inside, you'll want to keep coming back. Because unlike those big, austere galleries, the moment you walk into Number Thirty-Eight and hear the stereo blaring, you'll realise this is a whole new way to experience art.

Forget silence and speaking in hushed voices – Magda believes in having music playing (she has eclectic taste. Last week it was *La Bohème*; today it's Justin Timberlake), along with fresh coffee brewing and a popcorn machine. 'We are like the movies,' she cries to the curious members of the public who wander inside and find themselves being asked if they want sugar or salt on their popcorn. 'Here you can escape, be entertained, use your imagination. And even better, no Tom Cruise!'

Magda's passionate dislike of Tom Cruise ('If he jumped on my sofa, I would *keel* him!') is paralleled only by her passion for art, and her desire is to make it accessible to everyone. 'Remember, it's always free to look' is her mantra, and her enthusiasm is so infectious that people can't help but be seduced by it. In the few weeks that I've been working here, I've noticed regulars coming in just to hang out and enjoy the art, with no pressure to buy. It's not like any private gallery I've ever worked in.

'And I have decided . . .'

I focus back on Magda as she pauses for a silent drum roll.

'Yes?' I brace myself. I'm fast learning to expect the unexpected.

'It is time for us to do an opening. Show off our talent. Fling open our doors.' She throws out her arms. 'Fly in the face of this nasty recession!' Curling her lip, she snarls at me.

'Wow, er, great,' I enthuse, flinching slightly. 'That's an excellent idea.'

I feel a secret beat of relief. My boss's magnanimous attitude to art might be commendable, but we're not the MoMA or the Whitney. We do actually need to *sell* some of it to stay open. In the six weeks I've been working here, sales have been slow to the point of zero and I've started to worry a bit about my job.

I only got it because Rupert knows Magda from his Studio 54 days, back in the seventies, when he lived here for a brief period. When he discovered she needed an extra pair of hands, he suggested me. He knew I wouldn't turn down the chance to work in a New York gallery. 'Plus I owe Magda a huge favour,' he'd confided darkly, refusing to be drawn.

Not that I'd tried. To be quite honest, just learning that Rupert, in his navy blazer with gold buttons and pinkie ring, used to shake his thang at a world-famous disco was information enough.

'We will have wine, champagne . . .' she continues, then frowns ' . . .well, maybe not champagne, but the fizzy wine we can do.' Thanks to her generous divorce settlements, Magda is a very wealthy woman, but she's also frugal. 'I mean, who can tell the difference?' She looks at me, palms outstretched.

People who spend thousands of dollars on art, I'm tempted to say, but she's already run on ahead.

'And food, we must have lots of food,' she says, reaching for a bagel, then thinking better of it and putting it back. Despite her desire for everyone else to eat, I don't think I've ever actually seen anything pass Magda's suspiciously inflated lips.

'You mean canapés?'

Magda looks at me mistrustfully. 'What is this canopy?'

'Like, for example, mini-quiches,' I suggest. 'Or you could do sushi – that's always easy.'

'Pah! Sushi!' She wrinkles her nose in distaste. 'I don't get this sushi. These little pieces of raw fish and bits of rice.'

'Back in London we catered an exhibition with sushi and sake, and it was very successful,' I try encouraging. 'In fact, we got several compliments.'

'No.' She gives a dismissive shake of the head. 'We will do meatballs.'

For a moment I think I've heard wrong.

'Meatballs?' I repeat incredulously. The thought of inviting people to a gallery opening and serving meatballs is unheard of in the art world. I try to imagine Rupert eating meatballs while admiring a watercolour with Lady So-and-So.

Strangely I can't.

To tell the truth, I think Rupert would have a coronary at the *mention* of a meatball.

'Yes, I will make them myself. To my special recipe,' Magda is saying decisively. 'They will be wonderful. My meatballs are famous.' There's a pause. 'What? You don't believe me?'

I zone back in to see Magda looking at me indignantly.

'Oh, er, yes, of course I do,' I protest hastily. 'I'm sure they're delicious!'

Arms folded, she peers at me, nostrils flared. She reminds me a bit of a bull just as it stampedes. I know this because I grew up near a farm and there was a bull that had nearly trampled to death a rambler who dared cut across his field.

Right now I feel a bit like that rambler.

'Meatballs, *mmm*,' I enthuse, groping around in my head for something to say about meatballs and trying desperately to dismiss images of school dinners. 'How ... um ... meaty!'

Meaty? That's it, Lucy? That's all you can come up with?

I cringe inwardly, but if my boss suspects anything, she doesn't show it. Rather, the corners of her mouth turn up slightly and I see her visibly thawing.

'My favourite,' I add.

Well, in for a penny, in for a pound.

'They are?' Magda's ample chest swells.

'Absolutely.' I nod, crossing my fingers behind my back.

'In fact, I could eat them all day every day,' I continue.

Now I've started, I don't seem able to stop.

'You could?' Magda is positively beaming.

'Oh, yes.' I nod. 'In fact, if someone said to me, "Lucy Hemmingway, you can only eat one thing for the rest of your life," it wouldn't be chocolate or Ben and Jerry's Chunky Monkey ice cream. Oh, no.' I put my hand on my hip and waggle my finger theatrically, suddenly feeling a bit like when I played Annie in the school play.

'Dynamic,' was how the local newspaper described me. Mum has the cutting in a frame in the downstairs loo, along with a picture of me as Annie. Which is very unfortunate – me in braces and a curly ginger wig at thirteen is not a pretty sight, and not something I want to see every time I use the loo.

It's the reason I spent my entire teenage years whizzing boyfriends straight out through the front door, despite their bursting bladders.

'No. Do you know what it would be, Mrs Zuckerman?' I ask, throwing my arms out wide.

I'm now in full pantomime mode, complete with hand gestures and over-the-top facial expressions. I'm quite enjoying myself. Perhaps amateur dramatics would have suited me.

Had I actually been able to act, that is.

'No. Tell me,' whispers Magda with anticipation.

'Meatballs!' I declare dramatically. 'Nothing but meatballs!'

OK. Maybe I got a bit *too* carried away there.

Surprisingly, though, Magda looks like all her Christmases have come at once. Or, I should say, Hanukkahs.

'Oh, Loozy.' Reaching for my hand, she clutches it in her tiny one, which is encrusted with diamonds, courtesy of her ex-husbands. 'If only you were Jewish, I would beg you to marry my youngest son, Daniel. Nothing would make me happier.'

'Oh . . . um, thanks.' I smile uncertainly, not sure how to take this compliment.

Magda discovered my single status within thirty minutes of my first day at work. By noon she'd demanded my entire relationship history since primary school and by closing time had declared them all schmucks.

'You would be the perfect couple,' she says, reaching into her enormous tote and pulling out a concertina-type thingy, which she opens out like an accordion. It's filled with photographs of her family. 'See! Here he is!' She thrusts a picture at me.

I stare at it, my face momentarily frozen in shock.

Think Austin Powers in a yarmulke.

'I know, he's handsome, huh?' She beams, misinterpreting my reaction. 'Look at those green eyes! And that smile! Have you ever seen a smile like that before?'

'Um . . .wow,' I manage, trying to find a positive angle.

Then give up.

Well, really. I'm not shallow. I know looks aren't everything and that it's personality that counts, but, well . . . I glance back at the photo and his giant rabbit-sized teeth.

OK, sod it. Call me shallow.

'And an architect too!' Magda is swelling up so much I'm fearful she's going to burst with maternal pride.

'Wow,' I repeat. My vocabulary, it seems, has shrunk to one word. Not that Magda has noticed, mind you. She's too busy beaming at her son's photograph and polishing it with her sleeve.

'But it is such a shame because you cannot marry. The Jewish faith passes through the woman.' She takes a deep, heartfelt sigh. 'It is wonderful for the feminism but not for you and Daniel.' She turns to me, her eyes downcast.

'I understand.' I nod gravely, while inside I feel little bursts of joy. Like tiny fireworks going off inside me. I've always been an atheist, but now suddenly I'm a born-again.

'I'm so sorry.' She's still shaking her head.

'It's OK. Really, I understand.' I try to look as sad as I can, while stifling a giggle that's bubbling up inside. 'I'll survive.'

Any minute I'll start breaking out to Gloria Gaynor.

'It is a crime that a girl like you is single. A crime!' she repeats, passionately thumping the reception with her fist. 'But don't worry,' she quickly reassures. 'Leave it to me.'

I feel a beat of alarm. 'Leave what?'

'I married off my brother and three of my cousins. My family call me Magda the Matchmaker.'

Oh my God, this cannot be happening. It's bad enough having friends try to matchmake, *but your boss?*

'I even found someone for Belinda, my sister's daughter. A nice doctor from Brooklyn. And that was a tough one,' she confides, lowering her voice. 'The girl's a vegan and refuses to shave her legs. I mean, I ask you.' She throws her hands in the air. 'I said to her, "Belinda, we're not in Germany. Buy a razor!"'

I'm like a rabbit caught in headlights.

'Trust me, your single days are numbered,' she vows, throwing me a triumphant beam.

I stare at her dazedly. Never have I wanted to be part of a couple more than in this moment.

'Um . . . great,' I manage. 'Lucky me!'

She smiles in consolation. 'Well, it is no substitute for my Daniel, but it is the best I can do.' Then, taking one last lingering look at her beloved son, she snaps the concertina of photographs closed. 'OK, enough of this love stuff. We must go to work!'

Chapter Five

Thankfully I don't have any time to think about my near-miss with Daniel, or who else Magda is going to try to matchmake me with, as the rest of the morning is consumed in a whirl of activity getting things ready for the gallery event.

There's masses to do. True to form. Magda impulsively wants everything to happen right now and the date is set for this Friday.

'*This Friday?*' I squeaked in panic.

'You want Thursday instead?' was her reply.

And the scary thing was, I don't think she was joking.

So while she clatters around the gallery on her five-inch heels, firing off instructions, I start organising. First things first, I draw up a list:

```
1. Compile guest list.
2. Send out invitations.
3. Write promotional material.
4. Book caterer.
5. Hire waitressing staff.
6. Hang paintings ready to exhibit.
```

See. I might not have been born with the organisation gene like my sister, Kate, but I'm not *completely* useless at it. OK, so I admit I'd rather have a paintbrush than a computer mouse in my hand, and yes, I still type with two fingers (oh, all right, then, *one* finger), and it's true that until recently I thought a spreadsheet was that curtain-thingy on the bottom of the bed (apparently it's called a valance, which quite frankly is a really stupid name for it. Spreadsheet makes far more sense), but how hard is it to write down all the things you have to do, then tick them off when you've done them?

Feeling rather pleased with myself, I look back at the computer screen and my neatly typed list. Actually, hang on a minute, rewind that thought. I have to do all these things? By the end of this week?

Shit.

6. Panic.

But not right now. It'll have to wait until later, as it's lunchtime, I realise, seeing Magda's head popping out of the back office to remind me it's time to eat. *Again.* I swear I could set my watch by her. Bang on one o'clock she sends me out to Katz's, our local deli, for her usual order of a pastrami sandwich on rye and matzo-ball soup. Though with her tiny size-zero figure and twenty-inch waist, I have a sneaking suspicion it's Valentino, her Maltese, doing most of the eating.

Katz's is a New York institution that's been around for ever. For tourists and those new to the city like me, it's famous for Meg Ryan's faked orgasm in *When Harry Met Sally.* It happened right in the middle of the deli. There's even an arrow pointing to the exact table where it was filmed.

'God, I love that scene.' Taking a ticket, I turn to Robyn, who's just popped out between appointments to meet me with a set of keys she's had cut for the apartment. She works at Tao Healing Arts, not far from here, in Chinatown.

'Men don't.' She grins, also taking a ticket and following me to the counter, where, as always, there's a long queue. 'It scares them. Women who fake it are like the Tooth Fairy. We don't exist.'

I laugh. When she's not quoting Oprah, Robyn can be very funny.

'Saying that, I've never needed to fake it.'

I stop laughing abruptly. 'You haven't?' My voice comes out a little higher than intended.

'Nope, not me.' Shaking her head decisively, she leans closer. 'I'm like a hair trigger.' She snaps her fingers and I jump slightly.

'A what?' I ask in confusion.

'You know, I respond to the slightest stimulation,' she says cheerily. 'What about you?' She meets my eyes with that shiny, happy confidence that Americans seem to ooze from their pores.

'Oh, um. Just a few times,' I fib, pushing my sunglasses back on my head and flicking my hair about, like I always do when I'm avoiding. Well, I'm not going to admit I can't remember the last time to little Miss Hair Trigger over here, am I? 'You know, sometimes, when I'm a bit tired.'

'Have you tried sensual massage?' she suggests helpfully.

That's another thing about Americans – they are always so completely earnest. With fellow Brits, this conversation would have already descended into lewd jokes and leg-pulling, like the recent afternoon I spent in a bookstore with Kate sniggering at the illustrations in *The Joy of Sex*. She was going to buy it as a wedding gift for her friends, but after seeing the pictures of the hippy guy with the long beard and skinny legs, she was scared it might have a detrimental effect on their love life. She ended up buying them a set of steak knives instead.

Still, I am an adult, not a teenager. I should be able to have a conversation about orgasms and sex without being immature and having to make silly jokes, I tell myself firmly. I mean, I'm not that childish.

'It can really help get you in the mood.'

'What? The mood for lurve?' I joke, doing my best Barry White impersonation.

Robyn's steadfast gaze doesn't waver. 'You know, I've got some Chinese herbs you can take for that.'

'For what?' I say, pretending to look at the menu, even though after six weeks of doing the lunch run, I know it off by heart.

'Loss of interest in sex, lack of libido . . .'

'There's nothing wrong with my libido,' I snap, then blush with embarrassment. 'Thanks very much, but it's fine, honestly.'

'You know it's important to get in touch with your sexuality,' she continues matter-of-factly. 'You Brits can be so uptight. You're never going to come with that attitude.'

'I do come,' I gasp indignantly.

The queue of people in front of me turn to stare. I feel my cheeks sting beetroot. 'It's just been a while since I had great sex,' I hiss defensively, shuffling forwards.

'You and me both, honey,' mutters a fifty-something waitress, barging past with a tray of matzo-ball soup.

'How long's a while?' persists Robyn, looking concerned.

'Oh, you know . . .'

Ten years, pipes up a little voice in my head. *Ten years since Italy. Since Nathaniel. Since you had great, mind-blowing, knock-your-socks-off sex.*

'A few months,' I say firmly. Well, that's ridiculous. I must have had great orgasmic sex since then. What about Sean . . .? Or before that there was Anthony . . . Or even the fling with the Scottish guy on my holiday to Spain when I was twenty-five. I can't remember his name, but I remember he made this really funny noise when we did it, sort of like a *squeaking* . . .

Oh God. It's true. It's been ten years. Ten years without an orgasm.

Well, *not strictly*.

'Masturbation doesn't count, by the way,' says Robyn, interrupting my thoughts.

'It doesn't?'

The hope in my voice is audible.

'Nuh-uh.' She shakes her head, her eyes flashing with amusement. Then suddenly a thought seems to hit her and her face fills with comprehension. 'Oh my God, it's *him*, isn't it?' she says in a hushed voice. 'He was the last time.'

'Who?' I try to play dumb. I'm terrible. Annie was my only good role.

'The guy from Italy. Your everlasting love. *The One*.'

Put like that, it sounds more than ridiculous. It sounds pathetic.

'Don't be silly. He's not my everlasting love.' I give a scornful little laugh.

'But you said—'

'Hey, lady!'

Our conversation is interrupted by a loud holler and I glance up to see a sullen man behind the counter scowling at me. It's the same sullen man who serves me every day. I've never yet seen him smile or heard him grunt more than a couple of words. He jerks his bald head. This, I've learned, is my cue to order.

'One matzo-ball soup and a pastrami on rye,' I reply. I feel a beat of pleasure. Gosh, listen to me – I sound like a true New Yorker. *Pastrami on rye.* To think that not long ago I was in M&S buying a sandwich from the Count on Us range.

The sullen man grunts and starts carving up big chunks of pastrami.

'Oh, and a tuna melt,' I add.

As you can see, my Count on Us days are long behind me. Tuna melts, I've discovered, are *the* most delicious things. Who would have thought melted cheese on tuna could be such a winning combo?

He scowls, scribbles something on a piece of paper, which he stuffs through a hatch, and turns back to the heap of pastrami he's carved.

'Thanks.' I smile brightly and turn back to Robyn, who's having trouble deciding what to order. 'Look, I said a lot of things the other night,' I say dismissively. 'Like he married another woman, remember?'

She looks at me for a moment as if she's weighing me up. 'You know, if you're unable to reach orgasm, it might be because you're still in love with someone else,' she says pointedly.

'What part of "he's married" didn't you understand?' I say equally as pointedly.

She opens her mouth to protest, then thinks again and gives a reluctant sigh of defeat. 'Jeez, that sucks. It was such a romantic story,' she says sadly.

'So is *Romeo and Juliet*,' I reply, as we move towards the cash register, 'and that didn't turn out so well either.' I hand my receipt to the teller.

'That'll be twenty-two dollars and forty-five cents,' he says, ringing it up.

'Haven't we met before?'

In the middle of digging out my purse, I look up to see Robyn throwing a toothpaste-ad smile at the man behind the cash register. Well, I say man, but he can't be older than about twenty. Gawkily tall with dark hair and a bum-fluff moustache, he smiles nervously.

'We have?' he asks uncertainly. He looks slightly afraid. As if he's going to get busted for doing something.

'It's Harold, right?'

'Um . . . no, it's Anthony. You must have got me mixed up with someone else.'

'Oh. sorry, my mistake.' She smiles apologetically and turns back to me. The smile immediately falls from her face. 'Damn, he was kinda cute.'

'So you haven't given up yet?'

'Of course not!' She looks astonished that I could even ask such a question. 'If he's my destiny, I'm not going to stop looking until I find him. Because if I'm looking for my soulmate, my soulmate is out there somewhere looking for me.' Her green eyes flash with determination. 'I know you probably think I'm crazy . . .'

'No, I don't,' I protest a little too quickly.

' . . . but sometimes you have to take a leap of faith. Trust in the universe. Believe in the power of positive thinking and the laws of attraction. It's like *The Secret*. Did you ever read it?'

'No, I don't think—'

'Well, I did, cover to cover,' she continues, 'and I bought the DVD. It was amazing. Seriously. I made a vision board and everything.'

'What's that?'

Robyn turns on me incredulously. 'You don't know what a vision board is?'

'Um . . .'

I feel like the time I was ten and in the school playground and someone asked me if I knew what an erection was.

' . . . not exactly,' I try bluffing. 'Should I?'

'Oh my God. Totally!' she cries, eyes wide. 'A vision board is a visualisation tool that activates the universal law of attraction to begin manifesting your dreams into reality.'

'Right, I see.' I nod, not seeing at all.

Rather like when I was ten and asked my sister what an erection was and, after laughing her head off, she explained it's what you called a penis when it goes hard.

Only I didn't know what a penis was.

'Basically, it's really simple. You get a piece of foam board and you cut out pictures or words from magazines or wherever and you make a collage of all the things you want in your life,' she enthuses. 'It's actually kind of fun. You should try it.'

'Hmm, maybe.' I don't want to hurt her feelings, but really. A quiz in a magazine is one thing, but a *vision board*? My sister would have kittens. 'Only it's not quite my thing.'

'Lucy, you've got to stop being so negative,' she reprimands.

'I'm not being negative,' I protest. 'I'm British. We don't do vision boards or self-help books. Well, at least not in public,' I add, thinking about the couple I've got stashed on my shelf.

'Well, you should.' Robyn clicks her tongue and looks at me pityingly.

'Excuse me, miss?'

The teller is holding out my change.

'Oh, thanks.' Taking it from him, I put it back in my purse. 'Sorry, but I just don't believe in that stuff,' I say, turning back to Robyn.

'That's your problem right there.' She shrugs. 'You don't believe.'

Picking the takeaway bag of food from the counter, I hug it to my chest a tad defensively.

'Not everything can be explained or understood, you know, Lucy.' Tucking a shock of curls behind her ear, she looks at me beseechingly. 'Sometimes you have to trust in the mysterious power of the universe, in a greater energy, in a spiritual force, in something bigger than you and me.' Her eyes are shining and her face is filled with such conviction that for a moment I can almost feel my scepticism wavering. 'You just have to believe. And I believe that in this big wide world, in all these billions of people, if two people are meant to be together, they'll be together . . .'

As she's talking, something flickers deep inside. The part of me that used to believe it too, that used to think that Nate and I were meant to be together, that in this big wide world I'd found my soulmate.

'According to the laws of attraction, you attract what you think of the most. In which case, it's just a matter of waiting for Harold to show up.'

But you buried that part of yourself a long time ago, I tell myself firmly, pushing the thought out of my mind. Remember?

'So tell me,' I say, turning the conversation around. 'If you've been spending all this time waiting for Harold, how long has it been for you?'

Without missing a beat she rattles off, 'Thirteen months, eighteen days and –' she glances at her watch – 'about ten hours. I tell you, Harold better hurry up and put in an appearance soon.'

Rolling her eyes, she says to the sullen man who's still waiting to take her order, 'Actually, forget the chicken. I'll have what she's having.' And turning back to me, she laughs throatily. 'I've always wanted to say that in here.'

Back at the gallery, I'm greeted by a pile of wooden crates and a carpet of white polystyrene balls that have escaped from their packaging and are spilling all over the floor. Standing knee-deep in the middle is Magda, flapping her arms around like a flightless bird. She twirls round when she hears me enter.

'You're back!' she gasps excitedly. She's panting slightly and her face is covered in a sheen of perspiration. Her golden beehive, however, remains pristine. 'I have great news!'

Anxiety stabs. Oh God, what now? I've only been gone half an hour.

'You do?' I brace myself for what's about to follow, which, with Magda, could be anything.

'While you were gone, something wonderful happened.'

You took meatballs off the menu? Her son, Daniel, announced he was gay? Daniel Craig has finally discovered I exist and rung to ask if he could take me out for dinner in a limo? And yes, he'll wear *those* swimming trunks for me under his suit?

OK, I admit, that's a secret fantasy of mine.

'A man came in and bought our entire Gustav collection.'

I snap back. 'What? The entire collection?' OK, so it's not Daniel Craig, but it's a really big deal. The Gustav collection consists of several large works by a German artist whose paintings sell for thousands of dollars.

'Everything!' Magda flings her arms wide. 'It happened so fast. He walked in, looked around for a couple of minutes and then boom!' Polystyrene balls fly into the air.

'*Boom?*'

'He said he wanted to buy it all. Just like that. He didn't even ask the price.'

'Wow.' I try to imagine buying an entire collection of art without asking the price, but I can't. In fact, I can't imagine buying *anything* without first finding out what it costs. I even do a price check on shampoo before I put it in my basket.

Then again, I'm not someone who buys art. I'm someone who's forever up to her overdraft limit, late on her credit cards and running out of money before the end of the month. I've tried to learn how to budget, but I've also tried to learn how to play the piano and I'm totally crap at both.

I mean, what exactly is 'balancing a cheque book'? And why would you want to?

'Gosh, that's good news,' I say, feeling a beat of relief that we've finally sold something.

'And he paid with his American Express Black card,' says

Magda with the sort of hushed awe you'd use if you spotted Madonna in your local Starbucks.

'Is that good?' I ask innocently, perching on a stool and unwrapping my tuna melt.

Magda looks aghast. 'You are single and you don't know these things?'

'Um . . . no. Should I?' I ask, taking a bite.

She inhales sharply. 'Loozy! How are you supposed to find a rich husband if you don't know what to look for?'

'I'm not looking for a rich husband,' I reply, my feminist principles rising up in indignation.

'Pah!' She tuts dismissively. 'Every woman is looking for a rich husband.'

I swallow hard. 'None of my boyfriends has been rich,' I retort in my defence. 'In fact, with my last boyfriend I paid for everything!'

Hah! So there.

Magda's expression is incredulous. 'And you think this is a good thing?'

Put like that, I can feel my feminist principles faltering slightly. 'Well, it . . . um . . . gives you independence.'

See. I knew there was a good reason not to date a rich man.

'Independence?' Magda bats the word away like an irritating fly. 'What is this independence nonsense? What are you, an African country?'

My cheeks colour.

'You need to forget about all these silly things,' she continues firmly. 'You need to forget about romance and chemistry and the size of his—' She breaks off and crooks her little finger.

I can feel my cheeks, which are already red, deepen in colour. I'm not used to having these kinds of conversations with my boss. Rupert and I used to talk about London property prices and what happened on *EastEnders*.

'You need to look for three things.'

'I know, I know, personality, good sense of humour—' I begin reciting, but Magda interrupts with a snort of derision.

'What is this? *eHarmony?*' She pulls a face. 'No, no, no. It's very simple. Credit card, watch, shoes.'

I watch with bemusement as she counts them off on her fingers.

'Number one: credit card. No Visa or MasterCard.' She wrinkles up her nose as if there's a bad smell. 'Only American Express. And no green!'

'Why? What's wrong with green?' I ask, before I can stop myself.

'Because you want black,' she says firmly. 'Black has no credit limit. Black is perfect for when you want to go shopping at Bergdorf Goodman.'

I open my mouth to tell her that I've never been shopping at Bergdorf Goodman, but then think better of it.

'Two: watch.' She pauses. 'Rolex or Cartier are both excellent.'

'What about Swatch?' I ask, glancing at my own. It's bright yellow plastic and I've had it for ever.

'A Swatch is a four-storey walk-up in Queens,' she warns darkly.

'Oh, right.' I nod and quickly cover mine with my sleeve.

'Three: shoes.' She folds her arms and fixes me with a beady eye. 'What shoes did your last boyfriend wear?'

Oh-oh.

'Crocs,' I venture gingerly.

Magda looks like she's about to have a heart attack. 'The plastic gardening shoes? *With the holes?*'

I feel my cheeks redden with shame. And I wasn't even the one wearing them.

'They must be hand-stitched. Leather. And Italian.'

I don't think I've ever even *met* anyone who wears hand-stitched Italian leather shoes. Well, apart from Rupert, but he's gay. Hence his love affair with Pat Butcher.

'What about love?' I volunteer. 'Shouldn't that be on the checklist?'

'Trust me, if you find a man with all three, you will fall in love with him,' she instructs, and reaches towards a painting hanging on the wall. 'OK, now help me. We need to pack these quickly. He wants them delivering today.'

'Today?' I glance at all the packing boxes, my earlier excitement deflating slightly. 'Can't he wait until tomorrow?' I feel a tweak of irritation. Who does this guy think he is, coming in here with his black American Express card, thinking he owns the place?

I glance at our now almost empty walls. Saying that, I suppose he kind of does.

'And I want you to go with the delivery and make sure it gets there safely,' continues Magda, ignoring my last comment. 'I would go, but I need to visit my aunt Irena. She's moving into a nursing home. It's a good one, not a bad one. I say to her, "Irena, this is costing more than my apartment on Park Avenue."' She rolls her eyes. 'Anyway, you must go without me. Alone,' she adds darkly.

Suddenly it registers. She's trying to matchmake.

'Oh, no, Magda—' I begin protesting, but she doesn't let me finish.

'Number four: wedding ring. He wasn't wearing one.' Her eyes twinkle mischievously, and looking very pleased with herself indeed, she passes me a roll of bubble wrap.

Chapter Six

By the end of the afternoon all the paintings have been carefully packaged and are being loaded into a truck for delivery. As the last wooden crate disappears into the back of the truck, Magda turns to me.

'So the doorman will sign for the paintings, but they are to be delivered to the customer's penthouse. You must wait with them until the customer arrives. For insurance purposes, you understand?'

'But if someone's already signed, then surely—'

Magda silences me with an outstretched palm. 'You must wait,' she repeats in a tone that's non-negotiable.

I fall silent. I know there's no point trying to reason. She's determined to matchmake, I muse, reluctantly climbing into the front seat of the truck alongside the driver. And after her son, Daniel, I'm under no illusions.

'Y'all set?'

A thick Queens accent interrupts my spiral downwards into general gloom about being single, nudging thirty and at the mercy of well-meaning friends, relatives and now my boss wanting to try to set me up with anything that's got a penis and a heartbeat.

I glance up.

I feel my spirits lift. I've been so distracted I hadn't noticed my driver until now, but he's actually really cute. He's got a shaved head, dark brown eyes and the whitest teeth. In fact, they're so white they look almost luminous against his dark skin. And look at those arms! My eyes flick to biceps that are bulging out of his T-shirt like two huge watermelons as he grips the steering wheel. Crikey, I don't think I've ever seen arms like that in real life. They look like he's stolen them from *Rambo*, or *Rocky*, or one of those Stallone films, and he's got this amazing tattoo of a dragon.

Shit, I'm staring.

'Erm, yes . . . all set.' I smile brightly.

'Loozy.'

I snap back to see Magda at my side window, an expression of disapproval on her face. Without thinking I glance at the driver's feet. He's wearing Nikes.

Well, so what? I'm not looking for a husband, I think indignantly, peeking at his empty wrist and noticing he's not wearing a watch. Or anyone else's, I realise, before noticing he *is* wearing a wedding ring.

Bang goes my little crush.

'And remember to call me,' she instructs. 'I want to know everything got there safely.'

'I will,' I reply dutifully, as the driver turns on the ignition.

'And make sure—'

Thankfully her voice is drowned out as the engine fires up noisily.

Waving goodbye as the truck pulls away, I watch her figure getting smaller and smaller in the side mirror, and for the first time today I allow myself to feel a beat of excitement. I can't believe it. Me. Lucy Hemmingway. In sole charge of some of the finest artwork. Representing the gallery. It's a huge responsibility and a great opportunity to help me climb further up the career ladder.

Plus I get the chance to see inside a real-life penthouse in New York! With a doorman and everything!

Smiling to myself, I roll down the window and look out across Manhattan as me and thousands of dollars worth of paintings begin our journey uptown.

The traffic is bumper to bumper and it takes a lot of stopping and starting and cursing from my driver, who hangs one arm out of the window, yelling at cab drivers and gesticulating, before we reach the park. En route I'm given a running commentary by Mikey, my driver, who's full of anecdotes about each district we go through.

'SoHo's SoHo 'cos it's south of Houston and its neighbour is Tribeca, named for its shape – *Tri*-angle *Be*-low *Ca*-nal, get it? It used to be just full of abandoned warehouses until Robert de Niro set up the Tribeca Film Festival. Greenwich Village is just called the Village. It's always been this bohemian haven. See that café on the corner? That's where Jack Kerouac and Bob Dylan used to hang out.'

It's hot and humid and I stare out of the window and watch Manhattan slowly pass us by.

'Now Union Square. Man, that was nasty, full of drug dealers, but now it's totally cleaned up its act. Over there is where Roosevelt was born. Amazing, huh? Now Chelsea, that's famous for where Sid Vicious killed Nancy Spungen.'

As we move uptown, old brick warehouses covered in cast-iron fire escapes that cling like ivy give way to elegant brownstones with wide steps and polished brass doorknobs. Shafts of sunlight shine through the gaps in the buildings that tower overhead, and shopfronts change from discount 99-cent shops, busy markets and eclectic bookstores to fancy designer stores and expensive restaurants.

Neighbourhoods smarten up, as do the people. From the grungy guys, with their skinny jeans, piercings and White Stripes T-shirts, trawling through second-hand record stores on Canal Street, to the blonde ponytailed mums with their four-wheel-drive baby buggies and coffees-to-go on the Upper West Side, to the hordes of joggers and rollerbladers zigzagging in and out of Central Park.

'And finally we have touchdown . . .'

Amid a fanfare of horns the truck swings to a shuddering halt outside a large, modern high-rise towering over the park.

'We're here?' Dipping my head, I try craning upwards to see.

'Yup. Sure are,' nods Mikey, flashing me a huge grin. He glances at the building and lets out a whistle. 'Very fancy.'

I look across at the dark green awning, the square of carpet that spills out on to the pavement and the polished glass and brass door out of which a uniformed doorman hurries to greet us.

Wow. It's like arriving at the Savoy or something.

'Are you sure this isn't a hotel?' I call to Mikey, who's already jumped out of the truck and is hoisting up the back door with a loud rattle.

He laughs at my reaction. 'Nope, this is how some people live, lady.'

I feel a clutch of nerves. God, this is seriously posh. Nervously climbing out of the truck, I tug down my skirt and quickly smooth my hair, which has gone all poufy in the heat. That's another difference between my sister, Kate, and me. Whereas she's got thick, straight blonde hair, mine's fine and brown.

I swear I have the most boring hair colour in the world. I'll never forget the first time I dyed it. I matched it up against a colour chart in Boots, the ones where they give you little locks of hair to compare against, and guess what? It wasn't even chestnut brown or dark brown; it was 'normal brown'. Can there be a more dispiriting description?

Hence I've coloured it my entire life. I've been 'butterscotch', 'cinnamon', 'jet' and all the colours in between, including a dodgy period in my mid-twenties when I thought I'd try something different and dyed it 'bubblegum pink'. I'm currently a very sensible and mature 'chestnut'.

'Good afternoon. You're from the gallery?'

I turn to see the doorman. Wearing a dark green uniform, complete with peaked cap and white gloves, he nods briskly.

'Hi, yes,' I say, smiling brightly to cover up my nerves, before realising he's not smiling and I'm grinning away like a loon. I quickly match my expression to his very formal one. 'Lucy Hemmingway . . . um . . . senior coordinator.'

I just made that up. I don't actually have a title.

'I'm here to oversee the delivery and installation of a collection of artwork.'

I want to appear super professional. Like someone who's completely in control of every situation. Someone who's efficient, organised and, well, basically like my sister.

I do not – repeat not – want to appear like someone whose approach to problem-solving is ignoring something and hoping it goes away, who writes lists only to lose them and once hit 'reply all' to a friend's birthday evite and asked if she was still having sex with her ex.

'Ah, yes.' The doorman nods gravely. 'I've been given instructions to expect you.' Pushing his half-moon glasses up his nose, he flicks his eyes to the paintings, which are being unloaded on to a trolley by Mikey. 'I'm to take you up to the penthouse.'

My stomach gives a little flutter. It's that penthouse thing again. You can take the girl out of her poky little one-bed flat in Earl's Court, but you can't take the poky little one-bed flat out of the girl.

'If you'd care to follow me.'

With Mikey in charge of pushing the trolley, I dutifully follow the doorman through the doorway and enter a large marbled lobby, complete with trickling water feature, button-back leather sofas and oversized vases filled with the kind of exotic-looking flower arrangements that you know cost an absolute fortune.

'The elevator is straight ahead.'

I'm trying to appear completely nonchalant and unimpressed, but my head is swivelling from side to side like a barn owl. It's a bit different to my lobby, with its obstacle course of bikes, push-chairs and piles of mail to negotiate. And that's *before* you even begin to climb the three flights of stairs to mine and Robyn's apartment. Stairs, by the way, that are so steep they make the ones up the sides of the Mayan pyramids at Chichen Itza in Mexico seem like a walk in the park.

'Whoa, fancy,' whistles Mikey from behind the trolley. 'You must have some celebrities living here, right?'

'I'm afraid I'm not at liberty to disclose that kind of information,' replies the doorman stiffly.

Mikey throws me a look and mouths, 'Madonna.'

I break into a grin, despite myself, and stifle a giggle.

Ahead of us, I notice a lift, the doors of which are just about to close. 'Oh look,' I say, gesturing to it, 'just in time.' I make a dash towards them, but the doorman stops me.

'The penthouse has its own private elevator.'

'It does?'

He turns the corner, where another lift is waiting for us.

Crikey. There's posh and there's then *posh*.

Maybe Mikey's right. Maybe Madonna *does* live here.

Buzzing with anticipation, I step into the lift. It's quite tight inside and we have to shuffle up against each other as the door slides closed. The doorman presses the button with a ceremonious stab of his white-gloved finger and we start travelling upwards, climbing steadily higher and higher. I feel my stomach drop as we gather speed. Gosh, we really are going quite high, aren't we? Now my ears are even starting to pop.

I try swallowing to unblock them. Nope, they're still blocked. I know, maybe if I yawn . . . Hiding behind my hand, I give a couple of hippo-sized yawns, but nothing. My ears are still well and truly blocked. So much so I can't hear anything.

Out of the corner of my eye I notice the doorman. He's look-ing at me expectantly, the way people do when they've asked you a question and are waiting for your reply. Shit. Trying to look as natural as possible, I throw him what I hope looks like the confident smile of someone who knows exactly what they're doing, and not someone who can't hear a bloody thing as their ears are popping like crazy.

Honestly, you'd think I never go in elevators.

You don't, pipes up a little voice. *You hate them*.

My nerves wobble. With everything that's been going on, I've managed to block that out, but now I feel the familiar creeping anxiety. Still, it's no biggie. It's not like I'm phobic or anything. I just prefer to use the stairs.

Ever since you got stuck in one at art college and had to be rescued by the fire brigade.

I feel a flash of panic, but ignore it. I'll be fine. Totally fine. That was a crappy old lift in the student union at Manchester Poly. This is New York. Home of the skyscraper. People use elevators all the time here.

Elevators are just lifts in American clothing, and you're scared of lifts. You have nightmares about the cords snapping and plunging to your death.

I slow my breathing and stare fixedly ahead. I'm being ridiculous. I bet if you told a New Yorker you were scared, they'd think you were crazy.

I glance at Mikey for reassurance, but he's staring at his feet and muttering something under his breath. I notice he's wearing a small gold cross round his neck. And he's clutching it.

Fuck.

This is not good. This is not good. This is—

The elevator suddenly comes to a halt and the doors spring open.

Wow.

My fear instantly evaporates as I'm hit with the most breathtaking view of Central Park. Stretching out ahead of me, as far as the eye can see, is a vast carpet of trees. On and on it goes, as if someone just plopped a big piece of the English countryside in the middle of Manhattan.

'Holy shit.'

As we step out into the apartment, with its huge floor-to-ceiling windows, I turn to Mikey. Eyes out on stalks, he's gripping on to the trolley as if for support. 'I'm not good with heights. I get dizzy,' he mutters gruffly, a queasy expression on his face as he gazes out at the skyline and the towering skyscrapers we're now rubbing shoulders with.

'I would recommend putting the crates here in the hallway,' the doorman is saying in the background. 'That way, they're not causing an obstruction.'

'Sure, good idea,' nods Mikey. Immediately he gets underway unloading the crates in an eager bid to get out of here.

'It's very important not to cause an obstruction,' continues the doorman sombrely. 'Fire regulations, you know.'

'Um, yes.' I nod distractedly, my eyes flicking around me. Gosh, this place is enormous.

Wow. In my head I hear Lloyd Grossman's voice. *Who lives in a place like this?*

'Fire?' repeats Mikey. His voice sounds a little strangled. 'Did someone just say "Fire"?' He starts unloading faster, his biceps popping like pistons.

And white. Everything's white, I notice, glancing around at the white rugs, white sofas, white walls. I feel nervous just looking at it. Like I'm going to get this sudden impulse to chuck a glass of red wine everywhere.

Not that I go around chucking glasses of red wine everywhere, but I have been known to spill things occasionally. Not that I'm clumsy, I'm just—

Oh, who am I kidding? If I lived here, I'd have to take out shares in Vanish.

Anyway, I don't need to worry about that, I reflect, thinking about my cluttered little shoebox downtown with its clashing colour schemes and eclectic mix of East-meets-West-meets-thrift-shop. Which is something, I suppose.

'I like art, you know.'

I drag my eyes back to the doorman. 'Oh, really?' I nod politely.

'Van Gogh, he's my favourite,' he confides. 'Got any of his stuff?' He jerks his head towards the paintings.

'Er, no.' I smile apologetically.

The doorman's face drops with disappointment.

'OK, well, I'm all done here,' interrupts Mikey, straightening up. Digging out an invoice from his back pocket, he holds it out for me to sign.

'Great. Thanks.' I scribble my signature and pass it back.

'Right, I'm outta here.' Diving back to the elevator, he stands by the closed door with his trolley, waiting for the doorman. He reminds me of my parents' dog when it's time to go for a walk and he's sitting by the door, desperate to go out.

'If you'll excuse me, miss . . .' Clearing his throat, the doorman adjusts his peaked cap and strides into the elevator, like a pilot climbing into his cockpit. 'Any problems, buzz down.' He jabs at the button with a white-gloved hand. 'I'll be straight up.' And with that, he and Mikey disappear behind the sliding door.

I listen to the hum of the lift as it descends, gradually getting quieter and quieter. Then it's gone.

Chapter Seven

OK, so now what?

Alone in the penthouse, I stand motionless for a moment, looking around me. The owner might not be back for ages. What am I going to do now?

Out of the blue I get an image of Macaulay Culkin in *Home Alone*, rushing wildly from room to room, opening cupboards and jumping on beds.

Not that I'm going to do that, of course. I'm a professional twenty-nine-year-old woman, not an eight-year-old child.

Saying that, I'd love a quick snoop . . . Er, I mean a look . . . around.

Tentatively I venture down the hallway and into the spacious living room, still marvelling at the incredible 360-degree view. Quite different from the one you can see from my apartment, I muse, gazing at the Empire State, which is right there, as if someone moved it specially – a little bit to the left, a little bit to the right – so it's smack bang in front of the window.

To think I got all excited about cricking my neck to catch the teeniest of glimpses from Robyn's window. I feel a flash of embarrassment. This is like having front-row seats.

Awestruck, I turn away from the view and continue tiptoeing around, but I've only gone a few steps when a thought strikes. Swanky pads like this probably have some super-top-of-the-range security system. What if there's CCTV cameras and I'm under surveillance? And I'm standing on a pristine white shag-pile rug with my grubby old flip-flops . . . Looking down at my feet with dismay, I quickly step backwards. Only one of my feet has sort of stuck. Hang on, what's—

Chewing gum.

On the white shagpile rug.

Shit.

Dropping to my knees, I quickly pick at the greasy, grey blob with my fingers. Eugh. This is so sticky and disgusting. I pick harder, but it's welded itself to the rug and won't come off. I feel a stab of panic. Crap! I know, maybe if I use my nail scissors . . . I scramble around in my bag. I carry so much rubbish around with me that I've probably got a pair . . . Aha, here they are!

I start digging at the tufts of shagpile with one of the blades. If I just scrape those . . . Painstakingly I work on each tuft, scraping each one, until after a few minutes there's just a couple of stubborn little bits left. I know, what if I just trim those? No one will ever notice. It'll be as good as new . . .

Fuck. There's a hole.

I've made a hole!

With my heart thumping hard in my chest, I stop my frenzied topiary and stare at the rug in frozen horror. The hole stares back at me. Oh my God, Lucy! You're left on your own for five minutes *and this is what happens*?

In a desperate attempt I try ruffling it with my fingers, but it's no good – there's definitely a space where more tufts should be. It's almost like a bald patch.

Suddenly I have an idea. I know! What about doing a sort of comb-over?

Using my fingers, I get to work trying to arrange the tufts just so, but it's not easy. They keep springing back and I have to flatten them with my hand, then wrap a few more strands round . . . God, now I know how Donald Trump feels. Exasperated, I continue tugging a piece this way and that, until finally I seem to have it covered. OK, now it just needs to stay that way.

Rummaging around in my bag again, I pull out my little can of hairspray and give the rug a generous spritz. Perfect. You'd never even know the difference.

Triumphantly I survey my handiwork. I feel rather pleased with myself. Disaster averted! Still, perhaps I should just sit down and wait for the owner to arrive home, I think as an afterthought. It's probably safer that way. After all, I don't want any more accidents.

Padding barefoot over to the sofa, I perch gingerly on the edge of a cushion, being careful not to de-plump it. A fan of magazines is neatly spread out on the coffee table in front of me, but I resist the temptation to flick through them. I'm not going to touch anything, remember? I'm just going to sit right here and wait until the owner arrives. I'm not going to move a muscle.

Instead I glance at the titles, *Variety, Hollywood Reporter, Vanity Fair* . . . In my head I hear Lloyd Grossman's voice again, *Whoever lives in this penthouse is probably in the film business.* I feel a beat of excitement. Gosh, I wonder if it's someone famous. There was me thinking it was some boring old banker, but maybe it's a big-shot director. Or even an actor.

No, Magda would have told me, I tell myself quickly.

Wouldn't she?

Intrigued, I cast my eyes around for clues, but I can't see any photos or knick-knacks or unopened mail. I wonder if there's anything in the rest of the apartment . . .

I last about five seconds.

Then my curiosity gets the better of me and I'm up from the sofa and tiptoeing into the bedrooms. There are packing boxes strewn everywhere. So that explains it. Whoever lives here has just moved in, I conclude, playing detective. I feel a sudden sense of affinity with my mystery client. I wonder if he's new in town too.

I steal a look inside the fitted wardrobes. A sleek row of suits hangs neatly in various shades of grey. Underneath are several pairs of shoes. I pick one up. It's leather. Despite myself, I can't resist taking a peek at the sole: 'Made in Italy.' I feel a flash of excitement. Which of course is ridiculous, I tell myself quickly. As if I care where his shoes are made.

Quickly putting it back, I sneak glances into both bathrooms – large, white and marble, they're empty apart from an electric toothbrush and a couple of disposable contact-lens cases – and end up in the designer kitchen.

I glance around it nervously. My lack of culinary skills is something of a running joke in my family. Kate calls my style of cooking 'one, two, three, ping' in reference to the sound of the microwave when it's finished. Which is a *little* harsh (I once made Rice Krispie cakes *and* they were delicious). I admit I do find kitchens a bit scary. I mean, they're filled with endless equipment, and utensils, and ingredients, that I have no clue what to do with.

Take this one, for example. It's terrifying. Stainless-steel countertops, state-of-the-art gadgets, an intimidating cooker with a million different dials and knobs. It's called Wolf. How scary is that? And then there's that hulking great big fridge. What on earth do you need a fridge that size for? I take a look inside. There's nothing on the shelves apart from a few bottles of sparkling water, a bag of organic oranges, a tub of 0 per cent fat Greek yoghurt and some quinoa.

Quinoa? What's that? I read the packet. 'An ancient grain, filled with goodness and nutrition.'

Crikey, whoever lives here is seriously healthy. Where's the chocolate? The takeaway leftovers? The Diet Coke?

Er, in your fridge, Lucy.

Feeling a stab of guilt, I hastily close the door. I'll buy some ancient grains next time I go shopping, I tell myself firmly. Still, chocolate isn't *unhealthy*. I once read an article in a magazine about how it's filled with iron and ... I draw a blank. Well, anyway, it's ages since I read the article.

Exiting the kitchen, I wander back towards the living room to resume my position on the sofa. Boredom gnaws at me. I haven't found anything very interesting and the novelty of the penthouse is beginning to wear off. Plus I'm pretty tired. It's been a long day. I'd quite like to go home now, get in the bath and curl up on the sofa with tonight's episode of *Oprah* and the man who thinks he's a grizzly bear that Robyn's recorded. I laughed when Robyn told me about it, but now it's beginning to seem quite appealing.

Letting out a yawn, I'm padding back down the hallway when I notice a bookcase. I didn't see it before, but like everything else in the flat, it's still empty. Next to it are a couple of half-opened cardboard boxes. No doubt filled with books, I muse, kneeling down and lifting up the cardboard flap to take a look.

Not that there's anything much to see. Like I thought, just piles of books. Absently I leaf through a couple of political auto-biographies, several travel guides, a couple of dog-eared John Grishams, a book on Renaissance painters . . . I pause, my inter-est piqued. It's quite a heavy hardback, and tugging it out, I lie it on my lap and start flicking through the pages. *Michelangelo, Leonardo da Vinci, Botticelli* . . .

My eyes flick over each painting. It's like looking over photo-graphs of old friends. On some I think the brushwork is amazing; others it's the light; some I find a little too sentimental, or too religious.

As I turn the page, my heart skips a beat.

Portrait of a Musician by Titian.

I stare at the face looking out at me, my mind leaping back to the very first time I saw this painting. I was nineteen years old and wandering around the Gallerie dell'Accademia in Venice with a guidebook and the obligatory pair of earphones that didn't work when I'd stumbled across it, tucked away in a darkened corner.

It had been love at first sight.

With long, dark, messy hair swept away from his face, a beard, brooding eyes, soulful expression, strong forehead and unwavering gaze, he was one of the most handsome men I'd ever laid eyes on.

And a musician too! Which was just so typical of me. I've always had a thing about musicians. Show me a man with facial hair and a guitar and I'll show you a major full-blown crush. Evan Dando from the Lemonheads, the tragic Kurt Cobain, even Radiohead's Thom Yorke, they all leave me weak at the knees.

My mind spools back. I can remember it as if it's yesterday, standing in a little patch of sunlight, staring at him transfixed and thinking I'd found my ideal man, and what a shame he wasn't real. It was part of my course in art history – not the lusting bit – but the reason I was in Italy for the summer. I'd only been there a few days but already I'd fallen in love about a million times – with the huge plates of black truffle pasta, the faded ochre-coloured buildings and stunning piazzas, the sound of the water lapping gently against the banks of the canals . . .

And now with this painting.

'Bit of a cool dude, huh?'

It had been hearing a voice behind me that had finally caused me to drag my eyes away. Otherwise, who knows how long I'd have remained standing there, marvelling at Titian's skill as a painter and relishing the delicious coolness of the gallery after the baking midday heat outside. Those few words, spoken in an American accent, had made me realise I wasn't alone and I'd turned round, expecting—

Actually, to this day I'm not quite sure what I was expecting. Nothing really. Just another tourist with a camera and a guidebook. After all, the city was filled with millions of them. If anything, I was probably a bit irritated about being interrupted from daydreams.

And that's when I first saw Nathaniel.

Long, messy hair. Blond. Jeans and a T-shirt. Converse All-Stars.

And I just knew.

In the split second it had taken for my eyes to sweep over him, standing in the shadows, just a few feet away, with his hands in his pockets and a lazy smile on his face, I'd been hit with something so unexpected, so sudden, so unlike anything I'd ever experienced. It was like a lightning strike. A sense of certainty so powerful it had sent me reeling.

The Italians call it *colpo di fulmine*. Love at first sight.

This was it. He was the One.

What's that noise?

Abruptly zoning back, I look up from the book. I can hear a humming sound. A sort of high-pitched whining . . . Puzzled, I cock my head on one side, trying to figure out where it's coming from. It's down that way, towards the hallway, I decide, glancing at the crates of paintings stacked up against the wall and the elevator at the far end.

Oh shit.

The elevator.

That's where it's coming from.

No sooner has the thought struck than I see the light next to it ping on.

I feel a flash of panic. Oh shit, oh shit, oh shit. That must be him. The client. *He's back!*

Jumping up, the book falls from my lap to the floor with an almighty thud and I scrabble for it, while at the same time tugging at my skirt and trying to tuck my hair behind my ears. I want to look suitably professional and composed, and not like someone who's been snooping around the apartment for the last hour.

Shoving the book hastily back in the box, I turn to see the doors sliding open. OK, don't panic. Everything's cool. Just act normal. Right, yes, normal.

Only the problem is, there's nothing even *remotely* normal about being in a stranger's penthouse apartment while they rock up in the private elevator.

I glimpse the doorman first, the familiar flash of his dark green uniform, and then a figure appears from behind him. Tall, receding slightly, wearing a suit and sunglasses, he's looking down at some mail in his hand as he steps out of the elevator. I watch as the doorman goes back down in the lift, then glance back at the owner of the penthouse.

'Hi,' I quickly introduce myself, trying not to sound as nervous as I feel. 'I'm from the gallery.'

Suddenly aware of my presence, he looks up and slides the sunglasses on to his head. As he does, I see a flash of surprise in his eyes. Pale blue eyes with grey flecks around the irises.

It's like a ten-ton truck just crashed into my chest.

Oh my God, it can't be.

It just can't be.

Nathaniel?

Chapter Eight

'Lucy?'

For the briefest of moments I think I'm going to faint. As my mind goes into freefall, I try telling myself I've made a mistake. It's not him; it's a trick of the light. I mean, there must be a million people who have eyes with similar grey flecks around the iris, right?

Right?

But there's no mistaking that voice. It's the same voice I heard that day in the gallery. It was that voice that made me turn round and fall in love at first sight.

'Oh wow, Lucy, is that really you?'

It was also that voice that dumped me over the telephone.

'Hello, Nathaniel.'

I was aiming for cool, calm and collected, but it comes out a bit wooden and schoolteacher-ish. Still, they're words at least. Spoken out loud. Which is better than being utterly speechless with shock, which is how I'm really feeling.

Actually, I take that back. I'm not sure I can feel anything. It's as if my whole body's suddenly gone numb and I've got this weird floaty feeling, like the time I had my tonsils out and the anaesthetist told me to start counting backwards.

'It is you! I thought for a moment I was seeing things.' His face is breaking into a smile, creasing up the corners of his eyes.

Those are new, I can't help thinking to myself. He didn't use to have creases before. And his hair – it's so much shorter, and it's started to recede at the temples.

'I was, like, No way, it's impossible!'

I can hear him speaking, see him gesticulating, but it's as if we're separated by an invisible barrier, a sort of impenetrable shield between us, and instead I'm staring at this grey-suited figure in front of me with a certain detached disbelief.

He looks different. Older. Gone are the thrift-store suede jacket and the long, messy blond hair, and his teenage puppy fat has disappeared to reveal razor-sharp cheekbones and a much squarer jawline. But it's still Nathaniel. *Still Nate.*

As the thought fires across my brain, my heart gives a little leap. I quickly squash it back down. No, you don't, I tell myself firmly. Don't you go getting any ideas.

'Sorry, I haven't let you get a word in, have I?' he laughs, putting down his mail and scraping his fingers through his hair. 'So tell me, how are you? What's going on? What are doing here?'

I suddenly realise that despite the expensive designer suit and air of the successful businessman, he's nervous. Well, it must be a shock for him too, walking in from work and seeing me standing in his hallway after ten years. Like a ghost from his past.

'I brought your artwork,' I manage.

'My what?' Confused, he glances distractedly to the crates stacked neatly in the corner, not seeming to register.

'The Gustav collection,' I continue, keeping my voice steady. God, it's so bizarre. It's like a robot has taken over my body and I'm standing here stiffly, talking in some weird automated voice about art, when instead the real Lucy is flinging her arms up in the air and shrieking, *Oh my God, oh my God, oh my God*, on a loop.

For a moment he seems to stare in total bewilderment at the paintings. Then suddenly his brow unfurrows and he turns to me in a sort of 'eureka' moment. 'You work at the gallery,' he says quietly, and I can see everything starting to fall into place.

'Yes, I just transferred from a showroom in London.' I nod, still doing my R2-D2 impersonation. 'I'm the senior coordinator.'

Well, it sounded impressive first time around on the doorman.

'You are?' Nathaniel looks slightly dazed.

'It's a really good job,' I add quickly, suddenly feeling the urge to justify myself. 'I organise exhibitions, work closely with new artists, deal with clients . . .'

'But what happened to your own painting? I thought—'

'Oh, that's a long time ago,' I say dismissively, cutting him off and looking down to study my feet, which have suddenly become really interesting. 'Anyway, what about you?' I ask, changing the subject. 'What are you doing these days?'

What are you doing these days? Oh my God, Lucy, what kind of lame question is that? You sound as if you're hanging over the garden fence, passing the time with your next-door neighbour. Not talking to your first love, whom you haven't seen for ten years but have never stopped thinking about.

OK, I did not just think that.

'Oh, you know, this and that,' he says, his mouth twitching. His eyes flash with amusement as they search out mine and I feel something stir deep inside me. Like ice cubes when they start to melt. Shifting, splintering, thawing.

'Well, this and that must be pretty successful,' I reply, gesturing around me at the penthouse.

'Oh, this.' He shrugs modestly. 'It's just a rental.'

'Oh, really?' I say, trying to sound nonchalant, as if renting huge fuck-off penthouses in Manhattan is something I do quite regularly myself. When I'm not busy renting a room in a tiny shoebox downtown, of course.

Inside, though, I can't help feeling a stab of insecurity. God, he's obviously some major high-flyer, while I'm still broke at the end of each month.

'I've been living in LA, but now I'm moving here for work,' he adds in explanation.

'Don't tell me, you're in the movie business,' I say with a rush of excitement, before feeling my cheeks redden. 'I saw the magazines.' I motion vaguely towards the living room.

'TV.' He looks almost apologetic. 'I'm a producer.'

'Gosh, that's great.' I try to sound convincing, though I haven't a clue if that's great or not. Still, it sounds impressive.

Everyone always wants to work in TV, don't they? Well, apart from me. Art's only ever been my thing.

'Yeah, it's pretty cool . . .' He nods, then trails off.

There's an awkward pause and for a moment we just stand there in the hallway, looking at each other. I can feel the space between us thick with questions and emotions.

'Wow, sorry, I just realised, I haven't even offered you a drink or anything,' he starts apologising and rubbing his temples.

'Oh, don't worry,' I say hastily.

'I'm afraid I don't have much in, apart from some Evian.'

And that funny quinoa stuff, I think, remembering the packet in the fridge.

'Look, why don't we go out and get a drink?' he suggests all of a sudden. 'Catch up properly?'

I'm taken aback. Go for a drink? *Me and Nate?*

'Oh, er . . .' Flustered, I start trying to stall. 'I'm not sure . . .'

'There's a great little place on the corner,' he continues eagerly. 'Come on, how about it?'

He's looking at me expectantly, a big smile on his face, and out of the blue I feel a snap of indignation. My God, I can't believe it. He thinks I'm just going to trot off to a bar with him for a cosy chit-chat. After what happened? I should tell him to sod off.

I should, but of course I'm not going to.

'Let me just grab my bag.'

I've imagined this moment a million, trillion times: bumping into him again. What I'd say, how I'd look, exactly what it would be like. I'd look fabulous, *of course*. I'd be wearing my thin jeans. I'd be having a good hair day (well, I don't really have good hair days. I have at-least-it's-not-frizzy and phew-my-fringe-hasn't-kinked-yet days). Oh, and I'd have some amazing man on my arm.

Not that I believe you need a guy to make you feel good about yourself, but come on, enough of the feminist principles. You bump into the love of your life who married someone else, trust me, you don't want to be single and wearing your frumpy work clothes, or a pair of flip-flops that make your legs look completely dumpy.

Sitting on a barstool, I rub my legs self-consciously. Ugh, they feel all bristly. Which is when I remember that I forgot to shave them.

'I mean, what are the odds?'

Tugging down my skirt, I look across the bar at Nathaniel. Shirtsleeves rolled up, he's sitting opposite me, shaking his head in disbelief.

We're in a little French bistro on the corner of his street drinking red wine. I don't usually drink red wine. I don't actually like it. It makes my tongue feel all funny, like when I eat rhubarb. But I did that thing you do when you're a bit nervous and you say you'll have what they're having, so Nathaniel ordered a bottle.

Which took about twenty minutes, as he wanted to taste everything on the menu first, swirling each one round the glass and sniffing it. He obviously knows a lot about wine, unlike me. I don't know the first thing.

'It is a bit of a coincidence.' I nod, taking a large gulp of wine.

I feel absurdly nervous. As if I'm on a first date.

Quickly I scrub that thought.

'Just a bit.' He nods, rolling his eyes. 'It's incredible. I've always wondered if I'd ever see you again.'

'You have?' My voice comes out in a squeak.

'Well, yeah,' he says, looking down at his wine glass self-consciously.

My chest tightens and my stomach does this funny swooping thing. He's thought about me. During all this time he's thought about me. I feel a surge of validation. All this time I always wondered. *Always hoped.*

'Did you ever think about me?' He raises his eyes and gives me a long, searching look.

My stomach does a loop-the-loop again.

'Sometimes.' I shrug, trying to sound casual.

OK, so that's a fib, but I'm not going to admit the truth now, am I? That I can't *stop* thinking about him.

'Really?' He looks pleased. 'I thought you might have forgotten all about me.'

'Trust me, I tried.' I manage a half-smile and he blushes.

'Yeah, I didn't behave very well at the end, did I?'

'Oh, I don't know.' I take another gulp of wine, relishing the feeling of it weaving its way down into my stomach, soothing my jittery nerves. 'We were so young, and long-distance relationships never work out, do they? It was just one of those things. Inevitable, really. And breaking up with someone is never easy.'

Er, hello. Since when did I develop this super-mature attitude?

'I was a jerk, let's face it.' He flashes me a rueful smile.

'OK, you were a jerk.' I nod in agreement.

He laughs, his face crinkling up, and despite myself I can't help but laugh too. It's strange, but after all this time, all the years, all the wondering, the old hurt seems to melt away and it's just me and Nate sitting at the bar, like two old friends having a drink. Maybe it's true that time is a great healer.

Or maybe it's just the red wine.

'So . . .' he says.

I watch him fingering the stem of his wine glass, as if he's thinking hard about something. Then I notice. *He's not wearing a wedding ring.* It shoots out at me, like an arrow. Somewhere in the recesses of my mind I vaguely remember Magda mentioning it, but I didn't pay much attention – she was talking about a stranger. At least, I *thought* she was talking about a stranger.

I stare at his empty finger. Maybe he's taken if off and forgotten to put it back on. Or he could have lost it. Or maybe he's one of those guys who doesn't wear one, like my dad, who told Mum when they got married that he'd never worn jewellery and he wasn't going to start now. I think he even said the word 'poof', but the less said about that, the better.

Even as I'm thinking all these things, buried deep, down inside me a burst of hope is exploding in my chest like a firework.

'Tell me . . .'

I snap back to see him looking at me.

' . . . how long have you been in New York?'

The conversation seems to have moved away from dangerous ground and back to pleasantries. I feel a beat of relief.

'Not long, just a few weeks.' I take a sip of wine.

Don't let him see you looking at his wedding finger, pipes up a voice inside my head. Startled, I quickly avert my eyes.

'Wow, so you're new in town like me.' He smiles. 'What do you think so far?'

'I love it.' I smile, holding out my glass as he gives me a top-up.

It's very important I don't ask him about being married. I have to appear unconcerned. Like I'm not curious at all. Like I haven't even thought about it in years.

'Yeah, it's an amazing city. I visit a lot for work, but I've never lived here before.'

'Oh, really?'

Or tried to Google his wife to see what she looks like.

'Yeah, so I'm kinda excited to explore, get a real feel for it, instead of just being a tourist.'

And found nothing. Not even one lousy photo. I mean, you think she'd at least be on Facebook.

'So, how's married life?'

It's like an Exocet missile. Fired without warning from out of my mouth, it shoots straight at him and crash-lands on the bar. For a moment I have the weird sensation of being completely disconnected, an observer, an innocent bystander.

Then it hits me.

Oh my God, I did not just say that. I did not just say that.

Fuck. Fuck. *FUCK.*

There's a pause as Nathaniel takes a sip of his wine. It's like the moment between the crash and the impact. That stunned split second as you brace yourself for the inevitable.

Putting down his glass, he meets my eyes.

Please don't say it's wonderful. I cross my fingers under the bar. I mean, you can say it's good, and you're happy and all that, and I'll be pleased, really I will, but please don't go on and on about how wonderful it is, how wonderful *she* is.

'We're getting divorced.'

Now it's his turn to launch a missile. *Boom.* Just like that.

I look at him incredulously. I was prepared for a dozen different answers, but not this one. *Never* this one.

'Gosh, I'm sorry to hear that,' I say quickly, scrambling for something appropriate to say, but inside I'm reeling with shock. And something else. A secret tremor of joy that comes like the aftershock following an earthquake.

'Thanks.' He smiles ruefully. 'It's for the best. Beth and I should never have gotten married in the first place.'

My face doesn't flicker. I try to appear not really interested, but every cell in my body is like a finely tuned receptor.

'I met Beth when she was a freshman at college and the complete opposite of me – she was loud, confident, the life and soul of every party . . . We used to argue like crazy.'

As he tells me this information, I try to imagine it. *Nate? Arguing like crazy?* But I can't. He's always so mild-mannered, so laid-back. I don't think I've ever seen him lose his temper.

'We were only married a year and she moved out. Looking back, we should have called it a day then, I suppose.'

'Why didn't you?' I blurt, then catching myself, quickly add, 'I mean, if you weren't getting along.'

'I don't know. I suppose I didn't want to let anyone down. We had this great big wedding . . .' His voice trails off awkwardly.

'I know. You were in the *New York Times.*'

'You saw it?' He looks surprised and embarrassed.

As do I for admitting I've seen it.

'My sister, Kate, did. She lives here, you know. She showed it to me.'

The truth is, she tore it out and posted it to me, her reasoning being it was best that I knew all the facts. Secretly I knew she was hoping that by seeing his wedding picture I would finally stop mooning over him, move on, forget all about him. And it worked. Sort of.

'It looked like a good wedding.' I smile brightly and drain my glass.

I swear I have just turned into Miss Maturity. Look at me! All cool and calm and not even the teeniest bit jealous or upset. It's amazing. I feel noble. Magnanimous.

A little bit drunk, I suddenly realise.

'It was a big wedding.' He nods. 'We had three hundred guests at the Ritz-Carlton in San Francisco.'

'Wow,' I murmur, not because of the size of his guest list, but because I can't believe I'm sitting here, talking about Nate's wedding, *with Nate*. It's just so bizarre.

'Trust me, I don't think I even knew who half of them were. Still don't,' he continues, shaking his head. Picking up his wine, he looks at me thoughtfully. 'Anyway, enough about me. What about you? Who's the lucky guy?'

I feel my cheeks redden and for a brief moment I think about making one up, then decide to come clean. We never did play games, Nate and me, no point starting now. 'There isn't one,' I say, averting my eyes and looking down at my empty glass.

'What?' Now he's the one to look incredulous. 'Why not?'

Because I never got over you, because no one ever came close, because you were the One, whispers a little voice inside me.

Instead I just shrug my shoulders. 'I guess I'm still waiting for the right person.'

All the wine on an empty stomach is making me feeling light-headed and the bar has started to sway slowly. Lifting my eyes, I meet his.

'Smart.' He nods, looking reflective. 'I should've done the same.'

There's a pause as we look at each other. Neither of us speaks. Is it just me or is something happening here? *Is something going to happen here?*

Somewhere in my body a tiny pulse starts beating.

'Have you ever been back to Venice?'

My chest tightens and I feel my breath catch inside my throat. 'No, never,' I manage, trying to keep my voice steady. 'What about you?'

His eyes have never left mine.

'A million times,' he replies quietly.

My heart skips a beat. *So I didn't imagine it.* I feel a rush of emotion and for a split second it's like I'm suspended on the verge of something, wondering what he's going to say next, where this is going.

'I married the wrong woman, Lucy.'

His voice is low, but it's clear and composed. I feel myself reeling. Oh my God, I can't believe it . . . I can't believe it . . . Hearing his startling confession, I feel shocked, astonished, stunned and yet . . .

And yet there's something else . . . deep down inside . . . an overwhelming feeling of calm, inevitability, *destiny*.

'I made the biggest mistake of my life when I lost you and I've never stopped regretting it. I've thought about you for years. Wondered where you are, what you're doing, if I'd ever see you again. Sometimes I even used to imagine seeing you again, bumping into you in the street . . .'

I'm listening to him talking, but it could be me speaking. It could be my voice saying these same things. Because this is exactly what I've been doing all these years. It's like he's reading from my diary, talking about my life, and yet it's been his life too. All this time we've been leading parallel lives and we never knew it.

'It was crazy. I even went to see a therapist about it once.'

I snap back. 'A therapist?'

'Well, I was in LA.' He looks sheepish. 'I was depressed about work, but I just spent the whole time talking about you.'

Tiny darts of joy are pricking my skin, making me tingle all over. I never dared to imagine he would be thinking about me. I assumed that he never gave me a second thought, that I was long forgotten. Yet while I was in London thinking about him, there he was in LA thinking about me.

'Look, I know this sounds stupid, but . . .' His voice trails off. He hesitates, then looks back up at me, his eyes searching out mine. 'Do you believe in soulmates?'

Our eyes lock. My heart hammers in my chest. I feel dizzy. I've drunk too much wine. It's all too much. Everything is fuzzy.

Yet in that moment there's a flash of something so clear, so definite, so absolutely certain that I have no doubts.

'Yes,' I whisper. 'Yes, I do, Nate.'

And then it happens.

Leaning towards me, he reaches for my hand, and interlacing his fingers through mine, he pulls me towards him, slowly, gently. Closing my eyes, I sink into him. It's like nothing's changed. He feels the same, he smells the same, and as his lips brush against mine, it's as if the years simply melt away and we're right back on that gondola in Venice . . .

He kisses just the same too.

Chapter Nine

A shaft of sunlight filters through the gap in the blinds, warming my eyelids, stirring me from the deepest of sleeps. Blearily I open my eyes, expecting to see an embroidered Indian bedspread strewn with discarded clothes, clashing scarlet walls and piles of clutter. Instead I'm greeted with a vista of pristine white. An arctic landscape of clean sheets, bare walls and acres of empty carpet.

For a split second I wonder where on earth I am.

Then it comes back to me.

It's the morning after and I'm in Nate's bedroom. In Nate's bed. *With Nate.*

As it registers, I shoot out my hand to the other side of the vast mattress. Only he's not there. Momentarily I feel myself stiffen. Insecurities bubble up inside before I become aware of a faint whooshing sound. It's coming from the en suite. Of course. Nate must be in the shower. Closing my eyes, I sink back under the duvet. Cocooned within the soft, warm depths, I stretch and curl back up like a question mark, relishing the fresh linen sheets, the huge, plump mattress, the softest feather pillows, the memory of last night . . . It's like being in some super-expensive hotel.

OK, enough about the bed, Lucy. *What about the sex?*

A delicious shiver runs up my spine, sending little shockwaves all over my body. Like someone with a wonderful secret, I want to hug the memories to my chest and never let them go. To keep them tucked inside and think about them over and over, relishing them, reliving them, moment by delicious moment.

It was amazing, and yet completely natural, as if we'd never been apart. Everything just fitted together. Like two pieces of a jigsaw puzzle, we simply slipped back into place. That's what I remember the most, because the rest of my memories are hazy. Blurred by lust and alcohol, I vaguely recall coming back to the penthouse, kissing in the hallway, items of clothes being removed until suddenly we were both naked and tumbling into bed. The feeling of skin against skin, his mouth, fingers, thighs . . .

I blush at the memory, my stomach fluttering as sensations flood my body, my skin still tingling. A flashback of our limbs tangled together, followed by another, and another, and another, and—

'Lucy?'

Nate's voice snaps me back and I open my eyes to see him standing at the foot of the bed, wearing just a towel. His muscular body is still dripping with droplets of water and I watch a trickle run between his pecs, over his six-pack, weaving its way down to his navel.

Even with a hangover, my body responds. It's all I can do not to grab hold of him and drag him back under the covers with me. In fact, maybe I should.

Oh my God, what's got into me? Since when did I turn into some sex-crazed nympho?

Since last night, pipes up a little voice. Sex with Nate was always amazing, and last night proved nothing has changed. I feel my groin ache at the memory. Right, OK, play it cool, Lucy, play it cool.

Easier said than done when you're completely naked and in his bed.

'How are you feeling?' Padding over, he sits down on the side of the bed and gently brushes the hair out of my face, his face crinkling into a smile.

Horny. Happy. *In love*.

As the thought fires across my brain, I feel a stab of alarm. Whoa. Not so fast. This was just one night, remember? He could have cold feet. He could have changed his mind. He could be thinking this was one big mistake.

'A little hung-over,' I say, trying to sound casual, while my skin is tingling at the touch of his fingertips. 'What about you?'

'Pretty good.' He nods, his eyes meeting mine. 'Pretty damn good.'

There's a pause and a look passes between us, and in that moment I know that everything he said last night still stands. Nothing's changed. He feels the same. I feel a burst of euphoria that sends my defences crumbling.

'Yeah, me too,' I reply softly.

A grin flashes across his face. He looks pleased, and more than a little relieved. It's then that I realise he was probably as nervous as I was, if not more. After all, last night he was the one baring his soul to me, confessing that he'd made the biggest mistake of his life losing me, asking me if I believe in soulmates.

My stomach gives a leap.

'So, can I get you anything? Are you hungry?'

'Mmm.' I let out a little yawn. 'What time is it?'

'Six.'

My whole body recoils as if I've just been dragged under a freezing-cold shower. '*Six?*' I yelp in shock.

'Actually, it's nearly ten past,' corrects Nate, obviously missing the trauma in my voice.

Me? Awake? At 6 a.m.? I'm usually unconscious until 8.30. Noon if it's the weekends. I can't remember the last time I was awake at six o'clock in the morning.

Actually, yes, I can. I was twenty-three and clubbing in Ibiza, the difference being I hadn't yet *gone* to bed.

'How about I fix you some fresh juice?'

'Oh . . . um . . . yes, please. That sounds lovely.' I smile. OK, so it's a bit early for me – I stifle another yawn – but I'm awake now, and what better reason to *stay* awake than a semi-naked Nate.

'OK, coming right up.' Easing himself off the bed, he reaches for a pair of small wire-framed glasses on the bedside table and slips them on.

Gosh, he wears glasses now, I realise. I suddenly remember the empty contact-lens cases in the bathroom. So that explains it, I muse, trying to get used to this new, serious-looking Nate.

'Trust me, it's good freshly squeezed. I have a juicer.' He smiles, bending down and giving me a kiss.

God, he's still bloody cute, though, glasses or no glasses, I muse, feeling his soft mouth against mine.

'I'll get up and help you,' I murmur, making to get out of bed, but he pushes me back gently.

'Relax. I'll get it.' His mouth twitches with amusement. 'I know how much you like staying in bed . . . I don't think we ever got out of bed in Italy, did we?' He throws me a look and I feel a rush of delight. So he hasn't forgotten those lazy mornings we spent in Italy, lying spooned together for hours in my tiny single bed, listening to the world go by outside the window.

'True, but I can make coffee,' I suggest, and at the mention of coffee my taste buds ping awake. I love my morning coffee. It's my sacred ritual. Nothing comes between me and my strong latte.

'Sorry, I don't have any coffee.' He pulls an apologetic face.

'Oh, right, of course.' I nod, remembering he's just moved in. He probably needs tons of stuff. 'Well, no worries, I'll just run out and get some from—' I begin, but he cuts me off.

'Actually, I don't drink coffee.'

For a moment I just stare at him in disbelief, memories of us wandering around the backstreets of Venice and drinking endless espressos come flooding back. I think we lived on the stuff for the entire summer.

'You don't drink coffee?' I finally manage hoarsely.

'No, I gave it up,' he says matter-of-factly. 'Caffeine is really bad for you. You know it's more addictive than nicotine?'

'Um . . . no . . . really?'

'Totally.' He nods, his face serious. 'You should give it up, Lucy. You'll feel so much better for it.'

And with that he's disappearing out of the bedroom, leaving me lying in bed. *Nate's bed.* A blissful smile splits across my face.

I still can't quite believe it. That we're here, together, after all this time. It's amazing. Nothing's changed between us, and yet . . .

As I think about the coffee, I feel a slight niggle. Not everything is the same about Nate. Rolling over on to my stomach, I bury my head in the pillow. I wonder what else has changed.

'Are you certain you don't want me to ask my driver to give you a ride downtown?'

Less than an hour later and Nate and I are riding down in the lift together, along with the same uniformed doorman I encountered yesterday. I feel a flash of embarrassment. It's like the walk of shame, only in a lift. But if he recognises me, he doesn't let on. Instead he stares discreetly at his highly polished shoes.

'No, honestly I'm fine. I'll catch the subway.'

'Are you sure you'll be OK?' Nate looks at me, his face etched with concern. He's swapped his glasses for contact lenses, and his pale blue eyes search mine.

'Yes, I'm sure,' I say, and can't help laughing. 'I'm going to go straight to the gallery, start work early. I've got masses to do. We're having an exhibition on Friday.'

'Am I invited?'

'Of course.' I smile. 'If you want to come.'

'Try stopping me.' He smiles back, and wrapping his arm round my waist, he pulls me towards him. I feel a warm glow inside. I can't remember feeling this happy. It's like someone just dipped me in melted happiness.

The lift doors ping open, and as we walk out into the lobby, Nate's arm stays firmly round my waist. As does the smile that's plastered to my face. All the way through the revolving doors, and out on to the pavement, and the bright, early morning sunshine.

'Wow, the city looks so beautiful,' I exhale, feeling a wave of euphoria. Looking out across the park, I get a sudden urge to get up this early every morning. 'From now on I'm going to get up at six every day,' I declare firmly.

'Really?' Nate regards me with amusement. 'Six a.m.?'

'Yes, absolutely.' I nod, trying to stifle a yawn.

'So I guess this means you'll be wanting an early night tonight?'

I turn to see Nate looking at me expectantly and feel a stab of dismay. He's using this as an excuse. He obviously doesn't want to see me tonight, I suddenly realise. Which of course is OK, I tell myself quickly. I mean, I'm with him right now and I was with him the whole of last night, so it's fine if he doesn't want to see me tonight as well. I'm not disappointed or anything.

'Because you see, I was kind of hoping we could have dinner tonight.' Unlooping his arm, he turns to me. 'But I'm in the studio all day recording shows, so it might not be until fairly late.'

Like a kite caught on a blast of wind that sends it soaring upwards, I feel a rush of joy.

'Well, maybe not *every* day,' I say. 'In fact, I was thinking of giving tomorrow a miss.'

'Cool.' He breaks into a grin. 'I'll see you tonight, then.' And giving me a kiss, full on the mouth, he strides briskly across the pavement and disappears into the waiting black Lincoln town car.

I float downtown in a bubble of happiness, smiling at complete strangers, giving away my last ten dollars to a man spray-painted silver and dressed like the Statue of Liberty, and thinking about last night.

Snippets of our conversation provide the backing track as I glide through the turnstiles and into the subway station. I don't hear the rumble of the train, the screeching of the brakes or the thud of the sliding doors as I climb on board. Everything fades away, like a movie with the sound turned down, and all I can hear is Nate's voice. *I made the biggest mistake of my life when I lost you and I've never stopped regretting it.*

As the train rumbles downtown, I gaze into the darkness of the tunnel, my mind floating backwards. *I've thought about you for years. Wondered where you are, what you're doing, if I'd ever see you again.*

Until finally I reach my stop and I get off and climb up the steps, into the cacophony of city noise. *Sometimes I even used to imagine seeing you again, bumping into you in the street.*

I walk through the busy streets, dodging traffic, pedestrians, pavement cafés, and now I'm here at the gallery and I'm pushing open the door. *Do you believe in soulmates?*

'Loozy!'

Suddenly the sound comes back on, at full volume, and I hear Magda's voice blasting at me.

'What are you doing here? It so early!'

Dressed in her usual immaculate ensemble of black Chanel, diamonds and gravity-defying hairdo, she's sitting frozen behind the reception desk, a half-eaten bagel in one hand, an iced frappuccino topped with swirls of whipped cream in the other. She looks like a thief caught in the middle of the act.

Hastily dabbing away the smears of cream cheese from around her mouth with a scarlet fingernail, she drops the bagel and frappuccino like contraband goods and comes clattering over on her vertiginous heels. Valentino scampers along beside her, perfectly coordinated in a diamond collar and matching black jacket.

'I thought I'd start work on Friday's exhibition,' I say, my voice muffled as she grabs hold of me and gives me my usual greeting of two lipstick kisses. 'Make an early start.'

OK, so that's not *strictly* true, but I can't tell her about Nate, can I?

'You're wearing the same clothes!'

'Erm . . . excuse me?' On second thoughts, I might not have a choice.

'The same clothes as yesterday!' Her eyes are running over me like scanners. 'Did you stay out last night?' she persists. 'Were you with the client?'

'Well, actually . . .' I begin, my cheeks reddening. Oh shit, I've been busted. She knows I've spent the night with Nate and it looks really unprofessional. I feel a stab of panic. How am I going to explain this?

'Aha! I knew it!'

But if I thought she was going to be angry with me, I couldn't be more wrong. Clapping her bony hands together with glee, she beams delightedly. 'Are you seeing him again?'

'Tonight. He's taking me out for dinner,' I blurt before I can stop myself. I can't keep it inside. I just want to tell someone. Correction: I want to tell everyone.

Magda's face lights up like a hundred-watt bulb. 'What did I tell you?' She throws me a triumphant smile. Then her expression falls serious. 'Did you look at his shoes?'

For a moment I regard her in confusion. Then it registers. Of course. The checklist.

'Made in Italy,' I say, suddenly remembering my earlier snooping and feeling a faint flash of embarrassment.

Magda, however, has no such reservations. She couldn't look more thrilled if I'd handed her a winning lottery ticket.

'Loozy, this is *unbelievable*,' she gasps in a hushed voice.

Which is somewhat of an exaggeration. I mean, shoes do have a habit of being Italian, even mine, and they're only from Nine West, but still, I feel a ridiculous beat of pleasure that Nate is ticking off her checklist.

'And his watch?' She leans closer, her eyes wide.

'Um . . .'

I can't remember if he was even wearing a watch, but then it wasn't his wrist I was looking at, I muse, my mind darting off to a *totally* different body part.

'I'm not sure,' I say vaguely, but if I'm expecting it to put Magda off, I'm wrong.

'Don't worry,' she's saying determinedly. 'It will be fine. It will be more than fine! Trust me, I am never wrong when it comes to matchmaking. I even managed to fix up Belinda, my sister's daughter, once we'd addressed the waxing issue.'

Now I know why she's been so successful as a matchmaker: this woman is like Jason Bourne on a mission.

'Well, that's the thing, you see, you don't need to match-make . . .' I need to explain about me and Nate, about how we've already met, about everything.

But Magda's not listening. She's waving her skinny arms around like propellers and gushing, 'Oh, this is wonderful! Wonderful!' before putting them on her tiny hips and fixing me with an accusatory look. 'Is this not wonderful?'

'Well, yes ... but ...' I try again, then pause. Oh, what the hell. Why explain? I've met Nate again and it's fantastic – no explanation needed.

Breaking into a huge, delighted, over-the-moon grin, I nod happily. 'Yes, it's pretty bloody wonderful.'

Chapter Ten

The grin never leaves my face. I wear it all day, like a clown's painted smile, as I waft dreamily around the gallery. Nothing can pierce my good mood. Not the jammed printer that decides to chew up my guest list and get ink all over my skirt. Not the couple with the little boy who misreads the sign saying, 'Please don't touch,' so that it says, 'Please touch everything with your grubby, sticky fingers.' Not even the sullen man behind the counter at Katz's when I go to pick up our usual lunchtime order. Everything and everyone is wonderful. Life is wonderful.

Even my hair looks wonderful.

Well, OK, maybe not *wonderful*, but less fluffy and definitely shinier.

All through the day my phone beeps like a heart monitor as Nate sends me texts. Funny texts, flirty texts, romantic texts – plus quite a few suggestive texts that send me blushing to the bathroom to secretly respond. Magda might be the most broad-minded boss I've ever worked for, but there are still some things I can't do in front of her, and typing, 'Naked with whipped cream,' is one of them.

I float all the way home from work. I'm oblivious to the wail of police sirens and crazy rush-hour traffic, and when someone stomps on my foot, I barely notice. Neither do I notice the three flights of stairs that I usually pant up, cursing my lack of fitness. Instead, cocooned in my own little world, called Planet Nathaniel, I glide up them effortlessly, until here I am, unlocking the door of my apartment.

I discover the TV on, and Robyn lying on the sofa with Simon and Jenny. A braceleted arm waves from over the back of the cushions. 'You're just in time. Oprah's about to interview a man who had a baby.'

'Oh my God, I can't believe it!' I blurt, plonking myself down on the sofa.

'Well, it's not really a man, but she's got a beard and everything.'

'It's unbelievable.' I shake my head.

'No, don't you see? It's actually a woman who's been taking male hormones. I reckon she's doing it for the publicity.' She waggles the remote at the TV accusingly.

'I still can't believe it,' I murmur dazedly.

'No, Lucy, you're not getting it.' Turning from the screen to look at me, Robyn suddenly stops. Her brow furrows. 'Lucy, are you OK? You look funny.'

Hugging my knees to my chest, I'm staring into space, a dippy expression on my face. 'I had sex. It was amazing. I think I'm in love.'

Robyn looks like someone just hit her around the head. She stabs the pause button on the remote, freezing Oprah in mid-sentence. 'Whoa, whoa, whoa,' she cries, holding out both hands like one of the Supremes in a dance routine. 'Not so fast. Let's back up here a moment.' Tucking her curls behind her ears, she fixes me with her flashing green eyes. 'Sex? Love? *With whom?*' she demands.

'Nathaniel.' I smile dreamily.

Her eyes grow wide like dinner plates. 'You mean *the One*,' she gasps in a sort of hushed awe.

I nod, feeling a beat of joy. 'The One,' I repeat, feeling a swell of happiness.

There's a sharp intake of breath and Robyn shoots bolt upright, like something out of *The Exorcist*, arms flailing, eyes rolling, nostrils flaring. Simon and Jenny jump off the sofa whimpering.

'Oh wow, Lucy!' she shrieks. 'I can't believe it! Well, actually, I can,' she says quickly, as if arguing with herself. 'It's the power of the universe bringing you guys together. I just knew when you told me that story . . . you and Nathaniel are meant to be together. It's kismet.' Clutching at the crystal round her neck, she continues breathlessly, 'So come on, tell me, what happened?'

And so I tell her, in all the wrong order, and she asks me millions of questions, trying to fill in the gaps, as I jump in the shower, then out and start getting ready.

'Hang on a minute, so he's no longer married?'

'Separated, getting divorced,' I explain, twisting my hair into a towel and padding into my bedroom. I flick on the tangle of fairy lights around my wardrobe and light my aromatherapy candle.

'And he's moved to New York?'

'From LA, yes. He's filming some TV shows here. He's a producer,' I add with a beat of pride.

'What does a producer do?' asks Robyn, trying to clear a space on the bed to sit down, then giving up and sitting down anyway.

'Um . . . produce.' I shrug, reaching for my moisturiser. I have no idea what a producer does, but it sounds impressive. 'Oh God, Robyn, it was just amazing,' I sigh, daubing little dollops of cream on my cheekbones. '*He* was amazing.'

'Wow, it's so romantic.' She sighs dreamily.

'I know.' I nod, tugging off my towel and pulling on my bobbly old dressing gown. 'You know, he asked me if I believed in soulmates.'

'He did not!'

'He did.'

We exchange glances. Robyn looks like she's died and gone to heaven. 'Oh Jeez, Lucy,' she exclaims, her face flushed with happiness. 'I told you, you just have to believe. That's all you need to—' She breaks off and wriggles uncomfortably. 'Ouch, I think I'm sitting on something sharp.' Grimacing, she reaches underneath the embroidered bedspread. 'What's this?'

'I don't know. What is it?' I say abstractedly, without even looking. Having unearthed a pair of tweezers from my underwear drawer, I'm making a start on my eyebrows.

'Um . . . it's some kind of pendant, I think.'

'Oh, just chuck it with all my other jewellery.' I motion vaguely to my dressing table, which is strewn with nail polishes, loose change, a couple of sketchbooks . . . I make a mental note to add it to the list of things to clear up when I have a minute. Only I never seem to find that minute.

'It's made from a bit of a coin.'

In the middle of tweezing, I freeze. Hang on a minute, it can't be . . .

'Where is it?' I gasp, twirling round, my heart pounding.

Robyn sees my expression and suddenly the penny, quite literally, drops.

'Oh wow, is this . . .?'

'My necklace,' I gasp, catching it as it falls from her fingers. In disbelief I trace the broken edge with my thumb. 'I thought I'd lost it years ago. Where did you find it?'

'Just here, on the bed.'

'But that's impossible.' My mind is helter-skeltering. I only moved to New York six weeks ago and there was no way it was in my suitcases. OK, so my idea of packing is less 'capsule' and more 'chuck everything in', but even so, I would have noticed a necklace that went missing years ago. Especially *this* necklace. 'I mean, things don't just turn up like that,' I murmur, shaking my head incredulously.

Bewildered, I look up at Robyn, expecting her to appear as baffled as I am, but instead her eyes are shining with excitement. 'Don't you see? It's the legend,' she gasps, her face splitting into an ecstatic grin.

'The what?' I frown in confusion, not comprehending.

'The legend of the Bridge of Sighs,' she responds impatiently. 'It's coming true!'

As she says it, a warm gust of wind blows in from the open window, causing the flame of the aromatherapy candle to flicker and billowing out the length of red and gold sari fabric acting as a curtain. As the golden threads shimmer and dance, a shiver suddenly runs up my spine, and for an infinitesimal moment my imagination ignites . . .

Then just as quickly the gust of wind stills and my imagination is snuffed out.

'Don't be silly,' I retort. 'It's me being messy, never knowing where anything is. I'm always losing things.'

Inside, though, I feel jittery. Seriously, what has got into me? You're just nervous about tonight, I tell myself firmly. That's what it is. Nerves make you think all kinds of silly things.

'Anyway, on to more important matters,' I say, briskly shoving the coin pendant into my bag.

'Ooh, you mean like his star sign,' enthuses Robyn. 'Don't tell me. I bet he's an Aries.'

'No,' I gasp, grabbing a jumble of clothes. 'Like what am I going to wear?'

An hour later and I've tried everything on that's hanging in my wardrobe, which isn't very much, as I seem to have an aversion to coat hangers and instead prefer the back-of-the-chair approach to hanging up clothes. Plus everything that's lying crumpled on my bed, for when the back of the chair gets full. Plus everything that belongs to Robyn, even though she's about six inches taller than me and a fan of all things tie-dye.

And I'm still in my dressing gown.

'Oh God, what am I going to wear?' I wail desperately for the umpteenth time.

'What about this?' enthuses Robyn brightly.

Honestly, the woman is amazing. Now I know why she was chosen for the cheerleading team at college. Even in the face of defeat she remains amazingly upbeat.

'It looks great with leggings.'

Pausing from rummaging through a pile of tops that have gone bobbly, or have a mysterious stain on the front, or seem to have shrunk in the wash, I glance over. She's holding up a vicious purple tie-dye smock thing that looks like every other item of clothing she's already shown me from her wardrobe.

'It's nice, but . . .'

'But what?'

'I'm not sure about tie-dye,' I say carefully. Or the fact that it looks like a shapeless purple tent, I think.

'What's wrong with tie-dye?'

What's right with tie-dye? I want to reply, but I have to be tactful. Unlike most Americans I've met, Robyn spends her holidays travelling to far-flung corners of the globe, and her wardrobe stands testament. Forget the high street, hers is an eclectic mix of embroidered silk tunics from tiny hill villages in China, woven jackets from a tribe in Africa and baggy fisherman trousers from Thailand. And lots of tie-dye from India. The other day I caught sight of her underwear on the airer and saw even *that* was tie-dye.

'You've got to be a really special person to wear it. I mean, it looks amazing on you,' I gush, and see Robyn flush at the compliment, 'but I think I need something that's a bit more . . .' I search around for the right words ' . . . of a statement.'

'Right, I see,' nods Robyn thoughtfully. Sitting cross-legged on the bed, she wrinkles up her nose in concentration, the tiny stud in her nostril twinkling under the fairy lights. 'What kind of statement?'

'I'm not sure. Something that's feminine but not girly.' In desperation I start attacking the heap of garments on the back of the chair again.

'Something sexy,' grins Robyn wickedly.

'But not tarty,' I add quickly, feeling a beat of panic. 'I want him to think, Wow.'

'He already thinks, Wow,' she reassures.

I shoot her a grateful smile.

'Seriously, he loves you the way you are!' she exclaims. 'You could wear a trash bag and he'd still think you look amazing.'

'Actually, that's not a bad idea,' I groan, holding up a pair of black leggings that have gone all baggy at the knees. 'Do we have any of those?'

In the end, I opt for a lilac silk dress I bought on eBay last year. It's made of crumpled silk (so it's *supposed* to be creased), and I cinch in the waist with an amazing belt I borrow from Robyn.

'It's from the Amazon,' she says, fastening the strands of multicoloured beads round my waist.

'Have you been to the Amazon too?' I ask, impressed. God, Robyn has been everywhere.

'No, Chinatown,' she says matter-of-factly. 'They sell everything there.' Standing back, she looks me up and down appraisingly.

'How do I look?' I ask, angling my body into the mirror above my dressing table. I can see my torso and not much else.

'You look perfect,' she says, her face splitting into the whitest, toothiest smile. 'Just perfect.'

'Not too dressy?'

'Lucy, he's taking you to one of the best restaurants in Manhattan!'

'Argh, don't!' I feel a beat of excitement and alarm. Nate had texted me the name of the restaurant earlier, and when I'd told Robyn, she'd just looked at me agog and whispered, 'Oh wow, Lucy,' over and over until I begged her to stop as she was making me nervous.

'What time is the reservation?'

'Um . . .' Picking up my mobile, I scroll through the texts. Nate sent me dozens today, every one of which has been duly read and analysed by Robyn to much approval. 'Nine thirty,' I say, finally finding the right one.

'But it's twenty past now,' says Robyn glancing at my alarm clock.

'*What?*' I shoot a panicked look at the same clock. 'It can't be.'

I watch the digital numbers flick to nine twenty-one.

'Shit, I'm going to be late!'

'You'll be fine. Jump in a cab,' she says calmly.

'I can't. I'm broke. I'm still trying to pay off that Visa bill.' Scrambling around, I grab my bag.

'Lucy! This is your destiny!' she gasps. 'You can't make it wait while you catch the freaking subway.'

Actually, put like that . . .

'Here's twenty bucks for the fare,' she says, digging a bill out of her little embroidered purse. 'And I'm not going to take no for an answer.'

I give her a grateful hug. 'Thanks. What would I do without you?'

'I have no idea. Now, go have fun,' she calls after me, as I dash out of the bedroom.

Then dash back in again. 'I forgot my shoes,' I explain breathlessly. Snatching up my favourite pair of heels, I run barefoot out of the apartment, down the stairs and on to the street to hail a cab.

Chapter Eleven

According to my New York tourist guide, there are thirteen thousand registered yellow taxi-cabs in Manhattan. In addition there's all those other private-hire vehicles, and limos and black cars – I'm not sure exactly how many – but it's a lot. Which means that basically there's literally tens of thousands of taxis prowling the city.

And yet I can't bloody find one of them!

Fifteen minutes later I'm still standing on the pavement. Waiting. OK, don't panic, there must be a cab somewhere, there just must be, I tell myself, waving desperately at every passing vehicle in the hope that one of them might be a cab.

Oh look, one's stopping! Finally! Brilliant!

I feel a jolt of relief, swiftly followed by something else.

Er, actually, no, it's not brilliant. It's not a cab at all. It's some creepy man in a car. And now he's making a rude gesture.

Urgh ... Jumping away from the kerb, I march quickly in the other direction – not so easy in three-inch heels – and continue scanning the traffic for a yellow light. But nothing. The knot in my stomach tightens a notch. Shit. I'm going to be late. Like really late. Like my romantic-dinner-with-Nate-is-going-to-be-ruined late.

No sooner has the thought popped into my head than I see a flash of yellow.

Hang on a minute, *is that* ...?

Out of nowhere a cab appears and swerves up beside me. Oh my God, where did that just come from? For a moment I stare frozen in astonishment as it drops off its passengers next to me on the kerbside and flicks on its light. I mean, how can that be? One minute it wasn't here and then the next ...

Lucy, for God's sake, just get in.

'East Fifty-Seventh Street, please,' I say to the driver, jumping inside. Gosh, listen to me – I sound like a proper New Yorker. Then smiling happily to myself, I can't resist adding, 'And step on it.'

Robyn is right – it's super swanky.

Arriving uptown at the restaurant, the uniformed maître d' leads me through the intimate dining room, with its subdued lighting and murmur of chinking cutlery, to a candlelit table tucked away in the corner. And Nathaniel, looking immaculate in his dark grey suit.

He's chatting to someone on his iPhone. He sees me and smiles.

My stomach flips right over like a pancake.

'Sorry, Joe, can I call you back?' Then without missing a beat he says approvingly to me, 'Wow, you look amazing.'

'Thanks.' I smile, my anxieties about what to wear melting away. I don't know why I was so nervous. Nate's seen me in his boxer shorts and a sweatshirt, my hair scraped back and not a scrap of make-up. Admittedly it was ten years ago, but still. 'Sorry I'm late.'

'I'm glad to see nothing's changed,' he says, standing up and giving me a kiss.

I feel a tug of longing. Yup, he's right. Nothing's changed.

'So how was your day?'

Broken from my lustful reverie, I see the waiter pulling out my chair for me. 'Oh, you know,' I say, sitting down.

'Busy? Me too.' Nate nods consolingly, though that's not exactly what I meant. To be truthful, it all passed in a blur of butterflies and anticipation of this evening. 'We were filming all day in the studio. It was pretty exhausting.'

'What were you filming?' Knowing Nate, it's most likely some drama or documentary about history or politics, which is what he majored in at Harvard.

'A game show.'

'*A game show?*' I feel a snap of surprise, followed by something that feels like a tiny beat of disappointment. Which is ridiculous. I mean, there's nothing wrong with game shows. My parents watch them all the time.

'I know what you're thinking – what is Nate doing producing game shows? – but in terms of viewing figures . . .'

'No, not at all,' I protest quickly. 'I love game shows!'

So OK, that's a bit of a fib. I can't remember the last time I watched a game show. I think it was probably last Christmas at Mum and Dad's, when we watched *Who Wants to Be a Millionaire?* Kate was there too and she did her usual trick of answering all the questions before the contestant and getting them all correct. Me? I needed to phone a friend on the first one.

'Really?' Nate looks pleased. 'Which one is your favourite?'

Shit.

'Um . . . gosh, there are so many,' I say vaguely. 'It's hard to choose.'

'You never could make a decision,' he says with a smile, and reaches for my hand across the table. 'Remember Italy and the ice cream?'

His warm fingers wrap around mine and I feel a warm fuzziness.

'Well, there were so many flavours and they were all so delicious,' I protest, thinking about how I used to make him wait for me as I tasted a scoop of every single flavour. Meanwhile he chose vanilla every time. 'Saying that, the best ice cream I've ever tasted wasn't in Italy. It was in Paris, at this tiny little café up by the Sacré-Coeur.'

'When were you in Paris?'

'Last New Year's Eve.'

'Hey, so was I!'

'No way!'

We look at each other.

'Oh my God, what a coincidence. Did you watch the fireworks?'

'Over the Eiffel Tower, yeah.' He's nodding, his face breaking into a smile. 'They were pretty incredible, weren't they?'

'The bit where all the rockets shot out from the sides . . .'

' . . . and then the whole tower exploded at the stroke of midnight,' he finishes, and then we just stare at each other in disbelief.

'You were there,' he says after a moment.

'So were you,' I murmur.

My stomach flutters as my mind ficks back. To think that we were so close, that we were in the same city at the same time, watching the same fireworks burst into the same patch of sky – we just didn't know it.

'Wow, that's insane,' says Nate, grinning. 'You and me, both in Paris last year for New Year's Eve. What a total fluke.' He laughs at the absurdity.

'I know,' I agree, and ignoring my fluttering stomach, I laugh too. 'What a total fluke.'

After a few moments the waiter comes to take our order. Everything on the menu sounds delicious, though there are a couple of things that I've never heard of and I have to get the waiter to explain. I'm not used to eating in this kind of restaurant. Compared to my local Italian back home in London, with its red-and-white checked tablecloths and waltzy background music, this is a different world.

I try hard not to be fazed and plump for the wild mushroom pasta, whereas Nate opts for the fish and a green salad. 'And a bottle of champagne,' he says, shooting me a smile across the table.

My insides do a loop-the-loop. I swear at this rate they could rival the Red Arrows.

'What are we celebrating?' I whisper, as the waiter disappears.

'My decision to walk into a gallery.' He smiles and then looks at me thoughtfully, as if there's a lot of stuff going on inside his head. 'I wasn't going to, but if I hadn't . . .'

'So what made you?'

'I dunno.' He shrugs. 'It was totally random. I'm never usually in that part of town, but I was on my way to a business lunch and had five minutes to kill, so I was just walking around. In fact, I nearly walked right past it, but then . . .'

'Then what?' I ask, interested.

'I'm not sure.' He crinkles his brow. 'I suddenly had this desire to go inside. It was really weird.' He shakes his head dismissively, then laughs. 'Trust me, I don't normally go around buying expensive art on my lunch break. It's usually just a salad.'

I laugh, and at that moment the waiter reappears with the bottle of champagne, which he duly opens with a deft flick of his wrist and pours into two glass flutes.

'Here's to Venice,' Nate says, passing me a glass.

'To the gallery.'

'To us,' he adds quietly, holding my gaze as he clinks his glass against mine.

A tingle runs all the way up my spine, and I take a sip, savouring the sensation of the cold bubbles fizzing on my tongue.

I feel as if I'm in a dream, as if I'm going to pinch myself and wake up back in my old life. Instead of here with Nate, in some fabulously posh restaurant, sipping champagne and making eyes at each other across the table.

Suddenly we're interrupted by his iPhone ringing. He glances at the screen, then frowns. 'Sorry, Lucy, but do you mind if I take this call? It's work.'

'No, it's fine, go ahead,' I say happily.

He throws me a grateful smile, then picks up. 'Hi, John. So, as we discussed earlier, depending on the pilot, I would see this as a straight-to-network show and I'd be very happy to ensure that Regis takes a consulting, executive producer role and credit . . .'

As he starts talking business, I take another sip of champagne and glance around the restaurant. It's a well-heeled crowd. Mostly couples, and mostly older, the women all look the same, with their Hamptons tans and professional blow-dries, whereas the men are all salt-and-pepper hair and bespoke suits. Though there's a couple over there who look quite funky, I notice, spotting an unshaven man in the corner wearing a pair of dark sunglasses.

I give a little snort of derision. Honestly, who wears sunglasses inside a restaurant? Who does he think he is? Bono?

Absently I watch as he moves slightly to the side and I get a better look at him.

Oh my God, it *is* Bono.

I feel a sudden thrill. I can't believe it. A famous person, eating dinner in the same restaurant as me! See, this is what's so fantastic about coming to swanky restaurants in Manhattan. This wouldn't happen in my local Italian back in Earl's Court.

'OK, cc me in on the email and I'll call you tomorrow. Thanks, John.' Hanging up, Nate turns back to me. 'Hey, sorry about that.'

'Oh, it's OK.' I smile, then lean across the table and whisper, 'Guess what, Bono's sitting behind you!'

I'm expecting Nate to look excited and try to sneak a peek, but instead he just sort of shrugs disinterestedly and says, 'Oh, really?' and reaches for his champagne.

'Yes, I'm pretty certain it's him.' I nod, shooting another covert glance over his shoulder. 'I mean, he looks exactly the same.'

'Are you a big U2 fan?'

'Well, not really, but I saw them in concert once and they were amazing.'

'Yeah, me too. A friend of mine won tickets to the last gig of their three-night run in Dublin and took me along. It was a few years back now.'

'June 2005. The Vertigo tour,' I finish before I can stop myself.

'Wow, you *are* a fan!' he laughs.

I stare at him in astonishment. 'I was there.'

'Scuse me?' He looks at me as if he's misheard.

'My boyfriend took me to the same concert. Well, he wasn't really my boyfriend,' I add hastily. 'We just went on a few dates and—'

'You're kidding!'

'No, really, we were totally mismatched. He was into going to festivals and taking hallucinogens. OK, so I ate hash cookies once, but that's only because I thought they were real cookies—'

'I'm talking about the concert,' interrupts Nate, and I blush.

'Oh, right, I know.' I shake my head in disbelief. First New Year's Eve in Paris and now this . . . It's almost as if we've been meant to meet again. As if all these years we've been circum-navigating the globe, going to the same places at the same time, but we just kept missing each other.

Until now.

'Anyone would think you've been following me,' he says, breaking into my thoughts, grinning.

'Or you've been following me,' I protest indignantly. Goodness, I'm getting as bad as Robyn. Of course it's just a coincidence. There must have been thousands of people at that concert.

'By the way, that's not Bono,' he confides, his eyes flashing with amusement.

'It's not? How can you tell?' I look over to see he's standing up, ready to leave. I get a jolt of surprise. Oh my God, the man is a giant. Seriously, he must be about seven foot tall. I feel a flash of embarrass-ment. 'Well, the resemblance was very striking,' I say in explanation.

'I suppose you think that's Madonna sitting in the corner over there too,' he teases.

'And next to her are Posh and Becks,' I giggle loudly.

'Ssh.' He frowns slightly and gestures with his hand for me to keep my voice down. 'A little less on the volume.'

'Oh, sorry.' My giggles immediately disappear and I feel a bit awkward. As if I've just been told off. Still, I suppose I can get a bit loud and silly when I'm tipsy, and this champagne has gone straight to my head. That always happens when I drink on an empty stomach, I muse, feeling a flash of relief as the waiter arrives with our food.

'Mmm, this is heavenly,' I say, tasting a delicious mouthful of pasta. 'Do you want to try some?'

'No, thanks. I'm trying to stay off the carbs,' says Nate, making a start on his green salad.

'So you can't eat pasta?' I ask, momentarily trying to imagine life without macaroni cheese and failing.

'Or potatoes or bread.' He nods, spearing a lettuce leaf. 'And pretty much any baked goods.'

'So no biscuits?' I squeak.

'Well, I wouldn't be eating cookies, anyway. They're full of refined sugar.'

'Right, yeah.' I nod, trying not to think about all the packets of Hobnobs I've devoured over my lifetime. 'Absolutely.'

'When I think about what we used to eat when we were in Italy.' He rolls his eyes and shakes his head. 'All that pizza and ice cream. I mean, can you imagine eating that now?'

I don't have to imagine – it's pretty much all Robyn and I *do* eat. Our apartment is strewn with Domino's takeaway boxes and empty cartons of Ben & Jerry's. I feel a beat of alarm. What if Nate wants to come back to mine?

'God, no,' I say, and giving a little shudder, I make a mental note to nip to the loos to text Robyn and tell her to get rid of the evidence. Just in case.

'Since living in LA, I've adopted a much healthier lifestyle,' he continues, putting down his fork and leaning across the table towards me. 'I go hiking in the canyons. I run along the beach . . .'

Slow-motion footage of a muscular Nate running along the beach, suddenly springs into my mind and I feel a lustful twinge.

'What kind of stuff do you like doing?'

'Me?' I suddenly return from my daydream to see him looking at me expectantly.

'Yeah, to keep fit.' He smiles.

Nothing. Absolutely nothing.

Shit. Think of something quick. I don't want to look like I'm some kind of slob who sits on the sofa every night watching *Oprah* and eating biscuits. Well, not *every* night.

'Oh . . . um . . . I love rollerblading . . .'

OK, so 'love' is rather a strong word. I went once in Hyde Park and didn't know how to stop. I ended up crashing into a group of French tourists. Not good for Anglo-French relations.

' . . . and yoga.'

I've been once, maybe twice, but still, I love the *idea* of doing yoga. All that nag champa incense and a bendy pretzel body like Gwyneth's.

'Wow, really? Me too,' says Nate, looking pleased. 'We should do a yoga class together.'

Oh crap.

'Well, I'm not very good,' I say hastily. In fact, if the truth be told, the last time I went to yoga, I nearly put my back out trying to touch my toes.

'Don't worry, I can help you. I studied with a great teacher in LA,' he says, reaching across the table for my hand and giving me a smile that makes me feel all funny behind the knees. 'In fact, maybe we should have some private classes together, just you and me.'

Instantly I can feel my reservations vanishing as I imagine Nate and me doing sun salutations together every morning, going out for fresh juice afterwards, wearing all that fabulous gear to show off our amazing yoga-honed bodies. My mind starts running off with itself . . . Just think, we could go on those weekend retreats, or we could go live on a beach in India and spend our days going, '*Ommmmm.*'

Not that I particularly want to go live on a beach in India and go, '*Ommmmm*,' but even so.

'That sounds great.' I nod, smiling dreamily.

'It does, doesn't it?' He grins, and we fall silent and stare doe-eyed across the table at each other, like a couple of loved-up teenagers. Truly, it's horribly embarrassing.

Bloody fantastic, though.

The rest of the evening slips away in a hazy blur of delicious food, ice-cold champagne and flirtation. We skip coffee and dessert, as Nate doesn't drink it or eat them; instead he asks me back to his for a night-cap. By the glint in his eye, it's pretty obvious he's not talking about a cup of cocoa.

I feel a frisson of excitement as he asks for the bill.

Although the chocolate profiteroles with hot sauce did sound to die for.

'You OK?' he asks, stroking my hair as I lean against him on the back seat of the cab on the way back to his penthouse.

'Yeah, fine.' I nod. I can feel the hardness of his thigh pressing against mine through my flimsy silk dress. It's only a few hours since we were in bed together, but it already feels like eons ago.

'Sleepy?' Tracing his fingers underneath my hair to the nape of my neck, he moves them slowly down to my collarbone.

I swallow hard. 'No,' I reply, trying to keep my voice even. This feels like the longest cab ride ever. Filled with champagne and the anticipation of what lies ahead, every red light takes for ever, every block an eternity. I move my hand to his lap, feeling the hardness beneath. He flinches slightly and his breathing grows heavier. 'Are you?'

'No, me neither.' He reaches his hand down into my dress and I feel a shiver run down to my groin.

God, this is so surreal, both of us having this perfectly normal conversation, while at the same time not being able to keep our hands off each other.

It's also the biggest turn-on.

'So if we're not feeling sleepy, what shall we do?' I ask innocently, while untucking his shirt and sliding my fingertips underneath his waistband.

'Hmm, I'm not sure,' he says, still playing the game. 'We could watch a DVD.'

The breath catches in my throat. 'What movies do you have?' I manage. My entire body is pulsating and it takes every drop of self-control not to demand he has sex with me there and then, on the back seat of the cab.

I know. *What am I like?*

'Oh, I'm sure I've got something that you'd enjoy . . .' He trails off, his breath hot and ragged against my ear.

'Really?' I say thickly.

'Really,' he gasps, his voice trembling.

Then suddenly we're pulling up at his building, and Nate is paying the taxi, and we're walking in through the revolving doors and across the lobby. I'm so heady with desire I barely notice the doorman, or the ride up in the elevator. All I'm aware of is Nate's body standing close to mine, the warm musky smell of him, the sound of his breath, short and urgent against my neck.

Now the doors are sliding open and we're walking into the apartment and saying goodnight to the doorman, and it's just the two of us, alone at last.

'You know, I'm not really in the mood for a DVD.' I turn to him, feeling as if my whole body might explode at any moment.

'What are you in the mood for?' He looks at me, daring me.

I can't do it. I can't play this game any more.

'This,' I say, and pulling him towards me, I kiss him. Last night I was so drunk on red wine the sex was all a bit hazy. Caught up in the whirlwind of seeing him again, of being with him again, it all seemed to happen so fast.

But now I'm getting a glorious rerun, just in case I missed anything, I muse, feeling a shiver of delight as, kissing me back, he pulls me to the floor.

Afterwards we just lie there, dozing. Bathed in a warm fuzziness, I rest my head on his chest, listening as our breathing slows to normal. For a while neither of us speaks, then turning his head, he kisses me gently on the cheek and says quietly, 'I've got something to show you.'

'Oh, I think I've seen everything,' I say, raising an eyebrow and smiling.

He clicks his tongue reprovingly. 'No, you haven't.' He grins, pulling himself up.

Naked, he disappears for a moment while I lie on the white carpet, warm and contented. I stretch out like a cat and let out a yawn. I feel sleepy, spent, satisfied.

'I just found it today,' he says, reappearing. 'I thought I'd lost it years ago, but it just turned up out of the blue.' Propping myself up on my elbows, I gaze at him as he bends down to kiss me. 'A bit like you, hey?'

I look at him in confusion. What is he talking about? Then I notice he's wearing something round his neck. A pendant. *Half a coin.*

My heart leaps and I feel a shockwave of amazement, incredulity, excitement . . . and something else. This must be more than just coincidence. This must be Fate.

'Well, it's funny you should say that . . .' Rolling over, I throw out my arm and reach for my bag, which is lying discarded on the floor, along with my clothes. With my fingers, I fumble around inside, until finally I find it. My half of the necklace.

'Look.' Triumphantly I loop it round my neck and we exchange looks of delight.

'Hey, I wonder if they still . . .' Leaning towards me, he gently reaches for my necklace and puts it together with his. The two halves click into place, like two pieces of a jigsaw.

'It's a perfect fit,' I murmur.

'Are you talking about the necklace or . . .?' He raises his eyebrows suggestively.

'Nate!' I giggle, and swat him playfully.

'What?' he laughs, then pauses thoughtfully, tracing a finger across my shoulder. 'You know, now I've found you again, I'm never letting you go.'

'Yeah, right,' I tease, but inside I feel a burst of happiness.

'No, I'm serious.' His blue eyes search mine and he looks at me for a long moment. 'You're never going to get rid of me.'

'Well now, there's a coincidence . . .' Reaching up, I pull him down towards me. 'You're never going to get rid of me either.'

Chapter Twelve

The rest of the week slips away in a dreamy montage of romantic dinner dates in some of the finest restaurants in New York, a horse-drawn carriage ride in Central Park, an amazing bouquet of fresh white lilies delivered to work . . .

It's everything a girl could ever dream of and more. What's even more amazing is this time it's not happening to someone else. To some random celebrity I read about in a magazine on the subway, or a friend of a friend I hear about over drinks with my single girlfriends, but me. *Me*. Lucy Hemmingway.

I mean, who would have thought that only a few days ago I was trundling along in my normal life, doing normal things, like moaning about my cellulite to Robyn and doing my hand-washing, and then – *boom* – I bumped into Nate again and everything changed. Not that my life was terrible before, it wasn't at all. It's just . . . Well, put it this way, I'm not thinking about cellulite or hand-washing any more.

Now I'm too busy smiling as yet another slushy text beeps up from my phone, or lying giggling in his arms after we've had sex for about the millionth time.

As for my cellulite . . . the funny thing is, I don't think Nate's even noticed it!

Cocooned in our own little world called Nate 'n' Luce: Population 2, it's like no one and nothing else exists. In fact, it's all I can do each morning to drag myself away from his penthouse and catch the subway downtown to work. I want to be like John and Yoko and just lounge around in bed for a week, though my reasons are *slightly* less honourable. Well, ten years is a *lot* of lost time to make up for.

Saying that, as soon as I enter the gallery, I automatically switch into work mode. Wafting around in a heady, romantic state might be wonderful, but it's all-consuming and you can't get anything done, and there's loads to do, as this Friday is the opening at the gallery. Falling in love and having your first New York gallery opening to organise all in the same week is a bit intense, but I rise to the challenge. Switching back and forth between loved-up Lucy and work-mode Lucy, like Superman, only without the cape.

Until by Friday everything on my list has been ticked off with my brand-new highlighter pen. My sister, Kate, has always been a fan of highlighter pens. She carries one in every colour in her handbag – unlike me, who can never find a pen and usually ends up digging around until I find an old broken bit of charcoal I used to sketch with. This time, though, I'm determined to be more organised.

Compile guest list: *tick*. Send out invitations: *tick*. Write promotional material: *tick*. Book caterer: *tick*. Hire waitressing staff: *tick*. Hang paintings ready to exhibit: *tick*. Now all we need is for it to be a success, I tell myself, feeling a bundle of nerves as the first guests start arriving.

'Welcome to Number Thirty-Eight,' I smile, crossing their names off my list. 'Please feel free to wander around and enjoy the artwork, and if you have any questions, my name's Lucy and I'd be delighted to help you.'

Panic: *tick*.

Twenty minutes later and the gallery is buzzing. It's a hot, muggy evening in New York and the doors have been thrown wide open. People are milling around inside and spilling outside on to the pavement.

It's a diverse crowd. Magda has put together an eclectic guest list, from sombre-looking artists dressed in Birkenstocks and Elvis Costello glasses to some of New York's glitterati, including several pubescent-looking models, the odd actor and lots of older men with impossibly white teeth and impossibly skinny wives who are dripping in diamonds and designer handbags. And who all look suspiciously like they bought their face at the same place as Magda, I notice, watching them air-kissing with their strangely swollen lips.

'Wow, you clever girl, this is amazing!'

I glance up to see Robyn bounding towards me, her hair flying loose, a large smile sweeping across her face. I've barely seen her all week, as I've been at Nate's, and it's great to see her. She's wearing an embroidered kaftan and a pair of fisherman trousers, both of which are tie-dyed, and the longest, dangliest pair of earrings I've ever seen.

'And you look amazing! I love your hair!' Flinging her arms round me, she gives me a breathless hug. 'The colour looks great on you!'

'Thanks.' I grin. In honour of the occasion I popped into a salon this lunchtime and changed the colour of my hair from a boring chestnut to a spicy blackcurrant.

'Has Nathaniel seen it yet?' she asks excitedly.

What she really means is, has Nathaniel *been seen* yet? All week she's been dying to meet him, but I've been keeping him under wraps until tonight.

'He's running a bit late at the studio, but I'll introduce you as soon as he arrives,' I promise.

'Cool. I can't wait.' She grins. 'OK, I'm off to grab a drink before I die of thirst. Do you want one?'

'Oh, no, I'm fine.' I shake my head. 'Better not drink on the job.'

'OK, well, I won't be a sec.'

As she disappears into the crowd, I turn back to my guest list. More people are arriving and there's still more yet to come, including my sister and her husband, Jeff, though they left a message saying they'd be late. Something about an appointment. I can't complain. Knowing her, it's probably some mega-important multi-million-dollar lawyer thing. In comparison, mine is just a little gallery opening.

'Babe, sorry I'm late.'

My thoughts are interrupted by a familiar voice and I look up to see Nate. Instantaneously my stomach does its usual loop-the-loop. 'You made it,' I say, experiencing a rush of happiness as he bends down and gives me a kiss.

'Just. We had a bit of a nightmare at the studio.'

'Oh, is everything OK?' I feel a beat of concern.

'For now.' He nods, checking his iPhone. 'There was a problem with the presenter of one of the shows I'm working on. He's being a total prima donna, making all kinds of demands.' He stops and stares at me. 'Hang on, you look different.'

I feel a wave of pleasure. He's noticed my new hair.

'What do you think?' I do a bit of flirty flicking with my hand.

His brow furrows. 'Lucy . . . is your hair *purple*?'

'It's called "spicy blackcurrant",' I falter. 'Don't you like it?'

He looks at me, as if he's weighing it up carefully. 'Well, it's certainly interesting,' he says, but inside I feel disappointed.

He hates it. He hates my hair.

'Isn't the colour amazing!'

Hearing a voice, I swivel round to see Robyn reappearing with a drink, her eyes wide with excitement as she takes in both me and Nate.

'Robyn, this is Nate,' I say, quickly doing the introduction and changing the subject from my hair. 'My boyfriend,' I add.

Well, I can't resist. Just saying it gives me a little burst of happiness.

'Wow, I'm so pleased to meet you!' With a glass of champagne in one hand, she throws the other round him. 'I've heard everything about you!'

'Really?' Nate looks amused. 'Everything?' He shoots me a look over her tie-dyed shoulder and I blush.

'About Venice, and the bridge, and the legend.' Releasing him from her one-armed hug, she stands back and looks at us both, a huge soppy grin on her face. 'Just look at you two. You make such a cute couple.'

I blush as Nate squeezes my shoulder.

'No, but seriously,' she continues, her face falling suddenly solemn, 'you guys were meant to be together. You know there is a force out there that none of us understands, a bigger energy than either you or me . . .' She pauses, then lowers her voice to a whisper as if she's telling us a secret. 'Believe me when I say this, destiny is an amazing thing, and this is your destiny. This course was set out for you. It's kismet. You're puppets and Fate is pulling the strings, and—'

The jingle of someone's phone suddenly interrupts Robyn's monologue and Nate clamps his hand to his breast pocket.

'Sorry, excuse me.' Pulling out his iPhone, he glances at the screen. 'Do you mind? I need to take this. It's the studio.'

'No, no, go ahead,' bats away Robyn, snapping back to her usual vocal range, which is loud-verging-on-even-louder.

Clipping on his Bluetooth headset, he moves away. 'Hi. Yeah, Nathaniel Kennedy speaking . . .'

'Wow, Lucy, he's amazing,' gasps Robyn, as soon as he's out of earshot.

'You think so?' I say, trying to be modest, when of course I know he is.

'Totally.' She looks at me, suddenly welling up as if she's about to burst into tears. 'Oh, honey, I'm so happy for you.' Giving me a hug, she breaks away sniffling. 'Sorry I get so emotional . . . It's just . . .' She dabs her eyes with the sleeve of her kaftan and gives a little hiccup. 'I'll be right back. I'm just going to grab a napkin.'

Thrusting her drink at me, she turns and I watch her dashing off through the crowd. As it parts, I spot my sister. Carrying a briefcase and wearing a dark work suit and harassed expression, she couldn't look more out of place at a fashionable gallery opening if she tried.

'Hi, Kate.' I wave to attract her attention, and seeing me, she turns and marches over. 'I'm so glad you could make—'

But she cuts me straight off. 'Is that who I think it is?' she demands, bypassing the pleasantries and jerking her head towards Nate, who's still chatting away on his iPhone.

Oh shit.

I feel a clunking thud. The thing is, I haven't actually got round to telling my sister about Nate. It's not that I forgot as such. It's more . . .OK, I completely avoided telling her. She left me half a dozen voicemail messages this week, but I just texted back saying I was busy with work. Which is entirely true. I have been super busy with work.

I've also been super busy falling in love with Nate, but I couldn't tell her that. She's not exactly a paid-up member of the Nathaniel Kennedy Fan Club.

'Um . . .yes, it is,' I say, avoiding eye contact.

'The Bridge Guy!' she gasps incredulously.

'He's called Nathaniel,' I say, feeling defensive.

'I could call him a lot of things,' she replies, with a hard edge to her voice, 'and most of them aren't very complimentary.'

I feel my jaw set and I square my shoulders, just like I always do when I'm about to have an argument with Kate.

'Like, for example, *married*.'

'He's getting divorced,' I explain quickly. 'He and his wife are separated. He's living here in New York now.'

Kate's eyes narrow and she fixes me with the kind of look that terrifies vice-presidents of law firms across Manhattan. 'You're not seeing him again, are you, Lucy?' she demands, in a tone that makes grown men tremble.

By the look on my face there's obviously no need to answer.

'Oh my God, you are,' she gasps in disbelief.

'We're in love,' I say simply, trying to suppress a blissful smile, and failing.

'In *love*?' She staggers back as if she's just been shot. 'Since when?'

'Since I was nineteen,' I say, smiling ruefully.

Kate gives a little snort. 'Lucy, you haven't seen him for ten years. People change.'

'Well, he hasn't!' I say rather crossly. For goodness' sake, my big sister is always so negative. 'OK, so he doesn't drink coffee any more, and he does yoga, and—'

'Yoga?' gapes Kate.

'What's wrong with yoga?' I demand. 'It's very good for you. We're doing private classes together.'

'*You? Doing Yoga?*' She suddenly bursts out laughing. 'Lucy, you can't even touch your toes.'

'Yes, I can. *Almost*,' I say sulkily, thinking back to yesterday and mine and Nate's first lesson with Yani, our yoga instructor. He had long, dark hair and wore flowing white robes and reminded me a bit of Jesus. Especially when he kept talking about enlightenment, and spirituality, and discovering your inner soul. Unfortunately the only thing I discovered is that I have a body that does not bend. But like Yani says, it's all about the practice.

'Anyway, yoga's about the mind, not the body. Maybe you should try it,' I suggest, shooting Kate a look.

My sister looks back at me as if I'm an alien. 'Er, hello, can this robot who's stolen my sister please give her back?'

'If you're just going to make fun the whole time—'

'Well, c'mon, *Luce*.'

'No, there is no "C'mon on, Luce",' I snap hotly. 'We're back together again, and this time for good, and that's all there is to it.'

I break off, flushing, and Kate falls silent. 'Look, I'm not trying to spoil things for you,' she says, her tone much kinder, 'but are you sure about this?'

'I've never been more sure,' I say determinedly. Then I just can't help myself and gasp excitedly, 'Oh, Kate, this is it. The real deal. He's the One. He always *was* the One.'

I feel like when we were little and used to huddle excitedly together beneath the bedcovers, sharing our secrets.

But there's no flash of excitement across Kate's face this time. Instead she just looks at me, totally deadpan, and opens her mouth to say something, then thinks better of it and sighs. 'I'm just worried, that's all.'

'Well, don't be.' I reach for her hand. 'I'm really happy, Kate. Look at me. When did you last see me this happy?'

She pauses thoughtfully, then raises an eyebrow. 'When you got your picture taken with Daniel Craig?'

'You know I still have that as my screensaver.' I grin, thinking about the time I bumped into him outside Prêt-à-Manger on the King's Road in London and Kate took a photo of us on her phone. Me grinning like a loon. Him just looking jaw-droppingly sexy. 'It alternates between that and the shot of him coming out of the sea in his swimming trunks.'

'Lucky you. My screensaver's Jeff.' She smiles grudgingly. 'Though thankfully not in swimming trunks.'

I laugh. Unlike my sister, Jeff has zero willpower when it comes to diet and exercise. He likes to describe himself as cuddly. Kate, however, describes him as a lazy sod and is forever nagging him to join the gym. 'How is Jeff? Is he here?'

'Yeah, over there.'

My eyes swivel to the other side of the gallery, where I see Jeff hovering by *White Noise*, an abstract painting by one of our new artists, and peering at it unsurely. He's obviously been instructed to wait there until the coast is clear.

'Gosh, he's lost weight,' I say with surprise, as Kate waves him over.

'Has he?' She peers at him as he starts walking towards us, then shrugs. 'He looks the same to me.'

'No, he's definitely slimmer. What happened? Did you finally get him to join the gym?'

Kate snorts with amusement. 'Hardly. Jeff's idea of exercise is reaching for the remote. Isn't it, darling?' she says as he joins us.

'Totally.' He grins, having learned a long time ago to agree with whatever Kate says. Giving her a kiss on the cheek, he turns to me. 'Great exhibition, Lucy.' He hugs me. 'Though I'm afraid I don't know much about art. Just looks like a bunch of meaningless squiggles to me.' He shrugs apologetically.

'It's abstract,' I laugh. My sister and I might not agree on a lot of things, but one thing we do agree on is her choice of husband. If you had to look up 'good guy' in the dictionary, you'd see a picture of Jeff, an Irish-American with a heart of gold.

'Oh, so that's what it's called.' He smiles good-humouredly.

'Loozy! So there you are!'

We're interrupted by Magda, who's sporting a leopard-print dress and a beehive that appears to have taken on skyscraper proportions especially for the evening. She looks like a miniature Bet Lynch, albeit one with diamonds flashing on every appendage.

'This is Mrs Zuckerman, who runs the gallery,' I explain to Kate and Jeff, who are looking at her with slightly bewildered expressions. 'My boss,' I mouth over the top of her hairdo.

'Hi. So nice to meet you.' They both jump into action and go to shake her hand, but it's full of meatballs. A whole tray of them. True to her word, she's spent the whole week making them and is serving them up along with fake champagne.

Quite literally, I muse, watching her sticking the tray under their noses. Forget mingling with the guests, Magda has rolled up her leopard-print sleeves and is intent on serving up food like a good Jewish mother.

'Meatballs?' She beams, though it's more of an instruction and less of a question.

'Oh, no, thank you. We're going to go for dinner after—' begins Kate, but Magda interrupts.

'Nonsense. They are the perfect appetiser. Try some.' With characteristic pushiness, she thrusts them at her.

Kate shoots me a look. It's probably the only time I've ever seen her seem scared of anyone. Mutely she takes one.

'And you, you are far too skinny,' continues Magda, turning to Jeff.

'Oh, I don't know about that.' He laughs, looking bemused as he's handed a napkin piled high. 'Wow, that's a large helping.'

'They are *unbelievably* delicious,' she says, throwing her arms around and almost upsetting her tray. 'Are they not unbelievably delicious, Loozy?'

'Oh, yes, unbelievably delicious,' I repeat, nodding hastily.

'Aren't you hungry, Luce?' pipes up Kate.

That's my sister for you, absolutely no loyalty.

'Well, actually . . .' I stall. So far I've managed to avoid the famous meatballs by constantly flitting around and being busy, and for a split second I think my time is up, I can escape no longer, when I'm saved by the sight of more people arriving. 'Ooh, look, more guests!' And waving my guest list like a get-out-of-jail-free card, I quickly make a dash for it.

Of course, I can't go back until the coast is clear and so once I've ticked the new guests off my list, I go looking for Nate. I find him pacing up and down, gesticulating in the air, and talking to himself. At least, I think he's talking to himself, until I notice a tiny blue light flashing on his ear and realise he's wearing his Bluetooth headset and he's on the phone.

Still.

I suppress a tug of disappointment. He's been on the phone to the studio all evening and I've hardly spoken to him. Still, I suppose that's what it's like being some hot-shot TV producer, I tell myself. Seeing me, he throws me an apologetic look and I throw a 'No worries' one back. It's fine. I've got lots to do, anyway.

Turning, I go back inside the gallery. It's still pretty busy, and I do a bit of mingling, chat to a couple of journalists, shake lots of hands. Organising events isn't one of my strengths, and OK, I admit a couple of my emails bounced back because I'd sent them to the wrong people, and then there was the mix-up with the catering company.

Well, I say mix-up, but it wasn't my fault. How was I to know that Finger-Licking Fun wasn't a catering company? When I looked it up on the Internet, it talked about 'catering for your every need', so I sent them an email asking for their pricelist and I got a *completely* different menu of services than the one I was expecting.

Still, I have to say I've done a pretty good job here. Though a lot of them are more interested in the free food and alcohol than the artwork. Sometimes it's as if they don't even notice it, I muse in disbelief, looking around me in wonder at the amazing brushwork and kaleidoscope of colours we have displayed on the walls and feeling a familiar longing to paint again, to create, to let my imagination run away with my paintbrush . . .

But that's just me being silly, I think, sweeping the thought away quickly. After all, I tried that, remember, and look where it got me: broke and on the dole. No, this is much better. This way, I get to work in an amazing gallery in New York and organise events like this. I mean, how lucky am I?

I scan the crowd with a feeling of satisfaction. Pretty much everyone we invited is here. There's Mr and Mrs Bernstein, who are friends of Magda and huge art buyers, that super-model whose name I can't remember, a journalist from *Time Out* . . .Wait a moment, who's that?

My eyes land on a guy with a baseball cap out of which is sticking a shock of dark, curly hair. He's wearing a baggy green army T-shirt and a pair of jeans with rips in both knees. I look down at my guest list and scan the names, but everyone's ticked off. Apart from Jemima Jones, and he doesn't look much like a Jemima Jones.

I observe him for a few minutes. He's walking around gobbling up meatballs like Pacman and downing glasses of champagne. I watch as he drains one glass and takes another from a passing tray. Eating and drinking all the freebies without even a passing glance at the artwork.

I feel a stab of annoyance. I know his type.

Forget wedding crashers. This is a gallery crasher.

'Excuse me.'

As I tap him on the shoulder, he jumps, spilling his champagne, and turns round like he's been caught doing something he shouldn't be doing.

Which he has.

'Er, yeah,' he replies, his mouth full of meatball.

'I'm sorry, but I don't think I've ticked you off the guest list.' I smile politely.

'The guest list?'

'Yes, of all the people invited,' I say pointedly, and wave my clipboard.

He doesn't say anything. He just stares at me as if he's thinking about something.

I fidget uncomfortably. 'And your name is . . .?' I prompt.

'Hey, haven't I seen you somewhere before?' Narrowing his eyes, he waggles a finger at me.

I step back and look at him sideways. There is something vaguely familiar about him, but yet . . . 'No, I don't think so.' I shake my head dismissively.

There's a pause and then—

'Little man!' he says triumphantly, spitting a meatball crumb at me.

I remove it from my dress. 'Excuse me?'

'You told me not to cross until I saw the little man.' He grins.

'I don't know what you're—' I break off as I suddenly remember.

Oh God, it's him. Last week. When I was rushing to meet Kate and Robyn in the bar. The man when I was crossing the street. The man with the furry microphone and video camera. The man who I recited my stupid saying to, Never Eat Shredded— OK, enough. I cringe at the memory. How uncool.

'Oh, yeah, I remember,' I say, trying to sound all nonchalant.

'I thought it was.' He's full on grinning at me now, and his eyes are crinkling up and flashing. I notice he's got very bright, very blue eyes, and the longest eyelashes you've ever seen.

Like a girl, I think, realising I'm staring and looking sharply away.

'Hi. My name's Adam.' He sticks out his hand.

I ignore it and glance down at my clipboard. 'There isn't an Adam on the list.'

'I know. I was just passing.' He shrugs apologetically.

'Well, this is a private exhibition. By invitation only.' I stress those words, but he simply smiles, as if this is all really amusing.

'You're throwing me out?'

I falter. I suddenly feel like a bouncer. 'Well, if you want to put it like that.'

'OK, OK, don't worry, I'm going.' Polishing off his last meatball, he drains his glass. 'Compliments to the chef. Great meatballs.' Dabbing his mouth with his napkin, he puts down his glass. 'But by the way, next time you should get real champagne.'

I glare at him. The cheek of it!

'See you around.'

'I don't think so,' I mutter under my breath, watching as he turns and saunters off through the crowd.

'Who was that?' A voice in my ears makes me jump and I turn to see Nate standing next to me.

'Oh . . . um . . . no one,' I say, feeling flustered. 'Just some guy.' I quickly change the subject. 'How are you? Everything OK?'

'Bit of a nightmare at the studio, but it's sorted now.' He smiles, sliding his arm round my waist. 'How about you?'

'Oh, fine.' I nod distractedly. I feel jittery. Though that's probably to be expected. After all, not only is it a big night for the gallery, it's mine and Nate's first official outing as a couple.

'Only fine?' he asks, his brow furrowed, and as I look into his eyes, I suddenly remember all the years I've spent dreaming about him, thinking I'd lost him, wondering what would happen if I found him again.

And now we're back together and he's standing here with his arm round me.

And I'm saying I'm fine. Am I *completely* bonkers?

Smiling, I reach up and give him a kiss. 'No, everything's perfect.'

Chapter Thirteen

Well, perhaps not *everything*.

To be frank, I would have preferred it if Nate's iPhone hadn't kept jingling every five minutes for the rest of the evening, and he hadn't had to keep disappearing off to take calls from the studio.

And it was a bit annoying when afterwards we all decamped to a little Chinese restaurant round the corner and Nate wouldn't eat any of the dim sum that I'd ordered for both of us. Or the sweet and sour chicken. Or the fried rice. Something about MSG and E numbers, apparently, which was a bit of a shame, as his steamed mixed vegetables didn't look nearly as delicious.

Anyway, it's not like it was a big deal, I'm just saying. Like it said in my fortune cookie, 'Nothing will ever come between you and your lover.' What's a couple of phone calls and a few plates of dim sum between soulmates?

We all sit around a large table – me and Nate, Kate and Jeff, Robyn and Magda, who brings along her son, Daniel. Thankfully, it's apparent as soon as I meet him that he's one of those people who isn't photogenic, as in the flesh he looks nothing like Austin Powers.

Well, I wouldn't say *nothing* like, but put it this way, you wouldn't meet him and think he's going to yell, 'Whoa, baby,' and have a closet full of velvet suits and frilly shirts.

On learning Robyn's single and Jewish, Magda immediately rolls up her matchmaking sleeves, and before you know it, she and Daniel are sitting side by side while Magda keeps everyone entertained with her outrageous stories, including the one about husband number two and a tube of superglue, despite her son turning bright red and begging her to stop. It would seem that there is something a Jewish mother loves more than her son, and that's embarrassing him. At one point it was all he could do to stop her getting naked baby pictures out of her purse and showing everyone 'what a beautiful baby he was. It was unbelievable!'

And then, before you know it, it's late and we're saying our goodbyes. Nate and I catch a cab back to his, even though my apartment is within walking distance, but like he says, why stay in my tiny shared apartment when we've got his penthouse all to ourselves? This way, it's just us.

Plus about a million packing boxes, I note, stepping out of the elevator and coming face to face with another huge one that's just been delivered. I swear as soon as he unpacks one, another appears.

'Oh good, it's arrived,' he says.

'What on earth's in it?' I gasp, squeezing past the large cardboard monolith that's wedged in the hallway.

'My elliptical,' he says, as if I should know what an elliptical is. And of course I do. Sort of. Not.

'Oh, right.' I nod breezily. 'Great.'

Putting his keys and phone on the table, he takes off his jacket and hangs it over the back of a chair. Meanwhile I slide off my shoes and rub my sore feet. Normally at this point we'd be ripping each other's clothes off, but I'm exhausted. It's been a long day.

'Sleepy?' Nate catches me rubbing my eyes.

'Um . . . just a little bit.' I smile and stifle a yawn.

Well, I don't want to put him off completely, do I? Who knows, I might get my second wind in a minute. Nate seems to have that effect on me. This past week I've practically turned into a nymphomaniac.

Pulling off my dress, I pad into the bathroom in my underwear to brush my teeth. A few seconds later Nate joins me in the bathroom in his boxer shorts, and for a moment we stand side by side brushing. Like a proper couple, I think, feeling a beat of contentment as I look at us reflected in the mirror above the sink.

Which is when I notice Nate's boxer shorts reflected back at me.

No, surely not . . .

Until now I've been so busy ripping them off that I haven't given them a second glance, but now I do.

And they have pineapples on them.

'They're not pineapples, they're guavas,' he corrects, when I tease him about them.

'Where did you get them?' I ask, giggling.

'I don't know.' He shrugs, rinsing out. 'Beth bought them for me.'

I feel a sting. Beth is Nate's ex-wife.

'She bought you novelty boxer shorts?' I say, all jokingly, but my voice comes out a bit higher than usual. I don't know which is more horrifying – that his wife bought them or that he's wearing them.

'She bought all my clothes. She took care of that stuff.' Rinsing, he wipes his face on a towel and starts removing his contact lenses.

'Well, I think it's about time you bought some new ones,' I suggest, trying to sound light and breezy while plotting how to get rid of the ones he's wearing. 'What about some nice Calvin Klein's?'

'Why? These are comfy,' he grumbles.

Sliding my arm round his waist. I nuzzle the back of his neck. 'You'd look really sexy in a pair of Calvin's,' I murmur suggestively.

'What's wrong with these?'

'Nate, they have cartoon pineapples on them.'

'Guavas,' he corrects sulkily, disentangling himself and padding into the bedroom.

I let it drop and finish up in the bathroom, but there's a distinct change in the mood, and when I climb into bed next to him, he doesn't wrap his arm round me and pull me towards him, and I don't snuggle up and rest my head on his chest.

And there's not even a sniff of sex.

Instead we lie on separate sides of the bed and pretend like everything is normal.

'I'm really tired. I think I'm going to crash,' he says after a moment.

'Me too,' I say, even though now I'm wide awake.

'OK, well, night, then.'

'Night.'

Then he rolls over, turns out the light and the room falls into darkness. And just like that, things don't feel so perfect any more.

I must have fallen asleep because the next thing I know I'm being woken by a strange whirring noise.

Uh, what's that?

Groggily brushing my hair away from face, I tip my head slightly on the pillow to try to hear better.

Whirr, thump.Whirr, thump.Whirr . . .

Where's it coming from? Muffled and monotonous, it's like some strange kind of backing track. For a moment I think it's the neighbours upstairs. In my flat in London mine used to come in from clubbing on a Friday night and crank up the rave music. I bet that's what it is, except . . .

We're in the penthouse. There aren't any neighbours upstairs.

Flummoxed, I prise open an eye, as if maybe I'm actually going to see what's making this dull throbbing noise. The curtains are still drawn and the bedroom is in pitch-darkness – the only things in here are me and Nate.

And then I twig. It must be Nate snoring.

Not that he usually snores, but in my experience all a man has to do is roll on to his back and it's like someone just turned on the waste-disposal. Reaching out my hand, I go to push him over.

But he's not there.

Disconcerted, I sit up. Where's he gone? I crick my head and look in the direction of the en suite. Maybe he's gone to the loo, but nope, I can't hear anything and he can't have got up to do

a you-know-what, otherwise there'd be a crack of light underneath the door. That's another thing I've learned about men.
For some reason, never explained to me, they always have to sit
there and read a magazine *on the job, so to speak*.

I mean, *why?* Think of all the places to choose to catch up on
your reading material, like curled up on the sofa, or lying in bed,
or sprawled out on the grass in the park. Lots of lovely places.
But no. It has to be the bog.

I'm still mulling this point as I slip out from the covers and
pull on the dressing gown hanging behind the door. It's one of
those lovely white waffle ones that you get in expensive hotels,
and bears absolutely no resemblance whatsoever to my raggedy
old one that's covered in loose threads.

Note to self: remember to hide it when Nate eventually comes
over.

Opening the bedroom door, I pad into the hallway and catch
sight of the sunrise breaking over the Manhattan skyline, trig-
gering two thoughts: 1) Gosh, that's so beautiful and 2) Fuck,
it's early.

A hippo-sized yawn overtakes me, and distracted by the
noise, I turn my attention away from the window. The noise is
even louder out here, and is that . . .?

Feeling a ripple of apprehension, I pause to listen.

Panting?

Somewhere in the filing cabinet of my mind, my memory
throws up a story I once heard about a friend who stumbled in
on her boyfriend when he was watching a movie. Put it this way,
it wasn't the kind of movie you'd rent at your local Blockbuster.
It was *that* kind of movie.

Oh God. Alarm stabs as I get an image of Nate—

I quickly pull myself together. OK, don't panic. I'm a woman
of the world. I've been around. Well, not that *kind* of around,
but I've watched porn. Once, by accident, and for about two
seconds. It was years ago and I was staying at a hotel with my
parents and I pressed the wrong button on the remote. I don't
know who was more embarrassed, me or my mum.

Still, it's fine. I'm totally cool. Just as long as he doesn't want me to sit down and watch it with him, I think, suddenly remembering a letter I once read to an agony aunt and feeling a twinge of anxiety. I know, I'll just tell him I'm busy, that I need to make a cup of tea, or update my Facebook, or something.

Steeling myself, I pin what I hope is a sort of I'm-totally-open-minded-and-I-once-had-sex-dressed-in-nurse's-outfit-but-more-of-that-later expression on my face and head towards the living room. The panting is growing louder. And now there's a sort of *grunting*.

Oh fuck. I swallow hard. Be cool, Lucy.

Trust me, I have never felt less cool. I'm wearing a waffle robe and I have purple hair and I'm about to walk in on my boyfriend while he's—

' . . . and we should totally rethink our strategy of going out to the network with the pilot . . .'

On the phone and huffing and puffing up and down on a huge black exercise machine.

Frozen, I stare at him for a moment. I was prepared for all kinds of things, but this? Taken aback, I watch him. Red-faced and sweating profusely, he's gripping on to the handles for dear life, his legs pumping away. He's also naked apart from his pineapple boxer shorts, a Bluetooth headset, his glasses and a pair of very large, very white trainers.

Unexpectedly, a thought fires across my brain.

I don't fancy him.

It hits me, sharp and hard, in the solar plexus.

No sooner has it registered than I brush it aside. I mean, who *does* look sexy when they're exercising. I look terrible!

Well, if I exercised, that is.

'Hey.'

I snap back to see Nate looking at me.

'Hey, one minute, Joe,' he pants, as I give a weak sort of wave. 'You're up early.'

I nod lamely. 'So are you.'

'Well, now my elliptical's arrived I want to get back to my normal routine,' he puffs in explanation.

So that's what the big box was, I realise, watching as he presses a button and the whole thing starts inclining.

'Also I had to make a few calls to the London office.'

'On a Saturday?'

'TV never stops,' he grunts, tightening his grip on the handles and pumping his arms harder. 'It's twenty-four-seven.'

I watch the ramp getting steeper and steeper as he keeps striding.

'Anyway, I better get back.' He gestures to his earpiece.

'Oh, right, yeah, of course.' I nod. 'I'll go make some . . .' I'm about to say 'coffee', as it's such a force of habit, then remember that Nate doesn't drink it. ' . . . juice,' I finish.

'Great. There's some celery in the fridge.' Breathlessly he breaks off to wipe his face with a towel. 'I think there might be some beetroot too.'

'Fab.' I grin.

Celery? Beetroot?

With my smile still fixed to my face, I leave him huffing and puffing and pad into the kitchen, then pause as the enormity of what I've suggested sinks in. Me. In a kitchen. Using one of these gadgets.

Glancing around at all the scary-looking pieces of equipment lined up on the counter, my confidence deserts me. They look like evil torture devices. They *are* evil torture devices, I muse, remembering the one and only time I tried to use an electronic can-opener. It was like something out of *The Texas Chainsaw Massacre*. Trust me, I still have the scar on my thumb to prove it.

It takes a few minutes to locate the juicer. To be truthful, I'm not sure how I could miss it with a name like Hercules. It's a big silver monster of a thing and for a few moments I eye it warily, then screw up my courage. OK, so it *looks* scary and compli- cated, but how hard can it be? I'm making juice, for God's sake. Rolling up the sleeves of my dressing gown, I tug open the fridge and grab the celery and beetroot.

I mean, come on, it's hardly rocket science.

*   *   *

Ten minutes later I am deeply regretting that statement.

I've dismantled the machine, there are bits of it lying everywhere, and it's still not working. I look at it, lying dismembered on the countertop next to some mouldy-looking organic celery and a misshapen beetroot. Seriously, I would have more chance of building a rocket than making juice.

For example, what's this bit? Picking up a piece of the machine, I peer at it curiously. It's like a cog with a wiggly bit on the end. I pick up another bit. This piece is sort of round with a hole in it. I stare at them both blankly. Now I know why I flunked physics.

However, there is hope. Flicking through the instruction manual, which I managed to locate in a drawer, I turn to Chapter One: Getting Started. See, it's not all bad, I tell myself brightly. I've got the instructions: '1) Take the mesh strainer (part A) and attach it to the pulp extractor (part B), making sure the safety-locking clip (part C) is attached and the extra-large feed chute (part D) is in position.'

And I thought putting together cabinets from IKEA was difficult.

'Hey, how you getting on?' Nate yells from the living room, and I stiffen.

'Great,' I yell back, wishing I could do what they used to do in *Blue Peter* and produce one I'd made earlier. 'Coming right up.'

Fuck.

Frantically grabbing at different parts, I manage to stuff Hercules back together and grab the celery and beetroot. It says to 'feed them in one by one', but I don't have time for that and so I stuff the whole lot in together, then switch it on.

At exactly the moment I'm flicking the switch I spy another piece of the machine lurking by the side of the toaster. Oh, what does that bit do?

Argh.

Suddenly that question is answered as I'm sprayed with bits of celery and beetroot. Juice starts squirting everywhere, all over the countertops, all over me, all over everything . . . I dive on the machine, trying to switch it off. Only I can't even see where the switch is, as now I've got beetroot juice in my eyes, and the machine is making a loud grinding noise, and it's shuddering, and I'm getting soaked, and—

'Jesus!'

Abruptly the machine falls silent and I twirl round to see Nate. Standing in the middle of the kitchen, he's holding the flex, his face aghast.

'It looks like a bloodbath in here!'

Dazedly I take in the sight. It's like something from a horror film. Everywhere you look the walls are dripping with red liquid. It's sprayed over the countertops, the stainless-steel fridge, the cooker, the utensils . . . and then there's the celery pulp. Green clumps of it, flecks of it, little bits of it, all over his lovely pristine kitchen.

And me.

'What the hell happened?'

'Um . . . I-I was having a spot of trouble with the j-juicer,' I stammer in shock. Mortified, I start trying to wipe the splatters of pulp from my face with the sleeve of my dressing gown.

'No kidding.' Grabbing a few sheets of kitchen roll, he passes them to me.

'There was this piece missing.'

'You mean the lid?'

The tone of his voice makes me bristle slightly.

'Gosh, look, I'm so sorry. I'll clear it all.' Grabbing a dishcloth, I start frantically trying to clean up.

'It's probably going to ruin the marble countertop.'

'Oh God, I'm so sorry, really.'

'Marble's porous, you know.'

'Is it? Oh crap.' I wipe faster. 'Though it's a bit silly to make a work surface out of it, then, isn't it?' I can't help noting aloud as an afterthought.

'Well, they don't expect you to drown it in beetroot juice,' he retorts.

'I know. I'm sorry. It was just a total accident.'

And I've apologised three times, I feel like adding.

There's a pause and then he sighs. 'Hey, don't worry about it. I suppose it's not a big deal.' Picking his way through the debris, he tugs open the fridge and reaches for a bottle of Evian. 'I'd just forgotten how clumsy you are.'

Abruptly I feel myself prickle. OK, I admit I'm not the most coordinated of people, but still.

'What's that supposed to mean?' I reply stiffly, pausing from wiping the countertop.

'In Italy don't you remember you were always tripping over?'

'Have you ever attempted walking in high heels on cobbles?' I reply, trying not to sound defensive, and sounding defensive.

'Or breaking things.'

I look at him in disbelief. 'You're never going to let me forget that vase, are you?'

'It was expensive. It was Murano glass.'

'I didn't mean to drop it,' I gasp. 'It was all that spider's fault. It just appeared from nowhere and it was huge, with those big, hairy black legs.' I give a little shudder. 'Anyway, I bought you another vase.'

'True.' He nods. 'But they were all individually hand-blown. No two were alike.'

'I can't believe you're still holding this against me. It was ten years ago.'

'I'm just saying.' He shrugs, unscrewing the bottle of Evian and taking a swig.

I look at him leaning up against the fridge, casually glugging back water, while I'm standing here soaked in beetroot juice and covered in sticky bits of celery pulp, scrubbing down his kitchen, and feel a stab of annoyance. Actually, it's more than a stab – it's a great big dollop of fury.

'Well, don't,' I snap.

He stops drinking and glances at me sharply. 'This mess isn't my fault.'

'No, it's mine. I know, I'm clumsy.' Turning away, I continue furiously wiping the countertop.

'Well, if you were a bit more careful . . .' he retorts.

'If you bought juice in a carton like a normal person,' I say hotly.

He scowls. 'Oh, so I'm being blamed now.'

'No, you're just being patronising.'

There's silence as Nate and I stare at each other angrily.

'OK, well, I'm going to jump in the shower,' he says gruffly after a pause. 'I've got work to do today.'

It's like a boxer's jab. It's the weekend. We'd made plans to spend it together.

I reel slightly, then quickly recover. 'Yeah, I'm busy too,' I say stiffly. 'I'll just finish clearing up and then I'll go.'

Then before he can say anything else, I turn away sharply and start scrubbing the sink.

Chapter Fourteen

OK, so we've just had our first row.

But that's fine. All couples have them. It's perfectly normal.

In fact, it's not a bad thing at all. It's a *good* thing, I tell myself firmly. Arguing is healthy. It means we're a proper couple. I once read in a magazine that it's a really positive sign for the relationship.

Oh, who the fuck am I kidding?

It's horrible. I feel terrible.

An hour or so later I'm striding down Fifth Avenue trying to make sense of this sudden turn of events. Having finished clearing up the kitchen until there wasn't a splash of beetroot or a speck of green pulp left, and the marble worktop was spotless, I showered, dressed, then left the apartment. I didn't even hang around to dry my hair, I muse, glancing at my reflection in the windows of a store.

And immediately wishing I hadn't. My fringe has already gone *ping!* in the heat and I've got bits sticking out all over. And it's true. It does kind of look purple. Dismayed, I sigh miserably and look quickly away.

Nate didn't even say goodbye. He was on the phone when I left and he just nodded. And it wasn't a nice friendly 'Love you, babe' nod – it was a dismissive 'Whatever' nod. I've never really thought much about nods until that moment. I'd always assumed that one nod was pretty much the same as another. Until then. And trust me, that was not the kind of nod that is positive in a relationship.

Fighting back angry tears, I continue stalking down Fifth Avenue. Normally I'd be looking in all the glossy shops, revelling in a bit of window shopping and thinking, Look at me, I'm in New York! But now they barely merit a glance. Instead I'm just vacantly staring down at the chewing-gum-littered pavement, mulling over the argument in my head and thinking, Please don't look at me. I've just had an argument with my boyfriend and I think I might start crying at any moment.

No, you won't, Lucy, I tell myself sharply. You're angry, remember, and you need to stay angry.

Roughly wiping my eyes, I take a few deep breaths. Nate was behaving like such a smug, patronising, sanctimonious prat. Standing there lecturing me while he was wearing those criminal pineapple boxer shorts! Clumsy indeed! It was all that machine's fault.

Still, perhaps I shouldn't have left the lid off, I reflect, feeling a seed of doubt. I try to ignore it and keep walking, but it quickly grows into a prickle of regret. I mean, that *was* my fault. I push it briskly out of my mind, but it's rapidly turning into guilt. God, the kitchen was a right old mess.

In fact, by the time I've reached the edge of the park, all I can feel is full-blown remorse. I pause at the entrance and rest against the railings. I'm completely to blame. If I wasn't so bloody useless and pig-headed, we'd be looking forward to enjoying a lovely Saturday together picnicking in the park.

Instead I'm standing here on my own, looking at all the other couples on the grass doing just that, I think miserably.

I'm not sure how long I would have remained there, feeling sorry for myself, if someone hadn't walked past sipping a coffee. Catching a whiff, my taste buds immediately spring into action.

No wonder I'm feeling miserable, I realise, catching sight of a Starbucks across the street and dashing off in its direction. I haven't had my morning coffee. In fact, this whole week I've gone without, as I've been staying at Nate's and he doesn't drink it. I haven't felt any better, though. In fact, quite frankly, I've had a nagging headache all week. Nate says that's because I'm addicted caffeine and I'm going through withdrawal, that I just have to persevere and I'll feel like a new me.

Which is fair enough. Except, the thing is, I don't really want to feel like a new me. I want to feel like the old me who used to drink coffee and didn't have a nagging headache.

'A latte with two extra shots, please,' I say, smiling broadly at the woman behind the counter. I've come to the conclusion there are two types of people in this world: those who drink coffee and those who don't. And I'm not sure you can ever put the two together, I reflect, as she taps in my order.

On second thoughts . . . I feel a secret twinge of defiance. 'Make it three shots.'

Fifteen minutes later and I'm walking down the street sipping my coffee. I feel loads better. The sun is shining, it's a beautiful day, and I don't have to go to work.

OK, so now what?

It's still early and I can feel the whole day stretching ahead of me. I could go home, but Robyn's at her drumming circle and I don't feel much like sitting in an empty apartment: me, Simon and Jenny, and piles of my hand-washing. I could call my sister, but she'll either be at the gym or the office, or both. Or I could . . .

I draw a blank.

This is ridiculous. I'm in New York! The Big Apple! The city that never sleeps! There's masses to do. I've been so busy since I arrived that I haven't got round to doing any of the real touristy stuff yet. I could go up the Empire State, take a boat ride past the Statue of Liberty, go to Times Square.

All the things I wanted to do with Nate.

Suddenly my defiance takes a bit of a dip and for a split second I think about calling him, or maybe texting him. Then change my mind. I know, perhaps he's texted me. Perhaps I just didn't hear it beep. Hope flickers and I quickly tug out my phone and glance at the screen.

Nope. No text message. No missed call. No nothing.

For a moment I stare at my phone feeling upset. Then impulsively I turn it off. Otherwise I'll just keep checking it all day.

Shoving it firmly in my bag, I take a big gulp of coffee. I need
to do something that will cheer me up. Like brown-paper packages tied up with string did for Julie Andrews. Only in my case
my favourite thing's not raindrops on roses; it's art galleries.
As soon as I walk through the door, it's impossible to feel sad
or depressed. Surrounded by all those ideas, all that imagination, all that creativity, my problems seem to fall away and I lose
myself. It's like being a kid again.

When I was living in London, I lost count of the number of
hours, days, weeks probably that I spent at the National, the
Portrait Gallery and Tate Modern. And before that, growing
up in Manchester, the city's Art Gallery was my refuge as a
teenager. Art galleries are for me what Manolo Blahniks are for
Carrie Bradshaw. I go there when I'm happy and when I'm sad.
When I'm feeling lonely or I want to be alone. Not to mention
that they're the perfect heartbreak cure. Forget Bridget Jones
and her Chardonnay, give me a Rothko any day.

Like today, I suddenly decide, feeling galvanised. Today is the
perfect day to lose myself in a gallery, and where better than
here in New York? The city is stuffed full of them. I've already
visited quite a few since I've been here, but I haven't even *begun*
to scratch the surface. Plus I was saving the best until last: the
Museum of Modern Art is arguably the best modern art gallery
in the world.

I feel a buzz of excitement. Yes, that's what I'll do. Great idea!
Invigorated, I start striding off. Then a thought hits me: I have
absolutely no clue where I'm going.

I stop dead in the middle of the pavement and rummage
around in my handbag. Digging out my pocket tourist guide,
I look up the address: '11 West 53rd Street, between Fifth and
Sixth Avenues.' OK, well, that's easy.

Sort of.

I pause uncertainly. I think it's that way . . . but then it could
be that way . . . or even that way. Shit. I think about doing my
'Never Eat Shredded Wheat' rhyme, then think again. Well, look
where that got me last time.

'Spare any change?'

A voice next to me interrupts my thoughts and I glance sideways and see a homeless man sitting on a piece of cardboard, drinking a beer. He holds out a tattered old polystyrene cup, containing a few quarters.

'Oh, yes, of course . . .' Emptying my pockets, I find a couple of dollar bills and stick them in his cup. 'By the way, would you know the way to the Museum of Modern Art?'

OK, I know it's a long shot, but still.

He peers at me from underneath his shaggy eyebrows, then grunts, 'You mean the MoMA?'

'Oh, erm . . . yeah, the MoMA.'

That will teach you to judge, Lucy Hemmingway.

'Let me see . . .' He scratches his long, bedraggled beard.

'Is it that way?' I ask hopefully, pointing across the street.

He looks at me as if I'm slightly barmy. 'No, that way,' he rasps, and points in a completely different direction. 'Couple of blocks, it's on your right.'

'Brilliant. Thanks.' I grin.

'No problem.' He nods, then calls after me, 'Hey, lady.'

Walking down the street, I turn round. Taking a swig of beer, he flashes me a toothless smile.

'Check out the Rothkos. They're incredible.'

Wow.

That's pretty much all I can think from the moment I spot the three huge red banners emblazoned with 'MoMA' fluttering in the summer breeze. *Wow.* To walking into the striking modern glass building, with its amazing light-filled lobby, huge open-plan staircase and walls made entirely of windows. *Wow.* To the five floors filled with paintings, sculptures, drawings, prints, photographs . . . and all kinds of amazing things. *Wow.* It's like being in another world. As soon I step from the bustling street outside into the cool white open spaces inside, it's like stepping into Narnia. A world where time stands still and nothing else matters.

Not even rows with your boyfriend.

I spend the rest of the day wandering from room to room just drinking it all in. One room is completely round and holds a circular light-changing exhibit that you step inside to watch the ever-changing colours. It's beautiful, and fun, and it makes me laugh to see even a baby in a pushchair enjoying it, his eyes filled with wonder as the blues turn to green, turn to yellow, turn to red, and then letting out a loud approving gurgle.

Another room is entirely covered in scribbled cartoons, another with soft white feathers, another with an entire city made out of recycled cans. Then there are all the paintings: the Matisses, Pollocks, Dalís, Rothkos . . . I stop in front of one and smile. The homeless guy was right. They are incredible.

Lost in my own world, I lose track of time, until suddenly I look up and notice how busy it's become. When I arrived, it had just opened and it was empty, but now there are all kinds of people. Crowds of schoolkids, a little old lady, some mothers with their babies, a punk with his Mohawk, a gaggle of Japanese tourists with their obligatory cameras, a couple of students sketching . . .

Then there's him again.

The gallery crasher.

I stop dead. What's he doing here? There's no free food or booze. I watch him for a moment, trying to work out what he's doing, when unexpectedly he turns round and sees me, and looks right at me.

Fuck.

I dive behind a large sculpture of two cubes balancing on top of each other, but it's too late.

'Hey, it's you again.'

I pretend I haven't heard him and focus on examining the sculpture. Like I'm so engrossed in this amazing piece of artwork I haven't heard him. Hopefully he'll just go away.

He comes right up to me and prods me.

Or maybe not.

'Excuse me?' I turn and look at him, affronted. He's wearing the same baseball cap and the same jeans with the two big rips on the knees, but he's switched his T-shirt from the green one to a plain white V-neck.

Not that I really noticed what he was wearing last night or anything.

'From the gallery last night. You threw me out.'

'Really?' I frown and peer at him as if I haven't a clue who he is, then pretend to do a sort of slow register. 'Oh, yeah . . .'

Honestly, my acting is dreadful. Annie was my only good role.

'Well, you can't throw me out this time.' He grins, and digging in the pocket of his jeans, he waggles a ticket at me.

'You bought a ticket to get in here?' I stare at it for a moment. Sure enough it looks real. 'You spent twenty dollars to get into an art gallery?'

I'm impressed. Maybe I got him wrong. Maybe he's not all about the freebies.

'I didn't say I *bought* a ticket,' he corrects. 'I said I had a ticket.'

'You didn't pay for it?'

'No, it was free. A friend gave it to me.'

'Aha, I should have known,' I reply, it suddenly making sense. 'You know there isn't any free food or drink here,' I can't help adding.

He looks slightly insulted. 'I'm not just after free food and drink.'

'What, you've actually come to look at some art?' I say sarcastically.

'Actually, no. I came for the free films.'

'Free films?' For a moment I think he's got the wrong place.

'There's a special Tim Burton exhibition. They're showing some of his earlier work. You know, like *Edward Scissorhands*, *Ed Wood*, *Big Fish* . . .'

I'm looking at him aghast. 'You came here to watch movies for free?'

'Not just any movies,' he says, sounding offended. 'From one of the greatest directors. I mean, the man's a genius, the way he shoots, his camerawork, the way he explores film.'

'But this is the MoMA,' I gasp.

'So?' He shrugs.

'So you're telling me you haven't even so much as *looked* at Dalí, or Rothko, or Pollock.'

He stares at me blankly.

'They're artists,' I deadpan.

'Oh, that figures.' He smiles sheepishly. 'Well, seeing as you know so much about them, why don't you be my tour guide?'

His request catches me by surprise. It feels almost like a dare.

'And if I don't?'

'I'll probably go home, catch up on some shut-eye.' He yawns and stretches.

I waver. Part of me wants him to leave. I'm having a nice time on my own, and the last thing I need right now is having to show him around. Another part of me, however, can't let him leave without looking at any of the wonderful paintings. It would be a crime.

Let's make this clear, though, that's the only reason. It's got nothing to do with his strange mixture of geekiness and cockiness. Or the way he's kind of intriguing. Or those huge blue eyes of his with the crazy long eyelashes.

This is just about art. End of. Period.

'OK, follow me.'

'This is called *The Persistence of Memory* and is his most famous surrealistic work, as it introduced the image of the melting watches, which symbolise the irrelevance of time.'

Standing in front of the painting by Salvador Dalí, I turn to my eager student. Otherwise known as Adam, he reminded me, in case I'd forgotten.

I hadn't.

'Wow, pretty impressive.'

'I know, it's amazing, isn't it?' I say, my eyes flashing.

'You really love this stuff, huh?'

I feel my cheeks flush with embarrassment. 'OK, I admit, sometimes I can get a bit carried away.'

'A bit?' He grins.

I smile sheepishly.

'So how come you know so much about art?'

'It's something I've always loved, ever since I was little and I used to finger-paint. My choice of canvas back then was my parents' living-room walls.' I grin at the memory.

'So did you go to art college?'

I nod. 'I was always terrible at school, flunked all my exams except for art, but college was different. I started painting full-time and it was amazing. For once I was doing something I was good at, something I understood, you know?'

'I know.' He nods in agreement. 'So what happened after college?'

'I moved to London to be a painter, but that didn't work out, so I got a job in a gallery,' I say blithely.

'But you don't miss it? Painting, I mean.'

'Every day,' I say quietly, before I can stop myself. 'It all worked out for the best, though,' I add quickly, and yet even while I'm saying it, I feel as if I'm trying to convince him. Or is it, in fact, me?

I look across at Adam. He's studying me hard, an expression of thoughtfulness on his face, and feeling self-conscious, I suggest brightly, 'Why don't we go look at some Rothkos,' and start moving briskly away from the Dalí.

'You know, you should follow your passion. If your heart's in painting, you'll never be happy just working in a gallery.'

I feel a stab of defensiveness. 'It's not "*just* working in a gallery",' I reply shortly. 'I happen to love my job.'

'I know, I didn't mean . . .' he begins apologising. 'Look, I'm sorry, I guess I overstepped the mark.'

Now it's my turn to apologise. 'Oh, no, don't be silly.' I shake my head. 'It's me. I'm just being oversensitive.' I smile awkwardly. 'Anyway, I still can't believe you hadn't looked at any art,' I say, flicking the focus back on to him.

'Film's art,' he replies evenly.

It brings me up short. I hadn't thought about it like that. 'So are you a big film buff?'

'Just a little.' He smiles. 'I'm a film student at NYU.'

As we move into the next room, I shoot him a sideways glance. 'Really? Gosh, that sounds interesting.'

'It is, very.' He pauses for a beat. 'I love it there.'

'Wow.' I look at him with newfound intrigue, then peer at him quizzically. 'Aren't you a little old to be a student?' I tease.

'Probably, in the traditional sense' He nods. 'But I figure you're never too old to learn. That's when you become old, when you stop being fascinated by things, when you stop wanting to learn and explore . . .'

As he starts talking, his face becomes animated and I'm suddenly reminded of someone.

' . . . especially when it's something you have a great passion for, and for me that's film.' His face scrunches into a grin. 'I did it the opposite way round to you. I went straight from college into a job working on a magazine. I did the film reviews. It was a really good job. I got to see all the new movies, go to all the press junkets, interview the actors. I still do a lot of freelance stuff for them now. Just recently I did an on-camera interview for their website with Angelina.'

'You did not!'

'See, that got your attention, didn't it?' He laughs. 'No, not really. It was an interview with this amazing new Mexican director, but somehow I didn't think that would have the same effect.'

'It might have,' I protest, pretending to be offended.

'Are you interested in film?' He looks at me with interest.

'Of course. Everyone likes films.'

'So who's your favourite director?'

I pause. 'Um . . .' My mind's blank. I don't know the names of any directors, do I? Oh God, I must do. Quick, think of one. 'Scorsese,' I blurt. It's the first director's name that comes into my head. It's the *only* one.

'Wow, really?' He looks impressed. 'I would never have put you down as a Scorsese kind of girl.'

I feel both relieved and unexpectedly pleased.

'Which film do you think is his best work?'

'Well . . . um . . . there's so much work to choose from,' I say vaguely. 'I mean, it's hard to pick a favourite . . .' I'm hoping I can trail off and leave it unclear, but he's still looking at me, his face filled with interest.

He's waiting for an answer.

Oh crap.

Frantically I rack the part of my brain that has 'Films' written on it, but it's filled with sappy rom-coms starring Jennifer Aniston, and some really bad foreign-language films a long-forgotten ex used to make me watch. OK, forget that, try to do that association thing. Scorsese's a man. He's Italian . . .

'*The Godfather!*' I say triumphantly. See! I knew I knew it.

'That's Coppola,' says Adam, with a flash of amusement.

My triumph is short-lived. 'Oh, is it?' I am beyond embarrassed.

'But I can see how you thought it was. Italian, Mafia, violence . . .' He's talking earnestly, but his mouth is twitching. 'I mean, it's kind of easy to get two of the greatest directors in the world mixed up.'

'OK, OK.' I smile ruefully. 'I know I deserve it for giving you a hard time about art, but I know nothing about film, apart from renting DVDs and going to the movies. Even then I'm happy to see whatever. I'm usually more interested in the popcorn.'

'Maybe we should trade.'

I glance at him quizzically.

'You teach me about art and I'll teach you about film.'

'Well, I don't know about that . . .'

'OK, so tell me, what's your favourite film?'

'Oh, that's easy.' I grin. 'Anything with Daniel Craig in it.'

He throws me a look of horror. 'You've got to be joking! That's your criteria for going to see a film? If it stars Daniel Craig? Who, by the way, is not a great actor. The last Bond was pretty dismal.'

'I'm not looking at his acting.' I smile and Adam rolls his eyes in despair.

Taking off his baseball cap, his shock of black hair springs out. He scratches his head in disbelief. 'So let me get this straight. You haven't seen any of the classics. What about *Annie Hall, The Thin Red Line*, anything by the Coen brothers . . .?'

I'm looking at him blankly.

'Jeez, I'm going to have my work cut out for me.'

'You?' I say with indignation. 'What about me? What do you know about Cubism, conceptual art, Impressionism . . .?'

Now it's his turn to look blank.

There's a pause and then we both break into a smile. 'OK, deal.' I nod.

'Deal.' He grins as we shake hands.

'So now I've given you your first art lesson, when do I start to learn about film?' I ask.

'When are you free next week?' He looks at me eagerly. 'I'll take you to a great movie, one of my favourites. But the deal is, you have to get the popcorn.'

He laughs and smiles at me, but I pause. Put like that, it sounds like we're going a date, and for a moment I consider telling him I have a boyfriend. That just makes me look really arrogant, though. Like I think he fancies me, which I don't, *obviously*.

'Actually, I'm not sure,' I reply.

Well, that's the honest answer, isn't it? I'm not sure. I was planning on spending most of my free time with Nate, but then we had the row.

The row. Suddenly I realise I haven't thought about it all day. Followed by another thought. I haven't thought about Nate all day either.

'In other words, you've got a boyfriend.' He smiles and I blush beetroot.

'Sort of,' I hear myself saying before I can stop myself.

Sort of? Er, hang on a minute, Lucy. This is Nate, the love of your life, you're *sort of* talking about. Since when did he become your sort-of boyfriend?

I feel a twinge of surprise and guilt, all mixed up together. I quickly try to backtrack.

'What I meant to say—'

My voice is suddenly drowned out by a wailing siren and a loud announcement saying the gallery is closing. *Already?* I glance at my watch in shock. The day has flown by.

'Well, I better rush,' says Adam, interrupting my thoughts.

'Oh, yeah . . . me too.' I nod, but it's as if the easy mood has been broken by an awkwardness that wasn't there before.

'Bye.'

'Um . . . bye,' I murmur.

He strides away across the gallery. I watch as he turns briefly and waves, then disappears. And suddenly it hits me.

I know who he reminded me of back there. It was me.

Chapter Fifteen

When I switch on my phone, I discover I have eight missed calls and one, two, three . . . I start counting as all those little envelopes come beeping in . . . six texts.

All from Nate.

R U OK?
It's lunchtime. Where R U?
I'm sorry, babe. I was a jerk. Call me. xx
Hey, lovely. R U still mad at me? Love U xoxoxox
OK, U R obviously ignoring me. If you want to speak, U
    know where I am.
It's 6 p.m. Where the hell R U? I don't have time to play
    these games. Stop being so childish.

As texts go, it's a bit like going from the beginning of a relationship – polite and friendly – to the middle madly-in-love bit and ending up at the angry, pissed-off and arguing part. My emotions follow the same arc. I start off feeling pleased and relieved and thinking, Aw, isn't Nate wonderful? but by the time I've reached text number six, I'm back to being annoyed and indignant.

Which makes two of us, I muse, listening to one of his cross-sounding voicemails.

I call him straight back.

'Why haven't you been answering your phone?' he demands as soon as he picks up.

I bristle. 'I turned it off. I was at the MoMA.'

'All day?' He sounds disbelieving.

'Well, I had no other plans,' I can't help replying, then not wanting to argue, add, 'Anyway, I'm sorry I didn't get your calls.'

There's a beat, and then, 'Yeah, me too,' he replies, his voice softening. 'So how was the MoMA?'

'Amazing,' I gush, then catch myself. I don't want to sound like I had too good a day. 'I mean, the art was amazing, not the actual day . . .'

'I really missed you,' he says, sounding contrite. 'Did you miss me?'

'Of course,' I answer automatically. Only now, saying those words, it occurs to me that I haven't missed him at all. To be truthful, I didn't think about him once. But that's only because I was surrounded by such incredible paintings and I just lost track of everything, I tell myself firmly. It had nothing to do with Adam.

Adam? His name catches me by surprise. Why did he just pop into my head? What's he got to do with anything?

'So, when are you coming home?' asks Nate, interrupting my thoughts.

I feel a warm glow. See, we're back on course again. It was just a silly row. Nothing more.

'Well, I was going to head back to my apartment. I need to feed Jenny and Simon.'

'Jenny and Simon?'

'My roommate's dogs,' I explain, realising that of course he wouldn't know anything about them as he's never been to my apartment. 'She's away on a course all day and not back until late.'

'OK, well, a producer friend of mine is having a little drinks thing. It's nothing too fancy, just some TV people . . .'

Just some TV people? I feel a flash of nervous excitement.

' . . . I wondered if you wanted to go.'

'That sounds fun,' I hear myself saying.

'Cool.' Nate sounds pleased. 'Give me your address. I'll pick you up in an hour.'

*   *   *

One hour. Sixty minutes. Three thousand and six hundred seconds.

That's it?

To rush home, nearly have a heart attack racing up three flights of steps, feed the dogs, drag them round the block and almost choke them to death in an attempt to stop them sniffing every lamp-post. Then jump in the shower, shave my legs, cut them to ribbons, exfoliate, moisturise, blow-dry my hair, try my super new straightening balm, realise super new straightening balm is a total con and tie my hair up instead. Afterwards apply make-up, attempt smoky eyes like I saw in a magazine, end up looking like I've done three rounds with Mickey Rourke, agonise over what to wear, then wear only thing I can find that's not too creased.

Then finally charge around the apartment tidying up, abandon tidying up and shove everything under the bed or behind the sofa, jump a mile when the buzzer goes, panic, take deep breaths and greet Nate at door looking composed and utterly relaxed.

'You look nice,' he says approvingly, as he walks in and gives me a kiss. Then jumps back as Simon and Jenny come running, tails wagging, to greet him.

'Don't worry, they're super friendly.' I smile at his worried expression.

'I've just had these trousers dry-cleaned, that's all.' Bending down, he brushes a couple of hairs from the legs of his suit, where the dogs have rubbed against him. Jenny, thinking he's bending down to pat her, rewards him with a big slobbery lick. 'Eugh.' He jerks upright, looking disgusted.

'Ooh, sorry.' Hastily I try to shoo the dogs back into the living room.

'Do you have any antibacterial wipes?' he asks, wiping his face with his hand.

'No, I don't think so . . .'

'Where's your bathroom?'

'Just down the hallway on the right—'

Before I can finish he marches past me and I hear the taps start running on full blast.

'Is everything OK?' Shutting the dogs in the living room, I hurry down the hallway to find the bathroom door wide open and Nate stooped over the sink, washing his face.

'Yeah, fine.' Face dripping, he looks around for a towel.

Which is when I realise that in my mad rush to tidy up the flat, I totally overlooked the bathroom. Through the steam my eyes do a quick sweep and fall on several soggy towels I've left lying on the floor, together with the different products I'd used, all with their tops off. There's even my Bic razor just lying there on the shelf, full of shaving foam and bristles, I notice, feeling a wave of mortification.

I have a flashback of Nate's spotlessly clean bathroom, with his pristine white towels rolled up and stacked neatly on the shelves, like something out of *Elle Décor*.

Oh God, he must think I'm a total slob.

'I'll get you a fresh one,' I say, quickly scooping up the towels and shoving them into the laundry basket. I open the airing cupboard, but it's empty. Shit. Where are all the towels? Then I remember. I've got about five hanging over the back of my chair in my bedroom. 'Erm, sorry, we seem to have run out.'

'Don't worry, I'm practically dry now anyway,' he says, a little tetchily. 'Ready?'

'Nearly. I just need to finish my make-up.' Having wiped off my ill-fated attempt at smoky eyes after realising I looked like Ling-Ling the giant panda, I need to apply a bit of mascara.

'You've had an hour. What have you been doing?' He laughs, but I detect a twinge of irritation.

Or maybe that's just my twinge of irritation, I realise, resisting the urge to reel off the long list of everything I've been doing in a mad panic so I won't be late. Instead I say brightly, 'Do you want something to drink while you wait?'

'Just some water will be great.'

'I don't have any bottled. Is tap water OK?' I start heading towards the kitchen.

'You don't? Well, in that case, no.' Nate wrinkles up his nose. 'You know me – I only drink mineral.'

'Oh, of course.' I nod, feeling a bit stupid. We've moved into the tiny hallway and I'm suddenly aware it seems much more cramped and poky than usual.

'Shit. What's that?' He bangs into a carved wooden mask hanging on the wall.

'It's from a tribe in Ethiopia,' I say, hurriedly straightening it. 'My roommate got it. I think it's supposed to scare away evil spirits.'

'No kidding.' He studies it with a raised eyebrow.

'OK, well, I'll just grab my bag and then we can leave.' The sooner we get out of here, the better, I tell myself, pushing open my bedroom door. I dive inside and scramble around for my mascara. I'll put it on in the cab on the way to the party.

'So this is your room?'

I turn to see Nate standing at the doorway, his eyes glancing around him, taking everything in.

'Er, yeah, this is it. It's a bit small . . . and there's not much wardrobe space,' I add hastily, catching him looking at the piles of clothes on the back of the chair, 'but I like it.' I continue hunting for my mascara.

'It's very . . . colourful,' he says, choosing his words carefully.

'Well, I've always loved colour.'

Shit, where is that mascara? I look at my make-up, strewn all over my dressing table. It's got to be here somewhere.

'You've certainly got a lot of stuff considering you only moved to New York a few weeks ago.'

I look up from my dressing table to see Nate staring at my bookshelves, which are crammed with pictures, magazines, old sketchbooks and my collection of seashells, which I haven't got round to finding a place for.

'What's this?'

I watch as absently he picks up a magazine and peers at it, frowning. 'You've done some kind of quiz . . .'

Suddenly it registers. He's found *that* quiz. I feel a flash of embarrassment.

'Oh, that?' I say, trying to sound casual while hastily taking it from him. Yesterday I would have probably shown it to him, had a giggle over it – after all, Nate would probably find it cute – but now . . .

Out of the corner of my eye I spot my mascara on the bed and pounce on it.

Now something's different. I don't feel the same somehow.

'It's just a load of rubbish,' I say dismissively, and chucking it in the wastepaper basket, I grab my bag. 'OK, let's go.'

The party is already in full swing by the time we arrive. Well, I say 'full swing', but in reality it's just lots of people standing around drinking vodka martinis and talking TV. And by 'talking TV' I don't mean chatting about who they think is going to win *Dancing with the Stars*, but discussing the ins and outs of production, escalating budgets and viewing figures.

Apart from me, it appears that everyone here is in the industry, and whereas on the way over I'd been imagining a really glamorous party, it's actually a bit dull. In fact, at one point, while struggling to keep up with a conversation about production scheduling, I find my mind wandering and I catch myself wondering when we can leave. I quickly remind myself that I'm in New York at a TV party with Nate. A few months ago this would have been my dream scenario, and now I'm wanting to go home, put on my pyjamas and curl up in front of *Oprah*. I mean, Lucy!

I force myself to focus on the conversation.

'As I was saying, it's all about having integrity,' intones Brad, a short man in a shiny suit, who keeps putting his arm round my waist under the guise of moving me out of the way of waiters and then letting his hand linger. Not that Nate notices. He's too busy trying to pitch his new idea for a game show.

'Totally,' nods Nate, his face earnest.

I mean, please. He's talking about a game show, not an award-winning documentary.

'If you'll excuse me,' I say politely, trying to extricate myself.

'Why, what have you done?' chuckles Brad, highly amused at his own bad pun.

'Always the joker, Brad,' smiles Nate, playing along with the locker-room humour.

'Anyway, tell me,' says Brad, flashing Nate and me a broad smile, 'how did you two meet?'

'In Italy. We were both studying art,' I explain. At the memory of Venice I feel a familiar tingle.

'Oh, really? So are you an artist?'

I pause, briefly thrown by the question. 'I was, for a little while,' I say quietly.

'Then she realised she needed to live in the real world and get a proper job,' laughs Nate.

His words sting. 'Something like that.' I nod, forcing a smile, but deep down it's like something suddenly breaks inside me and at the first opportunity I make an excuse about popping to the loo and leave them laughing.

Making my escape, I wander to the far end of the room. The party is being held in an amazing loft in Tribeca, all exposed brickwork and pipes, and *über*-trendy furniture dotted around like art. Speaking of which, there's some amazing artwork on the walls, all of it no doubt original. According to Nate, the owner is someone high up at one of the networks, which doesn't mean much to me, except that working in TV seems to make people very rich.

After a few aborted attempts at trying to mingle, which make me realise that everyone is talking another language and I don't speak TV, I find myself outside on the balcony chatting to one of the waiters. His name is Eric and he plays guitar in a heavy-metal band. After twenty minutes of telling me all about his recent gig and how he spent the whole evening head-banging next to the speakers, he has to leave to serve canapés and I make my way to the loo.

This time it's genuine – I really do need to go – and finding the door unlocked, I push it open, only to see a couple of guys with their backs to me, one of whom is bent over the sink. It's pretty obvious he's doing coke, as when I walk in, he springs up. It's Brad. And with him, I suddenly realise, is Nate.

'Oh!' Feeling a mixture of shock and embarrassment, I stand there frozen for a moment as they turn round and see me. Then I remember myself.

'Sorry,' I blurt, before backing out.

'Excuse me, Brad,' says Nate, and quickly follows me out into the hallway. 'Where are you going?' He looks at me, his brow etched.

'I'm tired. I think I'm going to go home.'

'I'll come with you.'

'No, it's OK. You stay. You're obviously busy.'

Nate frowns. 'Oh, come on, Lucy, don't make a big deal of it.'

I look at him and suddenly I see someone I don't know. This isn't long-haired, pot-smoking, easy-going Nate. This is uptight, exercise-obsessed, workaholic Nate, who says coffee is bad for you and yet who's in the toilets at a party with a slimeball in a shiny suit doing God knows what.

'That's not the point. You're the one who's always going on about being healthy. I mean, you won't even drink tap water,' I say, thinking back to earlier.

'That's totally different.'

'No, it's not.' I shake my head. 'You're being a hypocrite.'

'And you're making a scene,' he shushes, glancing around at the other party guests to see if anyone has overheard us.

I bristle, but stop myself from retaliating. 'Look, I don't want another row. Let's forget about it.' I start to put on my jacket and turn to leave, but Nate follows me out.

'Lucy, wait. Let me say goodbye to a few people and I'll come with you.'

'It's OK. You stay. I'll catch a cab home.'

He shoots me a look as if to say, *Don't do this to me in front of all these people.*

'Just give me five minutes.'

I end up giving him over twenty as I wait in the doorway watching him working his way around the room, getting involved in conversations, laughing at jokes. At several points I come close to leaving without him, and part of me wishes I had done, because by the time he finally joins me and we climb into a cab, neither of us is in the best of moods.

'We always stay at yours – why can't we stay at mine for a change?' I ask, as he gives the driver his address.

'What? You'd rather stay at your place than mine?' He throws me a look across the back seat. Whereas before we'd be cuddled together in the middle, now we're sitting at opposite ends. It wouldn't take a body-language expert to see something is up.

'What's wrong with my place?' I feel a beat of irritation.

'Well, you can't really compare the two, can you?' He laughs lightly and raises an eyebrow.

If I was irritated before, now I'm annoyed. 'No, please, go ahead. I'm interested,' I say, folding my arms expectantly.

He lets out an impatient sigh. 'OK, well, one's a penthouse with a view of the park, and the other is a four-storey walk-up with a view of graffiti.'

'I happen to like it,' I bristle.

'Well, I don't.' He shrugs.

'Well, I don't particularly like your place,' I fire back.

'What's not to like?'

'All that white for a start. I like splashes of colour.'

'Splashes of colour?' Nate snorts. 'Your apartment looks like a paint factory exploded in there.'

I let out an indignant gasp.

'And as for all that voodoo stuff.'

'What voodoo stuff?' I demand hotly.

'Like that mask.' He pulls a face.

'That's not voodoo!' I exclaim. 'Anyway, at least there are interesting things in there. Your place is so minimalist there's hardly anything in it, apart from that epileptic machine.'

'It's an elliptical,' he corrects brusquely, 'and by the way, it wouldn't hurt for you to start using one.'

'And what's that supposed to mean?'

'Well, it wouldn't do your thighs any harm, would it? If you want to get rid of that cellulite.'

I inhale sharply. It's like a boxer's jab.

'And you put a hole in my rug,' he continues with a swift uppercut.

'What?' I'm still reeling from the last comment.

'I have security CCTV cameras as part of the alarm system.'

Damn, I thought he might have CCTV. What else has he taped?

'That's a really expensive rug.'

'For Christ's sake, it was an accident,' I gasp defensively.

'Like the juicer?' He glares at me.

My jaw sets defiantly. 'Well, I'm sorry I'm not as perfect as you. With your showroom apartment.'

'Your place is a mess. There's crap everywhere.'

'I'd rather be messy than anal.'

'What? So I'm anal because I don't leave Domino's pizza boxes lying under the bed?' he cries indignantly.

Shit. He saw them.

'No, because you fuss about how to stack the dishwasher, or which way to put a spoon in the cutlery drawer. You're so anal you even iron your pineapple boxer shorts! Speaking of which, what thirty-year-old *wears* pineapple boxer shorts?'

He scowls. 'Look, this was obviously a huge mistake.'

'A mistake?'

'You and me. It isn't working out. I want to break up.'

'*You* want to break up?' I cry indignantly. '*I* want to break up!'

He stares at me in disbelief. 'What? You're breaking up with me?' he retorts. 'No, I'm the one breaking up with you.'

'God, you always were a jerk!' I gasp contemptuously.

'You really haven't changed, have you? You're still pig-headed,' he yells.

'And you have changed. You used to be fun,' I yell back.

'Life's not all about having fun, Lucy. You need to grow up.'

'I am grown up!'

'You have purple hair!' he says scornfully.

'At least I have hair,' I fire in return.

There's a sharp moment of silence and he visibly winces.

'S'cuse me, where are you both going?'

In the middle of our break-up we turn, breathless from arguing, to see the driver looking at us quizzically in the rear-view mirror.

'I'm not going anywhere with him,' I say, throwing Nate a furious glare.

'And I'm not going anywhere with her,' he shoots at me with a scowl.

For a moment there's a stand-off in the back of the cab, both of us stubbornly refusing to move. Until, with an impatient gasp, Nate grabs the door and gets out, slamming it firmly behind him.

Chapter Sixteen

So that's it. Nate and I are finished. Our great love affair is over.

It lasted the grand sum of a week.

'Well, strictly speaking, it lasted less than a week,' points out Robyn blithely. Then seeing my expression, adds quickly, '*Ten years* and less than a week.'

It's Sunday morning and Robyn and I have taken the dogs for a walk in Battery Park, which basically means we're sitting on the grass in the sunshine eating ice creams, while Simon and Jenny snuffle around by our feet.

'I still can't believe it,' I say, taking a defiant lick of my ice cream.

'You mean about breaking up or what he said about . . .?' She trails off and gives me a look that says, *You know*.

I'd told Robyn about the argument and she'd nodded supportively and enthusiastically yelled, 'Go, girl,' at all the right moments. When it came to his comments about my thighs, she'd sharply sucked in her breath and gone completely silent with shock. Which for Robyn is saying something.

Or not, as it turned out.

'Both,' I answer, biting off another large chunk of my double-chocolate fudge whatever-it-is in an act of rebellion. 'And to think I was in love with him for all those years.'

'Better to have loved and lost,' remarks Robyn sagely.

'I haven't lost him!' I gasp indignantly. Simon stops snuffling in the grass and cocks up his ears, looking startled. 'I broke up with him!'

Robyn looks confused. 'I thought he broke up with you,' she says uncertainly.

'Well, he did . . . sort of,' I admit grudgingly. 'We broke up with each other. After we'd had that big argument in the cab.'

'Well, at least you agreed on something,' she says brightly.

Robyn never ceases to amaze me with her determination to see the positive in everything. Whatever disaster befalls her, she's never negative. She could get wrongly arrested for drug-smuggling in Thailand, be sentenced to life in prison and thrown into a jail where no one speaks English and she'd probably say how it was a wonderful opportunity to have some 'me-time' and learn a new language.

'I suppose so.' I nod doubtfully.

'Are you upset?'

I stop to think about it. Am I?

'No,' I say, after a pause.

As I say it, I feel a twinge of surprise. I thought I would be more than upset. I thought I would be devastated. After all, wasn't he supposed to be my soulmate? The man whom I couldn't live without. The person who completes me.

Er, no, Lucy, that's *Jerry Maguire*.

'Well, that's good,' Robyn is saying cheerfully. 'A break-up is one thing, but heartbreak is another.' She rolls her eyes as if to say she's been there, and I nod in recognition.

Only this time I don't feel heartbroken at all.

'I'm stunned, I suppose,' I confess. 'And disappointed. He's not who I thought he was. But then I suppose I wasn't either.' I look down at my ice cream. My defiance has melted along with it. 'I was in love with the idea of him. An ideal of him. Of who I thought he was. Of who he used to be.'

I'm thinking out loud now as my mind mulls over everything. Last week seems like a dream. A huge blur. A rollercoaster of emotions. It all happened so fast that I never really paused to think about it. I didn't *want* to stop and think about it. I was falling madly in love again and it was so exhilarating. Seeing him again. Discovering he still loved me. We both got carried away. We didn't even pause to think that maybe we were falling in love with different people. Caught up in the lust, the moment, the sheer thrill, it was like diving into the ocean.

And now, finally, I've come up for air.

'I was in love with the romance of it all, of getting back together with my first love. I think we both were,' I say eventually.

'We all were,' nods Robyn supportively. 'It was super romantic.'

'I mean, I really thought he was my soulmate, but now . . .' I trail off sadly.

'But now you've realised he isn't, and that's OK.' Seeing my glum expression, Robyn immediately springs into her cheer-leader role. 'So what if it's taken you ten years? Better late than never.'

'I thought you said Nate and I were meant to be together, that we were just puppets and it was the power of the universe, our destiny,' I say sulkily.

Robyn colours. 'Well, that's true. It did all seem like too much of a coincidence, like it was meant to be, and you did seem very cute together.' She pauses. 'Are you sure it's over?'

'A hundred per cent.'

'Hmm.' She licks her ice cream thoughtfully. She looks unconvinced.

'I suppose I'm also a bit angry,' I confess.

'You know, I'm sure he didn't really mean that comment,' Robyn says quickly.

I shake my head. 'No, not at Nate, at myself. I feel a bit stupid. All these years I believed that I could never be prop-erly happy without him. I'd built him up into this perfect guy, this great love.' I pause and tug at some tufts of grass. 'Now I feel like Dorothy in *The Wizard of Oz* when she pulls back the curtain and sees the wizard is just a little old man pulling lots of levers.'

'I felt like that when I went to my high-school reunion and saw Brad Poleski,' says Robyn supportively. 'When I was sixteen, I had the biggest crush. I couldn't even look at him. He was like a god. Then I met him again last year and he was just this little guy who ran a dry-cleaning company and lived in Ohio. He was just so *normal*.' She shakes her head, her green eyes flashing as she thinks back.

'It was like one minute I was crazy about him and then the next . . .' I trail off.

God, I didn't realise I was so fickle.

'It can happen,' nods Robyn. 'Once, it happened to me right in the middle . . .' She raises her eyebrows, like something out of a Carry On film.

'Middle of what?'

'When we were, *you know.*'

'Oh God, really?' Suddenly it registers. 'What happened?'

'He was a Hare Krishna and—'

'Can Hare Krishnas *have* sex?'

'Well, he wasn't great and the chanting was a bit distracting.' She pauses. 'Oh, you mean, are they allowed to have sex because of their *religious beliefs*?' She gasps, her eyes wide. 'Actually, I don't know.' She stops to think for a moment, her face screwed up in concentration. 'Anyway, where was I?'

'Having sex,' I remind her.

'Oh, yeah.' Brushing her curls out of her face, she looks at me intently. 'He was on top of me and I looked up and saw his bald head and suddenly, out of the blue, I got this image of Fred, my niece's tortoise. You know the way they stretch their little heads out of their shell . . .?' She does an impression. 'Trust me, it was never the same again. Which was a shame, as I used to like his cooking. All those mung beans. *Mmm* . . .'

As Robyn chatters away nineteen to the dozen, I feel myself cheering up. Well, it's impossible not to with Robyn around.

'Saying that, boy, did they give me gas.'

A giggle erupts from me. 'Haven't you ever heard of the phrase "Too much information"?' I laugh.

'Of course. I just ignore it.' She grins and then suddenly she sits up like a meerkat. Her body is on high alert, like when Simon and Jenny spot a squirrel.

'What have you seen?'

'A dark, handsome stranger. Two o'clock.' She gestures towards the lake.

Oh-oh. I know what this means.

'Harold?'

'Could be.' She nods, putting on her sunglasses and slinking down into the grass.

I suddenly feel as if we're on a stakeout.

'So what happened with Daniel the other night?' I ask, trying to steer the topic from an imaginary male into a real one. 'When I left, you were looking pretty cosy.'

'Oh, we had fun. He's cute,' she says distractedly, her eyes still fixed on the dark, handsome stranger. Any minute now I wouldn't be surprised if she dug out some binoculars. 'He asked me out on a date tomorrow night . . .'

'A date?' I repeat excitedly. 'You didn't tell me that!'

' . . . but of course I said no.'

'Because he's not Harold,' I say flatly.

'Exactly.' She nods, ignoring my obvious disapproval. 'I told him we had no future.'

I look at her aghast. 'You told him that? You told him about Harold?'

'Of course,' she says, as if it's the most normal thing in the world to tell a man she's just met that she can't date him because a psychic told her she was going to meet a dark, handsome stranger called Harold.

But then for Robyn I suppose it is.

'Why wouldn't I?' she asks.

Because he'll think you're a total fruitcake, I want to say, but instead opt for a more diplomatic 'But if you went on a date, you might discover you really like him.'

'Exactly. That's what I'm afraid of,' she says, shooting me a strained look. 'Because then what am I going to do when I meet Harold?' Quickly she glances back across the lake. 'Oh crap.'

I follow her gaze. The dark, handsome stranger has his hand round a heavily pregnant woman.

'Anyway, I've agreed to go out with him. Not on a *date* date, just as friends.' She sighs, brushing the grass off her skirt and standing up, ready to leave.

'Good.' I nod approvingly, hauling myself up. 'Maybe this way you'll really get to like him.'

'No, don't say that!' She looks panicked. 'That can never happen. What am I going to do when I finally meet Harold?'

Note it's not 'if', it's 'when'.

'But what if when you finally meet him, you and Harold don't get along?' I reason, as we start walking through the park towards the exit.

She throws me a look as if to say, *That's not very nice, Lucy*, and refuses to be drawn. 'Oh, by the way, a client gave me two free tickets for the theatre next week,' she says, swiftly changing the subject. 'That new play on Broadway, *Tomorrow's Lives*. I wondered if you wanted to go.'

'Ooh, yes,' I say eagerly. 'I've never seen a play on Broadway.'

See. I'm not going to sit around moping about you, Nathaniel Kennedy, flashes through my brain.

'But the thing is, I can't go. I've got a healing conference. So if you want to ask someone to go with you, like, oh, I dunno . . .' The name 'Nate' escapes silently from her mouth and hangs above her in a cartoon bubble.

'I'll ask my sister,' I say firmly.

Winding a curl round her finger, Robyn pauses thoughtfully. 'Lucy, I don't want to interfere, but are you certain this isn't just a lovers' tiff?'

'Definitely not.' I shake my head determinedly. 'In fact . . .' Suddenly remembering something, I stop walking, reach my fingers into my T-shirt and pull out my half-coin pendant. I haven't taken it off since Nate and I put them back on again. Looping it over my head, I chuck it into a nearby bin.

And turning to Robyn, who's staring at me in disbelief, I say, 'Now do you believe me?'

With endings come new beginnings, and later that day, back at the apartment, I decide to have a clear-out. Fresh start and all that. I've got junk everywhere and so I spend the rest of Sunday sorting stuff out and throwing lots away. Including my 'Nate file', which is full of old photographs, letters and mementoes that I've kept all these years and carted around with me wherever I've gone.

Now it's time to let go, I tell myself firmly, chucking the whole lot in the bin. Time to move on.

Before I go to sleep that night, I put my phone on charge. I haven't heard from Nate, but then I didn't expect to. For a brief moment I think about sending him a sort of goodbye-but-no-hard-feelings text, then decide against it. Things are still a bit too raw. Best leave it until the dust settles, then send an email saying something mature and philosophical about love and relationships.

Maybe even one day we'll become friends like Bruce and Demi, and go on holidays together with our new partners. Whenever anyone asks us, we'll talk fondly about each other and laugh and reminisce. I'll even laugh about those pineapple boxer shorts and how he's always on the phone. It will be endearing, as will my lateness and messiness and purple hair.

I'd still want to kill him about his comment about my thighs, though.

I wake up on Monday morning feeling positive. It's a new day, the first day of the rest of my life. After yesterday's cathartic throwing-away of the old, it's time to welcome the new. Just consider, I'm never going to have to think about Nate again. He's never going to pop wistfully into my head when a song comes on the radio, and I'm never again going to get a pang of 'What if?' when I see a couple cosying up together. It's incredible.

Like a whole weight has been lifted from my shoulders, I muse, happily sipping my extra-shot latte as I walk to work. Listening to my iPod, I stride down the street with a real spring in my step. I feel lighter, freer—

'I hear wedding bells!'

Pushing open the door of the gallery, I'm greeted by Magda charging over to greet me, her stilettos clattering loudly on the polished concrete like a drum roll.

'What?' Pulling out my earphones, I stare at her in confusion.

'You and Nathaniel! Can you hear them!' she exclaims, cupping her hand against her ear.

I stand still in shock, all thoughts of being lighter and freer and never hearing his name again vanishing into the ether.

'It will be amazing. You should have it at the Plaza. I have a friend, Ernie Wiseman, who can give you a fabulous deal on the flowers.'

I feel a sickening thud. How am I going to break the news to Magda that it's over?

'Actually, I don't think there's going to be a wedding,' I say tactfully.

Well, let's start with the obvious.

'I know, I know, you want a long engagement.' She shrugs her tiny shoulders, which are encased in two huge shoulder pads. 'You want time to plan, to organise, to make it all perfect, but let me tell you, you need to get him up the aisle in the first three months, three months I tell you.'

Faced with the ten-ton truck that is Magda careering towards me in full wedding-at-the-Plaza mode, softly-softly isn't going to cut it.

'We broke up,' I blurt.

For a moment Magda's mouth continues moving but no words come out. Then letting out a howl, like a wounded animal, her Gucci heels appear to buckle beneath her and she clings on to the reception desk.

'No, no,' she wails, finding her voice. 'This *cannot* be true!'

'I'm sorry. It just didn't work out,' I try explaining, but Magda's turned pale, even underneath that Hamptons tan and thick layer of pearlised blusher, and is staring at me with a stricken expression. Though that could be the result of a visit to her 'friend' Dr Rosenbaum, I reflect, spotting the telltale signs of bruising around her eyes.

'But he has Italian shoes,' she manages to croak.

'I made a mistake,' I fib desperately. 'They were from Banana Republic.'

Magda is undeterred. 'Don't worry, we can fix that,' she says, a look of pure determination in her eyes. 'I know the manager at Bergdorf. I can get fifty per cent off a pair of Pradas.'

'No, truly, it's fine,' I say hastily. 'We weren't right for each other.'

Magda looks at me like I'm speaking a foreign language. 'What does that have to do with anything?' she gasps, incredulous. 'I have had three husbands and none of them was right for me!'

She says this so indignantly that it takes a moment for it to register, and when it does, I'm not quite sure how it's supposed to lend support to her argument.

'At least the gallery opening went well,' I say cheerfully, deciding not to ask and instead changing the subject. Quickly skirting round to the computer, I flick it on and start checking our emails. 'Fingers crossed it helps business.'

'Hmm,' she says sulkily.

'And we've got a few emails here about the food, saying how delicious the meatballs were,' I continue, looking over for a reaction. There's a vague stirring of her head and her golden beehive tips slightly.

'Oh, and I saw my friend Robyn and she said she and Daniel are going out on a date,' I say, in a last-ditch effort. OK, so it's not strictly true. And I'm prostituting my friend. But give me a break. I'm desperate.

It works. Magda's head shoots up, like Jenny's and Simon's when you say, 'W.A.L.K.'

'They are? I knew it! What did I tell you? When it comes to matchmaking, I am never wrong.' She shoots me a pointed look, which I quickly deflect.

'Yes, isn't it great,' I enthuse. 'They seem like a really good couple.'

'A *good* couple? They are the *perfect* couple,' she boasts, raising herself up to her full height of four foot eleven. 'Though my son never tells me anything,' she grumbles as an afterthought. 'He thinks I will tell everyone, that I have a big mouth.' She looks at me, affronted. 'Me? A big mouth?' Clutching her chest, which, like everything on Magda, looks suspiciously pert, she gasps theatrically, 'I am the soul of discretion. The very soul.'

'Absolutely.' I nod gravely, clicking on an email from the photographer we hired for the opening. A whole set of pictures open up. 'Who's that?' I ask, peering at a photograph of a particularly attractive older woman. 'She looks very glamorous.'

I swivel the screen, so Magda can see, and she tuts loudly.

'Well, what do you expect?' she exclaims, rolling her eyes. 'That's Melissa Silverstein. She blackmailed her millionaire husband when she discovered he was having an affair.' Leaning closer, she lowers her voice. 'I shouldn't really say, as she told me in confidence, but she found him in bed with the gardener . . .'

After Magda has divulged the innermost secrets of her friend, giving proof, if any was needed, that perhaps Daniel does have a point and discretion and Magda don't go together, it's business as usual and the rest of the morning is taken up with admin and paperwork.

Then it's lunchtime and I'm going to Katz's for our regular order, being served by the same grumpy man behind the counter who never speaks and walking back to the gallery with Magda's hot matzo-ball soup and pastrami-on-rye sandwich. The only difference being that today I decide to skip my usual tuna melt and grab a coffee and an apple.

No particular reason. It hasn't got *anything* to do with Nate's comment about my thighs, for example. Or that I now know that tuna melts are hideously fattening because I Googled them earlier and they've got about a million calories or something and all that melted cheese is just waiting to hijack your thighs and cover them in dimples.

No, it's really strange. I just don't have an appetite today at all, I muse, sipping my coffee as I stride down the street. My stomach isn't gurgling because I'm hungry. It's just making a funny noise because . . . Well, I'm not sure why, but I'm sure there must be lots of reasons.

'Ow!'

I let out a yelp as someone bashes right into me, knocking my arm and spilling coffee all down my top. 'Watch where you're going,' I yell.

See, I'm becoming much more like a New Yorker. In the past it would have been an apologetic 'Sorry!', but not now, I think, looking down with dismay to see my top is covered in rapidly spreading brown splodges.

'Hey, why don't *you* watch where you're going,' yells back the person who just bashed into me.

God, what a cheek!

Looking up, I wheel round angrily. Hang on a minute, it was—

'*You!*'

We both say it at the same time. It sounds in stereo as I look at the man standing opposite me in a smart grey suit, the person who just knocked into me because he wasn't looking, who just ruined my top and scalded me with hot coffee because he was too busy yakking away on his phone to look where he was going.

And it's Nate.

He's staring at me, a shocked expression on his face.

'I'll call you back,' he says sharply into his Bluetooth headset.

I look at him in astonishment. I can't believe it. It's him. Of all people on the streets of Manhattan, I have to go and bump into him!

Correction: he has to *bash* into me.

Suddenly my astonishment is overtaken by anger. 'You need to look where you're going when you're on the phone,' I snap with annoyance.

His face clouds over. 'You walked straight into me.'

'No, I didn't!' I gasp. I feel a stab of fury. Trust Nate to make out it was my fault. 'You were chatting on your phone and not paying attention. Look, you've spilled coffee all over me!' Grabbing my now coffee-soaked shirt, which looks like something that's been tie-dyed by Robyn, I waggle it at him furiously.

If I was expecting him to be apologetic, I couldn't have been more wrong.

'Well, I did warn you about drinking coffee,' he says evenly.

I glare at him. 'What? So it's my fault?'

'Well, it's not my fault you're drinking coffee, now, is it?'

'It's your fault you were on your phone and walked straight into me,' I retort impatiently.

'You walked straight into me,' he fires back.

We're going round in circles and we both break off and glower at each other. I can't believe it. Until last week I hadn't seen him for ten years. And I'd spent those ten whole years fantasising about bumping into him and yet it never happened. Now here I am, randomly bumping into him in the street.

'By the way, you left a few toiletries at mine,' he says awkwardly, stuffing his hands in his pockets and jingling his loose change. 'I was going to post them to the gallery.'

'Oh, don't bother. Just throw them away,' I say quickly.

God, it's come to this. One minute we were ripping each other's clothes off, the next we're discussing the disposal of my toothbrush.

'OK, well, I guess that's it, then . . .'

'Yup, I guess so.'

For a moment neither of us says anything and then his iPhone starts ringing, like a bell calling time on the relationship. It's a fitting ending.

'Look, I need to take this . . .'

'Yeah, sure.' I nod. 'Goodbye, Nate.'

And leaving him standing in the middle of the street, I turn and walk away.

After all these years I've finally put him behind me, and this time there's no looking back.

Chapter Seventeen

'Do you want sake?'

Later that evening I leave work and hurry to Wabi Sabi, a tiny little Japanese restaurant tucked away underneath an antique shop in Chelsea, to find my sister already sitting waiting for me at the sushi bar.

'Erm . . . yes, great,' I say, puffing slightly after my run from the subway. I'd been determined to arrive first for once, and had even left the gallery early, but despite my best efforts she's here before me.

Now I know how a British holidaymaker must feel when they discover that despite getting up at the crack of dawn, the Germans have already got to the sun loungers.

'Good. Because I've ordered it.' She nods as I slide into the free seat next to her. 'I didn't wait. I knew you'd be late.'

That's my sister for you. Never one to mince words.

'Lovely to see you too.' I smile, giving her a hug, despite the fact that she doesn't really do hugs. Or kisses. Or in fact any shows of public affection. At school the boys used to call her 'Iceberg', which was a bit mean. And blatantly not true.

After all, icebergs do sometimes melt.

'Oh, before I forget I wondered if you wanted to go with me to the theatre next week. Robyn has two free tickets,' I say, breaking open my chopsticks and diving on the little bowl of *edamame*. I'm starving. I've only had coffee and an apple all day.

''Fraid not. I'm training,' she replies, shaking her head.

'Every night?'

'Well, the marathon is only a couple of months away.'

That's another thing. On top of the fourteen hours a day that my sister puts in at the office, she's currently spending her free time training for the New York Marathon.

I know. I feel exhausted just thinking about it.

'I have free passes for my gym. You should come,' she suggests, popping out the soybeans with her teeth. 'Now you won't be doing all that yoga.' She smirks and I swat her with a chopstick.

I've already told Kate about how I've broken up with Nate. I called her last night and filled her in on the details, at the end of which I'd drawn breath and waited for her response. It had come in the form of one word – 'Good' – and then moved briskly on to a conversation about her new bathroom tiles.

'Effusive' is not a word you could use to describe my sister. Sometimes I wonder if she views words like the rest of us view money and tries to save them up and not spend too many all at once.

'I think that was a lucky escape,' she continues. 'It will save you a fortune on chiropractic bills.'

'I'm not that bad at yoga,' I complain sulkily.

'Luce, how are you going to get into the lotus position when you can't even cross your legs? Remember that time in school assembly?'

Trust Kate to remind me of one of the most humiliating moments of my life. Aged twelve, I'd been sitting crossed-legged in the school hall, listening to our headmaster, and my legs had suddenly gone into cramp and I'd been unable to uncross them. I'd had to be airlifted out of assembly by Mr Dickenson, our PE teacher. I don't think I've ever got over the shame. For years after I was teased mercilessly with 'Don't forget to cross your legs', which took on a totally different connotation as I got older.

'Excuse me. Your sake.'

I look up to see a waiter return with a little bottle and two small ceramic glasses. Ceremoniously he arranges them on the counter in front of us.

'*Dōmo arigatō*,' smiles Kate, bowing her head respectfully.

The waiter beams. '*Dō itashi mashite*,' he replies, nodding profusely and backing away.

I stare at Kate in astonishment. 'Since when did you start speaking Japanese?'

'Since most of my clients are based in Tokyo,' she says casually, taking the sake bottle and pouring me some. 'I'm learning in my spare time.'

I look at her agog. My sister never ceases to amaze me. Sometimes I wonder if we really are sisters or if there was some mix-up in the hospital. I mean, can I really be genetically related to someone who *learns Japanese*? In her *spare time*?

There I was thinking spare time was for logging on to Facebook and sneaking a look at everyone else's photos, bidding on lots of things on eBay that I don't need and never fit properly, and watching TV with Robyn and discussing challenging subjects such as 'Do we order a twelve-inch pizza and garlic bread, or shall we just go for a sixteen-inch with extra toppings?'

'Now it's your turn. You have to pour mine,' she says, passing me the sake bottle. 'It's supposed to be good luck to pour each other's.'

'I thought you weren't superstitious.'

'I'm not.' She frowns as if I've just called her a bad name. 'It's tradition. Not superstition. There's a difference.'

'So tell me, how's work?' I ask, changing the subject. 'Any good . . . um . . . mergers and acquisitions happening?'

If there's one sure-fire way to snap my sister out of a bad mood, it's to ask her about work. It's her favourite topic of conversation. If she had it her way, it would probably be her *only* topic of conversation. Unlike my girlfriends, she's not interested in commenting on the fabulous new dress you just bought from Zara, speculating about what's going on in the Jennifer-Brad-Angie triangle or talking about relationships. Not even when it's her own.

In fact, the closest I think she ever got was on her wedding day, when someone asked her what the best part of being married to Jeff was and she replied cheerfully, 'Our new apartment. With two salaries, we can now afford a two-bedroom,' which I don't think was exactly the gushing response they'd hoped for.

'Exhausting but exciting,' she says, suddenly galvanised. 'The CEO is thrilled with the merger so far, which is superb on a performance note, but it looks like the Joberg-Cohen deal might need some extra . . .' She trails off as she sees my glazed expression. 'Are you interested in any of this?'

'Of course,' I protest. 'It's fascinating.'

And it would be. Truly, it would be. If only I had half a clue what she was going on about.

'Hmm.' She looks at me unconvinced, then suddenly stifles a yawn. 'Anyway, it's all good. Just the hours are pretty gruelling.'

I look at my sister closely. Beyond the power suit and immaculately groomed bob, there are dark circles under her eyes and the crease between her eyebrows is so sharply etched it's turning into a furrow.

'You look shattered,' I observe. 'You need a holiday.'

Kate looks at me like I just told her she needs to grow another head. '*A holiday?*' she snorts, as if the very idea is completely ludicrous.

'When did you last go away?' I persist.

She falters momentarily and I can feel her brain whirring backwards. 'We went to Mum and Dad's,' she says, with a flash of triumph.

'For Christmas last year,' I point out. 'Anyway, that was Mum and Dad. That's not exactly a holiday.'

'Luce, I don't think you understand,' she gasps impatiently. Tucking her hair behind her ears, she rubs her nose agitatedly. 'I can't go anywhere right now. I'm far too busy.'

'But you look like you need a break,' I say, squeezing her arm.

'No, what I need is to be partner,' she says determinedly, moving her arm away. 'And if I continue at this pace, there's a very good chance of being recommended at the next annual meeting.'

But can you continue at this pace? I ask myself silently, looking at her pinched expression and feeling uneasy. My sister has always been a crazy workaholic – 'over-achiever' is scribbled across her school reports – but she seems to be overdoing it, even by her standards.

'What does Jeff say?'

Her face clouds. 'Jeff understands. He knows how important this is to me.' Opening her menu, she says briskly, 'Anyway, we should order. It's getting late,' which is her way of saying the subject is closed.

She beckons over the waiter and orders for both of us. I'm not sure exactly what, as she does most of it in Japanese. 'Oh, and an extra miso soup to take away when we're done,' she says in English. 'For Jeff,' she adds, turning to me. 'I promised to bring him back some soup as he's a bit under the weather.'

'What's wrong?' I ask, feeling a beat of concern.

'Oh, nothing. Probably one of those seventy-two-hour bugs.' She shrugs, taking a sip of sake.

'He should go and see Robyn – she's got Chinese herbs for everything,' I suggest, thinking about the dozens of bottles that are randomly scattered around the flat. I'm forever tripping over things with weird and wonderful names like Yellow Croaker Ear-Stone or Long-Nosed Pit Viper.

'You have got to be kidding me!' gasps Kate.

'No, really. I know you don't believe in all that stuff, but she swears by them.' I stop as I see her making googly eyes at me.

'Are you OK? Is something in your eye?'

Now she's jabbing chopsticks at me and pulling this weird sort of strangled face. Suddenly it registers and I feel a flash of panic.

'Oh my God, are you choking?'

An image of me having to perform the Heimlich manoeuvre in the middle of the restaurant flashes across my brain. Shit. Why didn't I watch more episodes of *ER*? I got bored when George Clooney left.

'No, behind you,' she hisses, like a pantomime dame.

'What?' Bewildered, I frown, wondering what she's going on about, then turn sideways.

I don't believe it.

Because there, sitting right next to me, at the sushi counter, is Nate. He's with another man in a business suit and they've obviously just arrived, as they're ordering a couple of drinks. I stare at him in disbelief.

'Are you following me?' I accuse, finding my tongue, which had been held hostage by shock.

Hearing my voice, he turns and sees me. His face darkens. 'Are you following *me*?' he accuses back.

I can feel my hackles rise. 'I was here first,' I point out stiffly.

'Well, I made the reservation for the sushi bar last week,' he replies, as if to say, *Told you so.*

Not to be outdone, Kate fires back over my shoulder, 'We made ours the week before. You can check with my assistant.'

'Hello, Kate.' He nods in her direction.

'Nathaniel.' She gives him one of her scary looks.

For a moment there's a standoff and I can see Nate's business contact glancing uncertainly between us, like someone who just stumbled into a gunfight at the O.K Corral.

'Well, this is a coincidence,' says Nate evenly, for his benefit.

'Well, that's one way of putting it,' quips Kate dryly.

'Come on, let's move,' I say, turning back to Kate. 'There must be a free table.' Just then I glance around me and realise with dismay that the whole place has now filled up. There's even a queue of people waiting outside. 'Damn. Maybe we should leave,' I suggest.

Kate looks at me as if I've gone mad. 'I'm not leaving. I've just ordered seventy dollars worth of sushi.'

'We could get takeout,' I whisper.

She shoots me a look. 'It's crucial that you do not give the other party any cause to believe they have the position of power.'

'Kate, we're not talking about law now,' I say desperately. 'We're talking about my ex-boyfriend.'

She frowns and spears another *endamame.* 'If anyone's leaving, it's him, not us.'

'He won't – he's too stubborn,' I say pleadingly.

But she won't budge. 'Well, in that case, just ignore him.'

So I try. I try my very hardest. I talk about the gym, about the gallery, about anything to try to stop myself thinking about him, but it's not easy. I mean, he's *right there next to me*. Eating my miso soup, I can hear him asking the waiter to run through all the wines and then insisting on tasting every one. Before, it had impressed me, but now it annoys me. At one point I am about to turn round and yell, 'Just choose a bloody wine,' but thankfully my crispy salmon roll arrives and distracts me.

In fact, it's really bizarre, but through the course of my meal I discover that all the things I used to find cute and endearing now bug the hell out of me. Like the way he gels his hair into that little peak at the front, or makes that funny hissing noise between his teeth when he laughs, or mentions his game show *Big Bucks* about twenty million times.

'I mean, did he really go on about *Big Bucks* that much before and I never noticed?' I whisper to Kate.

Pausing from eating her tuna sashimi, she frowns. 'I thought you were ignoring him.'

'I am, I am,' I protest quickly. 'Except it's not that simple.'

'Well, don't worry, he's leaving now,' she says, gesturing behind me with a chopstick.

'He is?' Feeling a rush of relief, I turn round to see the seat next to me is now empty and he's walking towards the exit. 'Oh, thank goodness,' I sigh, my whole body relaxing. 'Bumping into him once was bad enough, but twice? In one day?'

'Unlucky,' says Kate simply.

I nod and turn back to my food, but something niggles. Is that all it is? Just an unlucky coincidence?

'Of course, there's always another reason,' says Kate.

'What?' I ask, snapping back.

'He's trying to find a way of getting you back.'

'What? By following me?' I frown.

'Bumping into you "accidentally",' corrects Kate. 'Remember like you did with Paul who used to deliver our papers?'

I'd forgotten all about that – well, more like blanked it out – but now I'm reminded and cringe at the memory. At twelve years old I had a crush on the paperboy and would find any excuse to bump into him: walking the dog along his route, accidentally on purpose being by our gate as he arrived, even resorting to following him around as he delivered the papers on his BMX. Oh, the shame.

'Nate wouldn't do that,' I say dismissively. 'He wanted to break up as much as I did.'

'Are you sure that wasn't just his pride talking?' Kate raises her eyebrows. 'Dump-before-you're-dumped kind of thing?'

I crinkle up my forehead, doubts forming. I think back to our argument in the taxi. 'No, trust me.' I shake my head decisively.

'Well, just a thought.' She shrugs. 'More sake?'

I'm reading too much into this. Bumping into Nate is a pain, but there's no big reason. It's just coincidence.

'Um . . . yes, please.' I hold out my glass.

Like Kate said, it's just unlucky.

Chapter Eighteen

Still, the next morning when I go to work, I'm on the lookout, and when I leave the office to get lunch, I make sure I carry my coffee ultra carefully, just in case. But nope, there's no Nate on his iPhone bashing into me. No sightings of Nate in restaurants. In fact, it's very much a Nate-free zone.

Admittedly a couple of times I spot a grey-suited man in the crowd and my chest tightens, but thankfully it's mistaken identity. Just me being jumpy and twitchy.

By the end of the day I'm feeling much calmer, and rather silly. OK, so what happened yesterday was a bit freaky, and very annoying – despite drowning it in Vanish, I'll never get those coffee stains out of my top, and I couldn't enjoy my sushi with him sitting next to me – but let's be rational, it was just a coincidence. Sod's law. Bad luck.

Call it what you want, it's hardly reason to think it's something more than that.

'I know it sounds crazy, but for a moment there I was getting a bit paranoid,' I pant breathlessly, looking across at Robyn, who's puffing away on the exercise machine next to me.

It's the next evening after work and Robyn and I have made the most of my sister's free passes to her private gym and are working out on the machines. I use the term 'working out' loosely. 'Near collapse' is probably a more fitting description.

Despite my sister's offer of free passes, she'd been taken aback by my eagerness. 'What? You're going *tonight*?' she'd said in astonishment, to which I'd rather curtly told her that I was keen to get fit and no time like the present.

What I didn't mention was Nate's comment about my cellulite, which had been scorching a hole in my brain like a burning cigarette. 'How dare he say I've got cellulite?' I'd harrumphed to Robyn approximately every ten minutes, and like the loyal friend she is, she'd harrumphed right back, 'How dare he! There is nothing wrong with your thighs!' I was a real woman, not some gym-honed stick insect. Besides, every woman has cellulite. Even Kate Moss. I mean, I'm sure I saw some on a photograph once.

OK, so it *could* have been a trick of the light, but still, I'm sure it was there.

Then after my vitriolic speech – Down with Nate, up with cellulite! – in which I'd marched around the living room in my knickers, waving the remote like a banner, I'd gone into the bathroom, looked at my bottom in the full-length mirror under the overhead lighting and made a startling discovery.

Someone had stolen my bottom! Not only that, but they'd replaced it with porridge in a string bag! I didn't know when, or how it happened, but I did know one thing: *I wanted my bottom back.*

Which is why I'm at Equilibrium, a super-trendy gym uptown, complete with exposed red brick and plasma TVs, nearly having a heart attack. And not just from the exercise. I feel like I've been thrown into a parallel universe. A universe where everyone is wearing designer Lycra, exposing gym-honed bodies and more six-packs than Oddbins. Strutting around wearing iPods, hand-towels casually thrown over their shoulders, swingy ponytails swinging, they positively glow with health and vitality. It's like landing on Planet Beautiful.

Meanwhile I'm in my old vest and shorts, puffing like a steam train, with a face like a giant tomato.

'What?' yells Robyn, in the way people do when they're wearing earphones and think they're talking normally but they sound like the drunks who spill out of nightclubs in town centres on a Saturday night.

'Oh, nothing. I was just thinking out loud.'

Screwing up her face in confusion, she tugs out one of her earphones. She's listening to a portable CD player. I don't think I've seen one of those since 1995. She's also wearing tie-dye. Next to her, I feel positively trendy, which is saying something.

'Sorry, I was miles away,' she gasps, yanking her ponytail tighter. Her hair is tied up on the top of her head and the curly brown strands are spilling outwards like one of those fibre-optic lights.

'What are you listening to?' I grunt. I'm on something called a cross-trainer, which has this huge control panel with flashing lights and dials. It's a bit like being in a cockpit. Not that I've ever *been* in a cockpit, but I'm sure it looks like this. Probably less complicated too, I muse, glancing at it now with trepidation.

After several false starts I've managed to set it to something called 'interval', as I liked the look of the little diagram at the side: high bits with lots of flat bits in between. It was the flat bits that swung it for me. It looked quite easy. After all, isn't 'interval' just another word for 'rest'?

Er, no, Lucy, I grimace, ten minutes in. It's apparently another word for 'torture'.

'It's this amazing CD,' gushes Robyn, looking invigorated.

'Oh, is it the new Black Eyed Peas?'

'Black Eyed Peas?' Robyn looks slightly baffled. 'No, it's all about miracles and how they can teach you the road to inner peace and enlightenment. It's totally fascinating. Do you want to have a listen? We can have an earphone each. I think they'll stretch . . .' She starts trying to untangle them.

'Um . . . no, it's OK,' I say hastily.

'Are you sure? There's this really cool bit about how you have to alter your perception of the world by imagining you're a tree and your arms are the branches . . .' To illustrate her point, she waves her long, skinny arms, resplendent with silver bangles, over her head. ' . . . and you're stretching your branches out into the sky and then up through the clouds and into the universe—'

'So how was the date with Daniel last night?' I cut her off before she narrates the entire CD. And she would. Trust me. 'You weren't back when I got in last night.'

Her arms flop back to her sides. 'It wasn't a date,' she corrects, wrinkling up her nose.

'OK, how was your non-date?'

She shrugs nonchalantly. 'Oh, you know, pretty good.'

I suddenly feel like a cop on one of those shows in which the perfectly innocent-looking granny does something suspicious. There's something wrong here. 'Pretty good' is not a phrase Robyn would use. 'Awesome', 'amazing' and 'wonderful' are Robyn adjectives.

Something's up. She's lying.

'Just pretty good?' I say, equally nonchalantly. Well, that's what they do in those cop shows, isn't it? Act all casual to try to catch the suspect out.

'Yeah.' She nods, but her mouth is twitching and I can tell she's dying to say more. 'He took me to dinner at this little vegan restaurant that's one of my favourites. The grilled tofu was amazing.'

'He did? Wow.'

'I know, isn't it incredible?' she gushes, flashing one of her megawatt smiles before quickly catching herself. 'Well, not that incredible, more just a coincidence . . .'

That's another thing Robyn doesn't do: use the word 'coincidence'. She doesn't believe in them. She believes in serendipity. Kismet. *Fate.*

I swear if I was a cop, I'd be ready to make an arrest.

' . . . Then we went to watch an African drumming band.'

'That's amazing,' I exclaim. Robyn's entire music collection consists of panpipes, African drumming bands and CDs with names like 'Sounds of the Indigenous Peoples' with soft-focus pictures of rainforests and rainbows on the front.

'Trust me, they were,' she gushes, unable to help herself. 'The rhythms, the music, Daniel and I were mesmerised . . .' She trails off, her eyes shining, and comes to a dead halt, unlike the machine, which keeps moving. She quickly starts again.

'You like him, don't you?'

'I do not!' she protests indignantly. 'I mean, yes, *as a friend* I like him, but that's it.'

Of course she's completely lying. I should be handcuffing her right now and leading her to the cells.

'When are you seeing him again?'

'I dunno . . . He invited me to see a play this evening. It's called *Celestial Awakenings* and it's all about angels.'

'*And you're not going?*' I look at her incredulously. One of Robyn's most beloved possessions is her deck of Angel Cards, as she believes in angels. Along with fairies, ghosts and Santa Claus. Actually, no, that's a fib, she doesn't really believe in Santa Claus, but sometimes I do wonder.

'No, I've got things to do.'

'Like what?'

'Um . . . just things.' She looks guilty.

I eye her suspiciously. 'Such as?'

'Such as planning for the future,' she says agitatedly. 'It's important.'

'Oh, OK.' I nod. Wow, I didn't realise that Robyn was so sensible. 'You mean like savings and pensions?'

'Yeah, something like that,' she says vaguely. 'Anyway, what are you doing tonight?' she asks, deftly turning the subject back on to me.

Which again is a total giveaway. Robyn never, I repeat *never* wants to stop talking about herself.

'There's a new gallery opening not far from here. I thought I'd pop over after my workout.'

'Ooh, that sounds fun,' she enthuses.

'Are you sure you don't want to come with me?'

She immediately stiffens. 'Um, no, I'm busy,' she says, avoiding my gaze. There's a sharp beep and she glances at the control pad of her exercise machine. 'Oh look, I've finished! Phew!' Her face flashes with relief as the machine starts slowing down. 'I think I might hit the steam room now.'

With wobbly legs she hastily climbs off the machine, tripping slightly. And this despite the fact she kept telling me earlier about how she'd climbed up to Machu Picchu, and 'if you've hiked in that altitude for seven hours, everything else is a breeze'.

Yes. Quite. When the Incas built Machu Picchu, they'd obviously never been to Equilibrium.

'I'll meet you there.' I nod, breathing heavily. 'I just want to do a few extra minutes.'

Which is a complete lie. I want to collapse on the sofa and eat an ice cream, but the image of my stolen bottom is preventing me.

'OK, well, see you in a bit,' she says, and hurriedly grabbing her CD and tie-dyed towel, she staggers off. 'Have fun.'

Fun? This is supposed to be fun?

With my heart thudding in my chest like a jackhammer, I glare at the cross-trainer. I can think of many different words to describe my experience for the past twenty minutes and 'fun' isn't one of them.

Torturous, agony, boring, please make it stop. Oh, no, that's four, isn't it?

Wiping away the beads of sweat that are beginning to trickle down my face, I grip on to the handles and ignore the fact that my chest feels as if it's about to explode. This is good for me, I tell myself firmly. It's healthy.

I glance at my reflection in the mirror opposite. I have a sweat helmet. My face is puce. My eyeballs are bloodshot and look as if they are about to burst from their sockets, like something out of a bad zombie movie. I don't think I've ever looked more unhealthy. Or more unattractive.

Thank God no one in here knows me, I think with a flash of relief. At least that's one good thing about being new in town. You're totally anonymous. You're not going to bump into someone you know.

No sooner has the thought fired through my brain than in the mirror opposite I see someone climb on to the running machine next to me.

My stomach drops. Literally plummets, like someone's just chucked me out of an aeroplane. Without a parachute.

Oh God, no. Please, no. It can't be . . .

But it is.

Nate.

For a moment I think I'm seeing things. It's impossible. There's unlucky and there's *unlucky*. Stunned, I stare at him in his shorts and vest, my brain not really computing. Is someone playing a trick on me? Am I on *Candid Camera*? I glance around quickly, then realise what I'm doing and pull myself together. It's just a coincidence, remember? Unfortunate, admittedly, but still a coincidence.

Pretending I haven't seen him, I surreptitiously reduce the speed on my machine. With any luck I can sneak out before he sees me and make my escape.

Out of the corner of my eye I can see him limbering up, stretching out his calf muscles, flexing his arms, bending sideways, back and forwards.

Oh, for God's sake, just get on with it. Show-off!

Then, unexpectedly, I feel a kick of stubbornness. Hang on a minute, why should I leave? I was here first! I've got as much right to be here as he has! Followed by a swell of competitiveness. Right, I'll show him.

Straightening up, I stick out my chest and start striding breezily, my feet bounding on the pedals like I'm taking a walk in the park, and isn't it wonderful? Next to me I can hear the machine starting up and feet pounding. I try not to look.

I keep staring straight ahead, but that's even worse as he's right in front of me, reflected in the mirror.

And there I am, right in front of him.

Catching sight of me, a look of shock flashes over his face, but he quickly recovers. 'Wow, fancy seeing you here,' he says tightly, in a way that says there's no 'fancy' about it.

'You too,' I say curtly, still striding out.

I feel like we're speaking in break-up language. There should be a phrase book, *Learn Break-Up*, in which common phrases could be translated from English. For example, in break-up a phrase like 'Fancy seeing you here' would be 'What the fuck are you doing here?' Then 'See you around' would be 'Over my dead body.' A simple word like 'Hi' would be 'Fuck, fuck, fuck!'

It would make things so much easier. You'd be speaking break-up in no time!

'So, I didn't know you were a member of this gym,' he says casually.

Also translated as 'What the fuck are you doing here?'

As you can see, in break-up many of the common phrases mean the same thing. It's a bit like Eskimos have a million different words for 'ice' when we've got just one. In break-up that one word is usually 'fuck'.

'I'm just trying it out,' I say, aiming to sound nonchalant. 'Seeing if it's up to my . . . er . . . usual standard.' I promptly jab a few buttons on the control pad in front as if I know exactly how it works. 'What are you doing here? I thought you had your own machine.'

Translated: 'Bugger off! I look like a big sweaty lump, I haven't got a clue what I'm doing on this dratted machine, which is now making a weird vibrating noise, and the last person on earth I want to see is you.'

'I like to mix it up,' he says.

'Oh, right, yeah . . . mix it up.' I nod, as if I'm always mixing things up.

There's a pause, and then . . .

'Look, about the other day, I said a few things I shouldn't have . . .' He trails off and his eyes sweep to my thighs.

I feel a stab of mortification. 'Yes, well, we both did,' I say hastily. I stare determinedly ahead, but out of the corner of my eye I can't help noticing he's barely breaking a sweat, while I'm starting to sound like a heavy breather on the telephone.

Taking a swig from my water bottle, I try to concentrate on my breathing – I remember reading an article about that once, though I'm not exactly sure what I'm supposed to be concentrating on. I mean, it's just in and then out, isn't it?

He's getting faster now, but I keep pace. See, I can do it. Though my legs are beginning to feel a bit like jelly. Did my knees just wobble? Oh shit, and now my machine seems to be starting to incline. Bollocks, what's going on? I glance down at my controls, trying to figure it out, then give up. It's too complicated. You'd have to be in Mensa to figure out all those buttons.

I can't believe it! Now he's speeded up!

Glancing up, I see Nate is springing along next to me at an alarming rate of knots. I take my eye off the ball for two seconds . . . Infuriated, I jab at the arrow marked, 'Up'. Aha! Take that!

I start striding harder – forward, back, forward, back – and swing my arms. Only the funny thing is, the machine doesn't seem to be getting any faster, just sort of *higher*. Flustered, I jab more buttons. I'm not going to let Nate win. I'm determined!

Sweat is now pouring down my face in rivulets, but I forge ahead. I'm picking up pace. I'm getting faster and faster. My feet are pumping furiously on the pedals. My heart is thumping in my chest. Next to me I can see Nate bounding along rhythmically. It's like a face-off. A dual. I glance at his controls.

He's on level 14!

I jab at mine. Up, up, up . . .

Suddenly I'm aware that my machine has started making a loud whining noise. Hang on a minute . . . alarm bells . . . Now it's going really fast . . . like really, *really* fast . . . like about ninety miles an hour . . . Oh God, and it's still getting higher and higher . . . I feel a stab of panic . . . How do I make it slow down . . .? How do I make it stop . . .?

Oh my God, oh my God, oh my—
Argggghhhhhhhhh!!!!!!

Chapter Nineteen

'Well, it's not broken.'

An hour later and I've left the gym and am en route to the gallery I wanted to visit, my phone wedged underneath my chin, my ankle twinging painfully. I'm talking to my sister, who called to see how my workout went. 'Oh, it certainly went,' I'd replied, limping out of the shower with an ankle the size of a watermelon. 'It nearly went all the way to Accident and Emergency.'

'Lucy, do you have to be so clumsy?' she's saying now, having spent the last fifteen minutes listening to how I'd gone flying off the cross-trainer, landed in a tangled mess by the rowing machine and had to be helped into the changing rooms by a very sweet personal trainer called Rudy, who'd advised me against 'trying to run before you can walk when it comes to fitness'.

The word 'embarrassing' doesn't even come close.

'I'm not clumsy,' I refute holy, pausing to check my pop-up map before continuing down a busy side street. 'It was Nate's fault.'

'Nate? What's it got to do with him?'

Up until this moment I'd avoided mentioning his involvement in my humiliating debacle. Partly because I was feeling sorry for myself and wanted some sympathy from my big sister – which is akin to being a contestant on *Dragons' Den* and hoping Duncan Bannatyne might take pity on you – and partly because I hadn't got round to that bit.

'Well, you're never going to believe it,' I gasp, 'but he was on the machine next to me at the gym. God, it was so embarrassing. He even tried apologising—'

'See! I told you!' She cuts me off, sounding triumphant. 'He's trying to make amends and find a way to get back with you!'

Oh God, she's still banging on about that. 'No way!' I refute, wincing as another pain shoots through my ankle. 'He looked as horrified to see me as I was to see him.' I pause to rub my ankle. 'How would he know I was at the gym, anyway?'

'He heard you talking about it in the sushi restaurant,' she fires back without missing a beat. 'It's perfectly viable.'

Now I know why my sister is such a successful lawyer.

'Viable, yes. Realistic, no. Trust me when I tell you that Nate did not look like a man who wants to get back together.'

'Well, what other explanation do you have?'

I pause, my mind momentarily throwing up something Robyn said about the legend.

'Sorry, Luce, I've got a call on the other line,' Kate suddenly says. 'It's the CEO from the loan-out company. Speak later.' And before I can say anything, she promptly hangs up.

Five minutes later I arrive at the address of the gallery to discover a hive of activity. Swarms of people gather outside on the tree-lined street, and the balmy air is filled with the sounds of laughter, chatter and the clinking of glasses. It's a sleek, expensive crowd, but then this is a sleek, expensive gallery.

Located in Chelsea, along with all the major blue-ribbon galleries, what used to be a garage is now this huge, lofty space that is home to big names like Damien Hirst and is famous for exhibiting large-scale installations.

Basically it makes Number Thirty-Eight look like my sitting room, I muse, making my way through the perfumed crowds and stepping inside. Huge white spaces. Huge impressive pieces of art. Huge price tags. Glancing in my catalogue at the price of one particular painting, I do a double-take at the number of zeros at the end. Nope, that's not a typo.

Tonight's opening is a showcase for a new rising star that I'd read about in one of the press releases we'd received at work and I was curious to come along. The artist is just a few years older than me. I know because I did that thing I always do when I read about an artist: I check their date of birth. It's silly, but if they're older, it somehow gives me comfort that I still have time.

Time for what? To have my own exhibition?

I bring myself up sharply. Even now it's like there's a tiny, secret part of me left that's still clinging to that dream. As if I can't fully let go.

I start making my way around the gallery. That's one of the great perks of my job: I get to hear about all the shows and can usually bag a free invite. Well, it was Magda who's bagged me the free invite, along with one for herself, but she wasn't able to come. She had to pay a visit to her elderly aunt, who's recently moved into a nursing home.

At the thought of Magda, I feel a twinge of anxiety. The last few days she's had this worried look about her. She won't say why, and whenever I've asked if everything is OK, she's replied with her usual 'Wonderful, wonderful', but I know everything is far from wonderful, and I know it's because the gallery isn't selling as many pieces as it should. In fact, despite our opening last weekend to drum up business, the only paintings we've sold recently are the ones Nate bought.

Nate. As his name pops into my head, I quickly shoo it back out again. No, I don't want to think about him. I've had quite enough of him. My ankle throbs painfully and I grimace. *Go on, scoot.*

A waitress wafts by with a tray of champagne. I accept a glass and take a sip. Savouring the cold bubbles, I glance around me. Now, what shall I look at first . . .?

Instead of my eyes landing on a piece of artwork, they land on a familiar figure in a baseball cap and faded T-shirt and jeans, hovering by one of the waitresses, who's carrying a tray of canapés. He's got his back to me, but I recognise him immediately.

The gallery crasher.

'Hi there.' Going up to him, I tap him on the shoulder.

He turns round and, seeing me, holds up his hands in surrender. In one is a glass of champagne, in the other a vol-au-vent. 'Guilty as charged,' he declares, grinning, before I can say anything.

'So how is it?' I smile.

I'm surprised by how pleased I am to see him. That's only because I'm here on my own, I decide quickly. At events like these it's always nice to see a familiar face, regardless of who it is.

'The art or the champagne?' he asks, his eyes twinkling with amusement.

'Both,' I laugh.

'Hmm, well . . .' He takes a sip from his glass and rolls it around his mouth. 'I'd say the champagne is pretty damn good, better than the last opening I went to . . .'

I shoot him a look. 'And the art?' I raise my eyebrows enquiringly.

He looks sheepish. 'I haven't looked yet.'

'Adam!' I cry, and whack him on the arm.

'You remembered my name.' He seems surprised.

'Um . . . yeah, my memory's not that bad.' I laugh self-consciously, suddenly feeling awkward. 'I think I need to hit you harder.' I try rescuing myself by resorting to violence a second time and punching his arm again.

'Ow, no.' He winces, rubbing his arm. 'I bruise like a peach.'

'Serves you right.' I smile ruefully. 'I can't believe you haven't bothered to look at any of the installations. They're supposed to be amazing.'

'I was waiting for you,' he says simply.

'Me?' Now I'm the one to look surprised. Not just by his answer, but by my stomach, which unexpectedly flips over like a pancake.

'Well, I figured you might show up, being such an art lover . . .' He trails off, smiling, and I can't tell if he's teasing me or not. 'I thought I'd wait for you to talk me through it. You did such a good job last time.'

So it's just because I know about art, I realise, feeling curiously deflated.

'Compliments aren't going to get you off the hook,' I say, quickly hiding my disappointment. 'Anyway, it's your turn.'

He looks at me, his eyes narrowed, as if now he thinks I'm the one teasing him.

'You want me to take you to a movie?'

'Wasn't that the deal?'

Abruptly I catch myself. Lucy Hemmingway, are you *flirting*? At the realisation I feel my cheeks flush. I am. *I'm flirting.* What on earth's got into me?

'Well, in that case, leave it to me . . .' He nods and chews his lip, clearly deep in thought.

'OK, whatever,' I say with a sort of noncommittal shrug, as if I'm not really bothered either way. Well, I don't want him getting the wrong impression and thinking I *fancy* him or anything ridiculous like that. Because I don't. Obviously.

We start moving around the gallery.

In fact, thinking about it, I wasn't really flirting. I was just being friendly. And jokey. Yes, that's it, friendly and jokey.

'Gosh, I'm starving,' I exclaim, trying to be all jolly and normal and steering the conversation on to something safe. Spotting a waitress, I help myself to a tiny wafer elaborately piled with slivers of lots of things I'm not sure I know the names of. I pop it into my mouth in one go. Well, it was really tiny. 'Mmm, this is delicious,' I murmur. 'You should try one,' I tell Adam.

'I've already had half a dozen.' He grins, swapping his empty champagne flute for a full one. 'But I suppose another couple wouldn't hurt.' Helping himself to more, we come to a standstill in front of a large red metal and mirror sculpture.

'So what exactly is it?' asks Adam, after a moment's pause.

I glance in the catalogue. 'It's called *Minanga*.'

'Meaning?' Glancing at me sideways, he looks at me expectantly.

'I have no idea,' I confess with a giggle.

His face creases up into a smile, making his eyes crinkle around the edges. 'How about getting some fresh air?'

'Good idea.'

We weave our way through the clusters of people, out on to the pavement and further along the street, until we reach the edge of the crowd, where it's quieter.

For a moment we both stand there, sipping our drinks. Then, after a long pause, Adam says, 'So, is your boyfriend coming here tonight?' with what feels like feigned nonchalance.

My chest tightens and I pretend to study the bubbles in my glass, but I can feel his gaze upon me. 'We broke up,' I say, forcing my voice to sound casual.

I sneak a look at his reaction. I might be imagining it, but I'm sure I see surprised happiness flash across his face. A split second and then it's gone and we're back to the feigned nonchalance.

'Oh, what happened?'

At least I think it's feigned nonchalance. Perhaps it really *is* nonchalance and he's not bothered and I'm reading this all wrong.

I suddenly feel about twelve years old again and confused about whether Robert Pickles likes *me* or he's kicking my chair in maths simply because he likes *kicking my chair*. I never did find out, but you'd think after all these years I would have learned something, discovered a few tricks, got better at this body-language stuff.

Instead I'm still completely rubbish, I think, feeling a stab of frustration. If only men were like New York taxi-cabs and had a light that they can switch on when they're interested and off when they're not available. Then you'd know exactly where you were and you wouldn't have to worry about getting it wrong and being horribly embarrassed.

Like now. I look at Adam. Is his light on or off?

For safety's sake, I go for the 'light off' option.

'It didn't work out.' I shrug.

Well, I'm hardly going to tell him the truth, am I? That I thought Nate was my soulmate. That we thought we couldn't live without each other, only to realise that we couldn't live *with* each other. And that we ended up having a huge row during which he said unspeakable things about my thighs and I made a hurtful comment about his receding hairline.

Exactly.

I think I'm going to stick with 'It didn't work out.'

'Sorry to hear that,' says Adam quietly.

'Thanks.' I give him a rueful smile, but somewhere deep inside I don't want him to be sorry to hear that I've broken up with Nate – I want him to be pleased I'm single.

Hang on, *what* did I just think?

As the realisation strikes, it suddenly triggers two more thoughts: 1) If I'm one of those cabs, my light has just been flicked on and 2) What on earth is that noise?

Abruptly I'm distracted by sounds coming from a shop across the street. I hadn't noticed it before. It's one of those stores that sells electrical goods and its window is filled with a jumble of toasters, kettles, hi-fis and TV sets, each showing the same programme. I look at them now, all the different screens ablaze with identical giant graphics, and there's a blasting sound of jingling theme music. Even from across the street I can hear the singsong voices booming out, '*Big Bucks* means big bucks!'

Big Bucks? Hang on a minute, that's the name of one of Nate's game shows, the one that, rather appropriately given its name, made him all his money. He told me about it one night when we were in bed, about how it was one of the most lucrative and popular on TV. At the time I didn't pay much attention – to be honest, I was more interested in what was under the covers than cash prizes – but now . . .

Now I watch, mesmerised, as a cheesy presenter bounds on to each and every screen, his neon-white teeth flashing, and feel myself recoil.

'Lucy?'

I tune back in. 'Oh, sorry, I got distracted,' I fluster, turning back to Adam.

'You OK?' He's looking at me quizzically.

'Sorry . . . yeah, I'm fine.' I smile, shrugging it off.

Bloody Nate, he's everywhere. If I'm not bumping into him, I'm being reminded of him. It's like there's no escape.

'Oh good, because I was going to ask you . . . um . . . if you'd like to . . .' He shuffles his feet self-consciously.

I feel a leap of nervous excitement. Oh my God, I think he's going to ask me out.

'Hey, it's Lucy, isn't it?'

Suddenly we're interrupted by a loud voice and I feel my heart plummet. Oh, no, go away. Whoever you are, go away!

'Yeah, it is you!'

I pretend I haven't heard. 'You were saying . . .' I prompt Adam, looking at him expectantly, but it's no good. The mood is broken.

'I think that guy knows you,' he says, gesturing behind me.

Hiding my crushing disappointment, I turn round and come face to face with a short man in a shiny suit, beaming at me. He looks familiar, but for a moment I can't place him—

'The TV party, the other evening. I said how cute your dress was . . .' He jogs my memory.

'Oh, hi . . . Brad?'

Of course, he was the creep who kept putting his arm round my waist and told one bad joke after another.

'Brad by name, bad by nature.' He laughs and lights his cigarette.

I falter. Normally conversations go back and forth, but there really is no answer to that. In desperation, I grab hold of Adam. 'Have you two met? This is my friend Adam. Adam, this is Brad.'

If I was hoping to be saved by this introduction, I'm wrong. Instead Brad grunts and shakes hands before immediately turning back to me. 'So, how's Nathaniel?'

I cannot believe this.

'Oh . . . um, I think he's OK.'

'He's an awesome guy. You make a really great couple.'

This is a bad dream. Any minute now I'm going to wake up.

'Well, actually—' I begin, but he cuts me off by turning to Adam.

'Seriously, they are so cute together.'

Oh my God. Make it stop. Please. For the love of God. Please make it stop.

'I'm just going to get a top-up,' says Adam, and moves away before I can stop him.

Fuck.

I think about draining my drink and following him, but I'm not quick enough, I realise, with dismay. Reluctantly I turn back to Brad, who's now droning on about himself. I try to look interested – 'Uh-huh ... really? ... Uh-huh ...' – but ten minutes later and I'm still caught in this stranglehold of a conversation. I keep smiling and nodding, but on the inside I'm crying with frustration. This is all Nate's fault. He completely sabotaged it for me. One minute I thought Adam was going to ask me out on a date, and the next up popped Brad and ruined it.

Talk about bad timing. I glance desperately over Brad's shoulder to see if I can see Adam. He's been gone ages. Where is he?

Then I spot him. Over by the entrance to the gallery. He's smoking a roll-up and *talking to a girl*. My heart thuds. A very pretty brunette. Heads bent low, they're deep in conversation, and I see her lightly touching his arm. My stomach lurches. Who is she? Jealousy stabs, followed by a crushing sense of disappointment as I watch them break into raucous laughter. They look intimate, comfortable, *together*.

'I'm sorry, will you excuse me?' Abruptly I cut Brad off mid-sentence.

'Oh ... yeah, sure.' He nods, slightly taken aback.

I turn away before Adam sees me looking, and quickly slipping away through the crowd, I hurry into the night.

'You're home early.'

I arrive back at the apartment to find Robyn sitting cross-legged on the floor of the living room, surrounded by piles of magazines.

'Yeah.' I nod glumly, plopping myself on to the sofa.

'How's your ankle?'

'Painful.' I wince, slipping off my sandal and rubbing my ankle. It's gone all puffy and a large purple bruise is starting to form.

'I've got some arnica gel for that.' Scrabbling around on the coffee table, on which more magazines are strewn, she unearths a tube. 'Rub it on three times a day and you'll be as good as new,' she instructs, passing it to me.

'Thanks.' I smile gratefully, then watch as she grabs a pair of scissors and starts attacking a magazine. 'What are you doing?' I ask curiously.

'Making a vision board.' She holds up a large piece of foam board on which she's pasted various magazine cuttings. There's a chocolate-box country cottage with roses around the door, some rosy-cheeked children, a couple of rescue dogs that look similar to Simon and Jenny. Across the top she's cut out letters that spell the words 'Harold' and 'soulmate'.

'I thought you'd done one of those already.'

'It didn't work, so I'm doing another one,' she says matter-of-factly.

I pause. I'm sure there's logic in there somewhere.

'This is the house I want to live in. These are all the children I'm going to have.' She starts pointing to the various pictures. 'These are my dogs.'

'And where's Harold?' I ask, playing along.

'Well, that's the thing – I can't quite decide. What do you think about this one?' She holds up a magazine, which is turned to an advertisement for aftershave, featuring a tall, dark-haired man in a suit.

'Er, yeah, he looks fine.' I nod, trying not to think about what we're actually discussing here.

'Oh good. I think so too.' She grabs the scissors and energetically cuts him out. Reaching for her Pritt Stick, she glues him slap bang in the middle of the board.

'You've cut out his face,' I point out, looking at the stranger, who now has a blank space where his face should be.

'Of course.' She nods, as if that's absolutely normal and not verging on serial-killer behaviour. 'We don't know what Harold looks like yet, do we?' Wielding her scissors, she continues flicking through the magazine. 'So I'll leave it empty until I do.' She glances up at me, bits of paper sticking to her hair, making her look like a crazy woman. 'It makes perfect sense.'

'Right, yes, perfect sense,' I agree, somewhat dubiously.

'Oh by the way, I've just remembered I've got something for you.' Rummaging around under all the magazines, she unearths an envelope. 'Theatre tickets!'

'Wow, that's great, thanks.' I smile, taking them from her.

'Who are going to take with you?' she asks, trying to sound nonchalant.

I hesitate. I know she still thinks I should take Nate, especially after what happened in the gym, which she declared was a 'sign' that the universe was trying to keep us together, that the legend was working its magic.

I agree. It was a sign. A sign exercise and I don't mix.

'No one,' I say defiantly. Briefly my mind flicks to Adam. I would have liked to have asked him, but after seeing him with the brunette . . . I force my mind to flick back again. 'I'm going to put it on eBay, auction it off for charity,' I say decisively.

Immediately her face lights up. 'Oh, Lucy, what an awesome idea.' She grins, all thoughts of Nate suddenly forgotten. 'I know just the one. It's an orang-utan sanctuary that I worked at when I was in Borneo.'

'Perfect.' I smile, stifling a hippo-sized yawn. It's been a long day, and not exactly one of my best. To tell the truth, I just want to go to bed and forget all about it. 'Well, I think I'll call it a day.' I haul myself off the sofa.

'OK, night.' Throwing me a little wave, she turns back to her vision board. 'How many "t"s in "serendipity"? One or two?'

I pause in the doorway. 'Um, one, I think.'

'Cool, thanks,' she mutters, and grabs her Pritt Stick and scissors. I leave her chopping up pages with a vengeance.

Fifteen minutes later I'm lying in bed with my laptop. Forget men, I want to marry my MacBook. It's dependable, reliable and you can even go shopping with it, I think, clicking on to eBay.

I go to the section marked, 'Sell,' and type in the description: 'One ticket for Broadway play to see performance of *Tomorrow's*

Lives.' I add a few details, then post the listing. Hopefully someone will bid on it, I muse, searching for things to bid on myself.
I'd really like a new bag ... I start looking through the vintage
section. Usually I can spend hours like this, but tonight my heart's
not in it. Instead my mind keeps sliding back to the gallery and
Adam. I feel a beat of sadness. I didn't even say goodbye.

Regret gnaws. I wonder what he's doing now. Probably with
the pretty brunette, I remind myself. In fact, they're probably
somewhere right now, having fun, while I'm here in bed with
my laptop husband. I stare distractedly at the ceiling and listen
to the droning hum of the fan on my windowsill.

Before I can sink even further into gloom, I'm distracted by
the ping of an email plopping into my inbox. I look at it absently.
It's from Facebook.

Adam Shea sent you a message on Facebook.

It's like someone suddenly plugged me into the mains. Adam!
The Adam. Adam-who's-suddenly-switched-my-light-back-on-
in-my-cab *Adam*?

Suddenly galvanised, I click on it and it takes me to Facebook
and his profile picture. I peer at it closely. It's a photo of him in
a silly hat and glasses. It's a good sign. You can tell a lot from
Facebook pictures. Anyone who has a black-and-white head-
shot, or a picture of themselves posing in a bikini (women), or
looking bare-chested and moody (men) is slightly worrisome.

As are all those people who have over hundreds and hundreds
of friends. I mean, they're not *real* friends, they're just people
they met randomly in a club one night, or in a queue at Tesco ...

I look at Adam's profile. He has fifty-seven friends – not
too few, not too many, just perfect, I think happily, feeling like
Goldilocks.

**Now it's my turn. Interested in seeing a really good film? You
disappeared before I could ask you. Say yes and all you have
to do is bring the popcorn.**

I stare at the message, feeling a mixture of delight and excitement. That will teach me to jump to conclusions about pretty brunettes. Quickly I type, 'Yes,' then smiling happily to myself, I snuggle down into my pillows and am about to log off when suddenly I notice a status update:

Nathaniel Kennedy is feeling on top of the world.

My ankle twinges in annoyance. Argh, is there no getting away from him? Quick! I need to defriend him.

I click on 'Remove from friends' and he's gone.

Chapter Twenty

Except it's not that easy.

Unfortunately real life isn't like cyberspace – I can't just press delete and erase him – and over the next few days Nate keeps popping up everywhere. Not a literal *boom!* he's right there in the flesh and standing next to me on the subway. Just small, random, apparently inconsequential things that by themselves seem like coincidences . . . but put together are starting to seem really *weird*.

Like, for example, I keep getting missed calls from him on my mobile. At first I just ignored them, but when one woke me up at 5 a.m., I finally called him back and demanded what he wanted.

'Nothing,' he replied angrily, before swearing blind he hadn't rung me and it must have been an accident.

'What? Twelve times?' I huffed, before telling him he needed to learn how to lock his iPhone and hanging up.

Which by itself isn't that bizarre. After all, who hasn't sat on their phone and accidentally dialled someone, or answered a call from a friend only to hear their footsteps walking down the street?

What *was* bizarre was Nate calling me back the next day complaining that I was calling him! Which is impossible, 'as my phone was locked', I told him indignantly. Only later, when I checked my call log, sure enough there were all these calls to his number.

Then there was this funny incident when Magda sent me uptown in a cab to fetch some 'supplies' from her friend Dr Rosenbaum, a peculiar-looking man in a white coat who has a pink, shiny face that doesn't move and huge offices overlooking the park. It was all very cloak and dagger. After punching in a secret code, I was ushered inside, asked to hand over the cash and given a bag of creams and potions. I felt as if we were doing a drug deal. Not that I've ever *done* a drug deal, but anyway, that wasn't the strange part. The strange part was on the way back.

One minute everything was totally normal. I was trundling along in the cab and the driver was cursing away on his phone in what sounded like Russian, when suddenly the engine spluttered loudly and we broke down. Guess *where* we broke down? Right outside Nate's apartment. I mean *right* outside. As if that wasn't enough of a coincidence, it was at *exactly* the same time as Nate was leaving the building! I had duck down on the back seat so he didn't see me. A few seconds more and it would have been too late. How weird was that?

And it doesn't stop there. Every time I turn on the TV, he's on it. Admittedly not him personally, but *Big Bucks* is always playing. What's even worse, I've now got the jingle in my head and I can't stop humming it. It's like there's no escaping him. It's the same with the radio. Only this time it's Bob Marley's 'No Woman, No Cry', which used to be 'our' song. Every time I hear it, it reminds me of Nate.

I haven't heard it for years. Normally it's Lady Gaga and Fergie and Katy Perry. Now suddenly, these past few days, every time I flick on the radio, it seems to be on every station. It's totally freaky.

So freaky that it gets me thinking about all the other things that have niggled me recently but which I've brushed off. Like Nate's confession that he had a strange desire to walk into our gallery one day, *for no apparent reason*, discovering that we'd been going to the same places for years and kept missing each other, both of us finding the pendants again, even though mine had been lost for years.

As one thought trips over another, like a row of dominoes, my mind starts whirring ... bumping into him in the street after we'd broken up, sitting next to him at the sushi restaurant, the incident at the gym – Manhattan's small, but not *that* small – and then the other night at the gallery, seeing all the TV screens tuned to his game show as I was talking to Adam, then Brad suddenly appearing just as Adam was about to ask me out on a date, mentioning Nate's name and making him disappear . . .

If I was superstitious, I'd almost think there was some higher force trying to stop me from going out with anyone else.

I'm not superstitious, though. I don't believe in all that rubbish, I tell myself firmly. OK, so I admit, I read my horoscope now and again, and yes, it's true, I once saw a fortune-teller, but it was years ago at a school fête and of course *I knew* all along it was Mrs Cooper, the chemistry teacher, dressed up in a belly dancer's outfit. There's absolutely no way I would ever be like Robyn and believe in something silly like, for example, a legend about eternal love. Just because I'm Googling it doesn't mean that I'm starting to have these completely insane thoughts about it coming true.

I type, 'Legend of the Bridge of Sighs,' and hit return. A page opens up:

> Local Venetian legend tells that lovers who exchange a kiss as they pass beneath the Bridge of Sighs by gondola at sunset while the bells of St Mark's are ringing will be guaranteed ever-lasting love and nothing will break them apart. For the rest of eternity they will never be parted.

Because, like I said, it's just insane. Ridiculous. Completely bananas. Hurriedly clicking off the page, I have a quick peek at Facebook to see if Adam has replied to my message, but instead all I notice is Nate. He's still there on my homepage! He's still my Facebook friend! I stare at his photograph with a mixture of disbelief and incredulity.

Feeling a seed of panic, I frantically hit my keyboard. *Delete! Delete! Delete!*

'It's like I can't break up with him.'

Fast-forward to the weekend and I'm in a nail bar the size of a letterbox, in Chinatown. It's Saturday afternoon, and together with Robyn and Kate, I'm ensconced in a massage chair, having my hands and feet attended to by two tiny Vietnamese ladies, who are furiously filing, clipping, cutting and scrubbing, while chattering away nineteen to the dozen.

This is my first time, but apparently this is a weekly ritual for every self-respecting female New Yorker. That probably explains the shocked reaction my nails received when I arrived. Do-it-yourself mani-pedis might suffice back in London, but in Manhattan it's a totally different story.

'What do you mean, you can't break up with him?' says Kate, not looking up from her BlackBerry, on which she's managing to type a work email with her free hand.

'I mean I can't get rid of him. He's everywhere I look.'

'Manhattan's a small place. Just ignore him,' she responds flatly.

'It's not that easy,' I try explaining.

'Yes, it is. I'm always bumping into my rival CEO from Lloyds Carter. Last night I even saw him at the doctor's.'

One of the Vietnamese women doing her nails slaps Kate's hand away from her BlackBerry. Frowning, Kate swaps hands and keeps typing with her thumb.

'No, it's more than that—' I break off. 'What were you doing at the doctor's?'

'Oh, I was with Jeff. He still hasn't kicked that bug. They think he might have some kind of virus.'

'What do you mean, it's more than that?' asks Robyn, glancing up from the book she's reading, *Cosmic Thinking Made Easy*. She's having tiny glittery flowers applied to each of her toenails.

'Well, it's not just about bumping into him. It's about all these little things that keep happening.'

'Such as?' Robyn studies me with interest.

'Such as I can't defriend him on Facebook,' I grumble with annoyance. 'It's been three days now and every time I log on, I'm greeted with his status update and profile picture.'

'What is it with everyone and this Facebook crap?' Kate

suddenly looks up from her BlackBerry. 'I don't have time for Facebook, yet I keep getting emails from friends saying they want to poke me!' She rolls her eyes in annoyance.

'I told you already. It's the power of the universe holding you together,' chimes Robyn, as if it's perfectly obvious.

Kate looks at her with open-mouthed scorn.

'It's true,' Robyn says indignantly. 'It's the legend of the Bridge of Sighs. Nothing can break them apart.'

'Have you been on the crystals again?' snorts my sister.

'It's true!'

'What a load of codswallop!'

'I don't know what that word means,' replies Robyn, her face flushing, 'but you know, you really need to open your mind.'

'I'm very open-minded, thank you very much. I'm just not insane,' retorts Kate dismissively. 'It's not the universe keeping them together – it's Nate! It's so obvious. He's trying to get back together with Lucy!'

I glance between my sister and my roommate hammering it out like boxers. There's Kate, in the rational-non-believing-bordering-on-completely-cynical corner, and there's Robyn, in the irrational-believe-in-anything-bordering-on-completely-away-with-the-fairies corner.

And me?

I'm somewhere in the middle. I swap corners. I go back and forth. I mean, Kate's right, she must be, and yet . . .

My mind throws up a memory of my conversation with Nate in the restaurant when we first got back together. The discovery that for all those years we'd been at the same events, it was almost as if something was trying to bring us together.

Something that now won't let us break apart.

Like the legend of the Bridge of Sighs.

As the thought zips through my mind, a shiver runs up my spine.

Which is ridiculous. Just ridiculous. There is no 'something'. It's just a silly legend. A bit of make-believe for the tourists.

I'm letting my imagination run away with itself. This isn't *The Twilight Zone*; this is real life. Things like that can't really happen. Can they?

I notice the magazine that's lying open in my lap. I took it from the dog-eared pile when I arrived and I've been absently flicking through it, but now suddenly I stop short. Because there, on the page, is a quiz. 'Is He the One?'

I inhale sharply.

'What's wrong?' My sister stops arguing with Robyn and glances over. 'Is it your cuticles? I always ask them not to cut mine.'

I shake my head dumbly and hold up the magazine. 'It's *that* quiz,' I say, my voice almost a whisper.

Robyn's eyes widen. Then, in the kind of voice they use for movie trailers, she says solemnly, 'It's a sign.'

Kate glances between us, her face incredulous. 'No, it's not a sign!' she says crossly. Leaning across, she snatches the magazine out of my hands roughly. 'It's an out-of-date copy of bloody *Cosmo*!' Tossing it in the bin, she shakes her head in exasperation. 'Honestly, you two!'

'You need to stop the legend coming true,' continues Robyn, ignoring Kate. 'You need to break the spell.'

'Spell?' Kate snorts loudly.

'It's more like a curse,' I mutter sulkily.

'Whatever.' Robyn clicks her tongue. 'You need to be exorcised.'

'Don't we all?' quips Kate, unable to resist the double-entendre.

'I said exorcised, not exercised,' says Robyn snippily.

'Whatever,' shrugs Kate. 'Jeff's not interested in either these days.'

She laughs dryly, but my antennae pick up on something and I glance over. Kate often makes jokey, sarcastic remarks about her relationship, but today there's something in her voice that's different.

'Is everything OK, Kate?'

She meets my gaze and I can almost visibly see her put up her defences. 'Yeah, fine,' she says flippantly. 'Why wouldn't it be?'

'With you and Jeff, I mean.'

She stiffens. 'Of course. He's just still got this bug, that's all. I reckon he needs some antibiotics, but you know what men are like with taking pills.' She shrugs brusquely. 'It's nothing.'

'Oh . . .OK.' I quickly drop it. I know better than to try to push my sister. If a subject is closed, it's locked, bolted and secured, and no one but no one is getting in.

'Right, finished.' One of the ladies doing my manicure and pedicure taps my leg lightly.

'Gosh, they look amazing.' I smile, wiggling my shell-pink fingers and toes in delight. They don't look like they belong to me. I'm used to having hands that are chipped, chewed or paint-splattered, but now they've been transformed into groomed New York hands.

I proudly waggle them at Robyn and Kate. 'Look!'

'Ooh, gorgeous, look at mine,' gushes Robyn, waggling her glittery toes so that the tiny flowers catch the light.

'Mmm, lovely,' I enthuse, and we spend the next few moments comparing, before remembering Kate. 'What about yours?' I ask, turning to her, but she's already putting on her sandals.

'They're fine.' She nods briskly, fastening a buckle. 'I just had clear polish, like usual.'

My sister is no fun sometimes.

'If you would like to pay . . .' The owner of the nail bar, a matri-archal figure in flowery pinafore, who's even tinier than all the other Vietnamese ladies, gestures impatiently towards the cash register and the long queue of women waiting for our chairs.

'Oh, sorry, yes.' Hastily I climb out of the chair and begin rummaging around in my bag. I fish out my purse. As I do, I hear a clink as something falls to the floor.

Probably loose change, I muse, handing over a twenty-dollar bill. Twenty dollars for a manicure and pedicure! Oh, how I love New York.

'Miss, you dropped this.'

I see one of the Vietnamese ladies picking something up off

the floor. She holds out what looks like a quarter.

'Oh, thank you so much.' I smile and go to take it from her, then abruptly realise it's not a quarter. It's a coin. In fact, *it's half a coin.*

My stomach goes into freefall.

'That's impossible.' I stare at it dumbly in the flat of my palm, my mind reeling.

'What is it now?' Kate looks at me uncomprehendingly.

'My pendant,' I stammer, holding it out. The chain has gone, but there's no mistake, it's definitely my pendant.

Robyn inhales sharply. 'But I saw you throw it away . . .'

'In the park,' I finish. 'I know, it's impossible.' I stare at the broken coin, my thumb running along the jagged edge. 'There must be some mix-up. It must have got caught on my clothing . . . dropped into my bag accidentally . . . got lost somehow.' I look back at both Robyn and Kate. For once my sister isn't saying anything. Instead she's staring at me, wide-eyed and silent with astonishment.

I can't ignore it any longer. I can't persuade myself it's not happening. Because as weird and incredible and crazy as it might be, there's something going on here, something very weird. I don't know what to call it, and I don't understand it, but there's no denying it: the legend is coming true.

Despite the heat, a chill brushes over me and goose bumps prickle my arms.

Oh God.

What do I do now?

Chapter Twenty-One

Just like when we were kids, my big sister comes to the rescue.

'You need a strategy,' she instructs, drawing herself up to full lawyer mode.

'Oh, you mean like reading her horoscope?' suggests Robyn brightly.

Kate throws her a withering look. 'No, I mean a plan of action to achieve a particular goal,' she explains briskly. 'We use them all the time in law. We have to apply one to your situation by creating a systematic approach to solving this current problem and methodically working through the aims until the desired outcome is accomplished.'

I look at her blankly. 'Can you say that again, but in English this time?'

She tuts impatiently. 'It's perfectly simple. You want to break up with Nathaniel, but something or someone appears to be preventing this from happening properly.'

'Like the legend,' pipes up Robyn.

'Or Nathaniel himself,' retorts Kate, who after a brief moment of astonishment has swiftly gone back to her original opinion.

'Look, I don't care what it is. I just want it to be over.'

'OK, follow me. Let's get to work. Magical legend or no magical legend, this will do the trick. Trust me, no one is going to stick around after this. And I don't care what you say about your universe,' she adds, throwing Robyn a stern look. 'Universe schmooniverse.'

Robyn looks offended. 'You can't alter the course of destiny,' she says stiffly.

'Just you watch me.'

'It won't work. The laws of our world have no bearing on the laws of the universe.'

'So do you have a better plan?' scoffs Kate. 'What are you suggesting? Hocus-pocus? Crystals? Chinese herbs? We need to get aggressive and tough.'

'I just think you're being very closed off,' says Robyn sulkily.

'What do you expect? I'm a lawyer,' she deadpans. 'I'm not paid to have an imagination.'

Kate doesn't waste any time, and armed with a briefcase full of notepads, biros and her famous highlighter pens in every colour, she marches us to a nearby diner to prepare our case. I've never seen my sister in action before and I'm scarily impressed. Swiftly turning a red vinyl booth into an office, she rolls up her shirtsleeves, instructs the hapless waiter to 'keep the coffee coming' and starts talking tactics.

Six intensive hours later, and buzzing with a heady cocktail of caffeine and exhaustion, she finally comes up with the Strategy. Underlined twice, and highlighted in fluorescent orange, it runs into a four-page, twenty-five-point document and is entitled 'How to Get Rid of the One.'

1. Take out a restraining order.

This was Kate's immediate suggestion – 'Well, having a lawyer for a sister and a cop for a brother-in-law has to count for something,' she'd argued – before reluctantly conceding that the courts might take a dim view of our case: 'My Honourable Judge, I'm here to request a restraining order to prevent the defendant, Lucy Hemmingway, being stalked by the accused, Nathaniel Kennedy, as her friend on Facebook, through his TV show *Big Bucks* and by their song, Bob Marley's 'No Woman, No Cry', playing on the radio.'

Exactly.

Better is her idea that I turn up at his apartment unannounced and:

2. Tell him you love him.

A sure-fire winner if ever there was one. The plan being that I declare my undying love and – *poof* – watch him disappear for ever.

Just in case extra ammunition is needed:

```
3. Don't shave your legs beforehand.
```

So that I can turn up in a skirt.

```
4. Grow your underarm hair.
```

Better still, team it with a spaghetti-strap top.

```
5. In fact, go the whole hog and grow your
   bikini line too.
```

Then cross my legs Sharon Stone style.

```
6. Leave off the deodorant.
```

It doesn't sound like much, but right now in Manhattan it's ninety degrees. Sweaty armpits are one thing, but *hairy* sweaty armpits are quite another.

```
7. Talk about periods.
```

As in 'Gosh, I'm so exhausted, but that's because I'm *on my period.*' Be sure to throw in lots of words like menstruating, bleeding, cramps, bloating, water retention, PMT and acne.

```
8. Even better, use the loo and leave super-
   super-plus Tampax lying around.
```

Men have a fear of Tampax. Like dogs are scared of thunder. It sends them cowering.

```
 9. On second thoughts, make that super-super-
    plus sanitary pads.
```

Then tell him I've had 'an accident' and could he pop out to the store and buy the aforementioned large tampons. Pretty pleasey-weasey, pumpkin.

Which brings me to:

```
10. Give him a pet name, and speak in a baby-
    waby voice.
11. Say you want to get married and suggest
    looking at rings.
12. Start showering him with phone calls,
    emails and texts.
```

Reason being, he'll think I'm a bunny boiler and delete my number from his phone faster than you can say, '*Fatal Attraction.*' Result: I'll never get a misdialled call again.

```
13. Ask him how many lovers he's had.
```

Then double the amount and say that's how many I've had. No, triple it.

```
14. Turn up at a sports bar when he's there
    with his friends.
15. Be wearing a fleece.
```

Together with no make-up, hair scraped up in a bun and leggings. Make that unwashed baggy-at-the-bum leggings.

```
16. Proceed to tell all his friends hilarious
    anecdotes about erectile dysfunction/prema-
    ture ejaculation/small penises.
```

Nudge, nudge, wink, wink.

```
17. Be clingy.
```

Think limpet. Think Posh with Becks.

```
18. Fart.
19. Belch.
20. Pick your nose.
21. And then eat it.
```

OK, so it's pretty revolting, but it's like doing a Bushtucker Trial on *I'm a Celebrity...Get Me Out of Here!* Only in this case it's *I'm Lucy Hemmingway...Get Me Out of This Relationship!*

```
22. Coo at babies.
23. Steal his iPod and put music on it.
```

Suggestions: James Blunt's 'You're Beautiful', the *Mamma Mia* soundtrack, *The Best of Take That*.

```
24. Cancel his pay-per-view for the big game.
```

One of Robyn's clients works for Direct TV and can hack – I mean 'look into' – customers' accounts.

```
25. Buy bridal magazines.
```

And carry them with me at all times.

Just in case I should 'accidentally' bump into him again, I muse, peering round a bookshelf to make sure the coast is clear and Nate's not lurking.

It's the following Monday and I've popped into McKenzie's, my local bookstore, on my way to work. Navigating my way through the aisles stuffed full of paperbacks and signed hardbacks piled high on tables, I head over to the magazine section.

Gosh, I didn't realise there were so many, I think, staring at a smorgasbord of wedding publications displayed on the shelves. *Bride This*, *Wedding That* ... I grab a handful. Ooh, maybe I should pick up some baby ones too, I decide, pouncing on one with a picture of a pregnant woman, along with the caption 'Broody!'

Well, no, it doesn't *really* say that, but that's definitely what Nate will think if he sees it, I conclude, grabbing a copy. Fingers crossed the Strategy works. Kate is convinced that it will. 'I've never lost a case yet,' she'd said determinedly as she'd passed me a copy. At this point I'm so desperate I'm prepared to try anything.

My phone starts ringing. I glance at the screen. Nate. *Again.* I've already had half a dozen missed calls from him this morning. He's still insisting he's not calling me on purpose, and it's hard to know what to believe. I press reject. I sincerely hope this isn't the first case my sister loses ...

'Hi. Have you found everything you're looking for?' A smiley-faced assistant interrupts my thoughts.

'Yes, thanks.' I smile back.

'Getting ready for the big day?' She gestures towards the bridal magazines.

'Er, yes ... something like that.' I nod, clutching them tightly to my chest. The big day when I can forget all about Nate, I tell myself, feeling my phone buzzing in my pocket. Oh God, not again.

This time I pick up.

'Hi, Nate,' I say wearily.

'Lucy?' he asks resignedly. Despite what Kate says, he doesn't sound like a crazy stalker ex – he sounds as fed up as I am.

'Yup.'

There's a deep sigh.

'Bye.'

'Bye.'

I hang up. I don't know what to think, or who to believe – Robyn or Kate – so I'm taking the belt-and-braces approach.

'Well, if you need any help, my name's Emily.'

I turn back to the assistant. 'Thanks.' I start moving off towards the cash register, past the self-help books, when suddenly a section catches my eye: 'Love and Romance.' My eyes glide over the spines of the hundreds of books. There's even a whole shelf about the One: *How to Find the One, How to Keep the One, How to Know He's the One, Is He the One?*

'Actually . . .' I turn back to Emily, the smiley-faced assistant. She beams eagerly. 'Yes?'

'Do you have any books on how to get rid of the One?'

Arriving at Number Thirty-Eight ten minutes later, I'm surprised to find the gallery closed. That's odd. Where's Magda? Standing on the pavement clutching my magazines and obligatory extra-shot latte, I stare, perplexed, at the electronic grilles, tightly laced over the windows. Not once in the whole time I've been working here has Magda not been here to greet me. I check my watch. Knowing me, I've probably got the time completely wrong. But no, it's just a few minutes after 10 a.m.

Puzzled, I balance my coffee and magazines in one hand, fish my set of keys out of my bag and unlock the front door. As I step inside the darkened gallery, the alarm starts beeping, counting down its twenty seconds or whatever it is for me to punch in the code. For an instant I panic. Shit, what is it? Then it comes to me in a flash. Of course, Magda's date of birth – I remember her telling me once.

One, nine, six, five.

The alarm falls silent, and pressing the button for the window grilles, I flick on the lights. A blaze of colour bursts out of the shadows as the artwork is illuminated and I feel a rush of pleasure. There's something magical about being alone in a gallery. Once, when I was little, I remember losing my parents in the Louvre in Paris and finding myself alone in a room filled with paintings. Most kids would have probably been scared, started crying, tried frantically to find their mum and dad, but I can still recall that feeling of excitement, of being surrounded by all the different faces, characters, colours. It was like being lost in a world of imagination.

Unfortunately my mum took a rather different view of it and I remember getting severely ticked off when she finally found me and being made to stick by her side for the rest of the trip.

Scooping up the mail, I walk across to the reception desk and dump it, along with my magazines, on the counter. Sipping my coffee, I flick on the computer and check our emails. There's nothing much of interest . . . a few press releases, an enquiry about an internship from an art student, an invoice from the caterer we used for the gallery opening, entitled 'Unpaid. Urgent.' I frown. I thought Magda had sent a cheque for that last week. I feel a slight twinge of anxiety, but I brush it aside. It must just be an oversight. The cheque and the email must have crossed, that's all.

I look up from the computer, but still no sign of a golden beehive, so I click on to Facebook. Well, I'll only be a minute . . . Feeling a flicker of excitement, I log in. Over the past few days Adam and I have been exchanging emails. It's all been very light and friendly. He sent me a few lines to tell me about the short film he's been working on; I sent a few carefully constructed lines back about my week at work.

Carefully constructed, as I want to appear keen but cool. Chatty but relaxed. Busy but not *too* busy. As in, if he wants to fix up a date to watch a movie, my diary isn't that full.

OK, the truth is, it's completely empty, but I can't let him know that. I can't let him know that I've been agonising over every email I've sent him, trying to make sure I get it *just right*.

God, it used to be so much easier when you just picked up the phone and spoke.

Ooh, look, I have an unread message in my inbox. My stomach flutters as I open it. It's from Adam.

I'm free this week if you want to hook up. Call me.

Underneath he's added his number. I stare at the message, as if trying to wring some more meaning from it, other than just he's free this week and he wants me to call him. Oh, for God's sake, Lucy, what are you like? He wants to see you! My stomach gives another nervous flutter. I don't know why I'm so nervous.

Because you like him, whispers a voice in my head. *And because this is the first guy you've ever really liked apart from Nate.* Reminded of him, I slip my fingers into my pocket and finger the Strategy. I'm not sure when I'll have an opportunity to put it properly into practice. Or even if it will work. Unlike my sister, I'm far from convinced she's right. I don't think it's that simple. Right now, though, I don't have any other options.

A shrill barking outside causes me to glance up from the computer screen, just in time to see the door open and Magda appear. Dressed in a fuchsia Jackie O-style shift dress and matching heels, she's wearing a pair of sunglasses so large they almost look like welding goggles.

'Morning,' I say brightly, rushing over to help her. Under one arm she's carrying Valentino and under the other a large package.

'Ah, Loozy!' she puffs, out of breath. 'Thank you, thank you.'

Taking the package from her grasp, I follow dutifully as she stalks stiffly across the polished concrete floor of the gallery, taking minuscule fairy steps because her dress is so tight.

'I'm so sorry I am late,' she continues, redundantly patting her hair to make sure every strand is still hair-sprayed into place. 'So sorry.'

'Oh, it's fine, don't worry.' I smile, then pause. 'Where do you want me to put this?' I gesture to the package.

'Anywhere, anywhere. I don't care.' She sniffs dismissively, waving her diamond-encrusted hand around her like an air-freshener spray. Reaching a chair, she folds herself carefully into it. 'Just as long as I don't have to look at it.'

'What is it?' I ask, propping it up against the wall.

'A painting. From my aunt Irena.'

'Ooh, she gave you a painting?' My curiosity is piqued and I peer at the package, wondering what the painting's like.

'If you can call it that,' she says gloomily. 'It was left to me in her will.'

'*Her will?*' I wheel round and look at Magda. I'd presumed she was wearing her sunglasses because she'd had more 'enhancement', but now I notice her face looks a bit red and blotchy, even underneath her layers of make-up. And she's sniffling. 'Gosh, I'm so sorry. I had no idea,' I say hastily. 'When did she . . .?'

'At the weekend,' she replies, tugging out a box of tissues from her tote and loudly blowing her nose.

'Oh, no.' I crouch down beside her and squeeze her hand supportively. 'Was it sudden?'

'Nothing is sudden when you're ninety-six.' She shrugs, her palms outstretched. 'She had a good life.'

'Are you OK?' I ask with concern.

'I make a living,' she shrugs, and blows her nose again.

'No, I mean about your aunt.'

'Oh, yes, yes.' She nods. 'Everything is wonderful.'

I study her blotchy face, half hidden under her sunglasses, and feel a protective surge. 'No, everything's not wonderful,' I suddenly hear myself saying, and feel a beat of surprise at my outspokenness.

As does Magda, who looks at me with a shocked expression.

For a moment I think she's going to be angry and I swallow hard. 'I mean, it's not, is it?' I say, trying to keep my voice from wavering.

There's a pause and then she seems to collapse inwards, folding up like a fuchsia ironing board, with only her shoulder pads and beehive sticking out. I watch as they both start shaking and suddenly I realise she's sobbing.

'Oh gosh, Mrs Zuckerman . . .'

I watch her, feeling completely useless. I don't know what to do. I'm trying to be polite and appropriate given that this is an employee-and-boss-type situation. After all, I can't just give her a big hug and say, 'There, there.'

Oh, sod being appropriate.

'There, there,' I soothe, diving to give her a big bear hug. I'd never realised how tiny she was, but it's like hugging a child. 'Don't worry, it's all going to be OK. She's gone to a good place now.'

Abruptly Magda stops sobbing and looks up. She pushes her sunglasses on to her forehead and stares at me, aghast. 'These tears are not for Irena.'

'They're not?'

'Oy! Of course not.' She frowns. Or at least tries to, but she's had so many injections in her face that it barely moves. 'Irena lived like royalty. She had servants, furs, diamonds.' She waggles her knuckle-dusters at me. 'Real diamonds, not like my fake ones!'

'They're fake?' Now it's my turn to look aghast.

Magda hiccups and lets out a pitiful sob. 'Everything is fake – the diamonds, the Gucci, the Louis Vuitton . . .' She thrusts her tote away from her as if she can't bear to look at it. 'I am broke, Loozy, broke!'

I look at her in alarm. 'But I thought . . .'

I'm not sure what I thought, to be honest. It's just that with the designer clothes, and the plastic surgery, and the Upper West Side address, I assumed . . .

'Appearances can be deceptive, Loozy,' she continues. 'That's what my aunt Irena used to say.' She shakes her head. 'The bank, they are thieves, they want to take everything from me, my apartment, the gallery . . .'

'*The gallery?*' I feel a flash of panic.

'I am terrible with money. I borrow this for that, and that for this.' She hunches her shoulders as she waves her hands around.

I stare at her, a cold, sinking dread washing over me. My first thought is for Magda. How terrible to think you might have to lose your home, and at her age. But I'd be fibbing if I didn't say I was worried about what it would mean for me if she lost the gallery too. And what about the gallery itself?

'This place can't close. It just can't!' I cry, before I can help myself.

Magda suddenly raises herself up to full height and, reaching for my hand, holds it aloft like we're two protestors. 'We will do our very best, Loozy,' she says in a rallying cry. 'Our very best. We will not be beaten. We will not be afraid.'

'Um . . . hear, hear,' I offer.

'All is not lost yet. There is a new up-and-coming artist. He lives on the Vineyard, but I think if we can meet with him, we might be able to show his work. He is incredible. Simply incredible! He will save us!' All fired up, she smacks her fingers against her lips.

Watching her getting her mojo back, becoming passionate again, I feel a swell of affection and relief.

'Sounds good.' I smile. Maybe she's right. Maybe everything will be all right.

'Oh, it will be, it will be.' Her eyes flashing, she stands up, dusts off her shift dress, smoothes down her hair and takes a deep breath. 'OK, enough of these tears. Irena would kill me. She'd say, "Magda, what are you doing, acting like a big baby?" She was my mother's twin sister, but she was more like a mother to me.'

Smiling, I go to turn away, when a thought strikes. 'Did you say Irena was ninety-six?'

'Nearly ninety-seven,' says Magda proudly.

I pause, doing the maths. 'And you were born in 1965,' I say, remembering the code for the alarm. 'So that means . . .' I frown. That can't be right. I must have got it wrong. 'Your mum was fifty-one when she had you?'

Magda colours. 'Um . . . yes, I know!' Clearing her throat, she pretends to look as surprised as I am. 'The doctors were amazed! I was a miracle baby!'

Chapter Twenty-Two

As I walk home from work later that evening, I can't stop thinking about Magda. Despite her rallying cry and cheery optimism that the gallery will be saved and everything will be wonderful, I'm worried.

Maybe it's the Manchester in me. The Northern pessimism instilled into me as a child that if things can go wrong, they bloody well will. Maybe it's the call I took from the Department of Water and Power, complaining that a payment was long overdue and we had twenty-one days to settle the account or be cut off. Or maybe it's that sometimes during the day I'd catch Magda, when she thought I wasn't looking, and despite her heavy-handed blusher she looked pale and frightened.

On my way home I stop to pick up laundry. After my huge clear-out at the weekend, I filled a large bin liner with crumpled clothes and, along with some of Robyn's stuff, dragged it to my local Fluff and Fold. I love Fluff and Fold. They're the New York version of our British launderettes, but they're so much more. It's a bit like comparing an Aston Martin to a Fiat Panda: they both do the job, but one does it with a super-fancy five-star service wash that includes fluffing, folding, ironing and giving it that delicious freshly washed scent.

Which is pretty amazing, considering next door is a Chinese restaurant, I muse, picking up a takeaway for me and Robyn.

'Food's up,' I yell, as I walk into the apartment. Slamming the door behind me, I'm hit by a sweet, pungent aroma. What's that smell? Following my nose, I wander into the kitchen to find it bathed in candlelight and Robyn sitting at the kitchen table, bent low over a large hardback book, the size of a telephone directory. In her right hand is a bunch of burning sage, which she's waving above her head.

To think I used to come home to find my flatmates watching *Coronation Street*.

Hearing me, she suddenly looks up, wild-eyed and with her hair all over the place.

'I've found a spell!'

Rewind a few weeks and I would have dropped my vegetable chow mein all over the kitchen lino in shock at such a statement, but now I'm fast beginning to get used to Robyn and her wacky ways. Saying that, a vision board is one thing, but this?

'*A spell?*' I repeat, for want of anything else to say.

Well, it was either that or, 'Ooh, what is it?' and I'm not officially crazy *just* yet.

'Yes! In here!' she says triumphantly, holding up the book, which has a deep red velvet cover and has the words 'Spells and Charms' embossed across the front in gold lettering. 'I borrowed it from my friend Wicker, who's part of this drumming circle I used to go to,' she continues in excitement. 'Well, I had to do something. I know your sister thinks the Strategy will work, but I'm afraid it's not as simple as that when you're talking about the power of the universe.'

Dumping my laundry on the side, I clear a space on the table for the takeaway and begin unpacking the little red and white cartons of food.

'So I've been thinking, I don't want to disagree with Kate,' she says, disagreeing, 'but when it comes to forces you don't understand, you need more than a document.' She wrinkles her nose sniffily. 'We're not talking law now – we're talking legends!'

There's a pause and I realise this is my chance to say something. Anything. Only, to be quite truthful, I haven't a clue what to say.

'It's called "the Good-Riddance Spell" and it's for getting rid of an unwanted suitor.' She looks at me, her eyes flashing. 'Can you believe it?'

'No, I can't believe it,' I say, finding my tongue. 'That's because it's *completely crazy*!' I waggle a napkin. 'Honestly, Robyn, *magic spells*? What is this, Harry Potter? It's insane!'

Robyn raises her eyebrows. 'I think it's a bit late for all that, don't you?' she says tetchily.

I open my mouth to reply, then fall silent. She has a point.

'So do you want to hear this spell or not?' she continues sulkily.

I sigh resignedly. 'Go on.'

'OK, well, it's a banishing spell, and banishing spells are powerful, intricate ritual spells, designed to break or undo spells or curses.'

'Like the legend,' I point out. Well, let's not be scornful. I'm the one walking around with a four-page, twenty-five-point document in my pocket because I kissed my soulmate under some bridge and now I'm stuck with him.

'Exactly,' says Robyn. 'They can also banish people away from you.' She thumps the table. 'Perfect! A double whammy!'

'Perfect.' I nod, playing along. 'Do we have any soy sauce?'

After all, if legends can come true, maybe there *is* something in this magic-spell business.

'In the cupboard on the right, middle shelf,' she instructs, turning back to her book. 'It says here that all banishing rituals are carried out at night using special magical ingredients . . .'

'Speaking of ingredients, I got you vegetable chow mein and spring rolls. Is that OK?'

'Mmm, perfect.' She nods.

I pull up a stool and sit down next to her.

'Whereas candle magic is a strong yet gentle magic, banishing and binding spells pack a faster, more powerful punch.' Dipping her spring roll in chilli sauce, she jabs it at an imaginary Nate like a spear. 'A powerful punch, *atta girl*!'

Flecks of sweet chilli sauce go everywhere and I pass her a paper napkin.

'So this is what you need to do . . .' Taking a bite, she chews furiously, then clears her throat. '"On a piece of parchment or recycled paper, write the name and date of birth of the person you are wishing 'away'. Use black ink for this. Many gypsies also say that it is best to use one of the old 'dip' pens and ink, rather than a modern ballpoint."' She breaks off. 'Shoot, I don't have one. Do you?'

'Um . . . yeah, I think so.' I nod, munching on a mouthful of chow mein, 'from when I used to do a lot of pen-and-ink drawings.'

'Great.' She nods, then pauses. 'You did pen-and-ink drawings?' She looks intrigued. 'Wow. Can I see them?'

'Oh, it was ages ago.' I shrug. 'I'm not sure where they are.'

'Huh.' She studies me hard for a moment, as if about to say something, then appears to think better of it and turns back to her spell book.

'OK, where was I . . .? Oh, yeah . . ."Let the ink dry – don't blot it. Then wrap a piece of his clothing round a hambone."'

I stop eating and pull a face. 'Eugh! Yuck.'

'Oh, that's easy. I have them in the freezer,' she says matter-of-factly.

I look at her in astonishment. 'I thought you were a vegetarian.'

'They're for the dogs,' she says, getting up and pulling open the freezer door. A little cloud of dry ice appears, and rummaging around, she pulls out a large frozen bone, wrapped in a plastic bag. Jenny and Simon start yapping frantically, thinking they are going to get a treat, but she shoos them away with a 'It's not for you. It's for Lucy, to get rid of the love of her life.'

They bark and start salivating. Memories of stories of people being found in their apartments half eaten by their German shepherds suddenly spring to mind. I make a mental note to keep my bedroom door firmly closed tonight.

'"Put the hambone in a plastic bag with two black feathers, ravens or crows preferably, add a pinch of one or more of the magical herbs – ash-tree leaves, clover, lovage, lilac, garlic – then take the paper with his name on it, fold it three times and pop that in too. Then tie the end tightly with red string."' She looks across at me and frowns. 'Are you making a list of all these ingredients?' she says crossly.

'Um . . .' Having been totally absorbed in eating the most delicious spring roll, I sheepishly grab a pen and a piece of paper.

'"Then take the bundle outside to a patch of earth, untie it and remove the piece of paper. Light a white candle and burn the piece of paper in its flame while thinking of the name of the person running away from you and saying . . ."' She pauses and affects a serious voice. '"Winds of the North, East, South and West, carry these affections to where they'll be best. Let his heart be open and free, and let his mind be away from me.""'

'And that's it?' Scribbling furiously, I glance up.

'No, then you have to bury the hambone.'

'Gosh, it's quite complicated, isn't it?' I groan. 'Maybe the restraining order might have been easier.'

'Oh, and you have to do this at exactly ten o'clock at night.'

'Why ten o'clock?'

'Because that's what the spell says,' she responds matter-of-factly. Scooping up a mouthful of chow mein with her chopsticks, she chews thoughtfully. 'There's one other thing.'

I throw her a strangled look.

'This spell must be performed during a waning moon.'

There's a pause as we both glance out of the open window. Mostly all we see is the brick wall with the graffiti, but there's a tiny sliver of a gap. Through it a crescent-shaped moon glows back at us.

'It's waning!' exclaims Robyn excitedly.

Panic stabs. I suddenly have an awful feeling I'm really going to go through with this.

'Have you finished?' Changing the subject, I go to clear away our cartons and chopsticks.

Robyn eyes me. 'Tomorrow night,' she says decisively.

'What about tomorrow night?' I say, trying to play dumb.

'That's when you need to do the spell!' she gasps, as if it's perfectly obvious that's what I should be doing on a Tuesday night in Manhattan.

I look at her for a moment and it's suddenly like sanity comes flying in through the window and wallops me on the side of the head. 'I'm not doing it tomorrow night! Or the next night! Or any night!' I cry, shaking my head as if shaking the sense back into it. 'I'm not doing any of this hocus-pocus nonsense.'

'It's not hocus-pocus,' says Robyn, looking offended.

'Whatever,' I gasp, then take a deep breath. 'I'm not doing it.'

'But if you don't get rid of Nate, you're never going to make room in your love cup for anyone else,' she tries to reason.

'My love cup?'

'It's how they describe it in the book I'm reading,' she says defensively, her cheeks pinking up. 'It has to be empty before it can be filled up again by anyone else. Like, for example, Adam.'

She raises her eyebrows and now I feel *my* cheeks pinking up. I'd told her all about Adam at lunchtime. Well, it was more a case of me showing her our email exchange and, her being the loyal good friend that she is, dutifully and carefully analysing each word until she came to the conclusion 'He likes you.' Which was hardly ground-breaking, but still.

'Look, I think we just need to get a grip here,' I say, trying to remain calm. 'My name's Lucy. I'm from Manchester. I wear knickers from Marks and Spencer. I don't *do* spells.'

'It's only a teeny-weeny one,' cajoles Robyn.

'Burying bones, lighting candles and chanting?' Pressing my foot on the pedal bin, I chuck the cartons in the recycling. 'No, I'm not doing it.'

Robyn's cheeks flush and she falls silent. For a few moments neither of us speak.

'I picked up our laundry,' I say eventually, to break the awkward atmosphere.

'Thanks,' she says mutely.

Then it's back to the awkward silence as I untie the plastic bag containing our laundry and begin unpacking it.

'Lucy, I really think you should reconsider,' she says after a moment. 'Don't dismiss the things you don't understand.'

'You didn't say that when you were trying to do your taxes,' I point out, piling the laundry up on the table. That's funny, I don't remember us having white towels with monograms.

'That's different,' she replies touchily.

'I don't care.' I shake my head. 'I'm not going out at the dead of night to bury a bone and do some ridiculous rhyme in order to get rid of my ex-boyfriend.'

Hmm, I really don't recognise these T-shirts either. Gosh, they do look rather large. I hold one up. 'Is this yours?'

Robyn shakes her head. 'But you have to fight magic with magic,' she argues.

I roll my eyes. 'OK, Dumbledore.'

'I'm serious!'

'I know.' I nod. 'That's what worries me.'

Hang on a minute, men's shirts? And trousers? I frown.

'I'm not the one who can't break up with their soulmate,' says Robyn tartly.

'Look, I'm not doing a magic spell,' I gasp. 'So that's that. Full stop.'

'Well, I think you're making a big mistake. There are greater forces than us out there, forces that we don't understand . . .'

I can hear Robyn talking, but it's like white noise. A buzz in the background, I've tuned out. I'm not listening. Instead I'm staring at my laundry.

Only it's not my laundry.

Astonishment mixes with confusion, mixes with resignation. I let out a loud groan.

'It's his.'

'What?' Breaking off from her speech, Robyn frowns in confusion. 'What's his?'

I hold up a pair of pineapple boxer shorts and wave them at Robyn. 'About that spell . . .'

'Do you have any white candles?'

Fast-forward to the next evening after work and I'm standing in the cluttered confines of Burt's Hardware Store with my shopping list. The sane, rational part of me that pooh-poohs horoscopes and strides determinedly under ladders still can't quite believe I'm going ahead with this, but the other part of me that dragged all of Nate's laundry back to Fluff and Fold is desperate.

Brenda, the assistant manager, couldn't understand how there'd been a mix-up. 'We have branches all over Manhattan, but I have no idea how this could have happened,' she gasped in bewilderment. Apologising profusely, she poked the computer keyboard as if it was personally responsible. 'Mr Kennedy is registered at an address over fifty blocks away!'

I actually felt a bit sorry for Brenda, and for a moment I was almost tempted to offer her an explanation. I say *almost*, but I decided that one involving centuries-old legends, Italian bridges and soulmates would only complicate things. Better that I play the role of the dissatisfied customer than that of the lunatic.

In the end it all got sorted out. If I had his clothes, then he must have mine. And sure enough, in the middle of Brenda jabbing at the computer, a text from Nate popped up on my mobile.

Let me guess. You have my laundry.

I text back.

Let me guess. You have mine.

'Here you go. Anything else?'

I zone back to see Burt scampering back down the ladder, clutching a pack of candles. For a man who looks to be in his eighties, he's exceedingly agile.

I glance back at my list. Robyn provided the hambone, garlic and all the exotic-sounding herbs. I already had some string. Now I've got candles. Which leaves . . .

'Do you sell feathers?'

'Feathers?' he grunts brusquely. 'What kind of feathers?'

'Black ones, preferably from a raven or a crow.'

Scraping his bristly chin with his fingernails, he peers at me mistrustfully. 'Did you not read the sign? This is a hardware store, not a pet store.'

'Oh, yes, sorry, of course,' I stammer, and I hastily pay and leave the shop. How embarrassing. I sound like a total fruit loop.

I set off walking back to the apartment. Well, that's that, then. If I can't find the feathers, I won't be able to do the spell. Feeling a secret beat of relief at being let off the hook, I turn the corner, where I'm hit by an unexpected gust of warm summer wind. Litter blows all around me, a plastic bag gets whipped up and twirls like a ballerina, and then I notice something flutter past and fall in front of me on the pavement. I glance down.

Two feathers. Two black feathers.

I'm not superstitious, but that's what I'd call a sign.

At nine thirty I'm all packed and ready to go. Well, almost.

'Feathers?' asks Robyn. Armed with a list of everything I need, she's going through a final check to make sure I have everything.

I tug them out of my bag and wave them.

'Check.' Robyn solemnly ticks them off her list. She's taking it all super seriously. It's almost like a military operation: Operation Good Riddance.

'Red string?'

I do the same again.

'Check.'

'Hambone?'

I dig it out of my backpack. It's wrapped in his boxer shorts. I'd returned Nate's dry-cleaning, but those I'd kept. Partly because I needed an item of his clothing for the spell, but mostly because Nate has no business wearing those boxer shorts. Not with me. Not with any girl. They have to go. I'm thinking of it as a strike for all womankind. Like getting the vote, or equal rights: no woman after me will ever have to suffer the horror of the novelty pineapple boxer shorts.

'Awesome!' Having finished her checklist, Robyn beams broadly. 'Well, good luck!'

'Thanks.' I smile uncertainly. Something tells me I'm going to need it.

I'd wanted Robyn to come with me, but she couldn't, as she was going to her reiki healing class. Plus she said that I had to do this alone, otherwise the spell wouldn't work. 'Magic demands that,' she'd informed me.

Magic, it seemed, demanded rather a lot.

I leave the apartment and set off towards a tiny park a few streets away. Well, it's not even a park, more a small triangle with a couple of benches, some flowerbeds and a patch of grass. In the daytime it's usually filled with people sitting on the benches eating their lunch, or sprawled on the grass chatting, reading the paper or just delighted to be soaking up a tiny spot of nature amid the steel skyscrapers, the flowers bright splashes of colour against the grey concrete.

But now, at night, it's completely empty and in darkness. Not that anywhere in Manhattan every really gets dark, with all the city lights. It's dark enough, though, I think, with a tremor of apprehension.

I try the gate. It's locked. I'm going to need to climb over.

Not for the first time I question my sanity, but like my sister instructed, I have to keep my eye on the bigger picture. 'Forget it's the journey, not the destination,' she'd barked. 'It's *all* about the destination! The journey is immaterial.'

A couple stroll past and I drop to the ground and pretend to be tying my shoelace. It's totally instinctive. I'm not even *wearing* shoelaces; I'm wearing slip-on ballet pumps. Gosh, I'm obviously a natural at this, I muse, feeling pretty impressed with myself. I stay crouched and wait until they've moved further ahead up the street. Then, taking a quick look around to make sure the coast is clear, I clamber over the gate.

There's a brief moment when I think I might get impaled and my sex life flashes before my eyes, but then I'm over and down the other side. I feel a flash of triumph. I'm in! Jittery with nerves and excitement, I quickly make my way over to the flowerbeds. OK, I need to get this over and done with as quickly as possible, then get out of here. Lighting my candle, I hold the flame to the piece of paper with Nate's name and date of birth on it. It immediately catches alight. Much faster than I thought it would, in fact.

Shit, where's the poem? I mean chant. Shit.

Frantically I dig around for another scrap of paper – and for a brief second there's a panic that I'm burning the wrong piece of paper – fuck – but then I find it. Thank God. I take a deep breath. Heavens, I'm like a nervous wreck.

"'Winds of the North, East, South and West . . .'"I begin rattling through it. Robyn told me I had to close my eyes and breathe in every word, but I race through it as quickly as I can. "' . . . and let his mind be away from me.'"

I watch as the piece of paper disintegrates into ash and is carried away into the night air.

Brilliant. That bit's done. Now I just have to bury the hambone. I feel myself relaxing. See, it wasn't so hard, was it? All that worrying for nothing. In fact, this magic stuff is pretty easy-peasy, I reflect, grabbing the ladle – we didn't have a trowel – and digging myself a hole.

Quite literally.

Because at that moment there's suddenly a loud whooping siren and I'm bathed in a harsh light. I twirl round, blinking in the brightness.

What the . . .?

And then a voice booms from a megaphone, 'Stay where you are and put your hands in the air. This is the New York Police Department.'

Chapter Twenty-Three

OK, don't panic.

One scary ride in a cop car wearing a pair of handcuffs later, and I'm sitting on a very hard plastic chair at a police station in the Ninth Precinct, being interviewed by a very hard-faced Officer McCrory.

On second thoughts, maybe I should panic.

'So let me get this straight . . .' Clearing his throat, he looks down at his notes. 'You trespassed on city property and lit a fire.'

'A candle,' I correct. 'A white candle.'

It's important to be completely clear and stick to the facts, I tell myself calmly. Otherwise I could be mistakenly tried for a crime I didn't commit. Like a robbery. Or a kidnapping. *Or even a murder.*

I feel a clutch of alarm.

Facts, Lucy. Remember, stick to the facts.

'And why was that?'

'I needed to burn a piece of paper and say a chant.'

'*A chant?*' His eyebrows shoot up like two thick, hairy, grey caterpillars scuttling up his forehead.

'Well, it was more a poem,' I explain. 'Gosh, what was it now . . .?' I try racking my brain, but I'm so nervous it's as if it's been wiped clean like a computer disc and there's nothing on it. 'Um, something about winds . . .'

'According to these notes, you were also caught attempting to bury a deceased animal.'

'It was a hambone,' I say quickly. 'My roommate keeps them in the freezer for Simon and Jenny.'

'Simon and Jenny?'

'Her dogs. Two rescues. Very cute. Well, Simon is, but Jenny has a dreadful underbite. That doesn't make her ugly, though. I mean, she might not win Crufts, but—'

'Miss Hemmingway, can you please stick to the question?'

'Oh, yes, sorry, of course,' I apologise hastily. 'Officer.'

Shit. I've seen those cop shows. Robyn is always watching *CSI*, in between *Oprah* and *The Secret* DVD. If I'm not careful, Officer McCrory is going to throw me in a cell with lots of deranged lunatics and prostitutes called Roxy who chew gum and seem tough but who are really kind-hearted and have a sick kid at home and are just trying to make ends meet. Actually, no, that wasn't *CSI* – that was an episode of *Law and Order*.

'And you were doing all this in order to break up with your boyfriend?'

I snap back. 'Ex-boyfriend,' I correct. 'We've already broken up.'

Frowning, Office McCrory puts down his pen, rocks back on his chair and, steepling his fingers, gives me a long, hard look.

Fuck. This is not good.

'Miss Hemmingway, you do realise that the New York Police Department has reason to believe you have violated the law on three points . . .'

Really not good.

'Trespassing . . . arson—'

'*Arson?* But I only burned a bit of paper with my ex's name on . . .' I trail off.

There have been times in my life when I really should have kept my mouth shut. Like, for example, the time when I was eighteen and got hideously drunk on Scrumpy cider and told Jamie Robinson, who I'd been on three dates with, that I was madly in love with him and wanted to have his babies. Suffice to say, there was no fourth date.

Then there was the time Mum bought me a yellow mohair jumper, the reasoning being that my favourite colour is yellow. Which is true, except yellow is my favourite colour because I think of sunflowers and sunshine, not big, fat, furry mohair jumpers that make me look like I'm seasick.

It was OK, though, because she told me that she would return it if I didn't like it. She wouldn't be hurt or offended. So I said it was a lovely thought but would she mind returning it?

Mum promptly burst into tears.

And now this is one of those times, I muse, looking at Officer McCrory with a beat of apprehension. If I say anything, I will deeply regret it. I need to keep my big mouth so firmly shut a can-opener couldn't prise it open.

'And resisting arrest,' he finishes gravely.

'No, I didn't!' I cry, before I can stop myself. 'Look, I know how that must appear, but I was climbing over the railings to get *towards* you, not run away from you.'

'Miss Hemmingway,' he says sternly.

'Officer McCrory.' I sit bolt upright. This is it. He's going to charge me.

'I need to say something.'

'I know what you're going to say,' I blurt. Well, what the hell. It's too late now. I know I'm going down.

'You do?'

I vacuum my throat nervously, then launch straight in. 'You have the right to remain silent. Anything you say can and will be used against you in a court of law. You have the right to speak to an attorney, and to have an attorney present during any questioning. If you cannot afford a lawyer, one will be provided for you at government expense.'

For a moment there's complete silence and he just stares at me blankly. Then, shaking his head, he lets out a low whistle. 'Jeez,' he says finally.

'My roommate is a huge fan of *CSI*,' I explain, my voice trembling fearfully. 'I know the score.'

Visions of me being carted off to the cells swim before my eyes. Flashes of my parents' shocked reactions, Kate campaigning as a lawyer to free me . . . I can see the newspaper headlines now:

BRITISH GIRL JAILED IN AMERICA –
LIFE SENTENCE FOR TRYING TO BREAK UP WITH THE ONE
'She thought she'd found her soulmate,' says former roommate Robyn
Weisenberg, 'but then she couldn't get rid of him. The universe wouldn't
let her. It's a tragedy.'

Still, I suppose that's one way of having closure with Nate. A life sentence.

'So, do you have any questions?'

I zone back to see Officer McCrory looking at me expectantly. My mouth goes dry. 'Do I get a phone call?' I stammer. My eyes are beginning to sting with tears and I feel slightly dizzy. 'Before I'm . . .' I can barely get the words out. 'Before I'm taken *down*.'

'Down?' He raises his eyebrows. 'Miss Hemmingway, did you not hear me? You're free to go.'

I stare at him in shock. 'Free?'

'I'm letting you go with just a warning.' He nods, shuffling his notes.

It takes a second to register and then . . .

'Oh my God, thank you!' I gasp in astonishment. 'Thank you, thank you, thank you!' Overwhelmed with gratitude and relief, I jump out of my chair and before I know it I'm flinging my arms round his stout blue-uniformed figure. Taken aback, Officer McCrory stiffens and stands statue-still, his arms out like a scarecrow.

'Gosh, I'm sorry. I was just . . .' Suddenly aware that I'm bear-hugging a police officer in the NYPD, I jump back. 'I'm sorry. I'm just so emotional.' I feel my eyes start prickling.

'I understand. I know how hard it can be to break up with someone,' he says, lowering his voice. 'My wife left me less than a year ago.' Reaching over to his desk, he grabs a box of tissues and holds it out to me.

'Oh, I'm so sorry,' I reply, taking one.

'Ran off with my best friend. But she's still in here.' He bangs his chest with a meaty palm, his eyes glistening, and reaches for a tissue for himself. 'It's like she's everywhere I go.'

'I know the feeling,' I say wryly.

Sniffing, he blows his nose loudly. 'I just want to forget about her.'

'Me too.' I nod wistfully, thinking about Nate. 'Forget about him, I mean.'

Officer McCrory and I meet each other's gaze in solidarity. Then, remembering himself, he stuffs his tissue in his pocket and says gruffly, 'Is there anyone you can call to come pick you up?'

'Oh, I'm fine. I'll catch a cab.'

'I'm not letting you outta here on your own – don't want you reoffending.' He looks at me, his eyes twinkling.

I think about Robyn. She's my obvious choice, but she was going to her reiki class tonight and it usually goes on late. Last week she was out until the early hours having her aura read, apparently, and no, I don't think that was a double-entendre.

Then there's Kate. I glance at the time. It's nearly midnight. On second thoughts, no, there isn't Kate. She will have been in bed for hours by now, earplugs in, wave music on, as she gets up at five every morning to hit the gym. She won't take too kindly to her little sister waking her up. Even less so when she discovers I'm at the police station downtown.

I rack my brains – Magda? Magda is the most liberated boss I've had, but there's liberated and liberated. Calling her at midnight to tell her I'm at the cop shop and could she please come and get me probably wouldn't be the wisest career move.

Which leaves . . . I scroll through the contacts list on my phone. *Adam.*

His number jumps out at me. I punched it into my phone after he sent it to me on Facebook. I stare at it for a few moments, toying with the idea, mulling it over in my head.

Well, he did say to call him.

'Lucy! Are you OK?'

Twenty minutes later I glance up from staring at the scuffed floor of the police station to see the fire doors swinging open and Adam appearing through them. Like a knight in shining armour, I can't help thinking, only instead he's wearing a scruffy T-shirt, baseball cap and ripped jeans. He looks at me, his face etched with concern, and my heart swells. I have never been so pleased to see anyone in my entire life.

'Yeah . . . fine.' I jump up from my plastic chair to greet him, then hold back, feeling suddenly self-conscious. 'Everything's fine.'

'You usually hang around in police stations for fun, do you?' he says, his mouth twitching with amusement.

My cheeks flush. 'Well, there was nothing on at the movies,' I quip feebly.

He laughs, an easy, relaxed laugh and, tilting his head to one side, surveys me from beneath the peak of his cap. 'Sure you're OK?' he asks quietly. Reaching for my hand, he squeezes it gently.

As his fingers brush mine, a little tingle rushes up my spine. 'Sure.' I nod, but as I'm saying the words, I feel my lips tremble unexpectedly. 'Everything's cool,' I manage, and then, to my absolute embarrassment, burst into tears.

Chapter Twenty-Four

Adam escorts me back to my apartment, where I discover Robyn and the dogs fast asleep on the sofa, snoring loudly, an episode of *Oprah* playing faintly in the background. Tiptoeing past, so as not to wake Simon and Jenny – nothing, I've learned, will wake Robyn, who doesn't so much fall asleep as fall *into a coma* – I grab half a bottle of wine from the fridge and a couple of glasses and go into my bedroom. It's a warm, muggy evening, and pulling open the rickety old sash window, we clamber out on to the fire escape.

'I'm so sorry about bursting into tears like that,' I say, for about the zillionth time, as I perch on a metal step and pour two glasses of wine. 'I'm so embarrassed.'

'Hey, no problem.' He shrugs, sitting one step up from me. Taking out his tobacco, he waves it at me as if to say, *Do you mind?* and I shake my head. 'I tend to have that effect on women.'

Laughing, I shoot him a grateful smile and pass him a glass.

'So, you had a lucky escape by the sounds of it,' he continues, licking the cigarette paper. 'Trying to rescue that cat and getting trapped in there . . .'

'Um . . . yeah, I know.' I nod, crossing my fingers behind my back. 'Lucky the police found me!'

In my defence, it wasn't me who came up with this story; it was Officer McCrory. On meeting Adam, he'd taken him to one side to 'explain the situation'. It was only afterwards, when we were leaving, with strict instructions to Adam to 'look after this young lady', that he'd thrown me a wink over his shoulder and I'd realised he'd been up to something. And it wasn't law enforcement.

'Thanks for coming to get me –' I smile shyly – 'and for being so nice about everything.'

'My pleasure.' He grins. 'I'm used to rescuing damsels in distress.'

'You are?' I peer at him in the darkness, the soft, twinkly glow from the fairy lights in my bedroom casting patterns across his face, and for a brief moment I get a wobble of insecurity. *Damsels?* What damsels? Who are the damsels?

'Oh, yeah.' He nods, his face serious. 'It's a little sideline I have going. When I'm not crashing gallery openings.' He looks up at me, his mouth twisting with amusement, and I punch him playfully on the arm. 'Hey, I've still got a bruise on the other arm from where you punched me last time,' he yelps.

'Well, now you have a matching pair.' I grin ruefully.

'This is my reward for rushing out halfway through a movie?'

I look at him in astonishment. 'You left a movie halfway through? For me?'

'A late-night screening of *Annie Hall* at the Pioneer Theater.' He nods, then seeing my face adds quickly, 'Don't worry, I've seen it a hundred times, so I know how it ends.' He adopts a funny voice: '"Well, I guess that's pretty much how I feel about relationships. You know, they're totally irrational and crazy and absurd and . . . but, uh, I guess we keep goin' through it because, uh, most of us need the eggs."'

Listening to him, I laugh, feeling a surge of amusement and affection.

And something else.

Out of nowhere I suddenly fancy him. Like *really* fancy him. Even with that ridiculous Woody Allen impersonation.

'No, this is your reward.' Impulsively I'm leaning forwards and kissing him on the cheek. His skin feels soft beneath my lips and he smells faintly of cigarette smoke . . . Then, realising I've lingered just that millisecond too long, I pull back, blushing.

How embarrassing. Why not just grab hold of him and snog his face off, Lucy, why don't you?

'Well, it's not much of a reward,' I add self-consciously, trying to make a joke of it. Honestly, could I be any more crap at flirting? If I'm not lunging at him, I'm making bad, clumsy jokes.

His eyes sweep over my face and for a moment I think he's going to say something, do something. Then he seems to think better of it. 'I accept cash and cheques,' he quips.

'I'm sure I can't afford you,' I quip back.

'Oh, I'm sure we can come to some arrangement,' he replies, and holds my gaze for a moment.

My chest tightens. He's flirting with me, right? That's definitely flirting. And yet all my confidence has deserted me and I'm not sure. He could be just being friendly, I reason. I mean, for all I know, his invitation to 'hook up and see a film' might simply be him returning the favour after I showed him around the MoMA. It could have been purely platonic.

As the thought strikes, so does another: Which means he's probably not interested in me like that at all. Followed by another: I've been reading it all wrong. And another: He's just being a gentleman, coming to rescue me from the police station . . . As the thoughts gather momentum, hope starts unravelling like knots: In fact, he's probably not single at all . . . He's probably got a girlfriend . . . I bet it's the brunette at the gallery.

'So are you single?' I suddenly have that discombobulated feeling of hearing a voice blurt out, wondering who it belongs to, then realising with horror that it belongs to me.

In the middle of sipping his wine, Adam pauses.

The shame. *The shame.*

'I mean . . . sort of . . . as in . . .' I scramble around desperately in my brain for something to say that will stop me looking like . . . like . . . Oh, this is awful. I can't even think of that word.

'As in, do I have a girlfriend?' says Adam evenly.

I stop scrambling and look at him resignedly. 'Yes, that's what I meant.' I brace myself. OK, so he's got a girlfriend, and it's the pretty brunette, and they're very happy together, but that's all right – we can be friends. Platonic friends. Like in *When Harry Met Sally.*

Actually, no, they ended up sleeping together. Oh crap.

'No, I don't have a girlfriend,' he replies. 'I did, but we broke up a while back.'

'You did?' I sound happy and relieved. 'I mean, that's tough. Breaking up is tough,' I add, trying to look suitably glum.

Though not as tough as *not being able* to break up, I think fleetingly, rubbing my wrist, which is still a bit sore from the handcuffs.

'Not really. She cheated on me.' He shrugs.

I'm shocked. I can't imagine anyone wanting to cheat on Adam. 'Gosh, that's awful.'

'Yeah, finding out wasn't fun, but once I did, well, it was over pretty quick.' He takes a drag of his roll-up. 'There's no point. You can never trust someone again after that . . .' He trails off as if deep in thought, then holds out his roll-up. 'You smoke?'

I hesitate. 'Only on special occasions.'

'Do you think getting someone out of jail is a special occasion?'

'Maybe.' I nod, playing along as he passes me the roll-up. I inhale. It makes my head spin slightly, but in a good way. I can feel myself gradually unwinding after the madness of the evening, and for a few moments neither of us speaks; we just sit together sipping wine and listening to the sounds of Manhattan, which are playing like background music.

'I guess this is a bit different from most first dates,' he says finally.

'Um . . . yeah, I guess so.' I nod, trying to keep my voice even, but it's zipping through my brain. *We're on a first date?* So he wasn't just being friendly. I feel a buzz of delight, quickly followed by a sudden pressure. Casually drinking wine on the fire escape and sharing a cigarette has suddenly turned all official. If this is a first date, aren't I supposed to have made an effort, washed my hair, put on some mascara at least? Aren't I supposed to be making flirty small talk, and flicking my freshly washed hair, and trying to be cool and impressive.

Honestly, I'm useless. Why didn't someone *tell* me this was supposed to be a first date? Instead I've narrowly missed being arrested, I've burst into tears, I'm not wearing a scrap of make-up, my hair is tied up in a scrunchie, and I just lunged at him.

And yet . . . I glance at Adam, sitting across from me on the fire escape, and my nerves disappear into the darkness as quickly as they appeared. And yet none of it seems to matter.

Well, maybe the hair scrunchie, I decide, hastily pulling it out. I'm trying to shake out my hair surreptitiously when I notice we've finished the wine.

'Oh look, all gone,' I say, standing up quickly. This is a good excuse to dash back inside and take a quick peek in the mirror, I realise. 'I'll just grab us another bottle.'

Actually, I don't know if we have another bottle, but I'm sure I can dig out some beers from somewhere.

'Hey, I can do that.' Adam makes to stand up, but I push him down.

'No, no, I'm fine,' I say urgently. 'I want to get it.'

'Oh, OK.' He sits back down, looking slightly puzzled. Never has anyone appeared so keen to go into the kitchen to get a bottle of wine as a girl who has suddenly realised she's on a first date and needs to put on some concealer and lip gloss. Pronto.

Leaving him on the fire escape, I climb back through the window and hurry into the kitchen. There's no wine. There aren't even any beers. There is, however, mine and Robyn's emergency bottle of tequila. I eye it for a moment, weighing up how this could be perceived, then grab it anyway, along with two shot glasses, then make a quick detour to the bathroom.

A few minutes, some concealer, a smear of raspberry lip gloss and some hasty scrunching of hair products later, I head back into the bedroom to join Adam on the fire escape. Only he's not there any more. Instead he's sitting cross-legged on my bedroom floor with his back to me, looking at something.

'Who did these?' he asks as hears me walk back in.

I glance over his shoulder to see what he's looking at. 'Oh, that's one of my old sketchbooks,' I realise. I hold out the bottle of tequila. 'I'm afraid we only have this.'

He ignores me. 'These are yours? You did these?' He's flicking through pages. Stopping at one, he holds it up to me. 'You drew this?'

'Um . . . yeah.' I shrug absently, put the shot glasses down on my dressing table and unscrew the tequila. I begin pouring it out. 'A long time ago.'

'Who is it?'

I stop what I'm doing and look back at the sketch. It's a pen-and-ink drawing of an old lady, her face turned to the light, her body in shadow. 'I don't know who she was. I saw her sitting on a park bench one day.' My mind flicks back. 'She was reading a book – I remember it was open in her lap – but she had her eyes closed and her face to the sun, as if she was lost in her own world.'

'It's amazing, Lucy.' Adam's voice is hushed. 'These are all amazing.'

I smile with embarrassment. 'Oh, don't be silly, they're just drawings.' I hold out a shot glass and he takes it from me wordlessly.

'Seriously, Lucy.' He looks up at me, his eyes wide. 'They're incredible. You're really talented.'

I feel myself blush under his praises. Taking a sip of tequila, I kneel down next to him.

'Are those all your sketchbooks?' He gestures over to a pile of books stuffed into my cluttered shelves. Despite my attempts at having a clear-out, they're still filled with stuff.

I nod. 'My canvases are back in England.'

'Canvases?'

'My paintings,' I explain. 'I couldn't bring them with me. I keep them at my parents', in their garage.'

'You keep them hidden away?' He looks at me, incredulous. 'You should have them out so everyone can see them.'

'You haven't even seen them,' I say, amused by his enthusiasm. 'You might not like them.'

'Don't you have pictures?'

'Um . . . somewhere I think I have some Polaroids.'

'Where? I want to see!'

I know that he's never going to rest until he sees them, and so, leaning over to my shelves, I scrabble around for a bit until I find an old shoebox. 'Here you go.' I pass it to him. 'The colours are probably a bit faded now, as it was a few years ago.'

I watch while Adam opens the box. It's filled to the brim with a jumble of photos. That's another thing I should really sort out, I tell myself, as he starts rifling through. I need to get a lot more organised . . .

'Wow!'

I snap back to see Adam looking at me. But he's not looking at me like he normally does; he's looking at me as if I have a little green man from outer space sitting on my head.

'I had no idea,' he's saying now, his eyes wide with astonishment.

That really I'm a complete pig and this tidy room is merely a temporary situation? I'm addicted to tuna melts and I have the thighs to prove it? My middle name is *Edna*?

'You're an amazing artist, Lucy. You have so much talent. The colours, the shapes . . .' He's waving Polaroids discriminately. 'I mean, this one is incredible.' He grabs another. 'And then this one. Just look at their faces . . .'

I watch him, feeling embarrassed by this show of eagerness, and yet . . . and yet I feel something else. An old excitement. A possibility. *A dream.*

'You really think so,' I say, my voice almost a whisper.

He stops looking through the Polaroids and gazes at me. 'Yeah, I really think so,' he says quietly. Reaching for my hand, he pulls me closer beside him, his eyes never leaving mine. 'I really think so.'

He leans towards me – or is it me who leans towards him? I can't remember. All I'm aware of is his lips brushing against mine, my heart racing in my chest, as we start kissing.

I close my eyes. I've been wanting to do this all evening. I lean closer.

Abruptly he pulls away.

'Lucy.'

I let out a little groan of dismay and try to pull him back towards me.

'What are those?'

Reluctantly I open my eyes. My heart is still racing and I can still taste him on my lips. 'What?' I murmur thickly.

'Those,' he says, only firmer this time.

I turn my head to see where he's looking, slightly woozy with desire, wondering what it is, surely not more sketches . . .

Oh. My. God.

Suddenly I see them. My backpack has fallen off the bed, spilling out the contents, and there, lying on the rug, mocking me, taunting me, ruining my evening, are Nate's—

'Boxer shorts,' I gasp, my face contorted into a rictus of horror.

'Is there something you're not telling me?' Adam shoots me a look. His usual easy-going expression is gone and his face is set hard.

'No,' I say hastily. 'I mean yes, but well, no.' Flustered, my mind is racing. I can't tell him the truth about this evening, about magic spells, and soulmates, and hambones wrapped up in boxer shorts. He'll think he's been kissing a crazy girl. 'There was a mix-up. I got someone else's laundry,' I gabble. Well, that's the truth.

A tiny little bit of it.

'OK . . .' he says slowly, seeming to accept the explanation, before asking, 'So where's the rest of it?'

'Um . . . I gave it back.'

'But kept the boxer shorts?' He raises his eyebrows.

Shit. He doesn't believe me. He thinks I'm sleeping with someone. *And do you blame him, Lucy?* pipes up a little voice. *You have another man's boxer shorts lying on your bedroom floor.* I cringe inwardly. This does not look good. I suddenly remember his story of his cheating ex. Fuck, this really does not look good at all.

'It's not what you think,' I say urgently.

'How do you know what I'm thinking?' he fires back contrarily.

'I don't . . . I'm guessing.' Taking a deep sigh, I raise my eyes to meet his. There's no point trying to explain. I can't. 'Look, I know it seems kind of weird, and I know how it looks, but you've just got to trust me on this one.'

There's a long pause and he looks at me for what feels like the longest time. Then slowly he gets to his feet. My chest tightens. So that's it. He doesn't believe me. I feel a heavy thump of dismay.

'OK,' he says after a pause. 'I trust you.'

'You do?' Relief surges. For a moment there I thought that we were over before we'd even started.

'There's just one thing . . .'

I look up at him, feeling a beat of apprehension.

'Why are they covered in pineapples?'

As his mouth twists up into a smile, I burst out laughing. 'Funny you should ask that. I've asked myself the same question . . .'

Chapter Twenty-Five

The next morning I arrive at work to be told I'm flying to Martha's Vineyard to meet with the new artist Magda's been raving about.

'What? *Today?*' Mid-sip of my latte, I freeze and stare at Magda, taken aback.

'No time like the present,' she breezes, tearing off a piece of bagel and feeding it to Valentino. 'We need to snap him up before someone else does.'

'But what about flights, somewhere to stay . . .?' I start throwing obstacles like a knife-thrower.

'All done.' She deflects them by handing me a large brown envelope. 'A friend at the health club has done it for me. Her daughter works in a travel agency. She owed me a favour – I found her a husband. And trust me, *not easy*.' Magda clicks her tongue. 'Forty-one, three cats, a Judy Garland habit. Y'know what I'm saying?'

Only I'm not really listening, I'm tearing open the envelope and pulling out my airline ticket. 'My flight's at two thirty this afternoon?' I gasp.

'Wonderful,' she says absently, tickling Valentino under his chin.

'Magda, that means I have to leave for the airport in . . .' I quickly do the maths ' . . . less than two hours!'

'I know. Shouldn't you be home packing?' She frowns, looking up at me as if surprised to see I'm still standing here. 'You don't want to miss your flight.'

'But . . .' I open my mouth and then close it again. It's pointless. When Magda wants something done, she wants it done yesterday.

'Oh, and here's some reading material for the plane.' Magda passes me a few pages, torn from a magazine. 'It's an article all about Artsy.'

'Who's Artsy?'

'Our new artist!' exclaims Magda, pausing from hand-feeding Valentino. He begins yapping loudly, and picking him up, she shushes him with a flurry of kisses. 'Remember, Loozy, the gallery is counting on you!'

I force a smile. Great. No pressure, then.

I catch a cab home and chuck some things into a holdall. I haven't a clue what to take. I've never been to Martha's Vineyard and have no idea what to expect. I vaguely remember reading something in my guidebook about how it's a little island off Cape Cod where American presidents go on holiday, but I haven't had time to Google it. I mean, is it an actual vineyard? Am I going to be bumping into Obama? Should I take my posh dress or a pair of shorts?

In the end I take both, plus lots of other things that don't go together, and jump into the waiting cab and drive straight to the airport. As Manhattan whizzes by outside, I look at the rest of the travel documents. My return flight isn't until Friday morning. Friday?! That's ages away.

Well, it's not really – it's only two days away – but it *feels* like ages because I'm not going to be able to see Adam until then. *Adam.*

As he pops into my head, I think about last night. Gosh, that was a close shave. For a moment there I thought I'd completely blown it because of Nate's stupid bloody boxer shorts, but thankfully I managed to rescue the situation. Though I'm not sure for how much longer. Feeling a beat of anxiety, I dig my phone out of my pocket and text Adam:

Thanx for last night.

I pause. I think about adding more, about what a lovely evening I had, how I'd like to see him again . . . I start texting, then stop.

Argh, no, I can't put that. It looks far too keen, I decide, quickly deleting that bit. I stare at my phone, agonising. Texting is so hard. It's like every single word is loaded with all this meaning and then you've got the whole decision about whether or not to put a kiss at the end or not.

I look back at my text and add an x. Well, I don't want to appear unfriendly. And I do want to kiss him. Even if it's only on a text. Quickly I press send before I change my mind.

A few seconds later one beeps up from him.

> Hey, trouble. Where R U? Don't tell me you've been
> arrested again . . .

I laugh to myself. By the speed of his response, he obviously didn't agonise over his text, I muse, hitting reply.

> No, in a cab going 2 the airport. Am flying 2 MV to meet a
> new artist.

Two seconds, then another text:

> When R U back?
> Friday.
> Keep Friday eve free. I have surprise 4 U.

I feel a beat of delight.

> What is it?
> If I told U that, it wouldn't be a surprise, would it?

I smile to myself and say bye, feeling more comforted. Perhaps it's actually a *good* thing I'm getting out of town for a few days, I reflect, looking at the positives. This way it will put some distance between me and Nate and I won't have to worry about bumping into him. Or think about him. And I can concentrate on Adam.

Cheered by this thought, I turn and gaze out of the window.

Hopefully by the time I get back on Friday, mine and Nate's relationship will just seem like a bad dream.

I arrive at JFK Airport and go straight to the JetBlue check-in desk, where I discover it's not a direct flight and I have to get a connection in Boston. But that's OK – Boston's only an hour away. I'll read my magazine article on Artsy, I decide, settling into my seat on the plane. Ooh, this is really nice. Plush leather seat, comfy footrest, my own TV screen with lots of different channels . . . Ordering a glass of wine, I fasten my seatbelt and settle back happily with my article. You know, I'm beginning to have a really good feeling about this trip.

The flight is so comfy I almost don't want it to end. I read my article, surf a few TV channels and then before I know it we're landing in Boston and I'm wandering around the airport shops, killing time before my connecting flight. I love airports. There's something about them that makes me feel like I've stepped into some parallel universe, where real life doesn't exist. All these people coming and going, the buzz of excitement, the sense of transience. It's like nothing matters.

Like, for example, money, I muse, picking up an expensive moisturiser. Normally, in the real world, I would baulk at the price, but somehow in Airport World ninety dollars is like Monopoly money. It doesn't seem to count, I reflect, cheerfully handing over my credit card. Ooh, and look at those cute little fridge magnets that say, 'Boston Red Sox,' on them. Spying them by the register, I put a couple in my basket. I'm not exactly sure who the Boston Red Sox are, but Robyn might like those as souvenirs, as she's always sticking horoscopes, vegetarian recipes and to-do lists all over the fridge. Speaking of souvenirs, what about that tea towel with the big red lobster on for Mum . . .?

I end up leaving the shop with two bulging carrier bags and am just wandering into another, which sells electronic gadgets (strangely I've never been even *slightly* interested in a vibrating neck massager or a sound machine to help you sleep, but here in Airport World they're fascinating), when I hear my name.

'Last call for Miss Hemmingway. Please make your way urgently to Gate 4B. Your flight is about to depart.'

And look at my watch.

Fuck. Seeing the time, my heart plummets. How did that happen? A whole hour and a half has suddenly vanished and now I'm late! I'm going to miss my flight!

Fuck, fuck, FUCK.

Cursing under my breath, I charge through departures, my carrier bags banging against my legs. Of course the gate has to be the furthest one away and by the time I get there I'm pouring with sweat and breathless.

'Miss Hemmingway?' A member of ground staff in a fluorescent-orange jacket is waiting for me. She has a walkie-talkie and a very cross-looking expression.

'Yes . . . that's me,' I pant. My heart is thumping against my ribcage and I feel as if I'm going to collapse.

'Hurry! The flight is about to depart,' she reprimands, snatching my boarding card.

'I know, sorry—' I begin apologising, but she quickly ushers me through the turnstile.

'The bus is waiting to take you to your plane.'

I glance out of the glass doors at the little minibus. 'Thanks,' I gasp, then pause. 'Erm . . . where's the plane exactly?' I'm scanning the runway for a jet like the one I just flew in on, but there's nothing, apart from a tiny little propeller thing.

'Right there,' she barks, as if I'm stupid, and points.

To the tiny little propeller thing.

Still, now is not the time to feel nervous, I tell myself firmly, as I hurry on to the waiting minibus and it sets off swiftly across the runway. The flight is only thirty minutes. How bad can it be? I'll be up and down before I even know it.

The propellers are already whirring loudly as I clamber up the metal stairs. Gosh, it's even tinier inside than it looks outside, I realise, glancing in through the porthole windows to see only a handful of seats. And so noisy! Ducking down so I don't bang my head, I climb in through the doorway, where a stewardess in a pair of headphones is waiting impatiently to grab my shopping bags from me and hurry me to the last remaining seat, before rushing back to close the door.

Flustered, I quickly sit down and fasten my seatbelt. Just in the nick of time. I've barely had a second to catch my breath or take in my surroundings before the engines grow even louder and suddenly we're off, accelerating down the runway. I close my eyes tightly, listening to the propellers whirring, feeling the wheels juddering on the tarmac, and then the nose of the plane tips up and we're in the air, climbing steadily.

I feel a beat of relief. Great, that's the worst part over.

'Would you care for a refreshment?'

I open my eyes to see the air stewardess, minus her earphones, standing next to me.

'Just some water, thanks.' I grab the in-flight magazine from the seat in front of me and start flicking through.

'And for you, sir?'

'Nothing for me,' he says gruffly.

I freeze mid-flick. *I know that voice.*

Up until now I've only been vaguely aware of a person in the seat next to me, as I haven't so much as glanced in their direction, but now every single cell in my body is on full alert and is plummeting downwards like I've just jumped out of a plane without a parachute. Actually, that's not a bad idea. At least that would be one way to finally escape.

Instead I continue staring at my magazine, willing it not to be true. For the person sitting next to me *not* to be the person who I know is sitting next to me. In fact, by not even thinking his name to myself, I can pretend it's not real. I'm hallucinating. Or having some kind of lucid dream, and any moment I'm going to wake up and find myself back in my apartment in New York, and not twenty-five thousand feet in the air, on a tiny nine-seater plane, sitting next to—

'You've got to be kidding me. *Lucy?*'

Bang goes my lucid dream.

Having slunk lower and lower behind my magazine, in an attempt to hide, I look up from behind its parapet. 'Oh, hi, Nate,' I say, trying not to meet his eye. As if somehow I can still act as if this is not really happening.

I mean, seriously.

THIS CANNOT REALLY BE HAPPENING.

But of course it is.

'Jesus, it is you!'

'There you go.' The stewardess reappears with my water.

'Oh . . . thanks.' Grateful of the interruption, I take a large gulp. This flight is only thirty minutes. We must have done five already. Briefly I consider trying to ignore him for the next twenty-five.

'What on earth are you doing here?'

Only it's not that easy when he's sitting inches away, staring at me aghast, and is insistent on talking to me.

'Flying to Martha's Vineyard,' I deadpan, turning to face him finally. 'How about you?'

He frowns. 'That's not funny, Lucy.'

'Trust me, I know,' I agree ruefully. 'Do you see me laughing?'

We both stare at each other. I've never actually seen Nate lost for words before, but now he genuinely seems at a loss for what to say or do. I know how he feels. This is getting beyond ridiculous. I mean, what am I supposed to do now? It's not as if there are any rules to follow in a situation like this, are there?

No, but there's the Strategy.

Suddenly I hear Kate's voice in my ear and stiffen. Maybe she's right. Perhaps it might work. After all, nothing else has. Robyn's spell was a complete disaster – I was lucky I didn't wind up in jail – and this *would* be the perfect opportunity to put the Strategy into effect . . . I pause, my mind turning. All my life I've listened to my big sister in times of crisis. She always knows best.

Sod it. That's decided. I'm going to go for it. I've got nothing to lose, except Nate.

OK, so first I need to refresh my memory. Grabbing my bag, which is tucked underneath my seat, I slip my fingers into the front pocket and surreptitiously pull out the four-page document. I've been carrying it with me everywhere, along with my bridal and baby magazines. 'Work,' I say casually to Nate, who's watching me with a frown.

Unfolding it, I have a quick scan of the twenty-five points. OK, so here goes, in no particular order, I'll just start with an easy one . . .

19. Belch.

As a kid, one of my party tricks used to be burping 'The Frog Chorus'. I haven't done it for years, so I'm not sure if I still can, I muse, gulping down a mouthful of air.

'Beurrggghhhh.' Abruptly I let out a loud burp.

Wow, so it still works, I think, feeling a flash of triumph.

I catch sight of Nate's shocked expression.

'Oops, sorry. Just a bit gassy.' I smile sweetly.

Looking appalled, he turns away and opens his briefcase. Pulling out some documents, he begins reading.

I do it again. 'Beurrggghhhh.'

He visibly flinches. 'Can't you take something for that?' he remarks stiffly.

'Well, not really. It's got to come out one way or another.' I force a rueful smile. 'Better from up here than down there.' I motion downwards.

Nate's nostrils flare and I can almost see him squirming in his seat. As am I. This is so excruciatingly embarrassing.

But necessary, I tell myself firmly.

Blocking out every last vestige of decorum, I continue with the Strategy and move on to point number seven.

'And I've got enough going on down there at the moment, what with Auntie Flo.'

'Auntie Flo?' His brow crumples in confusion.

'*My period*,' I gasp loudly in explanation. 'It's that time of the month. You know, cramps, acne, bloating.' I pull up my T-shirt and stick out my stomach as far as I can. 'I mean, just look at that! Buddha belly or what?'

Nate couldn't look more horrified. Turning ashen, he recoils, as if an alien is about to explode from my swollen belly at any moment and eat him alive.

'Seriously, have you ever seen anything like it?' I continue, raising my voice a notch so that it can be heard above the drone of the aircraft. Grabbing as much of it as I can in two fleshy rolls, I waggle it at him menacingly. 'I look almost pregnant.'

'Lucy!' he hisses, finally managing to find his voice and motioning for me to pull down my T-shirt. 'Please! People are looking.'

Which of course is the idea. Nate's worst nightmare is 'people looking'. God forbid you talk too loudly or do something silly and someone glances in your direction. I feel a twinge of mean-ness for torturing him like this, but quickly console myself. I'm being cruel to be kind. To both of us.

'Saying that, I wish I was pregnant,' I continue loudly. 'I'm so broody.'

Gosh, this is fantastic! I'm racing through the Strategy.

Several people turn round and crick their necks to look over at us. Nate goes puce and tries to ignore me by staring down at the documents he was reading. I notice he's gripping them so hard his knuckles have gone white.

'I'd really love to have a baby, wouldn't you?'

'I don't think this is the time or the place,' he mutters tersely, shuffling his papers.

I swallow hard, trying to gather up enough courage to go for my final jab. My *pièce de résistance*. The straw that hopefully breaks the camel's back. I glance around me and see we've got a captive audience.

'Just imagine if we had a baby. It would be so cute!'

A strangled expression flashes across his face, as the rest of the passengers watch for his reaction.

'I'd rather not,' he manages, his cheeks flaming.

'I like Daisy for a girl. What names do you like?'

Nate's jaw clenches tightly. He's really struggling to keep his cool. He scowls at his audience, then back at me furiously.

'Look, if you don't mind, I really need to catch up on some paperwork,' he says gruffly. If looks could kill, I wouldn't be twenty-five thousand feet in the air – I would be six feet under.

'Of course, pumpy-wumpkin,' I say, pouting playfully.

A pet name. In a baby voice. Brilliant.

'I need to catch up on some reading too.' Digging out my pregnancy magazine, I start flicking through the pages, which are filled with photos of bouncing babies. I see Nate glance over, then sharply away, and smile to myself.

With any luck we'll be broken up for good in no time.

Chapter Twenty-Six

Nate and I don't talk for the rest of the flight, and after touching down, we mutter our goodbyes – 'See you around', 'Yeah, you too', while both fervently hoping that's not the case – and grabbing my bags, I go outside to get a taxi.

'Menemsha Inn, please,' I say to the driver, as I climb inside and roll down the window.

It's a lovely warm evening and I turn my face to the slowly sinking sun. It's the magic hour. Everything is bathed in a honey-coloured light, and after the frenzy of New York, the island feels quiet and sleepy. Like the pace of life has slowed down, I muse, as we drive down country lanes bordered by handcrafted stone walls, by fields filled with wild flowers and past clapboard houses and quaint village stores that remind me of *The Waltons*.

According to the driver, I'm staying 'up island', which is the more remote side of the island and where Artsy has his studio. It's also much wilder, I decide, as we pass white windswept beaches with grassy bluffs and a lighthouse standing proud up on the cliff.

After thirty minutes we arrive at the small ramshackle fishing port of Menemsha – blink and you'd miss it – and the cab pulls up a gravel driveway. At the end is a pretty inn with a pitched roof, white-painted windows and a wooden porch complete with a rocking chair on which is curled a big, fat ginger tomcat, fast asleep.

As I pass him with my bags, I tickle his tummy and he stretches out like a draught-excluder and yawns languorously.

'Welcome to Menemsha Inn,' beams a stout, ruddy-cheeked woman when I walk into reception. 'I'm Sylvia.'

'Hi. I'm Lucy Hemmingway. I'm checking in for two nights.'

'One moment, please.' She taps cheerfully at her computer. 'Ah, yes, we've got you in the shell room. That's one of my favourites. It's just down the corridor in a separate annexe. It has an uninterrupted view of the ocean.'

'Super.' I smile happily. Despite the shaky start, I'm really looking forward to my time here on the Vineyard. It really is like turning back the clock, I note, glancing around at the vast stone fireplace, the framed black-and-white photographs of fishing boats, the grandfather clock ticking quietly in the corner.

'Oh dear.'

I turn back to Sylvia. Her smile has slipped slightly.

'Is anything wrong?'

'Erm . . .' She's still tapping at the computer keyboard. Only now she's not so much tapping cheerfully as jabbing frantically. 'I'm afraid we have a slight problem.'

I get a twinge of apprehension. I don't like how she uses the word 'we'.

'Problem?'

'We seem to have double-booked the shell room.'

'Oh.' I feel a beat of disappointment. After her big sell on the shell room I was looking forward to staying in it. Still, I suppose it doesn't matter. I'm only here for two nights. 'Well, never mind. I'm sure all your rooms are lovely,' I say placatingly. 'What else is available?'

There's an ominous pause. 'Well, that's the problem. There isn't anything else available. We're fully booked.'

I look back at her, not quite computing what she's saying. 'But I have a confirmation.' I waggle the documents that Magda gave me.

'I know, my dear, but so does the gentleman.'

I frown. 'What gentleman?'

At that moment the door swings open and my heart sinks. I should've known.

'Nathaniel,' I say stiffly.

'Lucy.' He nods curtly.

'Oh, you two know each other?' cries Sylvia, glancing between us in astonishment.

'Intimately,' says Nate, through gritted teeth.

A look of relief flashes across Sylvia's face. 'Oh, silly me, I didn't realise you were together.'

'No, we're not,' I refute quickly. 'Together, I mean . . . Well, we are . . .' I glance at Nate, who's typing an email on his iPhone ' . . . but we're not supposed to be . . .' I trail off. This is hopeless.

'Oh, I see.' Her eyes widen, then lowering her voice, she says quietly, 'Don't worry, here at Menemsha Inn we're very discreet. The Vineyard has a history of accommodating presidents and world-famous celebrities.'

I look at her blankly.

'Who just happen to be married,' she adds, raising a bushy eyebrow.

Suddenly it registers. Oh my God, she thinks we're having an affair! 'No, it's not like that,' I try explaining quickly, but she's pinned a coy expression on her face and is holding out a key.

'Very discreet,' she repeats in a whisper.

I glance at the key. For a split second I think about trying to demand another room, but it's been a long day and I'm exhausted. I just want take a shower and go to bed.

And if you don't grab that room first, Nate will, hisses a voice inside my head.

'OK, great. Thanks,' I say hastily, and snatching the key, I quickly set off down the corridor.

'The shell room is just to your left,' she calls after me.

Then I hear Nate's voice. 'I'm sorry, but I thought I was in the shell room . . .'

Five minutes later there's a loud rapping at the door. For a moment I consider ignoring it, pretending I can't hear, hoping it will go away.

Yeah, right. This is Nate we're talking about, remember.

Bracing myself, I open the door. 'Oh, it's you,' I say, feigning a look of innocent surprise.

'Of course it's me,' he snaps, brushing past me. 'This is my room.'

'And mine,' I fire back challengingly.

'So it seems.' He nods, glancing around at my stuff, which is already strewn all over the place. I don't know how I manage to do that. I can makeover a spotlessly tidy room in five minutes flat and make it look like it's been lived in for years. I could be on one of those home-makeover TV shows, only with a slight twist.

'I tried everything,' Nate continues, 'but it's August, their busiest time of year, and there's no availability anywhere on the island.' He drops his luggage on the floor.

'Meaning?' I glance at his suitcase nervously.

'Meaning one of us will have to sleep on the sofa.'

We both look over at it. Tucked into the corner, it's this tiny little wicker thing, with plumped-up cushions embroidered with seashells, in keeping with the room's nautical theme.

'I'm six foot three,' he says, turning to me.

'So?'

'So it will have to be you,' he says simply. He takes off his jacket and hangs it over the chair. Then kicking off his shoes, he flops down on the bed, picks up the remote and turns on the TV.

I watch him in amazement. 'Er, hang on a minute.'

Flicking channels, he appears not to hear me.

'I don't think so.'

'Don't think what?' he says absently, getting comfy on a pillow. Suddenly he pounds the bedspread with his fist. 'Oh great, it's the game,' he whoops excitedly.

'Me. On the sofa,' I say loudly.

There's no response. Not even a glimmer. It's like I'm not here. Marching over to the TV, I stand in front of it.

'What the . . .?' He glares at me and motions with the remote. 'I can't see!'

'I have a bad back,' I say, folding my arms.

'Since when?' he gasps exasperatedly.

'Since. I. Got. My. Period,' I repeat slowly.

He blanches. 'OK, whatever.' He sighs, throwing his hands up in the air. 'I don't want to argue with you.'

I'm thrown off balance. 'You don't?'

He pauses to lean across to the bedside table and deftly pop out his contact lenses. Then, reaching for his glasses, he pushes them up his nose and turns to me. 'Look, I don't know what's going on here. I don't know why we keep getting thrown together, and I don't like it any more than you do. For now, though, we're stuck with each other, so why don't we call a truce for the next forty-eight hours?'

I look at him suspiciously. Damn, he's being too reasonable. This is not supposed to be how it works. He's supposed to be furious. Appalled. Horrified. He's supposed to be grabbing his jacket and marching out of the room right now, slamming the door behind him and declaring he never wants to see me again. And if everything goes to plan, he never *will* see me again. And I won't see him either.

And we can both live happily ever after. *Separately.*

And yet . . .

I stifle a yawn. I'm dog tired. Tomorrow is a big day. I'm meeting Artsy at his studio and hopefully I'm going to convince him to show at the gallery. Anxiety twinges as I think of the responsibility that's on my shoulders. I really should get some rest. Maybe Nate is right. Maybe it's time for a ceasefire.

I hesitate, and then . . .

'Budge up.'

Nate looks momentarily surprised but shifts obediently to one side of the bed. I sit down on the other and lean back against the feather pillows. Oh God, that feels good.

'I'm going to order room service. Hungry?' he asks, glancing across at me.

'Oh, I don't think . . .' I begin, then pause as my stomach rumbles. 'Actually, yeah, I'm starving.'

'I hear the clam chowder is awesome here,' he continues.

I smile ruefully. 'OK, clam chowder it is.'

He picks up the phone and dials, then covers the mouthpiece. 'Just for the record, this is as painful for me as it is for you.' Then, turning back to the phone, he asks, 'You want crackers with that?'

After we've eaten two big bowls of the most delicious clam chowder, Nate declares he's going to call it a night. 'Do you want to use the bathroom first or shall I?' he asks politely.

'It's fine, go ahead,' I reply, equally politely.

See, we can do this, I tell myself, as he disappears for five minutes, then re-emerges in his T-shirt and boxer shorts. We're two mature adults. My eyes flick to his boxers and I get a fright – I got rid of the pineapple ones, but do these have *Rudolph* on them? Quickly I avert my gaze. Don't look, Lucy, don't look. Pretend like it's not happening.

I keep my eyes fixed determinedly on the TV screen. Only, instead of heading for the sofa, he heads back towards the bed and proceeds to get under the covers. Er, just a minute. Surreptitiously sliding my eyes sideways, I watch him snuggling into a pillow. *What the . . . ?*

Horror and indignation stab, but I remain calm.

OK, so I have two options:

1. Sod the truce, have a huge row and forcibly try to remove him from the bed
    (which, considering he's six three and about thirteen stone will not be easy).
2. Sleep on the sofa.

I eye the uncomfortable-looking sofa with annoyance. That is just so unfair. So bloody unfair. Why is it that I have to— In the middle of my cerebral ranting a third option strikes:

3. Take the Strategy one step further and share the bed.

Oh, no.
Oh, no, oh, no, oh, no.

Just the thought makes me shudder. Whereas only a few weeks ago I couldn't think of anything I wanted to do more than climb into bed with Nate, now I can't think of anything I want to do less. Like my sister says, it's always about timing. And my timing sucks, I muse, looking across at Nate.

What about our truce?

He broke the truce when he clambered into bed, argues the other voice in my head.

But—

All's fair in love and war, it reminds me. *Or when you can't get rid of your soulmate . . .*

Right, OK, that's it. I'm convinced. In for a penny, in for a pound.

Feeling like a soldier preparing for battle, I grab my washbag and my 'uniform' and march into the bathroom. I've got to make myself look as unattractive as possible, I tell myself, scrubbing my face clean of make-up. Two little piggy eyes stare back at me in the mirror. Hmm, not bad. I tie up my hair in an unflattering top-knot. Not bad indeed. Squeezing out toothpaste, I apply a couple of big dollops – one on my nose and one on my chin – as a make-do spot cream. Revolting! Excellent.

Now for my 'bedtime attire'. God, what a difference a couple of weeks make. Before, when I was sleeping with Nate, I was applying lip gloss, dabbing perfume on my pulse points and slipping into my special-occasion lingerie. Now I'm pulling on an old greying vest and the big, ugly pair of period knickers that I always carry with me in case of emergencies. And the same goes for Tampax.

Digging out a box, I scatter them freely around the bathroom, like some might scatter rose petals, along with a half-used tube of Canestan (another of my emergency supplies), which I leave in a prominent position next to the washbasin, with the words 'For fungal infections' face up. Genius! Then taking one last look in the mirror, and almost frightening myself to death, I go back into the bedroom.

Damn, he looks asleep. Spotting Nate spread-eagled in the middle of the bed and hogging the covers, my plans are suddenly in danger of being thwarted. I can't have gone to all this trouble for nothing . . . I have to think fast. Grabbing the remote control, I quickly flick on the TV. *Sleepless in Seattle* is now playing. Perfect. All men hate this film. In fact, another ex-boyfriend of mine used to hate it so much that every time Meg Ryan came on the screen, he'd come out in hives.

Hitting the volume button, I turn it right up.

'Huh?' Nate rolls over and opens his eyes. At the sight of me he visibly recoils. 'Jesus, what's that on your face?'

'Spot cream,' I say, tugging up my big black period knickers. I see his eyes sweeping over me. 'I'm really breaking out. I just had a good squeeze in the bathroom.' I pull a face. 'Honestly, the stuff that came out!'

He looks like he's about to gag.

Pulling back the covers, I slide into the other side of the bed, and then, for the briefest of moments, I suddenly feel a tremor of doubt. What if this get-up doesn't put him off? What if he thinks I'm coming on to him? What if he's – I swallow hard as panic begins knotting my stomach – *horny*?

As the terrifying thought strikes, so does another: What if Kate's been right all along and he *is* trying to get back with me?

Oh shit, I know . . . Quickly remembering the Strategy, I stuff my finger up my nostril and start picking my nose, just to be on the safe side. I needn't have worried, though. A look of terror flashes across his face and immediately he scuttles as far as possible to his side of the bed.

'Well, night,' I say, forcing myself to sound all breezy.

'Um . . . yeah, night,' he says gruffly.

I glance across at him. He's pulled up the covers tightly around his chin and is lying teetering on the far side of the bed. Breathing a sigh of relief, I remove my finger from my nostril. Thank goodness. For a horrible moment there I thought I was going to have to eat it.

Shuddering, I turn off the light.

It's going to be a long thirty-six hours.

Chapter Twenty-Seven

When I wake up the next morning, I find myself alone in bed.

He's gone!

For a split second joy pierces my heart like a silver bullet. Kate, you star! You were right! The Strategy worked! Overjoyed, I spread out starfish wide, relishing the feeling of space, freedom, triumph.

His suitcase. It's still here. *Shit.*

Feeling a clunk of dismay, I stare at it resentfully, before peeling back the covers and climbing out of bed. Oh well, like he said, it's only for a couple of days. It's not like it's for ever.

Or so you hope, reminds the voice of doom in my head.

Oh, shut up.

The phone rings, interrupting my thoughts. Reaching over, I pick up. 'Hello?'

There's a brief pause and then a female voice says briskly, 'Oh, I must have been put through to the wrong room. I'm sorry to bother you.'

'No worries.' I stifle a yawn. 'What room do you want?'

'Um . . .' I can hear the rustle of papers. 'I believe it's the shell room.'

'No, you've got the right room.'

'Oh . . .' She sounds confused. 'I was looking for Nathaniel Kennedy.'

'You mean Nate? He's already gone out—' I suddenly have a thought and break off. 'Hang on. He might be in the shower . . .' Putting down the phone, I quickly jump out of bed and try the bathroom door handle to see if it's locked. It's not, and the bathroom is empty. 'No, sorry. Can I take a message?'

There's silence on the other end of the line.

'Or you can try him on his cell phone. Do you have his number . . .? Hello?'

She's hung up. I feel a snap of annoyance. I hate it when people do that. It's so rude.

I stare at the receiver for a moment, feeling rankled, then determinedly shoving all thoughts of Nate and his rude friends out of my brain, I put it back on the cradle and dash into the bathroom. I have my big meeting with Artsy this morning. I can't be thinking about anything but that, I remind myself, as I quickly shower and get ready.

Nerves twist in my stomach. According to the article I read on the plane, he's described as 'an eccentric recluse', which, having dealt with lots of artists, is most likely the journalist's polite way of saying he's difficult, unfriendly and completely weird.

And I have to make friends and persuade him to show at the gallery, I think, giving up on my hair and rushing outside to my waiting taxi. Considering no one has yet managed to do this, it's not going to be easy. Perhaps impossible, I brood, thinking about Magda and how she's pinning all her hopes on this meeting.

The cab pulls out of the driveway, and as it heads along the coastal road towards Aquinnah, the most remote part of the island, at the southwestern tip, I can feel my spirits sinking to my default setting of Mancunian pessimism. My mind runs along ahead to a terrible meeting, unsuccessful outcome and breaking the news to Magda that I've failed, it's all over, she's out of a home and I'm out of a job.

Whoa!!!!

Screeching the brakes on my negativity, I quickly try to rally. This is no good at all. I can't turn up with that attitude. I'm supposed to be cheerful, hopeful, positive. Just the fact that Magda managed to get Artsy to agree to a meeting is hugely impressive. After years in the business, she knows a lot of people, and has asked a lot of favours, but apparently what clinched it is that she and Artsy share the same philosophy: art should be free to be enjoyed by everyone. Which is brilliant.

Saying that, his art isn't free. On the contrary, his pieces run into tens of hundreds of thousands.

Still, no need to split hairs, I tell myself firmly, as we reach a gate swung wide and off its hinges with the sign 'Keep Out' scrawled on it and turn down an unmade road. The cab driver seemed to know exactly where he was going when I asked him to go to 'Artsy's house' (the only address I had), and as I bounce around on the back seat, I see a ramshackle farmhouse ahead of me through the windscreen.

'This is far as I can go,' declares the cab driver after a couple of minutes.

'OK, great, thanks.' Paying him, I climb out, and as the cab reverses down the lane, I look around me.

When the journalist said remote, he wasn't wrong. Perched up high and hugging the edge of a cliffside, I'm surrounded by tufty hillocks and wild, unkempt farmland. I can't see anything for miles, apart from the ocean on one side of me and the farmhouse on the other. I walk towards it. Old and weather-beaten, one of the windows appears to be boarded up, and several chickens are running freely around it. Boldly I knock on the door. Nothing. I knock a second time. Again nothing.

I wonder if he's forgotten I'm coming. I stare uncertainly at the peeling paint on the door for a moment, unsure about what to do. I can't call him. Artsy has no phone – landline or mobile. Or email him – no Internet or email address either. Apparently Magda had to go through a long and complicated process in order to contact him, ringing various friends of friends on the island who passed secret messages back and forth, like something out of the French Resistance.

I wait a few minutes longer, but it's now abundantly clear there's no one in the house. It's strange for a recluse, but maybe today he's not feeling that reclusive. Maybe today he's gone out. Stepping back from the porch, I hesitate for a moment, unsure of what to do next, then decide to have a look around. Well, I'm here now.

Picking my way through the grass in my new sandals, I walk around the side of the ramshackle barns and outbuildings. There's an abandoned tractor, a rusty bicycle leaning up against a wall, a drum kit . . . A drum kit? What's a drum kit doing in the middle of a field? Shielding my eyes from the bright sunshine, I stare at it in astonishment, before being distracted by the sight of a man up ahead digging a vegetable patch.

Maybe he can help. I call over to him, 'Excuse me. Do you know where I can find Artsy?'

Straightening up, he turns round and, seeing me, strides over. Tall and broad-shouldered, he's wearing a deerstalker hat, plus-fours and argyle socks, and looks a lot like the bronze statue of Sherlock Holmes that's outside Baker Street Tube Station. It makes for a bizarre sight. Not helped by the fact he's got a big bushy beard and is smoking a pipe. While wearing flying goggles.

Taking them off, he peers at me. 'Who's looking for him?' he asks, in a gruff southern drawl.

'My name's Lucy Hemmingway. I'm from Number Thirty-Eight, a gallery in New York.' I realise I'm gabbling.

He throws out his hand, which is the size of a dinner plate. 'Artsy. Pleased to meet you.'

Of course. It had to be him. Who else would wear such an outfit? 'Oh . . . hi,' I stammer. Smiling, I shake his hand. He's not anything like I imagined, though I'm not sure what I did imagine, as he never allows himself to be photographed.

He hands me a shovel. 'You can help me dig for potatoes.'

Dig for potatoes? I look down at the earth and try not to think about the new sandals that I wore especially for our meeting. 'Um . . . thanks.'

Luckily it seems Artsy is not just an artist, he's also a true gentleman.

'Here, put these on,' and smiling, he holds out two plastic bags. 'For your feet, so they don't get dirty.'

For the next hour I dig for potatoes with plastic bags tied around my feet. Slightly surreal, and not exactly the first impression I wanted to make, but then Artsy is renowned for being eccentric and so it was never going to be me and him chatting over a cappuccino.

During the whole time we don't talk about art. Instead we talk about composting, organic fertilisers and the benefits of horse manure versus cow manure. Understandably he does most of the talking – my knowledge of cow manure extends to the fact I once trod in a cowpat on a farm near my parents' – while I listen politely and sneak sideways glances at him. The article didn't give his date of birth – he's very secretive about that, as he is about a lot of things – but underneath the beard and goggles, I ascertain he's probably in his thirties.

And attractive, I decide, noticing his piercing blue eyes and perfect white teeth, hidden underneath his beard and only revealed when he smiles. It's as if the beard and his wacky outfit are part of his disguise, his desire to remain anonymous, but if he shaved it off and wore a T-shirt and jeans, he'd actually be rather devilishly good-looking, I realise, as he rolls up his sleeves to expose large, tanned forearms.

After a back-breaking hour in the hot sunshine, he finally declares it's time we break for ice cream.

'Vanilla or pistachio?' he demands, as we troop into one of the barns, where a large fridge with the words 'Eat Me' is standing. He flings it open to reveal nothing but tubs of ice cream and stacks of cones.

'Vanilla, please.' I smile at his eccentricity.

'Coming right up.' Grabbing a cone, he scoops out a ball of ice cream and passes it to me, then does one for himself. 'Delicious, hey?' He looks to me for approval. 'I love these cones. They're made from actual waffles, you know?'

'Mmm, yummy.' I nod approvingly.

'So . . .' Taking a lick of his ice cream, he studies me.

'So . . .' I say, trying to sound all breezy and not really nervous, which is how I am feeling. I can't put it off any longer. I have to bring up his artwork. I take a deep breath and swallow hard. 'About your artwork . . .'

'Wanna see it?' He flashes me a grin.

Taken aback, I stare at him. Crikey, that was easy. 'Absolutely.' I nod, and feeling myself relax, I break into a broad smile. 'I'd love to.'

His studio is a large barn at the rear of the farm. Sliding back the door, shafts of sunlight flood inside, lighting up the dust particles, which twirl round like glitter in a snow globe. I'm filled with excitement and anticipation. Artsy is a hot new talent, a graffiti artist known for his ironic phrases and subverted images, and I'm entering his inner sanctuary, where he works, where he creates, where the 'magic' happens. I feel like an explorer about to discover a whole new world.

What I discover, instead, is a giant washing line. Strung the full length of the barn, it's hung with dozens of large white sheets, each stencilled with various graphics and slogans. On one is painted a giant heart in all its anatomical detail with the words 'Life is love' spray-painted across it. On another a picture of a series of hand-silhouettes that spell out, 'It's complicated.' Another is simply a plain white sheet and right in the middle, in lettering so tiny that you have to go right up to it and squint, is the word 'Why?'

'Wow, these are . . .'

'Different?' he finishes my sentence.

'Very.' I nod. 'Tell me, why did you choose to use sheets as your medium?'

I'm expecting a long, convoluted answer, but instead he just shrugs. 'Have you any idea how much canvases that size are?' He pulls a face. 'Total rip-off!'

I smile at his honesty. I'm beginning to really like Artsy. Like his art, he's certainly different.

'Sheets were perfect, but I used other stuff as well . . .' He walks further into the barn, past piles of paint cans, brushes and aerosols, to another washing line. This one is strung with shirts, trousers, socks and underwear – all dirty, and all painted with slogans and words.

'It's sort of a metaphor for airing your dirty laundry,' he's saying. 'Only I really am airing my dirty laundry.' He bends down to sniff a sock. 'Pheugghhh.'

'And why all the umbrellas?' I ask, amused, pointing to a whole washing line strung with them, all painted with different graffiti.

'Well, they make wonderful canvases, plus I thought I'd high-light the plight of the missing umbrellas.' He shrugs. 'Everyone's always losing their umbrellas. They're left on the subway, in cafes, in bars. But where do they all end up?' He looks at me beseechingly. 'Maybe there's some parallel universe where they're all propping up a singles bar, meeting other singleton umbrellas, creating mismatched waterproof couples . . .'

'Maybe.' I nod. He really is kooky-for-Coco-Pops, and yet there's something childlike in his imagination and enthusi-asm that's oddly appealing. Having said that, eccentric people always are appealing, aren't they? Like your crazy aunt who's in her eighties and wears feather boas and does the can-can. Actually, no, that's just my crazy aunt.

'So, what are you thinking?'

I turn back to see Artsy looking at me, his brow crinkled up, like a child waiting approval.

'I think the gallery would love to represent you,' I say, a little nervously. After all, he must have heard this a million times.

If he has, he still looks delighted. 'Really?'

'Yes, really.' I nod.

'Huh.' He smiles faintly to himself and seems to be turning the idea over in his head. I think he's going to say something, *anything*, but then suddenly he's sliding his goggles back down and holding out his hand. 'Well, I must get back to my potatoes.'

Our meeting must be over.

'Um . . . yes, of course.' I smile, hiding my disappointment, and shake his hand. 'It's been great meeting you, and thank you for taking the time—'

Before I can finish he's striding out of the barn. I hurry after him before I'm locked in. Trust me, I wouldn't put it past him.

'So, any last questions?' Padlocking the barn door, he turns to me. 'Speak now or for ever hold your peace.' Twirling his hand above his head, he does a silly, formal bow.

I don't move a muscle. There's nothing Artsy could do or say now to surprise me.

Except . . .

'Why all the secrecy?' I blurt, before I can stop myself.

His expression clouds and a large furrow appears down his forehead and runs underneath the glass of his goggles.

Oh shit, me and my big mouth. Immediately I regret my question. What on earth did I go and say that for? And just as it was going so well. Feeling a stab of panic, I try doing what I always do when I regret saying something, and that's say even more. 'I mean, no one even knows your real name.'

When really I should just shut the f*** up.

'Do you ask Sting his real name?' he demands. 'Or Madonna?'

'Actually, Madonna is her real name,' I can't help pointing out.

'It is?' Surprise flashes across his face, followed by one of his handsome smiles. 'Well, in that case I'll let you in on a secret. It's actually really embarrassing . . .' And pressing his bushy beard against my face, he whispers it in my ear.

Chapter Twenty-Eight

'His name's Harold!'

An hour later I'm in a café in town making a frantic call to Robyn.

'Lucy?' She sounds disorientated. 'Is everything OK?'

'Did you hear what I just said?' Ever since Artsy told me his real name, I've been desperate to get hold of Robyn to tell her the news, but the signal is so sketchy on the island that it's only now, back in town, that I've finally got reception.

'Um, sorry . . . say that again.'

'The artist who I've come to see in Martha's Vineyard,' I cry down the phone. 'You're never going to believe this, but his name's Harold!'

Robyn takes a breath. 'You met someone called Harold?' she whispers.

OK, so I'm *slightly* breaking the confidentiality agreement.

'But it's a secret,' I add quickly. I was always useless at keeping secrets. By their very nature, as soon as you know one, you have to tell someone. But this is more than just a secret, I think, in justification. This is her destiny. *This is Harold!*

God, I'm getting as bad as she is.

'What does he look like?' she asks quietly.

'Tall, dark, handsome . . .' I trail off. 'Well, he would be if he shaved off the big bushy beard and he wore some different clothes, but I'm sure you can sort that out.'

There's silence on the other end of the line.

'Robyn? Are you there?'

'Yes, I'm here.' She sounds bizarrely calm. I thought she'd be whooping excitedly down the phone. But no, *I'm* the one whooping excitedly down the phone. I know, maybe she's in shock, I suddenly realise.

'Hey, are you OK?' I feel a beat of concern. 'I know it's probably come as a bit of a shock.'

'No, not really,' she says evenly.

'It's not?' Now *I'm* the one in shock.

'Of course not,' she replies, sounding completely unfazed. 'I always knew he was out there and I'd find him one way or another. How could I not? He's my soulmate,' she says with absolute certainty. 'It was just a question of where and when. Like everything, it's all about timing and—' She breaks off. 'Sorry, D, I'm just on the phone. I won't be a minute.'

'Who's D?' I frown.

'Oh . . . um, Daniel,' she says, sounding cornered. 'We're at Rockaway Beach. It's super hot, so we came here for the day. You've never been, have you?'

She's changing the subject, which means only one thing: she's hiding something.

'What's going on with you and Daniel?' I ask suspiciously.

'Nothing,' she fires back innocently. 'We're just friends.' She lowers her voice. 'It's totally platonic.'

'Hey, Robyn, will you rub some lotion on my back?'

'You're rubbing lotion on him?'

'Sorry, Lucy, but I'm going to have to go.'

'*Go?*' I look at my phone in disbelief. Did I just mishear? She's been looking for Harold for months. She's visited a psychic. Made a vision board. Lit candles. Said her affirmations. Accosted strangers in the street. And now here I am ringing to tell her I've found him *and she wants to go*? 'OK,' I say reluctantly. 'Well, make sure to keep all your fingers and toes crossed. If he decides to exhibit with us, you'll meet him then.'

'Meet who?' she asks distractedly.

'Harold!' I gasp incredulously.

'Oh . . . awesome.'

Is it just me or could she have made that sound any *less* awesome?

'OK, well, have fun at the beach.' I shrug.

'Thanks! Bye.'

'Bye.'

Then she's gone and I'm left feeling slightly bewildered. Well, that didn't go quite how I was expecting. I never even got a chance to tell her about Nate being here, I realise. Oh well, I guess it can wait until I get back to New York, I muse. After all, it's not long now. My flight's tomorrow morning, so I'll be home by the afternoon.

Plenty of time to get ready for my date with Adam.

As the thought zips through my brain, I feel a delicious thrill of excitement and nerves. Since arriving on the island, I've tried not to think about Adam. I didn't want to be distracted before my big meeting with Artsy by thoughts of his crazy long eyelashes, the way he looked at me that night we sat on my fire escape, *that kiss*.

When I haven't been thinking about Artsy, my thoughts have been hijacked by Nate, I think grimly, rewinding back to last night, me and him, together in the shell room . . . before hastily fast-forwarding back to my date with Adam. OK, focus, Lucy, focus.

Briefly I think about calling him, but the beep of my phone battery reminds me that I've forgotten to pack my charger and I still need to ring Magda. I make a quick call to tell her how the meeting went, which brings into sharp focus that I still don't really have a clue *how* the meeting went – 'We dug for potatoes, ate ice cream and talked about umbrellas.' Then I drain my coffee, leave the café and walk down to the harbour.

A small ferry is making its way across the water. Plonking myself down on the harbour wall, I watch it for a moment. I feel unexpectedly wistful. OK, so I'm not going to miss having to share a bed with Nate, but it would be nice to spend a bit longer here. Explore a little. On the way back from meeting Artsy, I got a very chatty taxi driver who regaled me with stories about the island, including telling me about when Steven Spielberg filmed the famous scenes from *Jaws* here in Edgartown. Then he told me about the tragic car accident involving Teddy Kennedy and a young girl, who was killed when, late at night, coming back from a party in 1969, he drove off a bridge leading to the tiny island of Chappaquiddick.

That's where the ferry is coming from, I muse, watching it for a few more moments as it chugs calmly across the short gap between the two islands. I'm used to ferries being huge ocean-going vessels, but this looks more like someone cut a short piece of road and made it float on the water. Look, it can only fit three cars on it, I note, counting them, and just a few foot passengers.

As the ferry chugs nearer, my eyes flick across them. There's a couple with bikes, a woman with a toddler and . . . Is that Nate? I squint in the sunlight. Yup, that's definitely him – I'd recognise that combo of navy blazer, pale blue shirt and pleated chinos anywhere. When it comes to clothes, Nate doesn't do casual; he does middle-aged. He's chatting to a smartly dressed woman and I watch as they disembark and shake hands. Then he walks towards where I'm sitting.

'Hey, fancy seeing you here.' I manage a smile as he passes me.

He looks over and stops. He doesn't look best pleased. 'You again.'

I bite my tongue. Think mature. Think Bruce and Demi. Think one more night and then it's all over. 'Did you sleep well?'

Pushing his sunglasses up on to his forehead, he shoots me a look. 'I've had better nights,' he says with irony. 'What about you?'

My mind flicks back to last night, in *that* bed, being on tenterhooks and waking up every five seconds terrified I'd mistakenly spooned him in my sleep. 'I've had better nights too.'

'So we can agree on some things.' He smiles, despite himself. 'How was your day?'

'Pretty good.' I nod. 'And you?'

See. We're being so civil to each other. It's incredible.

'Pretty good.' He pauses. 'What was it you said you were doing here again?'

I didn't. I was too busy belching, picking my nose and throwing Tampax around the bathroom, I think guiltily. 'I was meeting with an artist.' Well, better not say too much.

If I'm worried Nate is going to ask me questions, I don't have to worry.

'Oh,' he says, but more out of politeness than any genuine interest. Nate never was particularly interested in my work. It was always his career we talked about.

'What about you?' I bounce the question back to him.

He waves some brochures he's holding. 'Looking at real estate.'

'You're buying a place here?' I gasp. Being curious, I peeked in a few estate agents' windows earlier just to see, and trust me, it is *not* cheap.

'Thinking about it.' He shrugs casually. 'For the summer.'

'Wow.' God, he really is loaded, isn't he? A rented penthouse in New York, a summer house in the Vineyard. For a brief second I imagine my life if things had worked out differently. Me and Nate at our stunning hideaway beach house, with our own private beach, just the two of us.

'Well, I'm going to take a walk back into town.'

'Yeah, me too.' I nod.

Actually, the way things are going, that might yet still happen, I think with a stab of fright.

We start making our way up the main high street. Lined with souvenir shops, art galleries and tourists, it reminds me of the Cotswolds. Everywhere you look there's someone eating fudge, or taking a photograph of something twee, or simply staring aimlessly into shop windows selling painted china cats, terrible art, antique jewellery . . . I watch a couple hover by the small bowed window, their arms wrapped round each other's waists, her leaning in, *him pulling away*.

And have an idea.

'Hey, look over here,' I pipe up, grabbing Nate by the elbow and steering him towards the store.

'Huh? What?' Regardless of the fact there's hardly any phone reception on the island, Nate has found a weak signal and is chatting away to his realtor about uninterrupted views and under-floor heating.

'What do you think?'

The couple has now moved away and we have the whole window to ourselves. It's just as I thought: it's a whole window of antique rings. *Antique engagement rings.*

'Sorry, Jennifer, one minute.' Slapping his hand over his iPhone, he turns to me in confusion. 'What have you dragged me over here for?'

'What about the pink sapphire with the baguette diamonds?'

God, I can't believe I know all this stuff. Baguette diamonds? Where did I get that from? Females must just absorb this stuff through osmosis.

'Yes, very nice,' he says, not even looking before going back to his phone call. 'Hi, Jennifer. Sorry – you were saying about the under-floor heating?'

This is harder than I thought. 'Maybe you could buy it for me?' I say loudly, and gaze beseechingly at Nate.

A sharp crevice splits down his forehead. 'You want me to buy it?' he asks, incredulous.

'Well, that's the idea.'

'Sorry, no, Jennifer, I wasn't talking about the Chappaquiddick house.' He glares at me. 'Look, can you give me a few minutes? I'll call you right back.' He gets off the phone, his face furious. 'Jesus, Lucy,' he gasps. 'What's got into you? Why the hell should I be buying you a ring, for Christ's sake?'

I widen my eyes pointedly. 'Why do men usually buy women rings?'

He stares in bewilderment. Then suddenly the penny drops. 'What the . . .?' He pauses, trying to contain himself. 'Have you gone *insane*?'

'No.' I shake my head. 'It's just . . .' The words stick in my throat and I swallow hard. OK, come on, Lucy, you can do it. Screwing up all my courage, I think about the Strategy. It was Kate's second suggestion. She said it couldn't possibly fail . . .

I screw my hands into tight fists and dive off the edge.

'I'm in love with you,' I blurt.

Nate looks at me like I've suddenly got two heads. The colour seems to drain from his face and a million different emotions flash across his features – shock, disbelief, horror, scepticism, before finally settling on suspicion.

'What are you up to?' Narrowing his eyes, he peers at me.

'Up to?' I feign innocence. Badly.

'You and I both know that's not true,' he says simply. 'I mean, please, *those granny panties?*' He pulls a face. 'No woman would wear those in front of a man she was in love with.'

I feel my cheeks flush. 'No, but . . .' I'm about to argue, but what's the point? It's not going to work. He doesn't believe, and who can blame him? 'OK, so you're right. I'm not in love with you.'

'Good. Because as you might have guessed, I'm not in love with you either.'

'I guess that's something else we agree on, then,' I say, feeling rather foolish after my outburst.

He throws me a withering look. 'Believe me, I'm as horrified as you are that we've been thrown together these past couple of days. When you sat down on the plane next to me, my heart just sank.'

'It did?'

'Are you kidding me? Like a rock.' He nods. 'It was bad enough bumping into you the whole time in New York, but trapped on an island together? I have to confess I thought you were stalking me.'

'*Me?*' I look at him with indignation. 'Stalking *you?*'

'Well, c'mon, there's coincidence and there's *coincidence.*' He raises his eyebrows. 'I thought you were trying to find a way to get back with me.'

I'm speechless. Totally speechless.

'A friend of mine said it was obvious. I mean, all those calls.' He throws me a pointed look. 'Apparently that's what girls do.'

'*That's what girls do?*' I repeat. I can't believe I'm hearing this.

'He said you were probably a psycho ex.'

I glare at him in disbelief. '*Me? A psycho ex?*' Oh my God, wait till I tell Kate.

'For a moment I almost believed him.' He pauses, as if steeling himself, then adds in a low voice, 'Until I saw those panties.'

He makes a scary face, but the corners of his mouth twitch in amusement and I can't help smiling.

'It's been hell for me too, you know,' I protest.

'I'm sure.' He nods. 'It's not pleasant for either of us.'

'You know, maybe we can end up being friends,' I say, as we move away from the jewellery shop.

'Hey, steady on,' he replies sardonically.

'OK, well, what about acquaintances? Our only contact can be a Christmas card every year,' I suggest. 'Unless of course I forget.'

'Or I delete your address. By accident, of course.'

I feel a shift, as if we've entered a new phase in our relationship, an understanding.

'Sounds perfect.' I grin.

'Doesn't it?' He grins back.

We end up staying in town and having dinner together. It goes fairly smoothly, apart from when I snap at him for making a fuss about wanting to taste their wine list (I mean, really. We're in Pappa's Pizza. They have two wines: house red and house white), and he snaps at me for using my fingers to eat the calamari starter we're sharing.

Then there's the bit when he tells me off for glancing at a text that beeps up from Adam – Looking 4ward 2 tomorrow x – and texting a reply – Me 2 x – and I accuse him of being a hypocrite for using his iPhone at the table, which results in him doing that thing with his hand where he tries to shush me for talking too loudly and I get infuriated and tell him to sod off loudly.

Followed by several long sulky silences from both of us.

All in all, though, it's pretty civil, and although it's not an experience I'd want to repeat, we both emerge alive, which, considering there were sharp implements of cutlery at the table, is saying something.

After the meal, Nate offers to give me a lift back to the inn in his rental car, which is lucky, as on leaving the restaurant, we discover it's started raining heavily.

'Probably a storm coming,' comments Nate, pausing in the doorway to put up his collar. 'You get some pretty big ones here in the summer.'

'Big storms?' I repeat. 'How big?'

'Oh, pretty big.' He shrugs, then dashes out into the blackness, holding his blazer above his head. 'C'mon, run!'

Fuck. Bracing myself, I race after him across the car park. A few seconds is all it takes, but by the time I get in the car I'm drenched.

'Didn't you have a jacket?' he says, stating the obvious.

'If I had, I'd be wearing it,' I gasp, slamming the door closed behind me and peeling off my soaking cardigan. I glance across at Nate. He's totally dry. 'You know, a gentleman would have lent me his.'

'Why should I lend you my blazer?' he remarks, putting the car into gear and heading out of the car park. 'It's your fault if you're not sensible enough to bring a jacket. That's the problem with you, Lucy. You're never sensible.'

My jaw sets hard. 'How was I supposed to know there was going to be a storm?' I reply, trying to stay calm.

'Didn't you check the weather report?'

'No, Nate, I didn't check the weather report,' I fire back.

'Well, there you go,' he says smugly. 'Let that be a lesson.'

Argggghhh! He's so patronising I want to hit him over the head with his bloody weather report, but instead I take a couple of deep breaths and, ignoring him, sit on my clenched fists and stare out of the window.

Outside it's pitch-black. The island isn't like New York – there aren't a million lights illuminating the sky – and we head out of town and start driving down a small road, into thick, velvety darkness. Nate puts on his high beams, but rain is pelting against the windscreen, making it impossible to see.

'Be careful,' I say after a moment. 'You need to slow down. You're driving too fast.'

'I'm not driving too fast,' he replies. 'It's fine.'

'Don't you know what happened to Teddy Kennedy?' I reply. 'In fact . . . are you related?'

He tuts impatiently. 'Just quit it, OK?'

My patience snaps. 'No, I won't quit it,' I cry above the sound of the windscreen wipers, which are beating furiously. 'Slow down!'

'Jesus, I'd forgotten what a nag you are!' he grumbles.

'And I'd forgotten what a bad driver you are!' I mutter, my mind flicking back to when we were teenagers and Nate drove me from Venice to Florence for the weekend and nearly crashed because he insisted on racing the Italian drivers.

He swerves to avoid a giant puddle spilling across the road and I'm thrown back into my seat by my seatbelt.

'Are you trying to kill me?' I shriek.

'Well, that would be one way of getting rid of you,' he yells, glancing sideways at me.

'What are you doing? Keep your eyes on the road!' I yell back.

'My eyes *are* on the road!'

'And slow down!'

'Lucy, am I driving or you?'

'You are, but you're going too fast.'

'I am not going too fast!'

A huge bolt of lightning splinters the sky, illuminating the inky darkness, followed by a deafening crack of thunder. Every nerve ending jumps and I grip the seat with my fingers. Shit, we're really in the eye of the storm now. Rain is lashing down, pummelling the car and flooding the road. I feel the back wheels skidding.

'Be careful. You're going to hydroplane!' I roar over the din.

'Of course I'm not going to hydroplane!' he roars back.

'Nate, be careful. Look where you're going.'

'*Argghhh!*'

Everything happens so fast. All I'm aware of is our voices sounding in stereo, me shrieking, him yelling, as suddenly he loses control of the wheel. Now we're being flung across the road. The car is spinning out of control. We're veering off into the blackness ... I hear the tyres screeching ... see flashes of fields, bushes ... feel the sensation of being thrown forwards.

And then ... *boom!*

Chapter Twenty-Nine

Dazed, I open my eyes and am immediately blinded by bright lights. Oh my God, so this is it. It's all over. I'm in heaven. Any minute now I'm going to hear piped musak, arrive at the pearly white gates and see my grandma, waiting for me with a big pile of her homemade coconut macaroons.

'Shit!'

I swivel sideways, but instead of Grandma and her coconut macaroons, it's Nate.

Seriously, there is no getting away from him. Not even in the afterlife.

'Are you OK?'

'OK?' I round on him in disbelief. 'You've killed me!'

'Oh, stop being a drama queen,' he snaps. 'You're fine. We hit a tree, that's all.'

There's a brief silence as I register this information. I'm not dead. Then . . .

'That's all!' I exclaim. 'You drive like a crazy man in a storm and crash into a tree and nearly kill both of us and *that's all*! I've probably broken my arms and legs because of you!'

'Well, have you?'

I wiggle my arms and legs. 'No, but that's not the point.'

'That's totally the point,' he replies, rubbing his forehead in agitation. Letting out a deep sigh, he hugs the steering wheel.

Reluctantly I feel a beat of concern. 'Are you OK?'

'Fine, no damage done,' he says stiffly. 'Not sure about the car, though.'

Following his gaze, I stare out through the windscreen towards the bright lights. Only now I realise, slightly shamefacedly, that they're just headlights, and they're shining brightly at the trunk of a large tree. Up against which the bonnet is completely scrunched.

'Well, it still starts,' he mutters, firing up the engine. 'That's something.'

Relief washes over me. Thank God. Soon I'll be back at the inn safe and sound, tucked up in bed.

I scratch that image. I'll stick with just being back at the inn.

Rain is still drumming hard on the roof of the car as Nate sticks it into reverse and puts his foot on the accelerator. My relief is short-lived. There's the high-pitched sound of the wheels spinning, but we don't move. He revs harder. The wheels scream louder.

'Fuck.' Slamming his fists on the steering wheel, Nate flings open the door and disappears round the back of the car. He returns a few seconds later, soaking wet. 'We're stuck in the mud.'

Images of the warm, snug inn quickly start receding. 'Who are you calling?' I ask, as Nate pulls out his iPhone. Please don't tell me it's the studio. Or his real-estate agent.

'AAA. We need a tow-truck.'

'But how will they find us?'

He looks at me like I'm a complete idiot. 'It's got GPS. I'll be able to locate exactly where we are.' He starts jabbing away at the screen.

'Oh, right . . . great!' The whole time I've hated that dratted iPhone, but now I take it all back. I feel a swell of gratitude. Thank God for Nate's iPhone!

'Except there's a slight problem.'

'*Problem?*' I look at him warily.

Peering at the screen, his jaw sets. 'There's no signal.'

After twenty minutes walking along an empty road, in the pouring rain and pitch-dark, we make out distant lights. My heart soars as we trudge towards them and I spot a sign: 'O'Grady's Irish Tavern.' Never have I been so happy to see an Irish pub.

Pushing open the door, we stumble inside, soaking wet and freezing cold, and are greeted by warmth, light and 'Fisherman's Blues' playing on the jukebox.

Spotting a payphone, Nate dives over to it, while I make my way, squelching, to the bar. The tavern isn't very big. At the far end are a few tables and chairs, around which are gathered what look like locals – I'm beginning to recognise their uniform of yellow sailing jackets and beat-up khakis. Running along one side is a well-stocked bar, behind which are wallpapered hundreds of faded Polaroids. No doubt taken on previous St Patrick's Day celebrations, I note, as everyone's wearing green and there are lots of four-leaf clovers. The luck of the Irish.

I could do with some of that luck right now, I think, wearily hoisting myself on to a barstool, where a puddle rapidly starts forming around me.

'Little wet out there, huh?' The moustachioed barman, a fifty-something Hell's Angel with a cut-off T-shirt and tattooed forearms, pauses from chewing a toothpick.

'Just a bit.' I sniff, resting my elbows on the bar.

He reaches underneath the bar and holds out a bar towel. 'Here you go.'

'Thanks.' Smiling gratefully, I wipe my face, then tip my head upside down and start towel-drying my hair.

'It's going to be a while.'

Hearing Nate's voice, I flick my head back up. He's standing next to me, looking like he's just taken a shower fully clothed. Even his blazer couldn't keep him dry, I think with a beat of satisfaction. I'm half tempted to let him drip-dry, but I take pity and pass him the towel. 'How long?'

'Apparently there've been a lot of accidents,' he grumbles, rubbing his face roughly, 'and there's only one frigging tow-truck.' With a face like thunder he slides on to the barstool next to me.

'Maybe we can call a cab,' I suggest.

'Oh, silly me! Why didn't I think of that?' He thumps his forehead in a sarcastic 'eureka' moment.

'I was only trying to help,' I reply archly.

'Well, don't,' he deadpans. 'There's, like, one cab service on the island and it's busy. We're just going to have to wait.'

'So, what can I get you guys to drink?' interrupts the barman cheerfully.

'A vodka tonic, please,' I say, thankful of the interruption.

'Make that two,' says Nate gruffly.

The barman moves away and there's an ugly silence. I cast around for something to say. 'Oh, by the way, some woman called the room for you this morning,' I remember. What with everything that's happened today, it had totally slipped my mind. 'She didn't leave a message.'

'Huh, it was probably Jennifer, my real-estate agent,' he tuts. 'That woman's like my stalker.'

You mean Jennifer who you were shaking hands with earlier and chatting to about under-floor heating, I'm tempted to point out, but I'm not going to go there. Instead I steer clear of his bad mood and, noticing 'Fisherman's Blues' has finished and the bar has fallen silent, ask, 'Do you have any change for the jukebox?'

For a moment he looks as if he's going to make a sarcastic comment. Then, seeming to think better of it, he reluctantly digs in his pockets and holds out some quarters.

'Thanks.' I force a bright voice and, leaving him sitting at the bar, dive off to the jukebox. I feel a wave of relief to be away from him. He's in a foul mood.

For the next five minutes I browse the playlist and choose songs. It's really quite fun. There are some absolute classics on here: the Eagles, Fleetwood Mac, Sister Sledge . . . and 'You're So Vain' by Carly Simon. I love that song! Humming away to myself, I pick some of my all-time favourites and then make my way back to the bar.

And Nate, who's sitting by himself, nursing his drink and scowling at his iPhone, as if willing it to work. 'So what did you choose?' he grumbles, looking up.

'Oh, a bunch of stuff,' I say vaguely, and reach for my drink. Boy, do I need this. Dispensing with the straw, I take a large gulp . . . and nearly choke as vodka blasts my tonsils. Wow, I always forget how strong the drinks are in the States compared to back home.

'Like what?' he persists.

'Wait and see,' I reply, refusing to be drawn. No doubt he will hate all my music and take great pleasure in telling me so. I don't like his taste either, though. Last time I was at his penthouse he was playing Hootie and the Blowfish.

I wait expectantly for the jukebox to start playing. I'm not sure what order my songs will go in. Oh, here we go. I hear the opening chords of a song strike up. Violins start blasting. Great. The Verve, 'Bittersweet Symphony'. One of my favourites. Only, hang on, this isn't the Verve. Isn't this—

'INXS?' snorts Nate derisively.

'What? I didn't choose this,' I say in confusion, as Michael Hutchence starts singing.

'You must have,' retorts Nate.

'No, I didn't.' I shake my head. 'There must be some mix-up. The jukebox must be faulty.'

Nate looks at me, quite obviously not believing me. 'Jesus, I hate this song,' he complains.

'Really? I love it,' I retort. Still, it's really weird. I honestly didn't choose this . . . Suddenly a thought stirs. 'Wait a minute, what's this song called?'

'Erm . . .' Nate crinkles his brow.

'"Never Tear Us Apart",' says the barman from across the bar.

Nate and I exchange looks as goose bumps prickle my arms.

'Talk about apt,' he mutters.

'Yeah, isn't it,' I murmur, feeling a shiver running up my spine as Michael Hutchence belts out the lyrics. What? Even the jukebox is in on this now?

'I'm beginning to feel like nothing can tear us apart,' he adds, through a mouthful of ice.

'Me too.' I nod.

'It's like we're stuck together.' He sighs gloomily, staring into his drink. 'For eternity.'

My ears prick up. 'Did you say "eternity"?'

'Well, it sure feels like it, doesn't it?' he says, taking a slug of his drink.

I look at him. Suddenly my heart is thumping like a piston. I want to tell him. I want to tell him everything. 'Well, it's funny you should say that . . .'

'Is it?' he quips wryly. 'I'm not laughing.'

I hesitate, chewing my lip, wondering if I should continue. He's going to think I'm an idiot. Oh sod it, he thinks I'm an idiot already. 'Do remember the bridge?' I blurt.

'What bridge?'

'In Venice. The Bridge of Sighs. We kissed underneath it, on a gondola.'

'Sorry, Lucy,' he tuts impatiently, 'but I'm not in the mood to be going down memory lane.'

I feel myself stiffen. God, he really is an arrogant little shit sometimes. I fall silent. I'm almost tempted not to bother trying to explain, but we're in this together – unfortunately – and it's as much his problem to sort out as it is mine, I think indignantly.

'This isn't about memory lane,' I respond, trying to keep my voice even. 'It's about the legend. Don't you remember? About how if you kiss underneath the bridge, at sunset, when the bells are chiming, you're guaranteed everlasting love.'

The song is still playing . . . *You can never tear us apart.*

Nate looks at me as if I've gone totally mad. Slugging back the rest of his drink, he turns to the barman. 'I'll have the same again. Make it a large one.'

The barman glances at me. 'Two of those?'

'Yeah, why not?' I nod, draining my glass.

'So what are you saying? That all this is because of some legend?' Turning back to me, Nate's face floods with scornful disbelief.

'Look, I know it sounds crazy. I thought the same thing at first . . . well, for ages actually,' I confess. 'In fact, I still think it's crazy—'

Nate cuts me off. 'That's because it is crazy.'

I exhale sharply. 'OK, so it's crazy,' I snap with annoyance. 'But don't you think it's crazy that we're here now? That we keep bumping into each other? That we get each other's dry-cleaning? Our phones call each other? We're booked into the same room? Next to each other on the same flight? Sharing the same bed?'

His cheeks flame. 'That wasn't my idea.'

'Don't you think it's crazy that we can't get rid of each other? That we've broken up, but we can't break up? That somehow something keeps bringing us back together?' My chest is heaving and I can hear my voice getting louder. 'Even the frigging jukebox is in on it,' I cry.

'What?' Nate looks at me in confusion.

'Listen!' I instruct, gesturing into the air. INXS has finished and another song has now started playing. 'Trust me, I didn't choose this song.'

'Velvet Underground, "I'm Sticking With You",' pipes up the barman, passing us fresh drinks. 'A true classic.'

'See!' I gasp impatiently.

There's a beat as Nate computes this onslaught of information.

'So let me get this straight . . .' Narrowing his eyes, he peers at me. 'What you're telling me is that a kiss, *ten years ago* has got us into this mess?'

'Exactly.' I take a large gulp of my drink.

He looks at me for a moment, then sits back on his barstool. 'You really expect me to buy that?'

I feel my cheeks flame. 'Well, do you have a better explanation?'

'Anything is a better explanation than that!' He rubs his forehead in agitation. 'C'mon, seriously.'

I heave a sigh and am casting around in my mind for a way to convince him, which isn't easy when I'm still having trouble convincing myself, when abruptly I'm distracted by what sounds like someone caterwauling.

'Christ, what's that noise?' curses Nate, glancing around. 'Don't tell me it's another song you didn't choose.'

'Thursday's karaoke night,' says the barman with obvious delight.

'No kidding.' Nate smiles tightly. 'This just gets better and better.'

'Yup, that's my girl, Shiree. Isn't she great?' The barman beams proudly.

'Um, yeah, great!' I enthuse, kicking Nate's calf.

He grimaces and fires me a furious look.

'Why don't you guys get up there?' he continues. 'We like out-of-towners giving it a go on the old mike.'

'Oh, no, I don't think so.' I shake my head hastily and begin hoovering up my drink.

'She can't sing – terrible voice,' confides Nate to the barman.

'I don't have a terrible voice,' I stay indignantly, putting my empty glass down on the bar.

'Oh, yes, you do.' He nods, gesturing to the barman for another round. 'I've heard you in the shower.'

'Huh! Me in the shower!' I cry. 'What about you!'

The barman puts down two fresh drinks. Grabbing mine, I take a large swig.

'I've got a great voice,' replies Nate. 'I used to be in a band.'

'You mean the time you played tambourine in college?' I scoff, my mind throwing up memories of him telling me all about it in Venice when we were teenagers.

'I did some vocals,' he says stiffly.

Giving a little 'humph' that is meant to translate into *Yeah, right,* I shake my head, then quickly grab the bar to steady myself. Gosh, I'm beginning to feel a bit dizzy.

'What? You think you're a better singer than me?'

'Absholutely,' I slur. Crikey, what's happened to my tongue? It's gone all floppy.

'OK, well, prove it,' he says challengingly.

'I don't have to prove anything,' I retort, glaring at Nate. Actually, make that two Nates, I think, seeing double.

'Hah!'

'Hah?' Trying to focus, I draw back my shoulders. 'What's "Hah!" supposed to mean?'

'It means you know I'm right,' he says arrogantly.

That's it. I've had it. I don't know if it's the vodka, or his smug expression, or more than twenty-four hours with him on Martha's Vineyard, together with the last few weeks, coupled with the last ten years, but something finally snaps.

Right, that does it. I'll show him.

'OK, you're on,' I say, rising to the challenge. 'Listen and weep.' And without a backwards glance I slide off the barstool and boldly head towards the microphone and speakers that have been set up in the corner of the tavern. Behind me I hear the barman whooping, 'Atta girl!' and jutting out my chin, I begin weaving my way among the tables.

I bash into a few accidentally. 'Oops, sorry.' I smile as people cling on to their drinks to stop them spilling. Oh dear, I'm feeling rather tipsy. In fact, I'm feeling a lot more than tipsy, I'm actually feeling drunk. The ground sways beneath me and I take some deep breaths. Make that *hammered*.

Reaching the speakers, a big-busted woman in a tank top asks for my request, then hands me the microphone. Normally at this point I'd be a nervous wreck, but it's almost as if I'm having an out-of-body experience and am not in control any more. Something else is operating my mind and my limbs, and it has no fear. It's full of confidence.

It's called three large vodkas.

I walk unsteadily on to the little makeshift podium and under the spotlight. 'Um, testing, testing, one, two, three.' I start tapping the microphone. Well, isn't that what people always do? It has an immediate effect. People stop chattering and swing round to look at me interestedly. 'This one's for my ex-boyfriend, Nathaniel.' In the shadows I can see him making stricken 'No, no, no' gestures. 'He's over there, sitting at the bar.'

Everyone twirls round and looks at Nate. Suddenly plunged into being the centre of attention, he looks like a rabbit caught in headlights: petrified.

'It's the classic from *Grease*,' I continue. 'I think you'll all know it.' There's a few murmurs of approval, and buoyed by my newfound confidence, courtesy of Smirnoff, I introduce it. 'It's called "You're the One That I Want".'

There's a murmur of approval.

'... but tonight I want to sing it a little differently ...' I pause as my eyes flit around my tiny audience. I see people looking at me expectantly, their curiosity piqued. 'Tonight "You're the One That I *Don't* Want".'

There are a few hoots of laughter and someone whistles. Over by the bar I can make out Nate shrinking down on his barstool in pure, undiluted mortification, and then the opening chords of the song start blasting from the crackly speakers.

I'm on!

Taking a deep, drunken breath, I start singing. I'm a bit wobbly at first, but I soon get going. It's actually quite fun, I realise, as I begin serenading Nate at the top of my lungs. Especially when the crowd starts joining in with the 'ooh-ooh-honey's in the chorus. I feel like Leona Lewis, or Mariah Carey, or one of those other big divas, I think, closing my eyes like you see the contestants on *X-Factor* doing. With a blast of exhilaration I grip the microphone and really go for it.

Wow, and now the crowd is going crazy. I can hear them wolf-whistling and cheering *and someone else singing*. I flick open my eyes. *Is that Nate?*

I watch him being pushed on to the stage, a microphone thrust into his hand, a look of horror on his face, as he's forced to warble into it. He shoots me a strangled look as he does the part of John Travolta to my Olivia Newton-John: 'You're not the one I want, ooh, ooh, honey ...'

The audience goes wild as we grimace at each other across the stage. Forget singing a duet, we're singing a duel. The karaoke equivalent of fighting to the death. I'll show him. Take that! Adrenaline pumping, I blast a line at him. I'll show her. Take that! Gripping the microphone, he lunges at me with another line.

Back and forth, back and forth . . .

'Excuse me.'

Until, in the middle of our song-fight, the music stops and I hear a voice. It's the bartender's. 'Guys, your tow-truck is here.'

Chapter Thirty

'Well, I guess this is goodbye.'

Walking through the gate at JFK Airport in New York and out into the busy arrivals hall, Nate turns to me.

'You hope so,' I caution.

'Oh, don't tell me, the legend is going to get me,' he mocks, waggling his fingers spookily and humming the music from *The Twilight Zone*.

'Ha, ha, very funny.'

'Well, c'mon,' he tuts. 'Do you seriously expect me to believe that?'

'Of course not.' I shrug. 'You never believe anything I say.'

He nods, as if to say, *Yes, that's true*, then winces and clutches his forehead. Taking out a blister packet of ibuprofen, he pops out two pills and swigs from his Evian bottle. 'Why the hell did you have to start me on those vodkas?'

'Why did you have to crash the car?' I retort, grabbing the water and tablets from him, and taking another two. That makes six already and my hangover is still throbbing.

'By the way, I'd prefer it if you don't mention to anyone about me, you know –' he lowers his voice – '*doing karaoke*.'

'Oh, you weren't that bad,' I tease.

He glowers and has opened his mouth to retaliate when his iPhone starts ringing. 'That's my driver,' he says, glancing at the screen. 'He's outside.'

'Bye.' I raise my hand in farewell. 'I hope I don't see you later.'

'You won't,' he says determinedly. 'I'll make sure to forget to send you a Christmas card.' He throws his bag over his shoulder, then turns sharply and strides off, swallowed up in the bustle of people.

I watch for a moment, barely daring to believe that this is it, he's really gone for good. Vanished, like a magic trick. I feel a beat of hopeful excitement. After so much false hope, so many false starts, it's hard to believe he could have finally left me alone. He's like the boy who cried break-up. But no, he really has disappeared, I reassure myself, looking into the crowd. He's not coming back.

My body sags with relief. Maybe Nate is right – maybe I was getting carried away by the legend, by all this magic stuff, and spells, and hocus-pocus. Feeling optimistic, I grab my bag from the baggage carousel and with a spring in my step head outside to catch a cab back home. Maybe, finally, this really is the end.

Arriving back at the apartment, I open the door and bump straight into Robyn, who's rushing manically around the kitchen.

'Hey! You're back.' She grins, giving me a bear hug. 'How was it?'

'Interesting,' I reply, flopping into a chair and kicking off my flip-flops. 'You'll never guess what—'

'Shoot, have you seen my keys?' she interrupts.

'Um . . .' I glance around the kitchen, my eyes flicking over the countertop. 'No.'

'Darn,' she gasps, tapping her foot impatiently.

Her stiletto-clad foot.

I look at it in astonishment. I've never seen her wearing anything other than her Havaiana flip-flops, of which she has a dozen pairs in all the colours of the rainbow. She's so tall and skinny she always says she doesn't feel the need for heels, but tonight she's wearing a fabulous pair of gold peeptoes that are to Havaiana flip-flops what a Matisse is to a paint-by-numbers.

'Are you going out?' I ask in surprise. Glancing up from her feet, I take her in for the first time and suddenly realise she's all glammed up. Wearing a long tie-dye dress, which shows off her impressive cleavage, she's piled her hair on top of her head to show off the most amazing choker. It's obviously from one of her exotic far-flung travels and is made from hundreds of tiny stones, which glitter and twinkle under the kitchen spotlights.

And there's me wearing a necklace from Accessorize.

'Wow, you look amazing,' I gasp.

She stops rushing around for a moment and stands still in front of me for my approval, so I can get a proper look. 'Do you think so?' Nervously she fiddles with her hair. 'I was thinking maybe it's a bit much.'

'No, you look great,' I say. I've never understood why Robyn covers up her figure in baggy clothes, but tonight there's no mistaking she's working it. 'Very sexy.'

Her cheeks flush. 'Thanks.' She grins, then, remembering her hunt for her lost keys, darts across to the countertop and picks up a pile of mail. 'Darn it, where can they be?'

'Don't worry, I'll hide my set.' Spotting a bag of Kettle Chips, I take a handful. 'I'll put them under the potted plant on the landing.'

'You will?' She throws me a grateful look. 'Oh, thanks, you're an angel.' She rushes for the door.

'Hey, but you still haven't told me where you're going—' The door slams behind her, sending something toppling from the top of the fridge with a crash. Bending down, I pick it up. It's her vision board.

'Or who with,' I murmur, staring at the pasted pictures of dark, handsome strangers and cut-out letters that spell the words 'soulmate' and 'Harold'. Something tells me it's sure as hell not with him.

Propping it back up on the fridge, I reach for my bag. I need to get ready for my date with Adam, though I still don't know what the surprise is, or where we're meeting, I reflect, feeling a flutter of nerves. Digging out my phone, I check again to see if I've got a text and notice the battery is completely dead. Damn, where's my charger? By the toaster, where you left it, I notice, hastily plugging it in. Instantly a message beeps up. It's from Adam.

It's a time and a place. Excitement buzzes and I glance at the clock on the microwave. Oh, no, it's that time already?

Dashing into the bathroom, I jump in the shower and spend the next thirty minutes doing what I call the 'transformation'. Out goes the frizzy hair, sweaty face, baggy T-shirt and leggings, and in comes natural-looking make-up, a vintage dress I got from a thrift store which is a bit tight under the arms but makes me look like I've got a flat stomach, and hair that OK, will never rival Jennifer Aniston's, but won't rival Donald Trump's either.

All done, I glance at myself in the mirror. Now I know how Jesus must have felt. Talk about performing miracles. So he made water into wine? Big deal. I can make a hung-over mess into something vaguely presentable. Maybe even a little sexy, I think, giving myself the once-over and feeling a tingle of excitement.

A thought zips through my brain, and rummaging in my chest of drawers, I pull out my 'special' underwear: a lacy thong and push-up bra that cost an absolute fortune from Agent Provocateur. I went shopping there last year after the Christmas party, when I was a bit drunk, and ended up spending far too much on sexy lingerie that I've barely worn.

The problem is, I'm worried I might look a bit, well, *up for it*. Looking sexy is one thing, but pre-meditated is another. As if I'm *expecting* to have sex with him. I want to look like I've just thrown this on, that it's my usual underwear, I decide, wriggling into it. I glance at myself in the mirror.

Oh, please. Like I usually wear a pink and black satin balconette bra that's squeezing my boobs together and hoisting them upwards to cleavage-busting proportions. I wear comfy flesh-coloured T-shirt bras from M&S that go with everything.

But I can't wear one of those, I think with horror, looking at the T-shirt bra discarded on the sink, like a beige jelly mould. It is the most unflattering thing you've ever seen.

I stare at it for a few seconds, an internal bra battle raging inside me, then make a decision. Nope, I cannot, repeat cannot, wear my jelly-mould bra on my surprise date. A man would never understand the excuse of comfort and that it doesn't show any seams. In fact, I remember once mentioning that very reason to an old boyfriend and he looked at me in bewilderment. 'What, you have to wear an invisible bra?' Which wasn't the point at all, but still.

In the end I go with the pink and black satin – just in case – and head to the subway. Adam has given me the address, it's on 12th Street, near Union Square, and I jump on a train. I'm getting pretty good at the subways now, I reflect, sitting down and glancing at the faces around me. When I first arrived, I used to feel so different, like an outsider, but now I'm beginning to feel like one of them. It's starting to feel like home.

But for how much longer? I muse, a seed of worry sprouting as I think about the gallery and Magda's financial problems. I just have to hope the meeting went well with Artsy. Whatever the outcome, we'll find out soon enough, I tell myself. Turning to stare out of the window, I brush my worry aside. For tonight, anyway.

Walking out of the station, I look for the address. Admittedly I have to take out my pop-up map – it might be starting to feel like home, but it's one I still regularly get lost in – and start navigating streets until I see a small art-house cinema. Neon light from the sign is illuminating the pavement, where a few people are milling about, including Adam.

I spot him first, leaning against a wall, smoking a roll-up and reading a magazine. It's like my eyes laser in on him. Why is it that before I barely noticed him? At the gallery opening that first night he only attracted my attention because he looked out of place. Now it's as if a spotlight is shining down upon him and I don't notice anyone *but* him.

On top of that, I notice *everything* about him. How the V-necked T-shirt shows off that little softy, fuzzy triangle of skin at the hollow of his neck. How the muscle in his tanned forearm flexes as he turns the pages of his magazine. The way a dark shock of hair keeps falling over his brow like a mischievous child, unwilling to behave. I watch him now, brushing it back with the flat of his hand.

'Adam?'

'Hey.' His eyes crinkle into a smile as he sees me. 'So you made it.'

'Sorry I'm late,' I begin apologising quickly. 'The plane was delayed and then my phone died, so I only got your text about an hour ago and—'

'No worries. I was catching up on some reading.' Cutting me off with an easy shrug, he puts out his cigarette, then rolls up his magazine and sticks it in his back pocket. 'I'm just glad you're here.' He looks pleased, and utterly adorable, and I feel my insides melt like chocolate. All my life I've been told off for being useless and late, greeted with an impatient tut or annoyed gasp. Adam is the first person just to be glad I'm here, like it's no big deal.

'Me too.' I smile and go to kiss his cheek. I don't want to be presumptuous, despite my choice of underwear, I think, ignoring the pinching of my G-string. Instead I sort of trip up on the paving stone and crash-land on his mouth. A tingle rushes all the way down to my feet.

Then I pull away awkwardly. 'Oh gosh, sorry . . .' I begin apologising again.

'Hey, no worries,' he says again. 'I was going to save that move for later, but if you want to go ahead now . . .' His eyes flash with amusement and I can't help but laugh, despite my embarrassment. That's another thing about Adam: even when I'm bursting into tears at police stations or lunging at him in public places, he always manages to put me at ease.

'So . . .' Grinning at me, we stand for a moment, facing each other on the pavement.

'So . . .' I say, raising my arms and then sort of flapping them back down against my sides. Rather like a penguin, I suddenly realise, quickly sticking them in the pockets of my jacket before he starts thinking he's gone on a date with Pingu.

'Shall we go inside?'

'Yes, let's.'

Looping his arm through mine, he leads me through the glass doors and into the foyer, with its faded maroon carpet covered in gold swirly patterns and zigzagging marks from where a vacuum has been run over it. On the walls are framed vintage posters advertising *The Godfather*, an old Bruce Lee movie, Alfred Hitchcock's *Vertigo*, along with chipped Art Deco mirrors. It smells of buttered popcorn and air-freshener, and the whole place is badly in need of a lick of paint, but it has that warm, shabby, lived-in feeling that you'd never get from a big, modern multi-screen cinema.

You can tell that everyone who comes here loves this place. And so do I, I realise, feeling a sudden fondness for it.

'This used to be an old fire station,' Adam is saying as we walk across the foyer. 'It's the oldest, longest-running art cinema in the city. It showed the first talkie in 1927, starring Al Jolson in *The Jazz Singer*. Look, there's a poster over there.' His voice is animated and his enthusiasm infectious. 'The reaction from the audience was immediate. They couldn't believe it. Can you imagine? They got to their feet and started clapping when it happened. It was in the middle of the film, during a nightclub scene, when Jolson suddenly spoke.'

'What did he say?' I ask, my curiosity caught.

He puts on a stupid voice. '"Wait a minute, wait a minute. You ain't heard nuthin' yet!"' He laughs. 'Kinda prophetic, huh?'

I marvel at him. 'How do you know all this stuff?'

'I dunno.' He shrugs. 'I guess because I love it. Film fascinates me.' He stops and looks at me. 'It's like you and art. It's whatever you're passionate about, right? It's the same thing.'

I glance at Adam. Thirty. A filmmaker from Brooklyn. Habits include doing silly voices and gallery-crashing for the freebies. We're so completely different and yet . . . I look at him again and get the same feeling I got that day at the MoMA: that fundamentally, underneath, we're the same.

'Yeah, it is.' I nod. 'It's the same thing.'

We continue walking, past the door that says, 'Screen One,' and towards another.

'So what's your favourite movie ever?' I ask, as we reach screen two. We pause outside. Briefly it crosses my mind that we haven't bought tickets.

'Wait and see.' He smiles enigmatically, pushing open the door.

'Is that the surprise?' Of course, Adam must have bought tickets earlier.

'Sort of.'

Pushing it open, we enter the darkened theatre.

'Gosh, there's no one here,' I say, glancing around the empty rows.

'I know.' He leads me down the middle of an aisle.

'Damn, I forgot to get the popcorn,' I tut, suddenly remembering. 'That was part of the deal, wasn't it? You get the tickets and I get the pop—' I break off as I spot something glinting in the darkness.

A silver bucket. *An ice bucket.*

'Is that . . .?' I glance up at Adam. In the darkness it's hard to make out the expression on his face, but as my eyes adjust, I see he's looking at me and smiling nervously.

'I hope you like champagne,' he says, producing a bottle from nowhere.

'But how?' I'm gobsmacked. Truly. For once in my life I'm lost for words.

'My friend's the projectionist. He owed me a little bit of a favour.' He starts unwrapping the foil.

'You mean we've got this whole place to ourselves?' I ask in amazement.

'Call it a private screening.' He grins as the cork suddenly pops. 'Oh fuck!' Champagne froths everywhere and he scrabbles to catch it in a plastic cup. 'Sorry, I totally forgot the glasses – I got plastic cups instead,' he says ruefully, passing me one.

'You know, I've always thought champagne tastes better in plastic.' I grin, chinking my plastic cup against his.

'Goes well with popcorn too,' he says, producing a large carton.

'What are you?' I smile, incredulous. 'A magician?'

'Something like that.' He smiles as I grab a handful of warm, buttered salty popcorn.

Happiness swells. 'Mmm, this is—'

He silences me with a kiss on the lips. 'Ssh . . . the movie's about to start.'

It turns out Fellini's *8½* is his favourite film, and for the next two and a bit hours I'm completely absorbed by the tale of Guido, an Italian movie director, whose flashbacks and dreams are interwoven with reality.

'It was amazing, really amazing. Though I didn't understand a lot of it,' I confess afterwards, while finishing my second slice of pizza. On leaving the cinema, we'd grabbed takeaway slices and were eating them on the way back to mine.

'Exactly like I feel about the art you show me,' he says, as we climb the stairs to my apartment.

'Can you like something you don't really understand?' I muse.

'Totally.' He nods, taking a large bite of pizza. 'You've got your whole life to figure it out. My grandfather once told me he'd spent his entire life trying to figure out my grandmother.'

'And did he?' Letting ourselves in, we pause in the kitchen.

'Not yet. Says she's like a mystery he can't solve.' Putting the empty pizza box on the table, he turns to me. 'Every time he thinks he's worked her out, she does something to surprise him and he sees her in a different way. I get that with films sometimes. I've seen them dozens of times and then I watch them again and I see something new.'

'It's the same with art. I can look at a painting one day and the next . . .' I trail off. There's no need to explain with Adam. I know that he gets it. *He gets me.*

'Hey, you got some grease on your chin.' He gestures.

'Oh, really.' I go to wipe it, but he gets there first with his paper napkin.

'You're a messy eater, aren't you?' he teases.

'I'm messy at everything,' I laugh, and for the first time it doesn't seem to matter. That I'm messy, or I'm late, or I'm eating pizza and dribbling grease down my chin, or that I talk too loudly, or that my hair is still that dodgy shade of purple from that bad dye job the other week. Because it doesn't matter to Adam.

'I think this is the best first date I've ever been on.' I grin a little tipsily.

'No, the police station was our first date,' he corrects me, smiling.

'That wasn't a date,' I retort.

'Well, that's when we had our first kiss,' he says.

At the memory of our kiss, all my nerve endings start tingling. 'So if this is our second date, does that mean we get to have our second kiss?' I reply flirtatiously.

Well, I haven't been suffering in this underwear all night for nothing.

'I guess it does.' He nods, sliding his hand round my waist and pulling me towards him. Before I know it he's kissing me. And I'm kissing him back. And he's sliding his hand up the back of my top. And—

Suddenly the buzzer goes.

I ignore it and keep kissing him.

It goes again.

'Do you think you should get that?' murmurs Adam.

'It will be my roommate. She lost her keys,' I say thickly. Flinging out my hand, I press the release buzzer for the main door and flick the latch. Gosh, Adam is a really good kisser.

I can hear footsteps pounding up the stairs. 'C'mon, we should go to my room,' I whisper, tugging at his T-shirt, worried that Robyn will walk in on us snogging in the kitchen.

'Just one more kiss,' he whispers, his soft stubble scratching my face as he pulls me even closer.

Suddenly there's a loud crash and the door slams wide open. I jump a mile. 'Crikey, Robyn,' I exclaim, laughing as Adam and I spring apart.

Only it's not Robyn. It's Nate.

It's like being wrenched from a dream into a nightmare. 'What on earth?' I gasp in horror, as his grey-suited figure comes charging through the door.

'What did you say to Beth?' he demands without any introduction.

I stare at him speechless with shock. I've never seen him look so angry.

'Who are you?' asks Adam in total bewilderment.

'What? When?' I cry, finding my voice.

'In Martha's Vineyard!'

'You were in Martha's Vineyard too?' Adam's brow creases.

Suddenly the penny drops. It wasn't Jennifer the real-estate agent I spoke to. It was Beth, Nate's ex-wife. *The* Beth. 'Oh shit, that was her who called our room?'

Adam turns to me, his face shocked. 'Our room?'

'She didn't leave a message. I had no idea,' I begin explaining, but my mind is reeling. All those years I built her up in my head to be this superhuman person, the girl Nate married, the one he chose over me, and yet she'd sounded so normal.

No wonder she hung up on me. She must have thought—

'You were together?' Adam looks at me, dumbstruck.

'Please, I can explain,' I try, turning to him, but Nate talks over me.

'We're *always* together!' he cries in exasperation. 'We're never apart.'

'That's not my fault,' I retaliate, wheeling round. 'It's as much you as it is me.'

'Now my wife thinks we're having an affair.'

'You're married?' Adam's voice is quiet and he's looking at Nate, his eyes flicking over him, his mind racing.

'I thought you were separated,' I gasp.

'We are, but . . . well, we've been talking . . .' Nate trails off self-consciously. For a moment he looks down at his feet, then back at me. 'We want to give it another try. At least she did. Before . . .'

There's silence for a moment. Nobody says anything. I don't think anyone knows what to say, least of all me. I feel numb, relieved, suddenly hopeful. If Nate wants to get back with Beth—

'You've been having an affair with a married man?'

Adam's voice snaps me back. 'What? No!' I spin round, shaking my head in furious denial. 'No, it's not like that at all.'

I meet his gaze, but gone is his warm faith in me. In its place is a cold, steely distrust. 'Save it, Lucy.'

'No, please, it's not like that.' I feel the panic rising. He thinks I'm like his ex-girlfriend. He thinks I've been cheating, that I've been unfaithful with another woman's husband. 'Please, I can explain,' I say desperately. Tears have begun prickling my eyelashes. I reach out to him. 'Trust me.'

But he brushes away. 'Like I trusted you before?' he says, his face splintered into anger and contempt.

'Adam, please,' I beg, but he just looks at me and it's the coldest, hardest look. Turning, he walks towards the door.

'Don't go,' I call out after him, but even as I'm saying the words, I know it's useless. He's already gone.

For a moment I stand motionless in the kitchen, staring at the empty doorway. Then slowly I become aware of Nate's presence. I raise my eyes to meet his, but if I'm expecting to see some kind of satisfaction, I'm wrong.

'I'm sorry. I was upset about Beth.' He looks at me with dismay. 'I didn't mean . . .'

'I know.' I shake my head wearily. My lovely evening with Adam is lying in tatters and yet there's no point blaming anyone. Nate's suffering too. He's probably lost Beth again now, just like I've lost Adam.

A sob rises in my throat. It's all such a mess.

Nate and I don't say any more; there's nothing left for either of us to say. He leaves, and closing the door behind him, I lean against it and sink to the floor.

And only then do I cry.

I cry my bloody heart out.

Chapter Thirty-One

'I've called a dozen times and left messages, but he won't return my calls.'

The next day I'm sitting in a café on the Upper West Side, having lunch with my sister. Over Eggs Florentine I've been telling her all about what happened, about Martha's Vineyard, about last night, about everything.

'I've tried emailing, texting, you name it, but nothing. I just don't know what else to do.' I heave a deep sigh and slump down into my seat. 'I can't believe Nate. He completely sabotaged everything with Adam. To think I did all those things on the Strategy.' I give a little shudder. 'It's like nothing works.'

I stare dolefully into the dregs of my latte. Last night, after Nate left, I went to bed but couldn't sleep. I spent the whole night tossing and turning, and woke up this morning still feeling horrible. 'But I'm not blaming Nate. I mean, it can't be nice for him either. Apparently he's trying to get back with his wife and give it another try, and now that's ruined too.' I heave an even deeper sigh and sink down further into my chair. 'It's all such a mess. We're doomed to be together for ever.'

'Lucky you.'

'Excuse me?' I glance up from my coffee cup to look at my sister. She's barely said a word since we met and has hardly touched her salad Niçoise. Instead she's spent the whole time staring off into space, as if her mind's on other things. Most likely mergers and acquisitions or her marathon training.

'Some people would love to be together for ever. I wish Jeff and I could be so lucky.'

'Aren't you the same person who called marriage a life sentence?' I remark. 'And you get your sentence shortened for good behaviour?' I look at Kate, expecting her to laugh, but her face remains passive.

'Jeff has cancer.'

Boom. Just like that.

I look at her in disbelief. '*What?*'

'Testicular. The doctor's finally figured out why he's been losing weight and feeling so unwell. He's got to have a chest X-ray and blood work to see if it's spread.' She says all this very matter-of-factly, in the same tone of voice she used to discuss what to have for lunch. 'He'll have his ball chopped off, of course, though that's OK – you can manage perfectly fine with just one.'

I'm staring at Kate and listening to her calmly talking, but I can't compute what I'm hearing. 'Oh my God, Kate, I can't believe it,' I manage finally. 'I had no idea.' I reach out across the table for her hand, but she pulls it away. I feel dreadful. There's me jabbering on about Nate and Adam and the whole time Kate's been sitting here with this awful news.

'I know, neither did I. I thought all he needed was antibiotics.' She falters momentarily – a blink of an eye and you'd have missed it – then, regaining her composure, quickly carries on. 'The good news is that there's a strong chance we've caught it early enough and the cancer hasn't spread, and by getting rid of the tumour, you get rid of it all. We don't know for sure yet, but they're running tests, so we'll know soon enough.' Affording a tight smile, she takes a sip of water. 'According to the oncologist, it's the best cancer to have. I didn't know there was a top ten of cancers you most want to have, but I guess you learn something every day.'

'And what if—' I stop myself. I don't want to ask the question, but Kate asks it for me.

'What if it's spread?' she says evenly.

I look at her mutely, almost shamefully. I feel disloyal for even thinking such a thing.

'Well, we have to deal with that if it happens,' she says

pragmatically. 'We'll have to go through the motions – radio-therapy, chemotherapy. I've been reading up on everything, but even for me, with my medical background, it's a whole new learning curve.' She's being incredibly calm. Spookily so.

'You're being so calm about everything,' I say to her in amazement.

She shrugs. 'There's no point bringing emotions into this. We need to deal with the facts. When it comes to medical matters, the body is like a car that's broken down and we need to figure out the best way to try to fix it.'

'But this isn't a car we're talking about – this is Jeff,' I say passionately.

'I'm acutely aware of that, Lucy,' she snaps, the strain show-ing for the first time.

I fall silent. I'm not sure what to do or what to say to try and comfort her. I know she's upset, but she refuses to show it. She refuses to put down the big, strong sister act and let anyone in, least of all me. It's so frustrating. I feel so helpless.

'How is Jeff dealing with it?' I say after a moment.

'He's been better. Obviously. His main concern seems to be that after the operation he's going to be flying solo.' She raises an eyebrow. 'But the doctor explained to him that you can get an implant.'

'An implant?'

'Apparently. I don't know if they come in different sizes like with breasts. My husband with the double-D testicles.' She smiles ruefully, attempting a joke. 'I'll be calling him "Jordan" next.'

We both laugh, but it's a hollow sound. This is cancer we're talking about, this is Jeff, and this is something that threatens the rest of their lives together, but she's refusing to go there, and so I don't go there either.

After lunch I leave Kate insisting she's OK. 'Don't fuss,' she protests. 'Everything's going to be fine.'

'I know, of course,' I say hurriedly. 'I didn't mean . . . Look, if you need anything, anything at all. If you want me to come with you to the hospital, keep you topped up with bad vending-machine coffee . . .'

'I'll call you.' She nods curtly, in a way that says she has no intention of calling me, or anyone for that matter.

She hitches her bag on to her shoulder and is about to turn away when instinctively I reach over and give her a big hug. I can't help myself. Despite her steely demeanour, she feels tiny and fragile beneath her cotton jacket.

She stiffens and awkwardly pulls away. 'Oh, and, Lucy, don't mention anything to Mum and Dad. You know how they worry about stuff.'

'Yes, of course.' I nod, thinking how that's so typical of Kate. Never wanting to be any trouble. Always determined to handle everything herself. 'I won't breathe a word.'

We say our goodbyes and I walk back to the subway and begin descending the steps, then pause. I don't feel like going back to the apartment, I feel like walking, and so, turning round, I climb back up again. I've no destination in mind, no clue where I'm heading. I just start walking aimlessly, paying no attention to my surroundings, the people who walk by, the shops that I pass, the neighbourhoods that I enter. Staring at the ground, I focus on putting one foot in front of the other, the rhythm propelling me forward, like a musician with his metronome.

I think about Jeff and Kate. About my sister's stoicism, her flippant remarks, the sarcastic humour that hides the true depth of love she has for him, but couldn't hide the shadow of fear I saw in her eyes. About Jeff and how he must be feeling. I try to imagine it, but of course I can't. How can I? This is life or death we're talking about. Not some silly legend about soulmates. I feel a stab of shame. Talk about putting things into perspective.

I'm not sure how long I walk for, but after a while I become vaguely aware that my legs are beginning to ache. As I slow down, I find myself outside a large art gallery: the Whitney, on Madison Avenue. It feels fortuitous. Galleries are where I always go to seek comfort. They never fail to make me feel better. They've never let me down yet. Right now I need them more than ever.

Seeking solace, I walk, as if on autopilot, in through the doors, eager to immerse myself in the art. To lose myself and block out everything else. Only today the paintings don't make me feel better; the sculptures don't lift my spirits; even Rothko's *Four Shades of Red* doesn't work its usual magic.

I think back to the last time I was at a gallery. It was after the row with Nate, when I bumped into Adam at the MoMA. As my mind flicks to him, I feel a tug in the pit of my stomach. What wouldn't I give to turn a corner and see him now? I reflect, as I wander from room to room, each time hoping to glimpse him, each time feeling a thump of disappointment as I realise he's not here.

I leave when the gallery closes. It's early evening, the clear sky is now a purplish bruise, and for the first time I can feel summer nudging into autumn. As if while I was inside the gallery there was a shift, a change, a coming to an end. I set off walking. My feet are sore and I'm not sure exactly where the subway station is, but somehow the feeling of being lost suits my mood.

I'll just keep walking until I come across one, I decide, zigzagging blocks, meandering past the park.

Until before you know it I'm in the Village and the streets are lined with busy restaurants and bars, and people are milling around outside on the pavement, smoking cigarettes and chattering, their voices filling the evening air. I keep walking, absently catching snippets of conversation, until all at once I stumble across another gallery.

I slow down. Sounds of glasses clinking, the hum of conversation, wafts of perfume and aftershave float towards me. Outside the gallery are gathered a small crowd of people.

For a moment my heart races. It's a gallery opening. Maybe Adam is here.

With my breath held tight in anticipation, I glance around, my eyes skimming the crowd.

Then I see a figure. He has his back turned to me, but he's wearing a T-shirt, baggy jeans, and he's got dark, floppy hair . . . My heart races. It's him. *It's Adam.*

It's like a shot of adrenaline. A jumble of thoughts shoots through my brain as I step towards him: relief, apprehension, hope, fear.

'Adam.' I hear an urgent voice say his name and suddenly realise it's me. 'I need to explain.'

He stops talking and turns round.

Only it's not him. It's a stranger with a passing resemblance to him. He looks at me questioningly.

'Oh.' I feel a crash of disappointment. 'I thought you were someone else.'

'Who would you like me to be?' he jokes good-naturedly, and his friend laughs.

I try to smile, but my face won't quite do it. Abruptly I feel tears prickling. 'I'm sorry. I made a mistake,' I stammer, and turn away sharply.

If only I could say that to Adam. But I'll probably never get the chance, I realise, with a heavy clunk of dismay. There are over eight million people living in New York – what's the likelihood of ever seeing him again?

And fighting back tears, I hurry away.

Chapter Thirty-Two

I arrive back late to the apartment with a giant bag of Kettle Chips and a bottle of Pinot Grigio. Usually they're my fail-safe, cheer-up, get-out-of-a-crap-mood card, but tonight not even New York Cheddar Cheese can make me feel better, I reflect, letting myself into the kitchen and putting the half-eaten packet on the table.

Maybe the wine will do better.

I screw open the top. I once read an article about why winemakers have started using screw-tops in the twenty-first century. It said something about being a better way of sealing the wine, as corks can go mouldy, apparently. Personally, I think that's a load of rubbish. Screw-tops are in demand because of all the heartbroken single girls who need to *get the wine faster*.

Pouring a glass, I glug half of it back, then pick up my discarded Kettle Chips in a resigned 'OK, let's try again stance,' like a weary couple giving things another shot, pad into the living room and flick on the light.

'Aaarrgh.'

I hear a strangled yelp and spot a couple lying entwined on the sofa. At exactly the same time they see me and spring apart in a flurry of adjusting bra straps, fiddling with belts and hastily brushing down hair.

'Oh, er, hi, Lucy,' murmurs Robyn. Face flushed, she smoothes her dress. 'I didn't think you'd be back so early.'

'Um, no, I guess not,' I say, frozen in the doorway. Now I know how my dad must have felt when he blundered in on me and Stuart Yates in the conservatory when we were fifteen.

'You've met Daniel before.' She gestures to Daniel, who's now sitting bolt upright on the sofa as if he's about to have tea with the vicar.

'Yes, of course.' I nod. 'Hi, Daniel.'

'Hi, Lucy.' He stands up to shake my hand politely and I can't help noticing his flies are undone.

'Um . . .' I gesture downwards with my eyes.

He looks puzzled and glances down. Seeing his zip, he turns beetroot. I'm not sure who's more embarrassed, him or me. Or Robyn, who's now vigorously plumping cushions like my mother when the relatives are coming.

'We were just watching a DVD,' she says briskly.

I glance at the TV. It's turned off.

'Great.' I nod, playing along.

'So did you have a nice day?' she asks brightly.

The conversation is so stilted it's like we're in a bad amateur dramatics play.

'Oh, you know . . .' I consider telling her about my sister and Jeff and Adam, but decide against it. Now's hardly the time to unburden myself. 'How about you two? How was your day?'

'Amazing,' beams Daniel enthusiastically.

'OK,' says Robyn, speaking over him with forced nonchalance.

Glances fly between them and I feel the air prickle as if there's a lot going on under the surface. I take this as my cue to leave.

'Well, I think I'll probably go to bed It's late.' I start backing out of the doorway.

'Oh, don't go on our account,' she says breezily. I notice she's still plumping the same cushion. As does Daniel, who prises it from her gently.

'Actually, I'm exhausted,' I say, and throw in a yawn for good measure. Which is true, I suddenly realise. It's been quite some day. 'Night.'

'Night,' they say in stereo, from opposite ends of the sofa, where they're standing awkwardly as if to prove there's nothing going on between them.

Proving that without any doubt there is something going on between them.

I go into my bedroom, flick on a couple of lamps and turn on my fairy lights. That's always a sure-fire way to make me feel better. I don't know why it is, but there's something about their soft, twinkly glow that never fails to lift my spirits.

Except for tonight. Tonight they have zero effect, I think glumly. Lighting an aromatherapy candle, I put on some cheery music, but it's hopeless. Not even my ludicrously expensive Diptyque candle, which I only burn on special occasions, and the *Mamma Mia* soundtrack Mum bought me can make a dent in my black mood.

Giving up, I resign myself to feeling miserable and ensconce myself on my bed with my wine, Kettle Chips and laptop. Maybe Adam's replied to my message on Facebook, I tell myself. Maybe now he's had time to think about things . . . Hope flickers, like the flame on my candle, and for a brief moment I feel a tiny pulse of anticipation, a ray of possibility. Maybe, just maybe.

Taking a large slurp of wine for courage, I check my emails. I have three. One from my mum asking me if I've spoken to Kate, as she can't get hold of her, and that it's 'boiling hot here. Everyone is wearing T-shirts.' Ever since I moved to New York, Mum and I have had an ongoing weather battle. For some reason she's determined to prove Manchester is hotter than Manhattan. 'You wouldn't believe how sunny it's been since you left!'

Quite frankly no, Mum, I wouldn't, I think, clicking off her email and on to the next one, which is an engagement party evite from a friend in London. 'Brilliant. Congratulations,' I type with two fingers, while glugging back wine. 'Sorry I can't make it.' Am in New York, becoming an alcoholic, I add mentally, pressing send.

The last one is from eBay, reminding me that the online auction for my spare theatre ticket is about to end tomorrow and that I've had several bids. I feel slightly cheered. Well, at least that's something.

And that's it. No email from Adam. I stare at my empty inbox, my mind turning, then log into Facebook. You never know, there could have been an error and his reply never got forwarded. That happened to a friend of mine once. Well, not an actual friend, a friend of a friend, or maybe it was in an article I read. I can't remember. The most important thing is, it did happen.

Not to me, though, I realise, looking at my profile page. No new messages. Nothing, apart from a status update from Nathaniel Kennedy:

Looking at real estate!

This time I don't even bother trying to defriend him. After all, what's the point? I think resignedly, logging out. Somehow it doesn't seem to matter so much any more.

My mind jumps back to this lunchtime and Kate's comment about wishing she and Jeff would be tied together for ever. Reminded, I feel a clutch of anxiety and take a sip of wine, trying to shake off the sense of foreboding that's threatening to envelop me like a heavy overcoat. Jeff's going to be OK, I tell myself firmly. Kate said it was the best cancer to have, and she trained to be a doctor, so she should know. Kate knows everything. She never gets it wrong. Why should now be any different?

I wake up on Sunday morning with one question and one question only: why, oh, why did I have that fourth glass of wine? Yet along with a thumping headache comes a new sense of determination. That's it. No more drowning my sorrows. I'm going to forget about men and relationships. I'm going to stop wasting time on all that stupid love stuff. Instead I'm going to focus on what's really important. Like family and friends, health, raising money for charity . . .

And a stonking great big cup of coffee.

Padding bleary-eyed into the kitchen, I find Robyn making herbal tea. Robyn is the queen of herbal teas, and we're not just talking bog-standard chamomile or peppermint that come as pre-packaged teabags from Ralph's Supermarket. She makes a whole *science* of herbal tea, brewing up spoonfuls of dried herbs with exotic-sounding names in her little teapot, stewing, sieving and straining through various filters and fiddly bits of gauze. All so she can produce the most foul-tasting liquid known to man.

Flicking on the kettle, I pull three cups from the cupboard.

'One for me, one for you and one for Daniel,' I say pointedly, giving her a knowing smile.

'Thanks –' she nods, ladling out dried herbs into a small ceramic teapot – 'but I'll only be needing one cup.'

'Sensible man. He hates that stuff too, does he?' I grin. I start unscrewing my little silver espresso pot. 'Maybe he'd like a coffee instead.'

'He's not here.'

Dumping the old coffee grains in the bin, I give it a quick rinse under the tap. 'Oh, has he gone to get croissants?'

Robyn and I live on the next street to this great little bakery that does the most delicious croissants. Every time I walk by I think of Nate's comment and tell myself, 'A moment on the lips, a lifetime on the hips.' And every time I can't resist popping in for an almond one. It's a stupid rhyme anyway. I much prefer 'A moment on the hips, a lifetime on the lips.'

'No, he's gone,' she says flatly. The kettle boils and clicks off and she starts pouring water over her herbs.

'Gone?' The way she says it, it's as if he's gone missing. I'm almost tempted to look under the kitchen table to see if that's where he's hiding. Then it suddenly strikes me that she means he's gone as in 'He won't be coming back.'

'But how? Why?' In confusion I watch her stirring her teapot, a strange sort of dazed look on her face. 'Last night you two seemed so . . .' I search for the right word. About to have sex? No, that's three. ' . . . cosy,' I finish.

She stops stirring and looks up. 'It's over.'

'Over?' I feel like the time I missed an episode of *X-Factor* and didn't realise that one of my favourites had been knocked out and spent the first ten minutes completely bewildered and trying to work out what had happened.

'Not that we were dating each other or anything,' she adds hurriedly.

'No, of course not.' I nod, playing along.

'We were just friends.'

'Good friends,' I suggest.

'Yes, totally,' she agrees, averting her eyes.

'So what happened?'

There's a pause and then she sighs. 'Harold. That's what happened. You told me you'd met him in Martha's Vineyard.'

Guilt thuds. This is all my fault. 'I didn't mean for you to break up with Daniel,' I protest quickly. 'I mean, not that you were ever together—' I try to backtrack, but she cuts me off.

'I didn't finish it. Daniel did. He doesn't think we should see each other any more.'

I stare at her incredulously. 'But I thought . . .' I hesitate, my mind whirring. 'I thought you two were having lots of fun together . . . the African drumming band, the vegan restaurant, last night . . .' I trail off thinking about them together on the sofa. Trust me, Daniel did not look like a man who wanted to finish things.

'We were.' She nods. 'We did.' She gives a little sniff and her large green eyes start to glisten. She blinks rapidly. 'But he said now that I've found Harold, he didn't want to stop me from being with him. From being with my soulmate.'

I pause, allowing for that to register. 'Can you just rewind that bit?' I fix her with a hard look. 'How does he know you've . . . I mean, *I've* found Harold?'

'I told him.'

'*You told him?*'

'Of course.' She nods. 'I told him about Harold from the very beginning, how I'm searching for him, how he's my soulmate.'

'You haven't even met him yet! He might be the completely *wrong* Harold,' I exclaim, waving the espresso pot around. 'I mean, there must be more than one unlucky sod in the world with the name Harold.'

Robyn stiffens slightly.

'And even if by some miracle he is the right one, you might hate him.'

'I don't hate anyone,' she reprimands hotly. 'Hate is wasted emotion. It will only bring bitterness into your heart.'

'That's not what you said about the man who left his dog in the car.'

Last week Robyn saw an article on the news about a man who'd nearly killed his Dalmatian from heat exhaustion by leaving it locked in his jeep in the midday sun. Thankfully it was found in the nick of time by a passerby.

'I don't hate him. I want to lock him in his car in hundred-degree heat without any water or air and let him suffer in agony for a very, very long time and beg for help and come this close to dying.' She pinches her two fingers together and scrunches up her face so that she looks pretty scary. 'There's a difference.'

'So what are you going to do?' I quickly change the subject. 'About Daniel, I mean, not the man with the Dalmatian,' I say hurriedly, before she reams off a list of torture devices. For a woman who's all about healing, she knows an awful lot of ways to inflict pain.

'Nothing.' She shrugs and stares dolefully down at the teapot. 'I would have had to finish it anyway. It was inevitable. It's meant to be.'

'Why? Because of what some stupid psychic said?' I feel a stab of frustration.

Robyn purses her lips tightly and lifts her chin. 'Wakanda is a Native American healer who can communicate with spirit guides. She has an amazing gift. Her Sioux name actually means "possesses magical power".'

I open my mouth to argue, then, realising it's futile, let out a groan. 'Oh God, why didn't I keep my mouth shut? I should never have told you about meeting the artist. It was supposed to be a secret.'

'But you did,' she says, reaching out and squeezing my arm in a don't-blame-yourself kind of way. 'You did tell me, and you did meet him. It's serendipity.'

'I thought that was a movie, not real life,' I quip ruefully.

She smiles and, turning back to her teapot, gives it one last stir and pours herself a cup of tea.

'So what are you going to do now?'

She pauses, and for a moment a look of sadness flashes briefly across her face, then it's gone and is replaced with one of determination. 'Do what I always do,' she says firmly, and tucking her hair behind her ears, she gives me one of her megawatt smiles. 'Leave things up to Fate.'

Chapter Thirty-Three

I've got a bone to pick with Fate.

Fate likes to portray itself as a genial character, a helpful soul, a guardian angel who will be there for you to lean on when the going gets tough. Don't know what to do? Leave it up to Fate to decide. Life in a mess? Let Fate sort it out – he knows best. Single and heartbroken? Fate's got something wonderful in store for you.

No wonder everyone is keen to put their feet up and let Fate look after them. It's rather like your granddad. Or a very hands-on organised person, sort of your own personal PA.

Only in my experience Fate is no such thing, and the same goes for his little brother, Destiny. Quite frankly they've made a real mess of things where I'm concerned. So from now on they can bugger off and stop meddling. I'm taking charge of my own life, and when it comes to love, Fate can mind its own bloody business.

Besides, like I said, I'm not wasting any more time thinking about that love stuff. That was then and this is now.

So, as Monday morning rolls around, it's a whole new me who wakes up before her alarm, puts on clothes that are hanging up and sets off for work in plenty of time.

'That was then and this is now,' I repeat to myself under my breath as I stride along the street. 'That was then and this is now.' Robyn says I have to keep repeating it to myself as an affirmation.

Robyn's big on affirmations. When I first moved in, I would find them stuck on bits of paper all over the apartment and hear her wandering around the house saying them. I have to admit

I'd thought she was a bit batty. 'It's about replacing a negative thought with a positive one,' she'd explained. 'So, for example, if you're worried about something and want to improve it, you say an affirmation.'

'I'm worried about this Visa bill,' I'd replied, waving my red, overdue statement at her. 'Got an affirmation for that?'

Closing her eyes, she'd pinched her nose as if in deep concentration for a few moments, then opening her eyes, replied solemnly, '"I pay my bills with love as I know abundance flows freely through me."'

Suffice to say, I got charged a late fee and a ton of interest.

But that was then and this is now, and although I still have my reservations, and I still think Robyn's a bit batty, the way I see it a few affirmations can't hurt. It's all part of my determination to turn over a new leaf, a blank page, plus anything else that I can get my hands on, and focus on what's important.

Like Kate and Jeff. His operation is scheduled for this afternoon and so I've arranged to work a half-day and meet Kate at the hospital.

'No, I'm fine, honestly,' she'd protested. 'You don't need to come.'

For the first time in my life I'd stood up to my sister. 'Tough – I'm coming.'

First, though, I need to deal with the fallout from my meeting with Artsy, I muse, reaching the gallery and pushing open the glass doors. I'm bracing myself for Magda's inquisition. Apart from the quick telephone call afterwards, we haven't spoken, and if I know her, she'll want all the details. And who can blame her? If he agrees to exhibit, the gallery is saved. And if he doesn't . . .?

Nerves twist in the pit of my stomach. I don't even want to think about it. Not yet, anyway.

Stepping inside the gallery, I wait for the usual cry of 'Loozy!' and for Magda to appear. Only she doesn't. I glance around the gallery. It's empty. Valentino scampers out from the back, snuffling and yapping, and jumps up at my legs.

'Hey, boy.' Magda's obviously here, but where? 'Magda?' I call out, walking past the reception desk and towards the office at the back of the gallery. My footsteps echo on the concrete floor. 'Are you here?'

I'm about to enter the office when abruptly the door is flung open and out jumps Magda. Wearing a white trouser suit and sporting a bright orange tan, she looks startlingly like an Oompa-Loompa.

'Oh my God.' I jump back, spilling my coffee and dropping Valentino, who gives a high-pitched yelp. 'You frightened the life out of me!'

'I'm sorry. I was ... er ... a little tied up.' She stands in the doorway looking all twitchy. 'I didn't hear you come in.'

'Oh well, never mind,' I say, smiling. 'Let me just hang my coat up.'

I go to enter the office, but she bars my way with an outstretched arm as if doing a stretch against the doorframe. Which is very odd. Magda doesn't stretch. Not even at her health club apparently: 'I go there to use the wonderful hot tub and watch the even hotter trainers,' she'd once told me unapologetically.

'Sorry, I just need to get through,' I say, making a gesture with my coat.

'Let me do it.' Flashing me a smile, she takes my coat from me. 'I'll hang it up for you.'

Now I'm really confused. Magda doesn't hang up other people's coats. She doesn't even hang up her own coat, for fear of ruining her manicure.

'Are you feeling OK?' I peer at her uncertainly.

'Who? Me?' She clutches her chest in exaggerated surprise. Trust me, her acting is worse than mine. 'I'm just a little preoc-cupied,' she explains, hopping from one white patent stiletto to the other. 'I have things on my mind.'

'Oh, of course.' I nod, suddenly understanding. She's probably spent a sleepless weekend fretting about the gallery, worrying if my trip to the Vineyard was a success. 'You mean Artsy.'

Her reaction is not what I'm expecting. Instead of nodding compliantly, she looks shocked. 'What about him?' she demands defensively.

'Well, I imagine you want to know all about what happened at our meeting. In the Vineyard,' I prompt. Gosh, she is acting really weird. Even weirder than normal.

'Ah, yes, yes, of course.' She nods vigorously. 'Your trip to the Vineyard.' The way she says it, it's almost as if she'd totally forgotten about it and was thinking about something else entirely. 'I'm all ears.' Putting her arm round my waist, she leads me across the gallery and over to the reception desk.

Basically moving me as far away from the office as she can get me, I can't help noticing. I glance at her sharply. What on earth's going on? Why is she acting so bizarrely?

'Go ahead. Tell me everything,' she says in a stagey voice, plonking me on to a stool.

'Well, he was really nice, not what I was expecting,' I begin, my mind spooling backwards, 'but then I'm not sure what I *was* expecting.'

'Mmm.'

'You know, when I first arrived, he had me digging his vegetable patch.' I smile at the memory. It seems so surreal now I'm back here in New York. 'Then he showed me his recent artwork, which really was quite . . .' I look at Magda. She's not even listening. Instead she's fiddling with her hair and looking around shiftily.

'Mrs Zuckerman?' I say in a firm voice.

It grabs her attention. 'Er, yes, Loozy?' She attempts an innocent expression, which quite frankly couldn't look more guilty.

'You seem preoccupied,' I say questioningly.

'I do?' Her eyes are rabbit-in-the-headlights wide and she hesitates before saying, 'One moment. I forgot something,' and scuttling back across the gallery and disappearing into the office.

I stare after her, perplexed. And more than a little bit peeved. Sod it, she's not even interested. I flew all the way to Martha's Vineyard to meet Artsy; I even shared a bed with Nate because of him, well, sort of, and all because Magda made out it was this huge big deal, that it was the only way we could save the gallery. Now I'm back here and she can't even be bothered to—

'Surprise!'

I snap back to see Magda re-emerging from the office door-way, then stepping to one side to reveal a tall figure wearing lederhosen, a white frilly shirt and a large-brimmed hat. His face is partly in shadow, but there's only one person I know who'd wear clothes like that.

'Artsy?' I gasp, taken aback. 'What are you doing here?'

'Exhibiting!' whoops Magda, before he can open his mouth to answer. 'Isn't that right?'

It's a statement, not a question, and I gape at Artsy. A bolt of relief, delight and God knows what else zips right through and threatens to erupt like a great big firework. Is it true? My eyes search his out under the brim of his hat. *Is it?*

'I do believe that's correct,' he replies with mock formality, then glancing at me, winks.

The firework erupts silently inside me. Fizzing and showering me with a million pieces of glitter.

I did it. He said yes. We're saved.

I want to punch the air, high-five Artsy, pick up Magda and swing her round, tickle Valentino's tummy, but instead I force myself into professional mode.

'That's great news,' I reply evenly, trying to silence my inner voice, which is shrieking excitedly in my head. 'The gallery will be very honoured, and I'm sure you'll find a very happy home here at Number Thirty-Eight.'

Magda shoots me a look of grateful appreciation. Something tells me she's been whooping, 'Wonderful, wonderful,' ever since he broke the news to her.

'I'm sure I will.' He nods lazily, chewing gum. 'Especially now I've met Mrs Zuckerman personally.'

'Please, call me Magda.' She blushes and giggles coyly like a schoolgirl.

A schoolgirl with a crush, I realise, glancing across at her.

'I'm sorry, it was all my idea.' Artsy turns to me.

'Sorry?' I look at him in confusion.

'The surprise,' he explains. 'I thought it might be kinda fun. I'm afraid I can a bit of a practical joker.'

'But you're not joking now,' I check hastily.

He grins and strokes his beard, which he's shaved into a point and plaited with tiny beads. 'No, this bit's for real.'

Magda and I exchange glances. She looks like she's died and gone to Gucci.

'After you came to see me in the Vineyard, I did some research, asked around, and I liked what I heard.' He glances at Magda and she puffs out her already inflated chest. 'So many galleries have sold out. They're not about the art any more. They're not about giving art to the people. They're just about money and profits and making the rich richer.'

'Yes, it's true,' agrees Magda. 'So true.'

'But you seemed different,' he muses, glancing at me. 'You seemed to care about what I was doing, about the art, about the process.'

'I liked your story about the socks.' I smile and he grins.

'I totally dig your philosophy,' he continues, turning to Magda. 'Everyone should be able to enjoy art. It should transcend all social classes, speak to the Proletariat, not just the bankers on Wall Street.'

'Absolutely,' nods Magda fervently. 'Those bankers.' She makes a disgusted tutting noise with her tongue. 'All they care about is money. They don't care about people, their lives, their hopes and dreams.'

I can see she's thinking about her own apartment being repossessed and the gallery being taken away.

'Yeah, exactly,' agrees Artsy. 'That's why I'm so excited to be exhibiting with you guys. I've never felt the need to show my work before, never wanted to, but now I know this is totally the right home, totally the right thing to do,' he enthuses, flinging his arms around.

'Great.' I smile. Gosh, this is amazing. Finally something is going right.

'Yeah, I'm totally stoked about the concept of having an exhibition and not selling my art but giving it away for free. I mean, it's genius!'

There's a pause.

'Excuse me?' Magda looks suddenly confused. 'Free?'

'Yeah, it's, like, your philosophy, right? Art should be for everyone, no matter if you've got a million dollars in your pocket or not even a dime.'

I feel a cold, creeping dread. He cannot be saying what I think he is saying.

'You want to give your art away?' I venture cautiously, the smile freezing on my face. I hardly dare speak the words. '*For free?*'

Making a gun with his fingers, he points it at me and pretends to pull the trigger. 'Bullseye!' He grins, looking pleased with himself.

'*Bullseye?*' croaks Magda in a strangled voice.

'Rather than sell it?' I persist, in dazed disbelief.

'Hell, yeah.' He nods, still grinning. 'It's the future of art. Art for the masses.'

I'm trying to remain calm, but inside I'm that little figure on the bridge in Munch's *The Scream*. I swallow hard. OK, don't panic, Lucy. You've got to turn this around. You've got to change his mind. Think, goddam it. *Think*. 'Yeah, it's an amazing idea, truly genius.' I summon my courage and take a deep breath. 'It's just . . .'

'Just what?' Pausing from bouncing cheerfully around on his big purple Nike trainers, Artsy looks at me and frowns. 'Temperamental artist' is screaming all over his pouting face.

I stall. It's just that this will mean that Magda will lose everything, because she's relying not only on the publicity that his exhibition will bring, but the commission on sales to save her business, her livelihood and her home. I glance across at her. Her face has paled and she looks slightly bewildered, like my nan used to look when my granddad had died, as if she can't quite comprehend what's going on.

I glance back at Artsy. How can I tell him all that?

I can't, can I?

'It's just such an incredible idea of yours,' I say at last, forcing a bright smile. 'Truly genius.'

It's like flicking on the flattery switch. 'I know, right?' His smile snaps right back on. 'OK, well, if that's all sorted . . .' He goes to high-five me and Magda. 'Later, peeps.' And striding across the gallery in his lederhosen, he disappears out of the door and on to the streets of Manhattan.

For a moment neither of us speaks. I'm still trying to absorb what's just happened. One minute everything seemed to be going so fantastically well and then the next . . .

Apprehensively I turn sideways to look at Magda. Crumpled into a chair, she looks tinier than ever, almost childlike.

'Magda, I'm sorry,' I begin falteringly.

For a moment I don't think she hears me. It's as if she's miles away, staring into space, and then her head tips slightly and she looks up. 'Sorry?'

'About the gallery, about everything.' I wave my arms helplessly.

Her heavily mascaraed eyes flick around the gallery, as if taking everything in, before turning to face me. 'Don't be sorry,' she says quietly.

'I know, but—'

'*Never* be sorry.' Her voice is still low, but there's a steeliness to it, and drawing herself up to her full height, she seems to summon an inner strength from somewhere. 'So I lose the gallery? Lose the apartment?' Her eyes flash with determination. 'So what? My relatives lost everything in the war. They lost each other.'

Our eyes meet and all at once I see a depth in Magda that I've never seen before. I've seen her being loud and outrageous, witnessed her exaggerations and dramatics, listened to her crazy stories and been amused by her innate humour, even when she doesn't realise it. But this is something else. Something different. Something noble.

Something pretty goddam special, I think, feeling a sudden surge of respect.

Seemingly galvanised, she takes a deep breath and stands up. 'This is not a reason to be sad. This is reason to celebrate,' she declares, beginning to pace around the gallery. 'We are going to exhibit the hottest artist in town. In the world most probably!' Flinging her arms out wide, she turns to me, her eyes flashing with exhilaration. 'This is wonderful, Loozy, wonderful!'

Her enthusiasm is infectious, and despite everything I feel myself getting swept up in it. She's right. Artsy is the hottest artist out there right now. No matter what happens afterwards, the fact that he's chosen our gallery to stage his first proper exhibition is a huge achievement. The publicity will be incredible.

'We'll have to have a really great party,' I say with a smile, 'and this time we're getting real champagne.' Even if it means putting it on my credit card, I tell myself determinedly.

'Real champagne, real everything! It will be incredible,' cries Magda. Bending down, she scoops up Valentino and hugs him to her tightly. 'People will talk about it for ever. This gallery will not close quietly. Oh, no, we will go out in a blaze of glory! Like *The Titanic*!'

'*The Titanic*?' I ask, slightly bewildered.

'It was sinking, but the band still played on,' she says, her lips quivering. 'The band played on to the very end.' She looks at me misty-eyed and, reaching for my hand, pulls me into a group hug: me, Magda and Valentino. 'That's what we'll do, Loozy. We will play on to the very end.'

Chapter Thirty-Four

The rest of the morning is spent brainstorming ideas for the exhibition, which is going to be in six weeks' time. That's if Magda can hold off the bank until then. Apparently they've issued her with a foreclosure notice, as she's been defaulting on the mortgage for months.

That's not all. Now that her finances are no longer a secret, she tells me about how she's been racking up credit-card debt, remortgaging her apartment to free up capital, gaining interest on the interest with no hope of ever being able to pay back the loan. As if that wasn't bad enough, the whole time this has been going on she's kept it a secret from everyone. She didn't want to worry anyone. She didn't want to admit how it was all falling apart, not even to herself, so she shouldered it alone.

'Have you told your children yet?' I ask, as she finishes telling me everything.

For the first time she falters. 'No, not yet.' She shakes her head. She's being remarkably upbeat, Olympian, in her determination, but I can see in her eyes that telling her children is the worst thing and my heart goes out to her. I have a great affection for Magda and I really respect her. I just wish there was something I could do, some way I could help.

But all I can do is be supportive and try to be positive. So, pinning on a happy face, I attempt to mirror her mood and be upbeat, but it's difficult. As soon as the gallery closes, I'll lose my job, and with it my visa to stay in America. I'll have to move back to London and say goodbye to New York.

At the thought I feel a stab of sadness and my mind flicks

to— I stop it, before it can even go there. Like I said, I'm not thinking about that stuff any more. That's it. I'm done.

With Magda's blessing I leave work at lunchtime and head uptown to the hospital, where I've arranged to meet Kate. According to her, it's one of the best, and I don't doubt it. Knowing my sister, as soon as Jeff got his diagnosis, she will have gone full throttle into research mode, finding out the best treatment, the best hospital, the best doctor. She will have made it her mission to become an expert on everything there is to know about testicular cancer.

Sure enough she meets me in the lobby clutching several colour-coordinated files and a briefcase that's bulging with paperwork.

'What's in there?' I ask, going to give her a hug.

'Research,' she says briskly, greeting my embrace with her customary statue-like stiffness.

My sister's husband might have cancer, but there's obviously no need to get affectionate about it.

'Where's Jeff?' I ask, glancing around.

'He went to the bathroom. He's nervous,' she says in a way that couldn't seem *less* nervous. 'I told him this was perfectly routine. I've got all the statistics.' She waves a green file at me. 'According to a recent study done by the National Cancer Institute, if the cancer hasn't spread outside the testicle, the five-year relative survival rate is ninety-nine per cent.'

But what about the one per cent? pipes up that tiny, terrified voice inside my head that likes to scare me with 'What if?'s. Determinedly I ignore it.

'He's going to be fine.' I nod.

'Of course.' She nods back. 'No question.'

'Hey, ladies.'

We both turn to see Jeff walking down the corridor towards us. He's lost even more weight since I last saw him and I try not to let the shock of his appearance show on my face as I go towards him and give him a hug.

'So, do you come here often?' he quips, injecting his easy humour into the situation as always.

I laugh. 'Is that the chat-up line you used on my sister?'

'No, she was the one chatting me up,' he replies, throwing her a mischievous smile.

She tuts indignantly. 'No, I was not. I remember it distinctly. It was at a Halloween party and you asked me if I'd ever kissed an Irish man.'

'And what did you say?' Amused by their quarrel, I turn to my sister. I've never heard this story before.

'I said, "Yes, several, when I worked for McGrath's law firm in Dublin."'

She says it completely straight-faced and I can't help laughing. That is so Kate. She has an answer for everything. Even cheesy chat-up lines.

'So what did you do?' I look at Jeff, who's loving this.

'Oh, you know, I hit her on the head with my club and dragged her back to my cave.'

'You did not,' gasps Kate, her feminist principles visibly rising up within her.

'No, she's right, I didn't,' he acquiesces with a grin. 'I told her that I'd never kissed a beautiful blonde English girl before, and could I?'

There's a pause as they exchange looks.

'You old romantic,' says my sister quietly, giving him a little squeeze.

I watch them. It's a tender moment. Her keeping it all together with her colour-coordinated files, sharp suit and business-as-usual attitude; him looking ready to fall apart, his face unshaved, his eyes betraying his fear. Two people lost in a moment while all around them the big busy machine of the hospital churns.

'Speaking of softies.' Jeff turns to me. 'I hear you tried to rescue a cat the other night, got into a little bit of trouble.'

Oh crap.

'Trouble? What kind of trouble?'

I swear my sister's ears are like a metal detector. They detect the slightest thing and that's it, she's off, bleeping away.

'Oh, there was no trouble,' I say hastily.

'I have a couple of friends working down the Ninth Precinct. One of the guys recognised the name, said it was a British girl and wondered if Kate was related.' He winks. 'I didn't realise we had a criminal in the family.'

'Lucy, what on earth have you been up to?' demands Kate accusingly. My sister is looking at me in the exact same way she looked at me when she caught me giving her Sindy doll 'a haircut'. Well, how was I to know it wouldn't grow back? I was four!

'Nothing,' I protest, shooting a strangled look at Jeff. 'There was a misunderstanding. The police didn't charge me.'

'Oh my Lord, you were arrested?' Kate almost shrieks.

'Well, sort of . . . but I was released without charge,' I add quickly.

'Lucy, I'm a lawyer!' she gasps. 'If my CEO finds out, this could potentially damage my bid for partner! My God, you're *always* getting into trouble.' She shakes her head and glares at me furiously. 'It's always been the same, me having to bail you out, me being the one to pick up the pieces, me being the one—'

'Hey, honey, it was no big deal,' interrupts Jeff, stepping in to defend me. 'My friend told me. No one's getting into trouble, OK?' He rests his hand on her arm and I see her calm down. She's like a tightly coiled spring, which under the circumstances is understandable, but still, I can't help feeling a bit hurt. 'Said some guy Adam had to come pick you up,' adds Jeff, turning to me, eyebrows raised.

His name stings.

'Who's Adam?' frowns Kate.

'I told you about him the other day,' I say quietly, in reference to our lunch at the weekend. 'You probably don't remember. I was going on about stuff, and you had a lot more important things on your mind.' I glance at Jeff, then stare awkwardly down at my sandals.

'New boyfriend, huh?' he says good-naturedly.

'No, we just went on a couple of dates. It didn't work out.' I shrug. I catch Kate's eye. She's looking at me and I can tell she's thinking of something to ask me, but I glance quickly away. I don't want to talk about Adam, especially not now. 'Not everyone's as lucky as you two,' I add with a small smile.

'He obviously didn't use the Irish line,' says Jeff with a grin.

'No, he didn't,' I say softly, my mind flicking back to the cinema, sitting together in the darkness, his fingers shyly interlacing mine. 'He didn't use any lines.'

'We should go up to your room.' Kate suddenly checks her watch and I snap back. 'You have your appointment with Dr Coleman in ten minutes.'

'OK, boss,' salutes Jeff, making a joke of it, but I catch him blanch slightly. He glances at me. I pin on my most encouraging smile and he winks. 'Right, ladies, let's do it.'

Dr Coleman is a kind-faced man with frameless glasses, a white coat, which sports about a dozen different pens in his breast pocket, and a patch of white bristles on the side of his chin that he missed when he was shaving.

It's odd how you notice these trivial details, as if your mind tries to distract itself by concentrating on the minutiae, rather than face the bigger picture.

This is Jeff's oncologist. He's a cancer doctor, and the only reason he's standing here now, in front of me, shaking Jeff's hand and making polite small talk with Kate, is because Jeff has cancer.

I leave the room and sit outside in the waiting area so they can have some privacy. The doctor is here to talk through the operation, which is scheduled for later this afternoon, and knowing my sister, she'll want him to answer all of her questions. As I left she was already pulling out sheaves of paper from various folders and asking him to 'clarify a few points', as if she's discussing a high-powered merger and not her husband's illness.

I flick idly through a bunch of magazines, not really paying attention. My heart's not in reading about celebrities and goggling over their bikini pictures. Putting them down, I look around the waiting room, my gaze landing briefly on the other people waiting for loved ones and family. I knew there would be a lot of hanging around and I meant to bring a book to read, but at the last minute something stopped me reaching for one of the dozens of unread paperbacks on my shelf and instead grab an old sketchbook of mine.

I pull it out now. It's all dog-eared around the edges and half the pages are filled with drawings from years ago, but I turn over to a fresh, blank page. I stare at its whiteness, momentarily nervous. It's been so long since I drew anything that maybe I've forgotten how to, maybe I can't do it any more. Nevertheless the same something that made me reach for this sketchbook makes me rummage around in the bottom of my bag and dig out a pencil. It makes me look around, at the different faces and their expressions, the different emotions – hope, fear, boredom.

And makes me start sketching again.

I'm not sure how much time passes. I vaguely notice the doctor leaving the room, but Kate remains inside, so I remain outside.

Finally I see two nurses pushing an empty stretcher into Jeff's room and a few minutes later he's wheeled out. He must be on his way for his operation. I don't get up. I don't want them to see me. Instead I watch as Kate follows him down the corridor to the lift, her head bent over him, her thick curtain of blonde hair providing a screen of privacy as she gives him a kiss. Then he's gone, disappeared into the lift and taken to theatre.

Then I'm there, right beside her, just as I promised, suggesting a walk outside and telling her not to worry, that he'll be fine.

'He'll be fine,' I say for the umpteenth time, as we sit outside in the quadrangle, drinking coffee. It's a universal thing: bad coffee and hospitals, the same the world over, I muse, as I sip the bitter dregs from my plastic cup.

'I know,' nods Kate for the umpteenth time. 'Of course.' She stares silently into her cup, chewing her lip, and then, unexpectedly, I notice a lone tear roll down her face and splash into her coffee. One tear, that's all, but it speaks volumes. I can't remember the last time I saw my sister cry. In fact, I'm not sure I can even remember my sister crying. *Ever.*

I stare at her in shock as she lets out a whimper. 'Oh, Luce, what if he's not fine? What if it's spread? What if—' She breaks off, unable to say the words.

'It's going to be OK,' I say quietly. 'The operation will be a success.'

'How do you know?' She rounds on me angrily. 'What if he's not OK? What if he's in the percentage that doesn't make it?'

I flinch slightly, but hold firm. 'Jeff's a fighter. He's not just some random per cent,' I say determinedly, forcing my voice to remain steady. 'He's married to you, remember. He's got to be made of strong stuff.'

She sniffs, despite herself, and gives me a small smile. 'I just haven't allowed myself to even think it, not for one moment,' she confesses almost guiltily. 'I've got to be capable. I've got to be the one who takes care of everything and everyone.'

'You don't have to be,' I say firmly but softly. 'No one expects you to be.'

'Yes, they do. You do, Mum and Dad do, work does, everyone does.' She adopts a different voice. 'Ask Kate. Leave it to Kate. You can rely on Kate.' She lets out a heavy sigh.

'True, we do,' I say, feeling guilty, 'and it's not fair. We shouldn't rely on you like that, but it's also up to you,' I add. 'You've got to tell us. You've got to stop taking so much on.'

'But if I don't, everything will fall apart.'

'You don't know that,' I argue.

'Yes, I do,' she replies obstinately.

'OK, so let it. Let it fall apart.'

Kate looks at me agog.

'Seriously, Kate. So what if it does? It's not life or death.' As soon as the words leave my mouth, I want to stuff them back in again. 'Oh God, I'm sorry, I didn't mean that, me and my big mouth—'

She cuts me off with a firm shake of her head. 'No, you're right,' she says, her pale grey eyes meeting mine. 'It's not life or death. None of it really matters. Not trying to make some stupid partnership, or training for a silly marathon, or whether to choose the grey penny tile or the white subway for the kitchen . . .' She trails off, and shakes her head as if in disbelief.

'Bollocks, Luce,' she curses, more to herself than to me. 'I've been so incredibly stupid. And blind. This whole time I've been thinking that all these other things were important, anxious about everything, worried about achieving stuff, and it's just meaningless crap without Jeff. He's what's important. Without him nothing matters. Without him I don't have anything.' She looks at me and now her eyes are glistening and her face is blotchy.

'All my life I've never failed at anything. I've been a straight-A student. I put in the hard work and the long hours and I get results, pass tests, run marathons and win promotions. It's simple. Easy almost. *It makes sense.* But this doesn't work like that. It's so random. There's no rhyme or reason to cancer, and it doesn't matter how hard I try, or what I do, I can't fix this. I'm completely helpless.' She shakes her head. 'For the first time in my life I don't know what to do.'

I've never seen Kate look so lost and frightened and I feel a clutch of anxiety. As long as I can remember she's always been this strong, capable sister. I've never seen her afraid and not in control, and until this moment I never realised how much I've taken that for granted. She's always been the one looking after me, and there's an unconscious security knowing that I'm the one who can get into scrapes and messes, and be frightened and upset, and despite everything she's always there to pick me up, dust me off and sort things out. Even if it is with a frown and an impatient sigh.

I suddenly realise how much I've resented her for that. For her life seeming perfect and always in control. Things never go wrong for Kate. Everything has always gone right. She's never failed at anything and always got what she wanted, be it the good hair or the exam grades. I feel like such a mess next to her. Her life seemed so sorted. Her emotions were in check. I don't think she's ever even been heartbroken. She met Jeff, they got married, and they have lived happily ever after. It's all seemed so easy for Kate.

Now I realise it's not easy; it's *never* been easy. She's just felt she had to be strong, to be there for me, and for all my life she has been. Now, though, it's my turn to be strong for her. I have to be there for her.

Putting my arm round Kate, I give her a hug, and for the first time she doesn't stiffen and pull away.

And I'm going to be.

For a few moments we remain like that, in the late afternoon sunshine, not saying anything, before finally going back inside to wait. After a while Dr Coleman comes to tell us that Jeff's out of surgery, the operation was straightforward, and they're going to keep him in overnight because of the effects of the anaesthetic.

'In the meantime I suggest you go home and get some rest, young lady,' he says to Kate, with a firm nod of his head. 'I'll see you tomorrow.'

He turns as if to leave, but she stops him. 'When will we know if you got it all?'

'We should get the results back from pathology in the next couple of days.'

'So you'll be able to determine the type and stage of cancer?'

He seems momentarily taken aback by her forthrightness, but this is the trained medic coming out in Kate, not the frightened wife.

'Yes.' He nods. 'And what further treatment, if any, will be needed.'

'Do you think he's going to be OK?'

But the frightened wife is here. Underneath her files and her candidness, she's right here and her hope is almost palpable.

Dr Coleman pauses. He must have been asked that question a million times. 'Let's just stay positive, shall we?' He lays his hand on her shoulder, then leaves.

I offer to go home with Kate and this time she doesn't argue or protest, just mutely nods her head and lets me take control as

I find us a cab and give directions. Once inside the apartment I run her a hot bath, make her a cup of tea, then change it for something a lot stronger. Whose stupid idea was it to make tea at times like this anyway?

Wordlessly she does as she's told. The old capable Kate would have made some comment about the teabags I accidentally leave in the sink, or the choice of towel I find for her in the airing cupboard, or the dirt from my shoes, which I forget to take off and trample across her rug.

The old Kate has been replaced by a girl with a helpless expression, who with clean, damp hair and pyjamas looks about ten years old, and who sits dutifully on the sofa nursing her whisky.

After a while she looks up. 'I think I'll go to bed now, Luce. I'm pretty tired.'

I nod. 'I'll come too.'

'Oh, no, you don't have to. I'll be fine on my own . . .' she replies automatically, then trails off, as if realising that actually, no, she's not all right.

'It'll be like when we were little,' I cajole. 'Remember how we used to share a bed sometimes?'

'So we could share secrets under the eiderdown with a torch.' She smiles.

'You used to kick me out in the middle of the night.' I grin. 'I used to have to creep back into my own bed and it was freezing.'

'God, I was a horrible big sister, wasn't I?'

She turns to me sheepishly and I laugh. 'Trust me, I was a pretty annoying little sister.'

We go into her and Jeff's bedroom. It's the polar opposite of mine. Uncluttered and painted a soft beige, it's all perfect linens and plumped-up pillows.

'All we need now is a torch,' I whisper, snuggling under the duvet.

'And some secrets,' she whispers back. Turning her face, she looks at me, her eyes searching out mine in the darkness. 'Want to hear one?'

I nod, as if to say, *Go on*.

'That life can change in the blink of an eye. All you have is right now. So don't ever put off telling someone how you feel about them, don't assume that they know, because they might not and it might be too late.'

I can tell she's talking about herself, about Jeff, but it resonates with me.

'I love you, Kate.'

'I love you too, Luce.'

She turns over and I spoon her, just like I used to, and as her breathing grows heavier and she falls asleep, I lie awake and think about her secret. I think about it for a long, long time.

Chapter Thirty-Five

'You have to help me. I need to speak to Adam.'

It's the next morning, and having dropped Kate off at the hospital to collect Jeff, I've rushed over to see Robyn at Tao Healing Arts, where she works.

'What? Who's Adam?' she hisses, all flustered.

And well she might be. I've just burst into her therapy room, where she was in the middle of sticking needles into a half-naked man. I don't know who was the most surprised, me, Robyn or the naked man, who suddenly got a needle somewhere he didn't expect.

'The guy from the gallery, the one who came to get me from the police station.'

Robyn stops indignantly waving around her braceleted arms, and two spots of colour appear on her cheeks. She's still feeling guilty about nearly getting me arrested.

'We went on a date and it went horribly wrong . . . Well, not the date. The date was perfect. Anyway, now there's been an awful misunderstanding because of Nate—'

'*Nate?*' Her ears prick up.

'Oh, I didn't tell you, did I? He was in the Vineyard. We slept together—'

'*Slept together?*' She looks aghast.

'Well, yes, *strictly speaking*, but not really, and Adam got the wrong idea, and we had this big row, and he won't answer any of my calls or emails, and, well, I saw my sister at the hospital—'

'*Hospital?*'

Robyn is uncharacteristically lost for words and has been reduced to an echo.

'And she told me that I must never wait to tell someone how I really feel, because I might never get the chance, and I want to tell Adam how I really feel.' I stop abruptly, gasping.

'Wow,' comes a voice from behind us. 'That's intense.'

We both glance over to see the man covered in needles. Lying flat out on the bed in his boxers, he's staring at us agog.

'Sorry, won't be a moment.' Apologising hastily, Robyn quickly pulls the door closed behind her, then turns to me. 'Lucy, why didn't you tell me any of this?' Folding her arms, she gives me her sternest look.

'Well, you've had a lot going on. We both have.' I sigh and look at my feet.

Robyn's face turns from impatience to guilt to sympathy and finally to determination. 'Listen, I'll do anything to help, you know I will, but what can I do? I mean, the last time I tried to help it didn't turn out so well,' she says in reference to the spell.

I look at her, my chest heaving, my mind whirring. 'That's just it – I don't know. I don't know what to do. He won't speak to me. He won't return my emails.'

We both look at each other for a moment completely at a loss.

'If only I could see how to make this right . . .' I murmur, trailing off.

'I know,' nods Robyn sympathetically. 'It's at times like these I always wish I had a crystal ball.'

'That's it!' I exclaim, suddenly hit with an idea. 'What about your psychic?'

Robyn looks doubtful. 'You don't believe in psychics.'

'But you said she can communicate with spirit guides and that she has an amazing gift,' I say pointedly. 'In which case she can tell me what to do.'

OK, so I'm clutching at straws, but I'm desperate.

'I'm just not sure it's a good idea,' says Robyn with a worried expression. 'I know – what about some cupping?'

'*Cupping?*' I exclaim.

'Or some tinctures?' she continues brightly. 'The effects can be amazing.'

'You're not going to fob me off with some old herbs,' I say determinedly. 'Remember I found Harold for you.'

'But that's blackmail,' she gasps.

'I know,' I reply unapologetically.

Tucking a loose curl behind her ear, she studies me, as if thinking hard about a lot of stuff, then asks softly, 'You really like this guy, huh?'

'Yeah,' I reply quietly. 'I really like this guy.'

Satisfied, she gives a little nod of her head. 'Let me get a pen.'

I spend the rest of the day in a pent-up state of nervous antici-pation about what Wakanda is going to tell me. Normally I'd need an appointment, but apparently in emergencies she'll squeeze people in, so the plan is to go there after work and beg her to give me an audience, or whatever it is psychics do. Robyn doesn't have her phone number, just her address, which she gives me, along with a lecture about how I have to keep my mind open and not be alarmed when she starts channelling and speaking in 'voices'.

'Voices?' I'd asked curiously. 'What kind of voices?'

'Just voices,' Robyn had replied casually. 'You know, different spirit guides.'

Actually, no, I don't know, but I'm prepared to leave my disbelief and cynicism at the door and find out. At this point I'll try anything, and if it means crossing some woman's palm with silver, then sod it, I'll do it.

'So which way is it?'

Having left the subway, I'm standing on the street corner. Despite detailed directions, including a printout from MapQuest, I'm utterly lost and on the phone to Robyn.

'Just walk east,' she's trying to explain.

'East? Which way's east?' I say in frustration. 'And don't say opposite to west.'

I twiddle my pop-up map around, and around again, then give up and start walking, my phone still wedged in the crook of my neck.

'Did you figure it out?' she asks after a moment.

'Sort of,' I fib, crossing my fingers and hoping for the best.

'There's a Laundromat at the end of the street, and then next door is this shoe shop with a funny sort of purple awning.'

'Oh, I see it!' Spotting the purple awning, I speed up.

'Number forty-three,' Robyn is saying in the background. 'It's got a silver sign.'

'Yes, nearly there.' Anticipation is buzzing. If you'd have told me a few months ago that I'd be going to see a psychic, I would never have believed it. But then there are a lot of things I would never have believed a few months ago, I tell myself, ignoring my ankle, which is still dodgy from my accident at the gym and is twinging in protest.

Slightly breathless from rushing, I finally reach a small shop with a glass window, across which are painted lots of stars and a sign: 'Psychic Readings.'

I feel a beat of triumph. 'Yup, found it!' I'm actually quite excited.

'Great!' she enthuses.

'Only it doesn't look open,' I say, trying the door and, finding it's locked, feel a wave of disappointment.

'Wakanda's probably just giving a reading,' she quickly reassures. 'Ring the buzzer.'

'OK.' I go to ring the buzzer, then pause as I notice a piece of paper pinned in the window. 'Wait a minute, there's a sign.'

'A sign?' Robyn sounds surprised. 'What does it say?'

I peer closer.

'Well?' persists Robyn.

'"Closed due to unforeseen circumstances."'

There's silence at the other end of the line.

'Well, some bloody psychic she was!' I tut loudly.

'Are you sure you're at the right place?' Robyn sounds bewildered.

'Positive. Number forty-three. Next to the shoe shop with the purple awning,' I repeat her directions back to her.

'I just can't understand it,' Robyn is murmuring to herself. 'There must be some mistake.'

'The only mistake is me coming here,' I reply, feeling suddenly foolish. Turning on my heel, I start heading back down the street towards the subway. 'You were right – it was a bad idea. I don't know what I was thinking.'

'You were thinking about Adam,' replies Robyn helpfully.

At the mention of his name I feel a tug inside. 'Well, I should probably give up thinking about him,' I say resignedly. 'He probably hates me anyway.'

'Bullshit!' protests Robyn.

I hold my phone away from my ear and look at it in astonishment. 'Did you just say "bullshit"?' I ask, putting it back to my ear. In this whole time I've never known Robyn to swear.

'Well, yes, I did,' she says, sounding embarrassed. 'And it is. Because he doesn't. And you mustn't give up.'

I smile gratefully. 'Thanks. I know you're trying to be sweet and everything, but I think I've lost him,' I say sadly.

'OK, well, in that case what would you do if you lost something else?' she replies, refusing to let my negativity dampen her unwavering positivity. 'Say your keys, like I did the other day.'

'Um . . .' Thrown off on this tangent, I have to think for a moment. 'Retrace my steps, I suppose.'

'Right, so let's retrace yours and Adam's,' she says briskly. 'When did you last see him?'

'It was after our date, when we had our row.'

'And why did you row?'

'Because Nate burst in and Adam got the wrong idea.'

'Nate. Exactly,' says Robyn. 'He's the cause of all this. So, first things first, you need to break the bond you have with Nate once and for all.'

'Tell me something I don't know,' I sigh. Only that day I'd received another missed call from him, and I've had to completely give up watching TV. Every time I turn it on it's *Big Bucks*.

'Seriously, Lucy, otherwise this will never get resolved and you might as well give up now.' She gives a little snort. 'It's like with Chinese medicine. You don't try to treat the symptom – you need to fix the cause: *you and Nate*.'

Walking along the street listening, I have to admit that for someone who believes in angels, she does talk a lot of sense sometimes.

'You need closure,' she says determinedly.

'And how do you propose I do that?' I sigh dejectedly. 'The Strategy didn't work. Nothing worked.'

'True,' she agrees reluctantly. There's a pause and I can hear the TV blaring away.

'What are you watching?' I ask absently.

'*CSI*. I'm getting ready to go to my new drumming circle, but I thought I'd watch five minutes. I'm just at the part where they've gone back to the scene of the crime to try to get some answers—' Suddenly she breaks off. 'Oh wow, that's it!'

'What's it?' I ask, puzzled.

'You need to go back to the scene of the crime! The answer's right there. You have to be like Catherine Willows. That's where you'll find your answer.'

'What do you mean?' My ankle has now started throbbing from all this rushing around and I flag down a cab.

'It means you have to go back to Venice.'

I almost drop the phone. 'Don't be so ridiculous!' I exclaim.

'It's the only way. Otherwise, forget it, wave goodbye to Adam.'

The cab swerves to the kerbside and I reach for the door. 'Are you mad? I can't go rushing off to Italy on a whim.' As I tug the door open, the opposite door is suddenly flung wide open and someone else jumps in the other side.

'Hey, this is my cab!' I cry indignantly.

'Lucy, you have to go,' urges Robyn on the other end of the line.

'Robyn,' I gasp into my phone, as I climb into the back seat, 'I'm not going to Venice!'

Just then I come face to face with the stranger who's trying to steal my cab.

Only it's not a stranger. It's Nate.

Chapter Thirty-Six

'I'm going to Venice.'

Walking into the kitchen the next morning, I find the radio playing, tea brewing and Robyn sitting cross-legged at the kitchen table in her tie-dye pyjamas. 'You are?' She looks up from buttering a slice of raisin toast and grins widely. 'Awesome.'

'Well, I'm not sure I'd call it "awesome", exactly.' More like desperate, I think, plopping myself down next to her. After my run-in with Nate last night, finding myself next to him on the back seat of a cab, my mind is made up.

'Wanna slice?' she proffers.

'Mmm, yes, thanks.' I nod, as she passes one to me.

'So when are you going?' She looks at me expectantly.

'Erm . . .' I pause. It suddenly hits me that I haven't thought about that bit yet. In fact, now I *am* thinking about it, I realise there's quite a lot of bits I need to think about. Like how I'm going to afford a flight to Italy, or pay for a hotel, or get time off work . . . Anxiety rumbles. 'I'm not sure yet,' I say vaguely, taking a bite of raisin toast.

'Well, you need to go as soon as possible,' instructs Robyn. 'You mustn't delay.'

'Right, yes, mustn't delay,' I murmur, chewing slowly, my mind whirring. God, this is all beginning to seem a bit overwhelming.

'And of course Nate has to go with you.'

I nearly choke on my raisin toast. 'What? You mean Nate *and* I have to go to Venice *together*?' I turn to her in astonishment. 'I thought the plan was to get rid of him, not fly off to Italy with him!'

Calmly taking another slice of toast from the huge stack on her plate, she begins buttering. 'It will only work if you both go,' she says matter-of-factly.

'Says who?' I cry, waving my slice around in exasperation. 'Is there a rulebook for legends?'

Robyn stops buttering and looks up. 'Look, if you and Nate being together made this happen, you have to be together to undo it.' She gives a little shrug. 'It's common sense.'

'In your world maybe,' I retort, wrapping my dressing gown round my knees and hugging them to my chest. 'I don't live in a world of magic and spells and ancient legends.'

'Oh, really?' Robyn raises her eyebrows and fixes me with a sceptical look. 'You could have fooled me.'

Indignantly I open my mouth to argue, then heaving a sigh, I drop my toast and bury my head in my knees. 'Oh God, this is hopeless,' I groan, my voice muffled in the folds of my towelling dressing gown. 'I've tried everything and everything's failed. We're still ruining each other's lives. Adam's never going to speak to me again, and Beth's probably never going to speak to Nate either. Going to Venice isn't going to work. It's a stupid idea.'

'Listen, Lucy,' says Robyn, with sudden steeliness. 'Do the one thing you think you cannot do. Fail at it. Try again. Do better the second time. The only people who never tumble are those who never mount the high wire. This is your moment. Own it.'

'Huh?' I glance up at Robyn, who's staring at me, her face flushed with determination.

'Oprah,' she says in explanation.

'But how am I supposed to own it? Nate will never go to Venice, not in a million years.' In the background I can hear a song playing on the radio: Neil Sedaka merrily warbling 'Breaking Up Is Hard to Do'. Leaning over, I flick it off.

'How do you know?'

My mind throws up a few jumbled images: sharing a bed in Martha's Vineyard, singing karaoke, yelling at each other in my kitchen when he accused me of sabotaging his relationship with Beth. 'Trust me, the last thing he wants to do right now is go on a trip with me to Italy. In fact, he'd probably rather have his eyeballs poked out with a sharp stick.'

'Well, you're going to have to persuade him,' says Robyn frankly.

I look at her. 'But how?'

'I dunno.' She tilts her head on one side and chews thoughtfully. 'You'll just have to think of something.'

'And if I don't?' I look at her anxiously.

'You're together for ever,' she says simply, and finishing off her toast, she grabs another slice.

With Robyn's words ringing in my ears I pluck up the courage to call Nate on my way to work. As I expected, he's not very happy to hear from me. Translated: he hangs up on me several times, calls me something unrepeatable, then finally agrees to listen 'for thirty seconds'. I get about ten before he cuts me off. No, he's not coming to Venice. Yes, I really am crazy, and don't I know it's the Venice Film Festival and I'll never get a place to stay as everything is totally booked up, so good luck with that.

Then he puts the phone down.

'So basically I'm stuffed.'

It's lunchtime and I'm with Robyn, standing in line at Katz's, waiting to order.

'Are you sure he's telling the truth? Maybe it's a ruse to put you off,' she suggests optimistically. Unwrapping a brownie from her pocket, she takes a bite.

'No, he's right – I Googled.' I sigh. 'It's the festival, so the flights are a fortune. I'll never be able to afford one.'

'That's easy – you can use my Air Miles. I've got thousands from all my trips abroad.'

'Gosh, Robyn, that's so kind of you.' I look at her with grateful astonishment, then frown. 'But even if I can get a flight, there's nowhere to stay – all the hotels are fully booked.'

'All of them?'

'All of them.' I nod. I did an online search that morning on Expedia, Travelocity and every other travel website I could think of. I even made up this whole story about someone I knew wanting to propose to his girlfriend in Venice and got Magda to ask her friend's daughter at the travel agent's, but nothing.

'Hmm, true, that's a tricky one.' She chews thoughtfully.

'Anyway, it doesn't matter. Nate won't come, so there's no point.'

Robyn looks pensive. 'You know what this is, don't you?'

'Hopeless?'

'No, it's the universe trying to keep you together,' she says knowingly. 'The power of the legend. It doesn't want you and Nate to go to Venice and break the spell of everlasting love. It's throwing obstacles in your path to stop you.' She looks proud of her detective work.

'Great.' I shrug as we shuffle forwards in the queue. 'Now when I think it feels like the world is against me, I know that actually, it really *is* against me. And not just the world, but the whole *universe*.'

'Where there's love, there's hope,' she opines, taking another large bite of brownie.

'Oprah?'

'No, I think I read it on a bumper sticker,' she says, shuffling alongside me. 'It's true, though. If you love Adam, there's hope. You just have to fight for him.'

'Like you fought for Daniel?' I raise an eyebrow.

Her jaw sets as she falls silent.

'What are you doing, Robyn?'

'Doing?' she replies tetchily.

'Mooning around the apartment, listening to the African drumming CD he bought you, comfort eating . . .'

She blushes and stuffs the rest of her brownie in her pocket.

'Why are you just letting him walk away like that?'

'He's not my soulmate,' she says firmly.

'Says who?' I cry. 'The psychic who couldn't even see into her own future? Great fortune-teller she was!'

Robyn looks all twitchy and starts fiddling with her stacks of silver bangles, determinedly avoiding my gaze.

Now I've started, I can't stop. 'I was like you once. I was convinced that I would know when I met the One, that I would just *feel* it. Everyone tells you, "You'll just know." Well-meaning friends, books, films, poetry. And although you don't know what it is you're looking for, and haven't a clue how it's supposed to feel, you convince yourself that when you finally find your soulmate, some magical alarm bell will go off in your head and you'll just know.

'When I met Nathaniel, I had all these intense, incredible feelings, and I thought, This is it. He's the One. I truly believed it, which is why I was heartbroken when we broke up. I'd lost the one person in the world who was meant for me, and without that person I could never be truly happy again. OK, so there'd be other guys, nice guys, funny guys, lovely guys, but not another Nate. I'd lost him, and that was it.

'So for years I carried on. I dated, had flings, a few boyfriends, but no one compared. Nate was always there in the back of my mind. Then, by some miracle, we found each other again and got another chance at it. And what happened?'

Urgently I look at Robyn. She's standing next to me, looking a bit shell-shocked, and I don't blame her. It's all coming pouring out, a decade's worth of feelings spilling out in the middle of a busy New York diner.

'I realised I didn't feel the same any more, and neither did he. I realised I'd got it wrong. Just like all the other millions of people out there who marry and end up getting divorced. I was lucky, though – if I hadn't had a second chance with Nate, I'd still be hung up on him now. I would have spent my whole life looking back with rose-tinted spectacles and I would never have noticed Adam. I would have missed him. Because the moment that I stopped focusing on Nate, and what I thought love looked like, was the moment I saw Adam.'

'Hey, lady.'

I hear a voice, but ignoring it, I heave a sigh. 'Look, I'm probably not making any sense, but I guess what I'm saying is that too many people miss out on real love because they're too busy waiting for the One to show up. For this fantasy figure who's going to complete them and who probably doesn't even exist. For a sign to say, "This is it." Just like you did. You've set your heart on Harold, your perfect soulmate, the dark, handsome stranger on your vision board. You're so focused on him you can't see you've got something pretty damned good already.'

Robyn seems almost to flinch, as if I've hit a nerve.

'There doesn't always have to be a sign, Robyn. You don't always *just know*. Sometimes it takes a while to see what's been in front of you all along.' I stop talking and realise I'm almost breathless with emotion. Even if it's too late for me and Adam, I don't want it to be too late for her and Daniel.

She looks at me as if there's a lot going on inside her head, then says stiffly, 'Whatever's meant to be will be.'

'Ugh, that is such a cop-out,' I gasp impatiently.

'No, it's not,' she protests hotly.

'It is, and your logic is all skewed,' I argue. 'You're telling me I've got to take on the universe, like I'm some superhero, but you're just going to sit back and see what happens?'

'Hey, lady, you gotta problem hearing or somethin'?'

A loud voice hollers right behind me and I turn round, slightly irritated, then quickly realise it's the sullen man who takes my order every lunchtime. 'Oh, right, yes, sorry.' I snap to. 'I'll have a matzo-ball soup and a—'

He doesn't let me finish. 'Nah, forget the soup,' he says gruffly, shaking his head. 'I heard you talking about Venice.'

I gape at him in astonishment. In all this time I've never heard this man grunt more than a couple of words, and now he's talking to me? About Venice?

'Erm, yes, that's right,' I say uncertainly, wondering where on earth this can be leading.

'I think I can help you.'

I can't believe this. Not only is he talking to me, he wants to *help me*?

'You can?' pipes up Robyn, speaking for me.

'My uncle owns a small *pensione* in Venice,' he says with a shrug. 'I'm sure they have room . . . if you want me to make a phone call.'

I'm still staring at him in disbelief. I can hardly believe what I'm hearing.

'Wow, that would be awesome,' enthuses Robyn.

'Um . . . yeah, great,' I murmur dazedly.

'OK, give me your number and I'll get back to you this afternoon,' he instructs, removing a pen from behind his ear. Taking the notepad from his breast pocket, he passes them both to me across the counter, and then, for the first time ever, he gives me a smile.

Chapter Thirty-Seven

I spend the rest of the afternoon at the gallery still reeling from this recent turn of events. I don't know which is more shocking, the fact he actually smiled at me or his phone call later that afternoon to say, yes, that's fine, his uncle has a room, and no, it's not expensive.

Mr Sullen's real name is Vincent and he's actually quite chatty once you get to know him. Thanking him profusely, I take down all the details and promise to pop in to the diner when I get back to tell him how it all went. So that's sorted, I think, hanging up. I've got my flight. I've got my hotel. All I need now is to get Nate to come with me.

That's a bit like saying, 'All I need now is a billion dollars,' I think gloomily.

On the back of a press release I'm writing about Artsy, I doodle a list of options:

1. *Kidnapping? No. Impossible to smuggle on plane. Carries life sentence if caught.*
2. *Threaten? What with? My stiletto heel? A bridal magazine? Weapons of mass destruction? No. Don't have weapons of mass destruction. Saying that, it's never stopped anyone before.*
3. *Bribery? No. Ditto above. What with? Once I've paid for the room in Venice, I'm broke.*

I'm just trying to think of another option when I hear the door and look up to see Daniel walking in.

'Oh, hi, Daniel.' I wave, quickly hiding my list. 'How are you?'

It's a redundant question. He looks totally miserable. Wearing a crumpled navy suit that looks like it's been slept in, he hasn't shaved and has dark circles under his eyes. 'Hi, Lucy.' He forces a smile. 'Is Mom here?'

'Yeah, she's in the back.' I gesture to the office. 'You two going out?'

'No.' He shakes his head. 'I came to pick her up and take her home. I'm helping her pack up her apartment.'

'She's moving out?' I look at him in dismay. 'Already?'

'Yeah, 'fraid so.'

'She didn't tell me,' I murmur.

I feel a wave of sadness. All day long Magda has been her usual indefatigable self, entertaining me with outrageous stories, being excited about the Artsy exhibition. Yet all the time, underneath, was the knowledge that she was packing up her home that very evening. Moving out of the place she'd lived in for the past twenty years.

'Where will she go?' I ask anxiously.

'She's coming to live with me,' replies Daniel, and smiles ruefully. 'At least that's something. You know it's every Jewish mother's dream to live with her son.'

Despite myself, I can't help smiling.

'So how's Robyn?' he says after a moment, trying to sound nonchalant and failing terribly.

'OK,' I say vaguely. I don't know what to say. Do I tell him the truth? That I think she's making a huge mistake, that I've tried and failed to talk some sense into her? Or do I keep out of it and not interfere? Take a leaf out of her book and accept that what will be will be?

'I guess she must be really happy about finally finding Harold,' he says, nudging for a reaction.

We look at each other, neither of saying what we are really thinking. 'Yeah, I suppose so.' I shrug non-committally. I bite my lip. Oh God, this is killing me. 'Look, Daniel, I think you two should speak,' I blurt, before I can help myself.

Well, I'm sorry. Sod leaving things up to destiny. If I'd followed the rule of what will be will be, I'd have flat stringy hair and thick bushy eyebrows. Sometimes you need to give things a helping hand, whether that involves hair products, tweezers or your best friend interfering in your love life.

If I'm expecting him to yell, 'You're right!' and rush off to declare his undying love, I'm sorely mistaken.

'No.' He shakes his head resignedly. 'She's in love with someone else. It would be unfair of me to come between her and her soulmate.'

'But he's not her soulmate!' I cry, a feeling of desperation rising up inside me. 'Robyn isn't in love with Harold. She thinks she is, but she's not. She's in love with—'

'Daniel, my boy!'

I'm interrupted by Magda appearing with a shriek of delight.

'Hey, Mom.' He blushes beetroot as she flings herself against him, burying her head in his chest as if it's their last goodbye.

'My boy, my beautiful boy,' she wails, clinging on to him. Then she pushes him away from her so she can get a better look. 'What's wrong? Why do you look so sad?'

'I'm not.' He pins on a smile. 'Everything's great.'

'Wonderful!' She beams, her face flushing. 'And how is Robyn?'

Watching them together, I suddenly realise he hasn't told her yet.

'Great. She's great.' He nods, flashing me a glance as if to say, *Please keep schtum.*

I run my fingers over my mouth as if to say, *My lips are zipped.*

'See, if you had trusted me with my matchmaking . . .' she says, throwing a pointed look in my direction. 'So where is Robyn? Is she coming to the apartment?'

'Oh, no, she's busy.'

'Busy?' Magda starts grabbing her plethora of bags and packages. 'No, you have to wait. Mommy is busy,' she instructs Valentino, who snaps around her heels, wanting to be picked up. She turns back to Daniel. 'What is she doing?'

'I . . . um . . .' Daniel looks incredibly awkward. 'Here, do you want me to help you?' He reaches down, but Magda bats him away.

'Not with your bad back, Daniel.'

'Mom, I'm fine.'

'Remember what Dr Goldstein said about your sciatica?'

Valentino is still jumping up and down trying to get attention. Daniel bends forward to grab a bag, and I'm not quite sure what happens, but suddenly there's an ear-splitting howl and Daniel goes flying, along with the bags and Valentino, who shoots out from underneath him like a bullet, and Daniel lands in a tangled heap on the floor.

'Oy!' shrieks Magda, rushing to her son's aid. 'Are you hurt?'

'I'm fine, Mom.' Throwing Valentino a furious glare, Daniel starts scrambling to his feet and brushing himself down, while Magda fusses around him. 'Seriously, I'm fine. Don't worry—' Suddenly he breaks off. 'Oh shit.'

'What is it?' gasps Magda, her eyes wide with concern. 'It is your back? Oy! I knew you would hurt your back, I knew it!'

'No, Mom, it's not my back.'

'Then what is it?' She's almost shrieking. 'Oh, no, is it your heart? It's your heart, isn't it? You're going to take after your father.'

'No, it's the painting.' His face is ashen.

Magda stops shrieking and frowns in confusion. 'What painting?'

With a stricken expression Daniel points to the wrapped package that was leaning against the side, along with some of the bags. It's the painting that Magda's aunt left her. She'd obviously brought it out from the back office to take back to Daniel's, but now the wrapping is all ripped off, and underneath the canvas is torn.

'Jeez, Mom, I'm sorry. It must have been when I fell—' he begins apologising, but she stops him.

'Oh, don't worry about that.' She quickly bats away his concerns. 'It was terrible.'

'What was it?' I ask curiously. I've been watching this whole thing unfold, and now as Daniel picks up the painting, the wrapping paper in shreds, I look at it with interest.

'Looks like a clown,' says Daniel, peering at it.

'I hate clowns.' Magda gives a little shudder. 'They are so creepy.'

'Maybe you could fix it,' I say, standing by Daniel's shoulder. 'I'm sure we could find a restorer.' Reaching over carefully, I peel back the torn flap of canvas with my fingers.

'No, I don't care. Throw it away.' Magda wrinkles her nose. 'I never liked it.'

'But it was from Great-Aunt Irena,' Daniel protests. 'She wanted you to have it.'

'Hang on, wait a minute.'

They both stop squabbling and turn to me expectantly.

'What?' asks Magda. 'What is it?'

'Look, underneath,' I say, feeling a beat of excitement. 'There's another canvas hidden beneath.'

'Oh wow, yeah, you're right,' nods Daniel. 'It's another painting.'

'Well, would you believe it,' gapes Magda. 'Aunt Irena always did say appearances could be deceptive.'

'I wonder what it is,' muses Daniel.

'Well, there's only one way to find out.' I glance across at Magda. 'May I?'

She throws her hands in the air as if to say, *Sure, go ahead*, and so, taking a deep breath, I tear back the tattered canvas of the clown, with its gaudy colours and amateurish brushstrokes, to reveal a whole new painting. A naked portrait of a woman, reclining on a cushion, while cherubic angels dance around her.

'That's kinda nice,' murmurs Daniel with approval, but I can't reply. My heart is thumping so loudly in my ears I feel dizzy.

The distinctive muted colours. The familiar religious subject. It can't be. It just can't be . . . With trembling fingers I turn it to the light and peer at the initials in the far corner. It is.

'Oh my God,' I gasp, my voice barely a whisper.

'What is it?' asks Magda.

'Your aunt was right, appearances *can* be deceptive.' Turning to her, I can barely say the words. '*It's a Titian*.'

After that it's bedlam. Daniel's straight on the phone to a renowned art expert at an auction house, Magda has to sit down before she falls down, and I just stare dumbfounded at a priceless masterpiece. I can't believe that it's been here all this time, propped up in the back office, being completely ignored, and would have probably remained stuffed somewhere out of sight for years unless Daniel had fallen against it.

It's like finding you've got the winning lottery ticket. If it's genuine, it will be worth millions. I mean, just imagine. It will be the answers to all Magda's prayers. It will change everything!

With all the excitement at the gallery, I lose track of time and it's only at the last minute I remember that the play Robyn gave me the tickets for is tonight. I'd almost forgotten. Reminded, I leave work and head to the theatre.

Despite everything, I'm actually quite looking forward to it. I managed to sell the spare ticket yesterday for a whopping hundred and fifty dollars, as it's supposed to be a really good play and all the tickets are sold out, so it will be a good distraction from everything. It will be nice to lose myself for a couple of hours in a totally different world.

One that doesn't involve Nathaniel Kennedy, I muse, glancing at my phone and toying with the idea of giving it one more try. I check my watch. I've got a few minutes before the play starts. It's worth a shot. Dialling his number, I wait for it to connect. He probably won't pick up, I tell myself, listening to it ringing. He's probably screening his calls.

'If this is to ask me to go to Venice again, the answer is still no,' barks Nate, picking up.

We dispensed with the 'hello's and the 'how are you's quite some time ago.

'Nate, please, just listen—' I try persuading, but he cuts me off.

'Lucy, how many more times?'

I heave a sigh, struggling to remain calm. 'Look, I know you think this is a bad idea.'

'I think it's probably the worst idea you've ever had,' he huffs down the phone, 'and that's saying something.'

I feel a twinge of annoyance crank up a notch. 'I really think you should think about it,' I reason.

'I have thought about it and the answer is no.'

I check my watch. Damn, the play's about to start. I need to go in.

'Hang on,' I hiss into my phone, and hiding it under my jacket, I give my ticket to the usher and walk inside the theatre. I'm momentarily taken aback. Wow, it's impressive. I feel a buzz. A real Broadway play. How exciting. 'Sorry, where was I?' I say, retrieving my phone.

'You were hanging up,' deadpans Nate.

'And that's it? You're not going to change your mind?' I begin walking down the aisle, checking the letters on each row.

'What part of "I'm not going to Venice" do you not understand?'

Finding my row, I start shuffling down it towards my seat number. I've got to get him to change his mind, but how? *How?*

'Anyway, I've got to go,' he snaps.

'No, wait. What about the cab the other day?' Excusing myself to the people already sitting down, I head towards the middle, where I can see two empty seats.

'What about it?'

'We've got to make it stop, once and for all, otherwise you and Beth—'

'Lucy, stop this. You've got to get a grip.'

'I have got a grip,' I retort, peering at the numbers on the back of the seats. Twenty-two, twenty-three, twenty-four . . . It's silent on the other end of the phone. 'Nate, are you there?'

'Yeah, I'm here.'

Gosh, how weird. For a moment his voice sounded like it wasn't coming from my phone, but right next to me. *Bingo.* There's my seat. I glance up, and come face to face with someone who's been working their way down the row from the opposite direction.

'Nate!' I stare at him in shock. 'What are you doing here?'

You'd think by now I would have got past the surprised bit, wouldn't you? But no, here I am, staring at him, open-mouthed.

'What?' Still on the phone, he looks up at me in bewilderment. 'I've come to see the play. That's my seat.' He points to the empty seat next to mine.

I glance at it in astonishment, then back at him, as suddenly it registers. '*You* were the person who bought my spare ticket on eBay?'

'It was your spare ticket?' He looks at me aghast.

There's a pause as we stare at each other, frozen, until the lights go down and we're forced to take our seats. The audience falls silent, waiting for the curtain to rise and the play to begin.

It's then that I hear a whisper in my ear.

'So when do we leave for Venice?'

Chapter Thirty-Eight

Venice, Italy, 2009

Nothing has changed. The summer heat creates a shimmering haze, through which Venice appears like a Canaletto brought to life. The dome of St Mark's Cathedral rises above the pastel-coloured buildings, with their peeling paint and time-weary elegance. Vaporetti buzz. Tourists throng. Among the crowds, children run in the square scattering pigeons; men in sharp suits and designer shades sit smoking cigarettes; a guide with his umbrella talks history to a group of German tourists.

And down a maze of alleyways, tucked away in a tiny old *pensione*, in a room with a pink frilly bedspread and a picture of the Blessed Virgin Mary, are two people. A stressed-out American in a suit mopping his brow, and an English girl trying to stay calm.

That's me and Nate. Back in Venice, ten years later.

And this time around, *everything* has changed.

'OK, so what's the plan?' Nate is saying briskly.

Having put down his suitcase and hung his jacket over the rickety wooden chair, he turns to me. Sweat and stress are oozing from his pores. He might as well have 'I don't want to be here' written across his forehead in thick black marker pen.

'Um, that's the thing . . .' I walk over to the window and open the shutters. Light floods in, sending dust particles swirling, and I pause to lean out and survey the tiny slice of Venetian life in the narrow alleyway below.

It's also quite a good delaying tactic.

Because you see, the thing is, I'm not quite sure how to break this to Nate, but I haven't finished formulating my plan yet. It's nearly there. It's just . . .

Oh, who am I kidding? There is no plan. The truth is, I haven't a clue what on earth to do next.

'Lucy?'

I turn round to find Nate is still looking at me, only now his face has set harder, rather like when food starts to go cold and congeals on a plate.

'Please tell me you have a plan.'

His voice is steely and impatient, but I can detect a twinge of worry.

'Well, not exactly a plan as such.' I stumble through my excuses while Nate's eyes are boring into me like lasers. 'OK, I don't have a plan,' I confess.

'You don't have a plan?' repeats Nate calmly.

As in *eerily* calm. As in the kind of foreboding calm you get as you're opening your credit-card statement, slowly unfolding it, before the inevitable 'Oh my God, *how much*?' hits you like a ten-ton truck.

It's *that* kind of calm.

'Yet,' I add, forcing a positive tone. 'I don't have a plan *yet*.'

Nate erupts in fury. 'What the fuck?' he cries angrily, throwing his arms in the air. 'You got me all the way here, to Venice, Italy, and you don't have a plan?'

'OK, OK, I think we both get it. I don't have a plan!' I snap impatiently. 'What are you going to do? Shoot me?'

Heaving a sigh, Nate sits down on the edge of the pink frilly bedspread and presses his temples. 'Well, that would be a plan at least,' he mutters under his breath.

I shoot him a furious look. Death in Venice is not what I had in mind. 'Look . . .' Taking a deep breath, I try to focus. What was it Robyn said? Ah, yes, something about the scene of the crime. 'Just meet me at the Bridge of Sighs at sunset,' I say on a whim.

'And then what?'

'Wait and see,' I say, with as much confidence as I can muster. 'I'll come up with something.'

Rolling up his sleeves, Nate dabs his forehead with a handkerchief. 'You better do, 'cos I'm going to be on the first plane out of here tomorrow morning.'

I grab my sunglasses and throw my bag over my shoulder. 'Don't worry.' I reach for the door. 'I've got it all under control.'

Except, of course, I haven't.

I stumble outside into the bright Italian sunshine, my heart hammering in my chest. My mind is racing. Fuck. Bloody fuck. What on earth am I supposed to do now? I haven't the *faintest* clue. Anxiety grabs at my stomach like a pickpocket snatching at my purse. Under control indeed. What am I talking about? Everything is completely *out* of control. My life is spinning off its axis. I'm falling off gym machines and nearly breaking my ankle, performing magic spells and getting arrested, nearly killing myself in a car crash and doing karaoke.

And now I'm here, in Venice, with Nate.

And I'm still going to be with him in a hundred years' time if I don't think of something, and fast! A bolt of fear zips right through me, as I set off through the cobbled backstreets. I'm going to be tied to my ex-boyfriend for eternity. I'm going to die a shrivelled-up old maid who on her deathbed will still be trying to lose her ex.

A sudden vision of me croaking, 'You're chucked!' and Nate as a wizened-up old bachelor with no teeth, bald as a coot, in novelty boxer shorts, croaking back, 'No, you're chucked!' flashes through my brain.

Shuddering, I try blocking it out. I mean, at this rate he's going to sabotage my life for ever, I think with panic. A memory of Adam's face pops into my mind – how excited he'd looked that night in the cinema, rapidly followed by how hurt he'd looked later, in my kitchen, when Nate had stormed in. I'm going to sabotage Nate's life too, I sigh, thinking back to my phone call with Beth, his ex-wife. Nate's never going to be able to try again, because she's never going to take him back.

Because I'll still have him.

A cold chill grips my heart. We're going to be locked together like conjoined twins.

I won't be able to go anywhere without him. He won't be able to do anything without me. 'You complete me' will stop being the most romantic line in a movie and will become the most sinister. We'll be like those couples you read about who have been together for sixty years and have never spent a night apart and make you go, 'Aw, what an amazing love story.'

Yet no one will know the truth.

That it's not a love story; it's a *horror story*.

Maybe it's the same for those other couples too, I think with alarm. Maybe those couples we all read about have spent the last sixty years desperately *trying* to spend a night apart and dreaming of one day having the duvet to themselves. Maybe those couples kissed under a bridge in Venice and have been trying to lose each other for their entire lives.

OK, now stop, Lucy. You're getting paranoid.

Turning a corner, I find myself plunged into a mass of tourists. Abruptly I realise I'm in St Mark's Square. I pause to glance around me, my mind suddenly emptying of everything but the sheer beauty and majesty that is Venice. The way the sunlight is bouncing off the cobblestones, a gap in the crowds revealing glittering water, the rich scents of espresso, aftershave and cigarette smoke, the passionate scramble of Italian that always sounds to my non-Italian-speaking ears like someone playing scales on a piano.

God, I love Venice. I'd forgotten how much because it's been so long. Like an old photograph, faded by time, my memories of the city have dulled. Over the years it's become simply a backdrop, against which the more important story of me and Nate and how we first met was set. The moment we left, it was as if Venice stopped, ceased to exist. As if it was just there for us, until we went back to college, when it folded itself back up and was packed away.

I smile fondly at my foolish arrogance. In my teenage mind I was the first person to discover Venice, and Nate and I were the only two people to have ever fallen in love in among its canals, intertwined piazzas and maze of backstreets. No one had ever, and could ever, feel like us.

How wrong I was, I realise, walking across the square. Venice has a life of its own, a sense of history that overshadows anything that Nate and I created, a magic that draws lovers to it, I muse, watching the dozens of couples strolling by, hand in hand, no doubt feeling exactly the same way Nate and I once did. Like the only two people in the whole world. That's the magic of Venice – it makes everyone feel special.

Turning another corner, I head into the labyrinth of alleyways. This is the first time I've been back in ten years, and although I've changed, the city hasn't. I start wandering in no particular direction, enjoying the sensation of rediscovering the maze of canals, shadowy piazzas and sounds and smells that are Venice.

I've been so focused on Nate, on getting him here, on getting both of us here, that I've never stopped to think about actually *being* back here. In my head it was simply the scene of the crime, the baddy, the cause of this whole mess, but now I can't help falling in love all over again.

Only this time it's not with Nate; it's with Venice itself, I muse, glancing up at yet another beautiful building. I don't know the name of it, but a whole bunch of paparazzi are crowded outside. It's the film festival and everywhere the banners are flying, posters are advertising films, tourists have their cameras at the ready, hoping to spot a movie star. Apparently Penélope Cruz was spotted earlier on the Rialto Bridge, and the man checking us in at the hotel swore blind Tom and Katie were staying in room twelve.

Though somehow I doubt it. All the celebrities are staying at the magnificent Gritti Palace. We passed it earlier, coming from the airport on the Vaporetto, and there was a big stretch of red carpet running all the way up from the jetty to the terrace bar right on the canal. There was tons of activity, dozens of black-and-white uniformed waiters, like an army of penguins, flitting around getting everything ready for the big film première party that's happening tonight. Though I haven't a clue which film it's for.

Adam would know, pipes up a voice in my head.

I feel a familiar lurch in my stomach. I've been trying not to think about him, but now his face pops into my consciousness and my mind spools back to that first time I saw him on the street, with a camera and a furry microphone. To the time in the MoMA, talking animatedly about his love of films. To the night we met in the art-house cinema and how excited he was to be sharing his favourite movie with me. He'd love it here, I reflect, glancing around, feeling the buzz of the festival.

For a split second I think about calling him, telling him where I am.

But of course there's no point, is there? I doubt he'd even pick up the phone. Even if he did, how would I explain what I'm doing here? *Oh, hi, I'm here at the Venice Film Festival with Nate, trying to break an ancient legend. Wish you were here!*

Yeah, right, Lucy. Great move.

I keep walking. Sadness aches and I try cajoling myself. Perhaps once this is all over we could start where we left off . . . but I know that's not going to happen. He'll never trust me again, and why should he? Anyway, let's face it, it was over before it had even begun. What was it? A couple of kisses, two dates, that's it. He'll move on, so will I. It's no big deal.

Only it *felt* like a big deal. It wasn't just about a couple of dates; it was about more than that. It was about listening to him talking and thinking he reminded me of someone and realising it was me. It was the feeling I got when he walked into the police station that night and I discovered there was no one I'd rather see than him. It was seeing him sitting cross-legged on my bedroom floor, looking excitedly through my sketchbooks and telling me to follow my dream. Small, simple, fleeting things, and yet they made a huge impression on me. At the time I didn't realise it, but now . . .

Now it's too late. Whatever happens with Nate, Adam and I are over. This time there are no second chances.

I keep walking, hands stuck deep into the pockets of my shorts. Everywhere around me are the sounds of laughter and excitement, but they only serve to throw into stark contrast my own mood.

After a few moments I slip into a shadowy backstreet. It's quiet here, no fancy galleries, *gelata* stalls or souvenir shops to tempt the tourists, just the odd cat sitting on a doorstep, and a washing line strung high above. It reminds me of Artsy and his washing line of art. I think about his upcoming exhibition. It's definitely going to go ahead now. I spoke to Magda at JFK, just as we were boarding, and sure enough the painting had been verified and it was a Titian.

'Which of course I knew all along!' she'd declared. 'I said to Daniel, "I knew Aunt Irena would not leave me penniless, I knew!"'

Which isn't the exact truth, but who cares? She was so happy, and I'm happy for her. The painting's going to be put up for auction and with the proceeds Magda will no doubt be able to pay off her debts and save the gallery. Moreover, she'll most likely be able to keep herself in genuine designer goods for the rest of her life. Everything, it seems, has worked out for her.

Reaching a small piazza, I pause. In the middle there's a fountain with an elaborately carved fish spouting water, and a wooden bench in a patch of sunlight. It looks tempting. I'm tired and my sandals are starting to rub in the heat. Despite being the beginning of September, it still feels like summer. Gratefully, I sit down. Gosh, this is much better. Slipping off my sandals, I wiggle my toes and close my eyes for a moment, relishing the peace and quiet. Just the sound of the trickling fountain.

'*Scusi.*'

And a voice.

Snapping open my eyes, I look up to see a man peering over me. He's blocking the sunlight and his face is in shadow, so I can't distinguish his features, but I can make out the outline of his hat. A white fedora.

Deep within a memory stirs and I feel a tingle run down my spine. There's something about him. He's familiar. I know him, but how?

He motions to me, as if to say, *Do you mind if I sit down?* and I gesture back as if to say, *No, of course not.* As he eases himself down beside me, his face turns to the light.

And suddenly I place him.

'It's you!' I say, more to myself than to him.

He looks at me quizzically.

'You're the man who sold me the pendant, who told me about the Bridge of Sighs.' I scan his craggy face for a sign of recognition. 'Do you remember?' I look at him with eager anticipation, awaiting his reply. This could be it. This could be the answer I've been looking for. Hope swells inside and I hold my breath tight inside my chest.

'I tell a lot of people that story,' he confesses, his eyes crinkling into a rueful smile.

'You do?' I feel a curious stab of disappointment and look down at my lap so he can't see it on my face. All these years I'd imagined Nate and I had been special, yet now, abruptly, I realise we were just one of hundreds of couples to whom he told the story. Foolishness prickles. There was me thinking that somehow he could hold the secret, that he could somehow give me the answer.

'So did the legend work its magic?' I glance up to see him looking at me with an amused curiosity. 'Are you still together?'

'Sort of.' I shrug miserably.

He frowns at my expression. 'I'm sorry . . . my English.' He throws out his upturned palms. 'I don't understand.'

'It's a long story.' I smile apologetically.

He looks at me for a moment, his eyes searching my face, as if for clues. 'You are both in love with someone else? Is this it?'

'Yes, it is.' I nod, thinking about Nate. Earlier at the airport I'd heard him on the phone to Beth, still trying to convince her to give things another shot, and my heart had gone out to him. He was clearly in love with her, and it was even more clear that it was only now he'd begun to realise it. Never has the old adage 'you don't know what you've got till it's gone' seemed more true. But then, isn't that true for a lot of people? I muse sadly, thinking about Adam.

'And what about you?'

I snap back. 'Me? No,' I protest, shaking my head determinedly. 'No, not in love . . .' The words catch in my throat as my mind thumbs through the snapshots of mine and Adam's brief relationship. It wasn't love. Of course not. How could I be in love with someone I barely knew? And yet . . .

And yet you can spend a lifetime with someone and still be a stranger to them, but on the flipside you can meet someone briefly who can see inside your soul. Can you measure love by time? By anything? Or is it something inexplicable that has no rhyme or reason, no scientific explanation. Something that just happens. *Like magic.*

As the thought hits, I suddenly realise that I'm not convincing anyone, least of all me.

'Yes, I am,' I say, turning to look at the old man. My voice is quiet but unfaltering. 'I am in love with someone.'

'Well, then, do not worry.' He smiles reassuringly. 'The legend is indeed powerful, but do you know what is more powerful?' He looks at me, his dark eyes seeming even darker, and I feel goose bumps prickling my arms, just like all those years ago.

'*Love*,' he says simply. 'The power of love.'

I look at him, a million questions racing through my head. 'But—'

'Goodbye, Lucy.' Before I can finish, he stands up, tipping his hat. 'Say hello to Nathaniel for me.'

'Yes, I will.' I nod absently, watching as he turns and walks away. Then a thought strikes. 'How did you remember our names?'

But he's already gone, disappeared down an alleyway, leaving me with a jumble of thoughts and unanswered questions.

Chapter Thirty-Nine

I'm still sitting alone on the bench, trying to make sense of it all, when my phone rings. It's my sister, Kate. I pick up.

'How's Venice? Got rid of him yet?' she says with characteristic bluntness.

'Not yet,' I say blithely, but reminded of why I'm here, I feel a clutch of worry. 'So, anyway, how are you?' I ask, sweeping it under my cerebral carpet.

'Well, do you want the good news . . . or the good news?'

'Huh?'

There's a pause and then . . .

'We got the all-clear!' Jeff and Kate yell in stereo down the phone, their voices so loud I have to hold my mobile away from my ear.

'Oh my God, that's brilliant!' I gasp, feeling a tidal wave of emotions wash over me – relief, joy, delight . . . I want to punch the air, high-five a stranger, hug someone, but there's no one here, just me, on a bench, in a tiny piazza in Venice, listening to my sister and Jeff speaking nineteen to the dozen down the phone, telling me all about the results. It was stage one and he didn't need chemo. 'Just a holiday,' Kate is enthusing, 'a bloody long holiday.'

Listening to her speaking, I can't stop smiling, and it's not just because Jeff's got the all-clear. It's because of the change in my sister. Hearing her excitedly talking about taking a holiday, it's like a new Kate. Gone is the sister who used to spend every spare moment she had in the office or the gym, who was so focused on making partner or running the marathon that she lost sight of who and what are important in life. She was left behind that day in the hospital, and somehow I don't think she's ever coming back.

'We were thinking a safari, or maybe even diving on the Great Barrier Reef, or Jeff said why don't we just go crazy and take sabbaticals from work and do both . . .'

As she's talking, I'm distracted by a couple who've wandered into the piazza. Absently I watch them taking each other's photograph by the fountain, before the guy notices me and walks over.

'Excuse me,' he begins, then realising I'm on the phone, falters. 'Oh . . . sorry.'

'It's OK.' I smile. The glow from my sister's good news feels infectious. I mean, come on, here's a couple in love, in one of the most romantic cities in the world, and they want a photo together. 'Hang on, Kate,' I say to my sister, who's now wondering if they should buy round-the-world tickets and take in the Pyramids as well. 'I just need to take a photo.'

'No worries. Let's speak later,' she says cheerfully, saying her goodbyes and hanging up.

No worries? I stare, astonished, at my mobile for a moment. Something tells me this new sister of mine is going to take a bit of getting used to.

'Thank you so much.'

I turn back to see the girl in the couple smiling at me and holding out her camera. It's one of those big proper ones, with the lens that you focus manually, not like my little digital one that just takes snaps.

'Would you mind taking it over here, against the sunset?' she asks.

'No problem.' I smile, taking it from her and looking down the lens.

Then suddenly I pause. Rewind. Did she just say . . .?

'*Sunset?*' I gasp.

'Yes, isn't it amazing?' Her face lights up as she gestures towards it. 'Like the sky is on fire.'

Her voice is drowned out by the sound of my own heart pounding loud and fast in my ears as I look up. And there it is.

Like a huge cinematic backdrop. A pomegranate sky streaked with pinks and reds and oranges, and the sun is a fiery orb slowly sinking down low behind the buildings.

Oh my God.

The legend. I have to meet Nate.

I turn back. The couple are still smiling at me, their bodies posed for a photograph, but now I'm all fingers and thumbs. I can't even see to focus. 'I'm sorry, I have to go,' I gabble, quickly taking a picture and shoving the camera back at them. 'I hope I didn't cut your heads off.' I throw them an apologetic smile, and leaving them looking at me in confusion, I turn and start racing down the alleyway.

I can't be late. For once in my life I can't be late. I have to be there on time. I have to—

Shit, where I am going? I stop dead, my heart racing, my mind helter-skeltering. Suddenly, in all of this, I realise I haven't a clue in which direction I'm supposed to be heading. I haven't a clue where the Bridge of Sighs is.

It gets worse. I haven't even a clue where I am now. I'm lost. Without a map. And I can't speak Italian.

Panic rises a notch and for a moment I stand stock still, like a rabbit caught in headlights. Even my Shredded Wheat rhyme isn't going to save me now. Come on, think, Lucy, *think*. But I can't think, my mind is blank, and in desperation I just set off running down twisting alleyways, past shops and restaurants, crowds of tourists and paparazzi.

'Excuse me, do you know the way to the Bridge of Sighs?' I pant breathlessly to other tourists, but they shake their heads apologetically.

I spot a bunch of men who look distinctly Italian. '*Ponte dei Sospiri?*' I gasp desperately.

'Ah, *sì, sì.*' They nod and with a series of hand gestures point me in the right direction.

Relief floods, and thanking them profusely, I set off running through the crowded streets. It's really busy now. The film parties are gearing up for the evening and paparazzi and film crews are buzzing everywhere. The whole town is lit up. Even the canals, I notice, reaching the water and spotting a gondola up ahead, the bright lights of a film crew on board shining on some celebrity or other.

And the bridge, I realise, looking past the gondola and seeing it arching across the canal. It's the Bridge of Sighs.

I feel a rush of anticipation and wonder. It's so beautiful. The white marble is like a blank canvas, reflecting the colours of the sunset and the ripples of the water beneath, and for a moment I stare at it, transfixed. The effect is almost magical.

I can't stand here all evening, though. I've got to find Nate, and snapping back, I scan the crowds. I see him. A few hundred metres away upstream, he's standing waiting by one of the smaller bridges from which you can catch the gondola. Even from this distance I can see the expression on his face and he doesn't look best pleased. Spotting me, he glares at me furiously and throws his arms in the air as if to say, *Where the hell have you been?*

I rush towards him. Shit, I'm running out of time. The sun's going to set. I'm going to be too late. *Too late for what?* pipes up a voice in my head. *You still don't have a plan.* I ignore it. It's not over yet. I've still got a few minutes, I tell myself frantically. There's still time for a miracle.

Excusing my way through the crowds, I head towards Nate, but it's hard. There are so many people milling around taking photographs of the Bridge of Sighs, of the sunset, of the film crew on the canal.

'Ooh, look, it's that actor,' coos a voice, as I push past.

'He's in a gondola,' cries another voice, as I squeeze through a gap.

I look fleetingly over to see who're they're talking about and snatch a glimpse of the gondola I saw earlier. It's some pretty-boy Hollywood actor with bright lights shining upon him. A young guy in a baseball cap is interviewing him.

Oh my God.

The breath catches in the back of my throat. It can't be . . .

As the gondola glides past, I see his face.

'*Adam?*' Reeling with shock, I hear my voice call out his name. I see him glance up at me.

'Lucy?' he gasps, bewilderment flashing across his face.

Our eyes meet for a split second, and thrown off balance, I don't look where I'm going and suddenly I feel my foot slip. Stumbling, I throw my arms out to grab hold of something, but they clutch at thin air and I feel myself falling . . .

I can hear someone scream as I hit the water. Or is it me screaming? I can't tell. I think I've hit my head. Everything has gone woozy. Now I'm swallowing water and I'm trying to swim, but my arms are flailing and I'm going under. I can hear my heart pounding in my ears, feel the panic rising in my chest. Oh God, I'm going to drown. I'm going to—

Suddenly, out of nowhere, a pair of arms grab hold of me and I feel myself being pulled out of the water and on to the gondola. Spluttering and coughing, I'm fighting for breath, but it's as if everything has gone dreamy, as if I'm seeing the world through a blurry film of Vaseline. Around me I can see people's mouths moving, hear muffled voices, but I can't respond. My eyelids are growing heavy. My limbs don't feel as if they belong to me. The world seems to be receding.

'*Fare la respirazione bocca a bocca!*' the gondolier is shouting over and over. '*Fare la respirazione bocca a bocca!*'

'The kiss of life,' translates a voice. 'Give her the kiss of life.'

Adam's face flashes above mine, bathed in the golden glow of the sunset. I notice his wet hair, water trickling down his face, his urgent expression. I feel the gondola fall into shadow as we drift underneath the Bridge of Sighs. I'm so tired I want to go to sleep. Exhausted, I close my eyes . . .

Suddenly I feel someone's lips on mine, their mouth pressed urgently against my own. Jolted awake, I snap open my eyes to see Adam. Relief flashes in his eyes and he breaks off from kissing me. For a moment we just stare wordlessly at each other, a million questions hanging between us.

Then I hear them, in the distance, softly chiming. I listen harder. Is that . . .? Could that be . . .?

'*Bell*s,' I whisper, as Adam looks at me quizzically.

'Have you heard about the legend?' asks a thick Italian accent, and we both turn to see the gondolier grinning at us.

'What legend?' says Adam, still holding me tightly.

I smile the biggest smile. 'Oh, it's a long story,' and wrapping my arms around him, I lean in for another kiss.

EPILOGUE

Bundled up inside my thick winter coat, furry hat and woolly scarf and gloves, I hurry along the snow-covered street, my breath forming white clouds, like steam puffing from a train. Dusk has fallen and it's freezing. Icicles hang like chandeliers from the fire escapes, and snowflakes twirl around me, as if I'm in a real-life snow globe.

Shivering, I wrap my coat tighter around me. I probably should have caught a cab, but I love to walk. I adore this time of year. New York has turned into a winter wonderland of festive decorations and lights twinkling in windows. Anticipation hangs in the frozen air. I can't believe it's going to be Christmas in just a few weeks. It only seems like two minutes since I was in Venice, I muse, my mind spooling back to the warmth of the Italian sunshine.

It's been three months since Adam kissed me under the Bridge of Sighs, and since then it's not just the seasons that have changed. I still can't believe he was there to rescue me when I fell into the canal. Afterwards he took me back to his hotel to dry off and we stayed up for hours talking about everything.

He told me how he'd got an invite at the last minute to fly to Venice to film some interviews. How he'd never stopped thinking about me. How he missed me so much he thought he'd conjured me up out of his imagination when he saw me on the bridge. How he felt when he'd seen me fall into the canal. It all came pouring out.

Then it was my turn. I had a lot of explaining to do, about why I was in Venice with Nate, what we'd been doing together in

Martha's Vineyard, and how no, we weren't having an affair. He took some convincing.

Three whole days in his hotel room in Venice, in fact. I had no idea convincing someone could be so much fun.

My heel slips on an icy paving stone and I have to fight to keep my balance. That's the problem with wearing high heels, I reflect, glancing down at my new red satin stilettos and feeling a rush of delight. Totally impractical, ridiculously high and utterly gorgeous. But then I couldn't wear wellies to a swanky exhibition featuring the works of renowned artist Artsy, now, could I?

'Loozy, there you are!'

Arriving at the gallery, I'm greeted at the doorway by a flash of paparazzi cameras and Magda, resplendent in head-to-toe Gucci, with Valentino tucked under her arm.

'Sorry I'm late,' I gasp, giving her a hug.

Then again, not everything has changed.

Inside, the gallery is buzzing with an air of feverish excitement. Artsy's first ever exhibition has caused quite a stir and there are crowds of people, tons of journalists and even a few celebrities milling around his artwork. The exhibition has been the talk of the art world and we've had masses of publicity. Magda has been interviewed in the *New York Times*, the gallery has been featured in *Vogue*, and there's even been a rumour *Vanity Fair* might want to do a piece.

Standing on tiptoes, I quickly scan the crowd. Crikey, is that Madonna? I feel a leap of excitement, but I move swiftly past her, my eyes searching out a familiar figure. Then I see him, standing in the corner, waiting for me.

Adam.

'Fancy seeing you here.' He smiles, slips his hand round my waist and gives me a kiss.

I feel a beat of pleasure. 'So what do you think of the art?'

'Hmm, well, I'm not sure about the dirty laundry –' he gestures to Artsy's washing lines – 'but I think these are amazing,' he says, moving towards a series of charcoal sketches hanging on the walls.

'Really?' I study his face with interest. 'And why's that?'

'I love the way they capture people's expressions, their emotions, their hopes.' He points to a large one of a woman, half dozing in a hospital waiting room, rosary beads clasped tightly in her lap. 'There's a whole story, a whole history, and it's been captured in one fleeting moment with just a few strokes of charcoal.'

'You know a lot about art.' I nod approvingly, my mouth twitching.

'I had a good teacher.' He grins, turning back to me. 'Plus it helps when you know the artist.'

Pride swells in me, and my face splits into the widest smile. Because, you see, those are my sketches hanging on the gallery wall. Tonight's exhibition isn't solely for Artsy, though of course he's the main attraction. It's also a chance to showcase new talent. *New talent*. My heart skips a beat and I almost have to pinch myself.

It was Adam who encouraged me to follow my dream of being an artist, so when I came back from Venice, I started sketching again properly. It was like I'd never stopped. Soon I didn't go anywhere without my sketchbook, and evenings and weekends were spent exploring the city, capturing expressions, moods, moments. Until one day I plucked up courage and showed them to Magda, who threw up her arms, declared them 'Wonderful!', reprimanded me for being a dark horse and offered me my first exhibition.

Well, I say 'offered', but it was more a case of her insisting and me speechlessly grinning like a loon. I've been doing a lot of that recently. I'll be walking down the street and I'll suddenly remember that I'm in an exhibition – *me*. Lucy Hemmingway – and I'll start grinning to myself. I've had some funny looks. I'm sure other New Yorkers think I'm some kind of crazy person.

But I don't care. I'm finally following my dream and I've never been happier. I'm even hoping to go part-time soon at the gallery so I can concentrate on my art. Who knows what might happen. It's scary, but it's also exhilarating, and that nagging feeling has gone. The part of me that always felt as if something was missing. Because finally I've found it. I've found it and a whole lot more, I muse, glancing sideways at Adam, who's studying one of my sketches, his arm still wrapped tightly round me. Proof that dreams really do come true.

'Well done, sis!'

Hearing a voice, I twirl round and see my sister and Jeff. At least I think it's my sister, because she's almost unrecognisable. Gone is the grey pallor – her face is suntanned and covered in freckles – and her immaculate bob is tousled and streaked almost white-blonde. Even more shocking, the power suit and heels have been replaced by a pale blue silk dress and flip-flops. And is that *silver* nail polish on her toes?

'You're back!' I gasp.

'We just flew in from Bali this morning.' They grin excitedly.

'How was it?'

'Amazing. You'll have to come and see the photos,' enthuses Jeff, radiating health and happiness. 'The one of your sister doing a bungee jump in New Zealand is incredible.'

'Kate? Doing a bungee jump?' I stare at them both in astonishment. 'Actually, on second thoughts are you *sure* you're my sister?' I joke, peering at her suspiciously, and Kate swats me good-naturedly.

'Bubbles?'

We're interrupted by Magda bearing down on us with a tray of champagne flutes. Despite a flurry of waitresses, she still insists on serving the drinks herself. 'Who wants bubbles?'

It's not the kind of question that requires an answer, and she thrusts a glass of champagne in each of our hands. I don't think I've ever seen her so happy. Not only has she saved the gallery, bought herself a swanky new apartment and is hosting the hottest exhibition in town, but she's treated herself to a brow lift, lipo and lip implants.

Apparently Dr Rosenbaum had a three-for-two offer. Magda might be a millionaire, but she also likes a bargain.

'How are you?' asks Kate politely. 'You look well.'

'I'm wonderful, wonderful!' beams Magda, launching into her story about her amazing rescue of the Titian, which, like all her stories, has now become so exaggerated it involves the Mafia and a possible kidnapping.

'Wow, this is so cool!' cries Robyn, arriving and saving me from hearing Magda's story for the umpteenth time. She greets me with a huge bear hug. 'I'm so proud of you!'

'Thanks.' I smile, my cheeks flushing.

'I had no idea I had such a talented roommate. Soon-to-be-ex roommate,' she corrects, and beams at me and Adam. I feel a flutter of excitement. Like I said, there have been some big changes since I returned from Venice, and one of them is that Adam and I have decided to move in together. 'So how's the apartment search coming on?'

'We can just about afford a shoebox in Hell's Kitchen.' I smile ruefully.

'Well, at least that's your shoes sorted,' grins Robyn. 'That's the most important thing.'

Adam rolls his eyes. 'I think I'll leave you girls to catch up. I'm off for more champagne.'

I laugh. Some things never change.

'So what do you think of Artsy now you've finally met him?' I ask excitedly, as soon as we're on our own. I've been dying to ask that question all night.

'I think he's gay,' she replies evenly.

'What?' I look at her in confusion, then follow her gaze to where Artsy is standing, his arm wound firmly round a tall man with a shaved head and tattooed forearms. At exactly that moment he leans over and kisses him.

'That's his boyfriend,' deadpans Robyn.

For a second or two we both look at each other, neither of us saying anything, then burst into laughter.

'Harold has a boyfriend?' I giggle, shaking my head at the irony.

'Yup, I was chatting to him earlier. He's interested in join- ing my drumming circle when they're in town.' Robyn looks thrilled. 'Apparently he's amazing on the djembe.'

I look at her blankly.

'It's an African tribal drum,' she explains.

'So are you finally going to admit he's not your soulmate?' I raise my eyebrows pointedly.

She stops smiling and looks sheepish. 'Well, you see, that's the thing,' she says slowly, winding a curl round her finger. 'When I listened back to the tape of my psychic reading, Wakanda never said that Harold *was* my soulmate. She said I was going to *meet* my soulmate and I had to be on the lookout for a dark, handsome stranger called Harold. There's a big difference.' She stops talking suddenly and I see her blanch.

It's Daniel in a dark blue overcoat, snowflakes still glistening in his hair. He's just arrived and is chatting to his mum and Artsy. I haven't seen or spoken to him in months. No one has. Apparently he's been 'away on business'. Well, that's the official line. Though judging by his expression as he glances over and sees Robyn, I'm not so sure.

'Are you OK?' I ask, turning back to her with concern.

'Yeah, fine.' She nods, obviously not fine at all. 'I knew I'd see him tonight. I've been preparing myself.'

I look at her, fiddling agitatedly with her bracelets. She looks totally unprepared.

'Why don't you go over and say hi?' I suggest.

She shakes her head. 'I don't think he wants to talk to me,' she says sadly. 'It's been three months and I haven't heard from him once.'

'And did you want to?' I ask quietly.

Her eyes glisten. 'I've been such a total idiot, Lucy. You were right. I've missed him like crazy, but now I think it's too late.'

She looks miserable and I squeeze her hand supportively. 'You don't know that.'

Heaving a sigh, her eyes meet mine. 'What could possibly bring us back together?'

No sooner has she spoken than suddenly Artsy makes a beeline for us and, after a bout of air-kissing, announces loudly, 'Robyn, I want you to meet someone.' Before I quite know what is happening, I see a familiar figure in a blue overcoat standing next to him. 'Robyn, this is Daniel.'

For a split second glances fly between them and they both blush.

'Hi. Nice to meet you, Robyn.' Playing along, he holds out his hand.

She hesitates for a moment, then takes it. 'Nice to meet you too, Daniel.'

Their eyes meet and, still holding hands, they exchange a smile. The kind of smile you get between two people who feel like they're the only two people in the whole room.

And all at once it hits me.

It's not what could bring them back together. *It's who.*

Artsy.

Otherwise known as Harold.

Of course. Harold was never meant to be her soulmate; he was simply the person who brought her together with her true soulmate: *Daniel.*

I look at them now, both grinning madly at each other. You know, maybe that psychic was on to something . . .

Making a discreet exit, I leave Robyn and Daniel, and wander off by myself. Alone, I take a sip of champagne, relishing the few moments to look around the gallery, at Artsy, Magda, Daniel and Robyn, Kate and Jeff, Adam . . . I feel a glow of content-ment. After everything, it's all worked out.

And Nate? I haven't seen him since Venice. I noticed on Facebook that he'd changed his relationship status to 'married to Beth' and given his address as LA, but that was ages ago. Since then he's defriended me, I've stopped bumping into him, and there've been no more mysterious missed calls.

Maybe it's simply because he's moved back to LA, or maybe it really is because we went back to Venice and broke the spell. I'll never know for certain, but if you believe in destiny like Robyn, then it was all meant to happen this way. I was meant to kiss Nate in Venice ten years ago, to meet him again, to break up, then *not* break up, which forced me to return to Venice, because that's how I came to be with Adam. All these events led me to Adam. It was all written in the stars from the very beginning.

Or maybe you're like my sister and think it's all a load of nonsense. There's no such thing as magic and legends and Fate, that it was just a string of coincidences that kept throwing Nate and me together, that I let my imagination run away with itself.

Personally, I like to think the old Italian was right, that nothing is more powerful than love, and by falling in love with Adam I finally broke the spell that Nate had over me. I was able to move on.

And the legend? Is it real? Nobody knows, but if it is, Adam and I are now tied together for eternity and can never break up. We'll have to spend the rest of our lives together.

I look across at him, and seeing me, he flashes me a smile.

And I couldn't be happier about it.